TWISTED RIVER

~

Kelsey Gietl

Purple Mask Publishing
St. Charles, Missouri

Quotations within this book are sourced from the following public
domain works:
All's Well That Ends Well by William Shakespeare
The Comedy of Errors by William Shakespeare
The Legend of Sleepy Hollow by Washington Irving

ISBN-13: 978-0-9991105-3-9
ebook ISBN: 978-0-9991105-4-6
Library of Congress Control Number: 2018961907
First Edition

For my grandparents, George and Amelia,
and a 70-year love story that inspires me every day.
Thank you for everything.
I won't forget to smile.

ACKNOWLEDGMENTS

As ALWAYS, THANK YOU to my readers. Each and every one of you is incredible—never forget that.

To my husband, Scott, and our children. Thank you for continuing to encourage my crazy dreams and providing me with the best happy ending a woman could ask for.

To my parents, Ken and Ruth, and my in-laws, Mark and Sharon. I am so blessed to have you! Thank you for your constant support!

To my critique partners: Mary, Susan, and Tanya, for listening to me obsess about historical facts, character arcs, and the perils of marketing. God gave me a gift in each of you!

To my beta readers: Heather and Katherine. You rock!

To my online international author groups. I still find it amazing that we found one another oceans apart. Technology is truly magical.

And most importantly, to my Lord and creator, Jesus Christ. Without Him, none of this could be.

~ ~ ~

GOOD RIDDANCE, BEATRIX ARCHER thought as she watched her husband's labored breathing strain against his ribcage. Twenty years she had given to this sad infuriating man—the entirety of her twenties, into her thirties, the most fertile years of her life. Somehow he loved her, a complete absurdity. She had done nothing to encourage him to do so.

Laurence's chest rattled from the fluid lodged in his lungs, slowly reaching up to strangle the man whom it seemed none but she could ever cause to cower. It would not be long now. Within an hour, perhaps two, he would be gone and she a widow. Thank heavens her slender figure was even more comely draped in black.

Admittedly, she had often pictured this day—not his death of course, but rather the freedom it would bring. She sensed it then as a great relief, never the reality of a ragged man, pale-faced and gaunt. Even so, there was still a sense of victory in it.

"Bea." The dying man exhaled in barely a whisper, but it echoed in the stale silence of the room. As though drawn by a string, she moved towards him, only a final sense of propriety arranging her on the bed beside him. He cradled her palm inside his.

"Bea," Laurence said again. A strangled cough erupted, and his grip slipped momentarily from her hand. Once he recovered, he gave her fingers a gentle squeeze to match his thin smile. "Even after all our miserable days, I would not redo a one."

1

Which day would you redo? It was the question he always asked someone when he met them, the question he believed could determine any person's worth.

"Not a one?" she asked. "Not even—"

"No. Not even then." His skin grew colder against hers, and fear lined his gaze. "I would not change the life you gave me. It was a good life even if it was not one we both wanted. And yet ..." Another round of deep coughs emitted. He turned his face into the pillow and she realized he wanted to spare her even now.

There was no need. Compassion was a cruel friend long lost. She had become hollow nearly fifteen years ago.

"And yet ..." He continued slower this time, more calculated with his words. "What we have is based on deception. Yours. Mine. Ours. It is perhaps my only regret."

"It was at your insistence that we bury the truth." Tossing his hand off, she rose to her feet. "I do not bear the blame alone."

Laurence shook his head, the motion little more than a thrust of his chin. "No; however, the time will come—the time *has* come—to tell the girls. Promise me you will."

With a deep scowl, she retreated, a hand high on either hip. It was a battle stance he would be all too familiar with. "Why must I? Even now you try to mar my own daughters' opinions of me?"

"You have done that yourself."

The terrible thing about his words wasn't that they hurt her—for they didn't—or even that they were false—for they weren't—it was that he said them without an edge of malice. There was a soft peace in his voice and a simple hope. The faith that she could air the remains of their soiled past and from the destruction form a new life with their daughters.

Except it was far too late for that.

Her daughters were incapable of understanding the sacrifices she made to obtain the life she wanted or the lengths she would go to maintain it. Vicious rumors would spread like wildfire, a blaze that would burn their family name to ash. It was one sacrifice a young widow could not afford. She would not lose everything for a past which, like her husband, was about to be long dead and buried.

Laurence's golden eyes reached out to meet her blue-grey ones, a plea in his stare as well as his voice. "Promise me, Bea. When they ask, you will tell them everything."

Promise me, Bea. His pet name for her. He had only used it a handful of times over their years together: on their wedding night, when their daughters were born, and the night they moved from London. She stood over him, full of fury that even now he dared try to control her with it.

"Very well," she spat. She would fulfill his dying wish, but on her terms. "Maggie and Tena will know the truth, but only if they ask."

His fingers reached for hers, and she focused on those shaking fingers rather than Laurence's wondering voice. "I love you, Beatrix. Did you know? At the end of my world, I still love you."

She knew. Only there was always someone he loved more, and she had always resented him for it.

By the time Laurence Archer drew his last breath, he was alone. His wife lounged in the Winchesters' drawing room playing whist and sipping wine in a toast to the end of her worries. Her husband had taken their secret to his grave, and her daughters would never even think to ask.

PART ONE

~~~

Upstream

ONE

MEN CERTAINLY WERE A BAFFLING SPECIES.

Leave it to a man to drive the blade when a woman was already at her lowest. Leave it to a man to still consider a lady enticing when she appeared anything but.

Maggie Archer wiped the back of her hand across her mouth, flicking sordid saliva to the pathway after heaving her minimal breakfast into the bushes of Shaw's Botanical Garden. Meanwhile, the dark-haired man in the boater hat continued to openly eye her from across the path. Yet another lout anxious to—as last week's Billy Cranzton suggested right before her heel not so innocently collided with his shin—"instill his wisdom in her."

If she had a nugget of wisdom for every man who ever offered, she would be more intelligent than Sir Isaac Newton.

Ignoring the man, she quickened her steps. Even at eleven in the morning, St. Louis's summer sun blazed against the deep black mourning cloth which had draped her shoulder to ankle since her father's passing last February. Sweat slicked her shoulder blades, pooling along her spine where her dress quickly soaked up the moisture.

Summers in her English hometown of Fontaine were never this stifling. Even her wide-brimmed garden hat couldn't diminish the effects of rising humidity, and she braced herself against the nearest tree to keep from fainting. That was her fault for considering water

7

and a biscuit a suitable breakfast. But, confound it, her appetite was non-existent and an extra hour's sleep won out. Exhaustion had been a constant companion as of late, often from chores she wouldn't have batted an eye at a month ago.

Her stomach flipped, sending her dry heaving into the grass. Hands pressed to her middle, her insides convulsed with the strain of expelling food that wasn't there. With each heave, her hard little lump of abdomen swayed, proof in the pudding that she finally took her usual seditious antics one step too far.

At last the nausea relented, leaving her throat raw. Her chest strained against her corset, swollen breasts pinched within ties already severely loosened. She shouldn't even be wearing it, but what was she to do—go without any support? That would be a scandal unto itself.

Although, truly, what did another indignity matter now? Her horrid reality already screamed like a street newsie shouting about *Titanic*.

The girl who never wanted children was with child. Not merely with child, but unmarried and uncertain even as to which man was the father.

She had entertained three men in the same number of weeks, the last two within twenty-four hours of each other and forty-eight hours after *Titanic's* sinking. Calculating from the time passed since her last cycle, the most realistic culprit was half a world away in London. Derby, the smooth-talking, charming, second footman who had seen the inner workings of almost every one of Lady Alexander's maids, and she had been no exception. Despite a physique that stoked her fires, he was as capable of being a suitable father as Beatrix Archer had been a caring mother to her, which was to say not at all.

Yet, while Derby fit the bill based on timing, Maggie couldn't discredit two other possibilities: Reuben Radford, whom she met in their hometown cemetery on May Day two years past, and Lloyd Halverson, Reuben's archenemy whom she slept with for information that, in hindsight, should have been left deeply buried. After that night on the steamship *Höllenfeuer*, everything escalated in a rapid course of events that now left her with secrets of her own.

Secrets, secrets, are no fun. Secrets, secrets, hurt someone.

A mere childhood rhyme and yet, a line never rang truer for Maggie's life. Every secret sought, every truth forced, had gained nothing except heartache and ruin. After Reuben explained his past, he nearly died in the frigid waters of the North Atlantic. After her sister, Tena, revealed her clandestine relationship with German-born Charles Kisch to their anti-German mother, it resulted in both sisters' dismissal from the Archer family. What damage might be done when Maggie told her sister she was expecting or informed Reuben that he might be a father?

It was why she regularly paid for shoddy hotel rooms where she slept alone despite being the conquest challenge of the city. There was a time not too long ago when she would have given in simply to break her mind free of life. Every dinner or moving picture or dance hall would have led back to those same hotels only not alone and definitely not for sleeping. She would have lavished in the intimacy, and he would have praised her for walking away in the morning.

All she desired now was undetermined paternity for her baby.

If Reuben even so much as suspected she was with child, his honor would demand they marry. Despite being a complete mismatch, he would remain in an unrequited marriage exactly like her father. He would shower her and their baby with love she could never reciprocate.

Swiping her sleeve across her sweat-baked brow, she opened the door to the Linnean House. A long rectangular building, it contained botanical specimens ranging from citrus trees to ferns. Nearly floor length windows drew excess heat into the greenhouse—necessary for the plants to thrive, but also able to send her into radical sickness.

"Where did you wander off to?" Tena asked, making her way to the door. She pushed damp honeynut tendrils from her face. "Are you feeling ill again?"

Maggie waved her off, wishing desperately that she could undo the buttons at her wrists and scrunch her sleeves past the elbows. "Felt a bit faint from the heat, so I fancied a walk into the shade. I'm afraid I'm not yet used to the weather here."

Tena frowned. "I heard you vomiting in the toilet again this morning."

Well, blast. All her discretion and it appeared someone *had* noticed. Of course, it would be her sister. Birthdays only ten months apart, they shared a bedroom for the first four years of Tena's life until their father's banking career led them from London to the quaint town of Fontaine and a much larger dwelling. Even so, four years sealed their fate. Closer than blood, when it came to Maggie, Tena had eventually learned all her sister's darkest secrets.

Except for one.

"I told you, Tena, it's merely the weather."

Tena shifted her handbag and offered Maggie her arm. "I'm not convinced; however, it's far too warm to argue the point out in the sun. While you were away, the gardener told me about a research library at the other end of the garden. Would you fancy a look?"

"I suppose." In truth, Maggie had no interest in spending hours cramped between shelves while her sister carried on with her imaginary book beaus. But between sharing a room with Tena and sharing a living space with the Kisch family and Reuben—who staunchly refused to relocate—life had been beyond tense. She didn't want to ruin the one pleasant afternoon they had shared in months. So she swallowed her annoyance down a throat now raw from vomiting and accepted her sister's arm.

Vibrant with color and sweet with floral fragrance, the walk carried her back to her favorite summer days. Chasing after their family's gardener as a little girl, she sat in the grass while he worked, eager for an explanation of each flower and its meaning. Every May Day, she and Tena mixed up bouquets for the annual festival, the day her sister declared just for them.

What Maggie wouldn't give to be a child again. What she wouldn't give to have her father back. What she wouldn't give to have never read his final letter to her.

The words were branded on her brain, she had read them so often. The letter started out in her traveling case, tucked safely under the bed she shared with Tena until she found herself stealing away to her room nearly every day to read it. Then it took up residence in her skirt pocket, safely hidden if her sister decided to go prying in her things. Tena knew about the letter and also knew that she hadn't received one.

Dearest Maggie,

It saddens me that my time grows short. I find myself with many fears these days, in particular I fear what type of life I leave for you to endure.

There is a secret your mother holds, and once I am gone, she will not hesitate to tell you. I am sorry I cannot explain myself. It is her secret to reveal, although I fear she will attempt to destroy you with the truth.

Know this, Maggie: I have cherished you and Tena all your lives. I loved you more than any father could. Your happiness was all I ever wanted above my own.

Claim your happiness, my little girl. Love will find you one day. Ensure it is with a man who understands your heart.

Love always,

Father

Secrets, secrets are no fun. Secrets, secrets, hurt someone.

Her father wouldn't lie to her. It hadn't been in his nature to manipulate or ruin. Whatever lay between the lines of his letter would be exactly as he said, enough to destroy them ... a truth so unpleasant even their heartless mother had, as of yet, deemed it unspeakable.

Maggie breathed a sigh of relief as they pushed through the doors of the Herbarium-Library building. An assistant directed them to a room lined with bookshelves and cabinets labeled in fine print. At one of several small desks, a young man quietly pored over a stack of thick volumes.

She stepped nearer to extract one of the cabinet drawers. In neat little rows lay flower varieties pressed flat between two square panes of glass, each labeled in Latin. She smiled, the knot in her stomach beginning to unfurl. She wasn't familiar with the ancient language, but she didn't need to be. These were all plants in the market at Covent Garden. The flowers purchased there adorned her sparse upstairs room during her employment for Lady Alexander. Their scent brought her through nearly a year without her family, reminding her of the sister she left behind.

Her stomach fluttered with a feeling unrelated to pregnancy. Excitement wasn't an emotion she had felt in a long time.

"Have you found what you're looking for?"

The young researcher had abandoned his volumes and now stood at her elbow. Facing him, she instantly quavered. One shelf over, the leering stranger in the boater hat drummed his fingers against the book edges while darkened eyes stared intently at her. Correction, into her. As if she were one of the specimens and he a botanist anxious to dissect her.

"Everything all right, miss?" asked the researcher. He slid the drawer closed which she had been viewing. The stranger didn't move an inch. He didn't even blink.

She swiveled in search of Tena, but her sister had disappeared into the stacks like the ridiculous bibliophile she was.

"There's a man watching me ..." Maggie trailed off when her eyes flitted back to the stranger's location and found only books staring back. She turned a complete circle, but for all she was aware, the mystery watcher had been engulfed by the shelves around them.

"Which man?" the researcher asked. "We appear alone."

The breeze from a closing door swung her around.

"Excuse me, please." She hurried out of the Herbarium, a blast of summer heat knocking her back at the exterior door. Throwing an arm up to shield her eyes, she scanned the area. The mystery man hurried down the path into the garden, now holding his hat in his hands to reveal dark close-clipped locks. He stepped off the path into the trees.

When she followed, he was gone. Not a whisper, not a sign. It was as if she imagined it. As if he never was.

TWO

THROUGH THE BOOKSHELVES, Tena watched Maggie chase after Mr. Tall, Dark, and—from what she could observe—Older than their father. Probably the next stop on her sister's trail of one-night interludes. New country, but same distasteful parade of suitors as before.

She had hoped her sister's volatile flirtations would cease once they settled into their new home and Maggie understood how deeply Tena hurt from her fiancé, Charles's death on *Titanic*. That what happened between Maggie and Reuben could become water under the bridge, Tena would forgive, and they could finally begin to heal. But how could she heal, how could she forgive, when her sister remained so unfeeling towards the repercussions of her actions?

In under two months, a dense tension had filled the Kisch house like thunderclouds. No one was immune from Maggie's narcissistic mania. She and Reuben were constantly at each other's throats, which left Tena to claim sides between her sister and her closest friend. Inviting Maggie to the Botanical Gardens had been her last-ditch effort to salvage what was left of her sanity and their sisterhood. But it seemed that even Maggie's love of flowers couldn't quell her desire for masculine comforts.

While Maggie was detained with her most recent conquest, Tena quickly penned a note explaining her absence—assuming her sister even noticed—and slid a quarter to the Herbarium researcher to pass it along. As luck would have it, the streetcar clanged down Shaw Avenue at that moment, and she was able to climb aboard as she reached the street. Pressing a coin into the conductor's hand, she claimed an empty seat alone.

Alone—what a word, what an awful depressing word.

She closed her eyes and imagined Charles's hand in hers, his breath warm on her cheek, his lips soft against hers. *He's simply waiting at the stop*, she thought. *Merely standing around the corner. Just count the minutes, Tena. You'll be together soon.*

Such fantasies coaxed her feet out of bed in the morning and throughout the day. Pretending pushed her to the market, kept her fingers patching garments, and cooking dinner with Charles's mother, Elsa. Every time Charles's father, Karl, asked Tena how she was, she laced him with a lovely smile and replied, "Perfectly well, thank you."

Physically she was; her body felt perfectly healthy. It pressed on day after day without signs of fatigue. She hardly sat except for meals, and when she did, she ate with fervor. Always busy, never lax. It was pure and uncompromised denial and also the best recourse for grief she could muster.

The sailors buried Charles at sea. His body had been too disfigured to send home, especially when resources must be saved for first class passengers. So they gave him back to the sea that claimed him. They buried him, and she wasn't there. As much as she hated the sight of her father's dead form, one couldn't argue with the pallor complexion of a corpse. So who then could insist she give Charles up, to believe his death when she hadn't seen it?

The White Star Line could, along with their white canvas bag hidden in her bedroom closet.

Tena exited the streetcar, walked the final few blocks to 1282 Lemp Avenue, and climbed the thirteen stairs to the bedroom she shared with Maggie and Winnie, the Kischs' eleven-year-old daughter. This time of day the house lay empty. Karl would return from work at six o'clock with his sixteen-year-old son, Emil. Twenty-year-old Friedrich lived in the heart of the city while studying at university. Elsa and Winnie would be at the market fetching dinner.

Silence hung heavy when she opened the bedroom's closet door almost as if the space could feel her heart.

Lowering herself to the oak floorboards, she lifted the white canvas bag into her lap. Marked with the number 332 and a red seal, the rough fabric scratched her hands like the rope ladder she had climbed from *Titanic*'s lifeboat onto the rescue ship, *Carpathia*. After that day—the only time she ever experienced sedatives and determined she also despised them—Tena forced all raw emotions into some deep dark hole where hope goes to die.

Then this bag arrived two weeks ago, placed by the hands of the handsome postmaster into her own without so much as a condolence. He knew its meaning; how could he not? The news plastered the newspapers as the world waited for bulletins of more recovered bodies, more information about the infamous wreck.

Reuben read them aloud each night at dinner. Instead of listening, Tena focused on the back page advertisements. *"When you buy at Famous & Barr, you buy clothes of the uppermost quality!"* Karl and Elsa waited anxiously for news of their son's recovered body, never knowing Tena's closet held the solace they so desperately craved.

Breaking the bag's seal, she thrust her hands inside and retrieved each item—silver pocket watch, cigar case, soiled billfold, gold engagement band—everything in Charles's possession before they surrendered him to the ocean.

She hadn't kept it from the Kischs to be heartless. They were as close to parents as she had. But she simply wasn't ready to relive that night, to hand over the last pieces of her fiancé she would ever hold.

"Please, Tena, step into the lifeboat," Charles had pressed as they stood under *Titanic*'s deck lights in the midnight hour of April fifteenth. An hour had passed since encountering the iceberg, and the lifeboats were lowering, but she didn't understand why he insisted she enter one without him. The situation couldn't be as dire as all that. It simply couldn't. Ships these days were designed to be their own lifeboats. Other ships stayed afloat with limited resources until they could be towed to shore; surely *Titanic* would too.

Tena rolled her eyes and pulled his fingers to her lips. "Charles, you're overreacting."

"Overreacting, am I?" Charles shook his head with a thin smile. "What must I do to make you see reason?"

"I'll see reason when you make me see it." She smoothed their clasped fingers across the stubble on his cheek, and he closed his eyes with a sigh.

"You are the best decision I ever made."

Bending, he pressed a kiss to her lips and an object into her hands. Looking down, she found her fingers wrapped around a lovely new book with only a small dent in the corner of the blue linen cover. She ran her fingertips delicately over the title stamped in gold print. In all of her nineteen years, she had never owned a new book; all of her father's books were well-read and well-worn, unlike the one she held now. This one was pristine.

"I know how much my darling loves to read," Charles told her. "I stole this for you from the ship's library. Think of it as some good company while we are apart."

Tena's eyes widened. "Thief!"

"They will not miss it, will they?"

Tena's fingers caressed the cover's lovely linen. "I suppose not."

"Good." Charles stole her arm with a gentle tug. "Now, will you please go?"

"If I go, will you miss me?"

He tilted her chin upward, and her resulting shiver had nothing to do with the freezing night air. "Every second we are apart," he promised. "Now please, Tena, you must leave. I will find you."

With another quick kiss, she accepted his hand and stepped into the lifeboat. Taking a seat beside a young mother and her tiny son, she sought out Charles as the boat lowered, not once believing it would be the last time to see him. *Titanic* had precautions: safety compartments and watertight doors. Mechanisms she didn't understand but still trusted.

Her eyes took in Charles's dishwater blond hair and his lips raised into a broad smile. *Nothing is wrong*, she thought. *See how he smiles.*

Denial. It could be the strongest force on earth. Then again, so could love.

"*Ich liebe dich*," she called in German.

"I love you," he returned.

It was the first and only time he ever declared his love in her native tongue. He saved it for the only moment that would ever matter.

Tena stared at the book in her hands now, hidden in the recesses of her closet since she arrived in St. Louis, the final lost item in the contents of Charles's twenty-one-year-old life and the heaviest weight she would ever hold. Seventy-three pages of paper and half a heart.

Slowly, she bent open the cover and ran her fingers across the title, *Lilac Lilies: A Collection of English Poetry*. To know Charles, she would never be surprised that he enjoyed the poets. Every word from his mouth flowed like spoken song. Or at least that was how she always heard him.

She flipped the pages, the sound reminiscent of the wind on deck during their last night together, and stopped at the only dog-eared page.

Wait not the night for me / If the sun refuse to shine
If the grass does cease to grow / If the music loses rhyme
Wait not the night for me / If my tomorrow never starts
If the dark goes on forever / If death has pierced my heart

The book slipped to the floor with a hollow thud.

Charles knew, she thought. He marked this page on purpose intending for her to read it. He understood how dismal *Titanic's* situation was, and he still continued to laugh and assure her they would be together soon. But with every breath, with every false smile, he broke every promise he ever made. For better or worse, that was how it was supposed to be. Together or not at all.

Charles was dead, and Tena, in her unfathomable ignorance, left him to face it alone.

She wanted to scream and pummel his chest until her fists ached with the effort. To hold him in her arms and flood his shirt with her tears. Let him steal her pain away. Kiss him with a fervor she never would have dared before. One final touch, one last laugh, one more ... anything. She longed to speak to him in the very German she never mastered, but nonetheless always stole her heart.

But wants and wishes were for children.

Tena was no longer a child. And the last remnants of her girlhood dreams were at the bottom of the Atlantic with Charles's body.

THREE

ADJUSTING HIS FLAT CAP, Reuben Radford exited the crowded streetcar and purchased the *St. Louis Post-Dispatch* from one of the newsboys yelling headlines on the sidewalk. He always read the front section on his three-block walk to work and stashed it in his satchel until he could read the rest on the ride home in the evening. His fellow reporters at *The Mid-Mississippi Daily* would butcher him if they learned he spent his wages on a competing newspaper.

Except truth be told, the *Post-Dispatch* was the best news outlet there was. They could scoop stories the *Mid-Mississippi* couldn't hope to grab, including breaking news regarding the recent *Titanic* sinking, a fact that Reuben's chief editor found infinitely annoying.

"Why do I keep you boys, if you let the *Post-Dispatch* take all the decent news?" Eric Smithson yelled the day Reuben walked in for his interview. Smithson sailed a pencil through the air, hitting a bald reporter flat on the head. "Get me something decent on *Titanic* or I'll fire you all!" he roared. "And nobody gets a reference."

Reuben held up a hand. "Excuse me, sir. I believe I can help you there."

That was how Reuben landed a job at the *Mid-Mississippi*, for the same reason every other paper hadn't hired him—by simply mentioning that his writing portfolio went down with *Titanic* and he conveniently missed the boat. Smithson had been so intrigued as to have Reuben write a special interest story then immediately after shoved him on obituaries between marriage announcements and advertisements for ladies' shoes and gentlemen's cravats.

"Obits?" Reuben admonished after Smithson delivered the abysmal downgrade. "My *Titanic* piece was smashing. We had higher sales on that edition than any other day this week."

Smithson ground his cigar in the ashtray on his desk. "You still don't have a portfolio, Radford," he growled. "One article isn't enough for me to cast all my lots on you." He pointed his cigar in Reuben's direction then at the door. "You'll take obits or you can take your pretty British behind back to the street."

Folding the front page of the *Post-Dispatch* over, Reuben scanned for any more information on *Titanic*. He had watched the news day after day since he arrived in St. Louis, sharing updates with the family over dinner and hoping one of the recovery ships would find Charles's body soon. Tena usually remained quiet while he read, and it split his heart wide open the few times she said, "If they haven't found his body yet, then perhaps there's a chance he's still alive."

No one believed that, and nearly everyone in the Kisch family told her as much, but insisting she see reason only resulted in her lips tightening. Two weeks ago, she stopped commenting on the news articles altogether. Reuben could never bring himself to tell her what he thought, even during all the nights they stayed up talking long after the others went to bed, her head resting against his shoulder until the living room fire reduced to embers.

If she wanted to be in denial, he would let her. Her nonsensical hope might be the only way to bring them all through Charles's death in one piece. Or at least many pieces held together in the name of family.

"Good morning, Mr. Radford," Miss Newton called out from the reception desk as he pushed through the *Mid-Mississippi*'s revolving door. She held up a battered portfolio folder. "Mr. Frye left some more photographs. Looks like they're from yesterday's Independence Day celebration. Would you mind taking them up to Mr. Smithson?"

"Certainly, Miss Newton." Reuben took the folder on his way to the stairs, flipping through black and white photographs sure to impress Eric Smithson, and he was a difficult bloke to please. The man even made his feature writers cry in the alley on their lunch breaks. Nevertheless, if there was one thing Smithson approved of, it was positive numbers and the smell of cold hard cash. In the months since Hugo Frye began selling his photos to the paper, they had seen a significant increase in sales, especially in editions when Mr. Frye's work landed on the front page. Enough of an increase to even temporarily quell Smithson's rants about the *Post-Dispatch*. It was a lousy shame then that he refused to pay the photographer even a fraction of what his work was truly worth.

Reuben sprang up the next two flights of stairs, past the composition shop of the second floor and on up to third. Right on cue, the left side of the typists' room looked up in excitement at his entrance: Phoebe, Rosalea, Hazel, and Luella. Far younger and vastly prettier than the other matronly typists, they were reduced to fervent fits of giggles when he strolled through the office on his first day ... and every day after.

Despite being unfairly deposited on the lowest rung of the reporting ladder, he genuinely enjoyed his job. And not only because he garnered the attentions of four lovely women every morning. His minuscule desk was still his own even while crammed in a room far too small to comfortably seat twenty-two men. His fellow reporters— all solid born and bred American men—harped on him for his youth and his "redcoat" accent on day one, but Reuben earned their trust the minute he joined in that first cigar. After that, he was as much a part of the newsroom as the perpetual smoke and coffee-induced haze they worked in.

Sliding his fingertips along his hat brim, he threw the typists his usual winning smile. "Good morning, ladies."

Four cheery voices sang back in unison, "Good morning, Mr. Radford." As he reached the frosted glass wall of the newsroom, he caught Hazel Vine's usual follow up of, "Have a fascinatin' day, sir!" With a final glance over his shoulder, he cast her a sly wink and closed the newsroom door behind him.

"What are you smilin' 'bout?" Stanley Leonard asked as Reuben dropped his satchel under the desk which butted against his own.

As usual, paraphernalia covered Stanley's desk from his current assignments along with yesterday's publication of the *Mid-Mississippi*. The newest edition of *The New Websterian Dictionary* saved the stack from blowing out the open windows. All around them other reporters bent over their desks, either scribbling with or chewing on their pencils, while the furious *click clack click ding* of typewriters kept pace from the other side of the frosted glass.

"Wouldn't you like to know?" said Reuben with a smug grin that sent Stanley's bottlebrush brows straight into his wide forehead and curly brown hair. He certainly wasn't a substitute for Reuben's nearly twelve year friendship with Charles, but in only two months, the twenty-eight-year-old features writer had become his fast friend.

"You know," Stanley said. "One of these days those girls are gonna riot for some real affection from you." He jabbed his pencil in Reuben's direction. "And all I'll say is I told you so."

"Riot, Lee? Honestly?" Reuben retrieved his notepad from his satchel and skimmed over yesterday's interview with the family of recently deceased William Wainwright. He tapped his pencil against his lips as he spoke. "Why must you turn everything into an extreme? Keep that up and I'll have Smithson remove you from the homicide beat."

"Oh, I'm sorry," Stanley smirked, "you mean the front section? Would you even know how to find it, Obituary Boy?"

Reuben scowled at him. "Your words are like weapons, Lee."

"That's why I write about the violence and you cover the aftermath."

It was true that Stanley wrote the best statements of death and destruction Reuben had ever read. He made brutal stabbings sound as poetic as they were gruesome. Not that Reuben had much to go off of from his time at the *Fontaine Gazette*. Back home, the subject of murder wasn't so much unfit for print as it simply didn't happen. When he did almost commit murder five years ago trying to avenge his sister's stolen virtue, his father—and the *Gazette*'s chief editor—paid off the rat, ensuring all proof vanished before the newspapers could print so much as a word.

Life had become muddled without his sister, Mira. Even though hallucinations of her had driven him to the brink of mental destruction, he still missed her. Now he lived in a too cramped house with Charles's grieving family, Charles's fiancée, and Maggie, the one woman he wished he could remove from his thoughts. The daily tension between them stunk like ozone before an impending storm, with one ill-timed remark enough to put everyone on edge. Even Emil's impudent humor wasn't enough to save it.

Night was the worst. Alone in his bed, listening to Emil flip over in the bed opposite his, Reuben had too much time to think. He missed Maggie—if pressed, he would admit to a fair amount. Their night together on the steamship *Höllenfeuer* replayed constantly in his mind, wondering what he could have done differently, wishing he could take it back. Eventually he sank into sleep, and dreams would take over. Wonderful, often times sensual, they left him furious when he woke in bed alone and irritable all the way through breakfast.

"Reuben!" Stanley hissed. Reuben jerked, his chin sliding out from the hand he had propped it up in.

Eric Smithson stood by his office door, arms folded and veins pulsing in his temple. "Radford, are you deaf? Do I look like your secretary? Notes!"

Reuben shook his head, hastily grabbed his notes, and searched frantically for a pencil. "No, sorry, sir, I have them. I'm getting it together." His hands flew over the desktop and came up empty.

Stanley threw his pencil onto Reuben's desktop and picked up another from his own. "Get it together faster."

"Mr. Radford?" Reuben spun in his chair at Miss Vine's voice. She stood in the newsroom doorway, cheeks flushed.

"Shucks boy, you're pretty popular for being my lowest writer." Smithson's scowl shot in the young girl's direction. "What is it?"

Miss Vine paled. She held up a folded notepaper. "Miss Newton sent this up. Mr. Radford has a visitor."

Smithson turned his sights back on Reuben, stomping down the row to glower over him. "No breaks until one, Radford. Unless you have a corpse to write about. You know the rules."

"This isn't the *London Medical Journal*, Mr. Smithson. I write about people, not corpses."

"Don't give me your fancy pants British lip, Radford." Smithson's glare deepened, a purple sheen flaring his skin.

"Yes, sir, I know the rules."

Smithson jabbed a finger at the folder sitting on Reuben's desk. "That from Frye?"

"Yes, sir. Photographs from Independence Day." He offered the folder and Smithson swiped it.

He pointed it at Reuben. "I want to see an obit on my desk in an hour, Radford, or you'll be emptying garbage bins with your teeth."

"Yes, sir," Reuben replied, but Smithson had already disappeared into his office and slammed the door.

~~~

One o'clock could not arrive soon enough. Smithson was in right form the remainder of the morning, which was saying something given his already consistent propensity for crankiness. The *Mid-Mississippi* only published a single daily edition. Reuben could only imagine the height of the editor's stress if he needed to oversee an evening edition as well.

Retrieving their lunches, Reuben and Stanley left the newsroom. With renewed energy from their own lunch breaks, the typists sat up straight at their desks, long fingers tapping out the rhythm of tomorrow's news. Their eyes followed them to where Reuben stopped before Miss Vine. Her fingers stilled, her hazel eyes lifting to his through her lashes.

"Sir?"

Reuben smiled, well aware that the other ladies were listening. "I wanted to say thank you for delivering my message. Smithson can be a brute. It was quite brave of you to chance it."

Miss Vine's blush was as pretty as her coppery hair pinned into a loose chignon at the base of her neck. "It wasn't anything much, Mr. Radford."

"Rubbish. It meant a great deal to me."

He cast his gaze over the other typists, everyone now leaning in with bated breath. Not one bothered to turn away. In fact, Rosalea threw him a cheeky smirk. Reuben chuckled. "I'll return in thirty minutes, Miss Vine. If I have another message, would you care to intercept it, please?"

She nodded and the blush in her cheeks stretched her entire face. Reuben turned on his heel, clutching his lunch in one hand and his satchel triumphantly with the other, pleased that he could be so badly wounded by a woman like Maggie Archer and still manage to draw the attention of another so lovely as Hazel Vine.

Stanley spun after him, walking backwards as he waved goodbye to the girls. Another resounding round of laughter followed them down the stairwell.

"Holy smokes, that Hazel's one fine lass!" Stanley commented, nudging Reuben. "For fits and fiddles, Reuben, when do I get to wrap you around her?"

"I'm good, Lee. My mind's still wrapped around someone else right now, and I don't have the fortitude to take on any more."

"So all that flirtin' and 'Pleasant afternoon, ladies'," Stanley drawled. "You bein' Mr. Casanova. That's all just for show?"

"You've captured the idea."

"*Bull*," Stanley coughed into his fist. "Who's this lass you can't get over? Is she the bloomin' actress, Mary Pickford? No, and even if she was ..." Stanley paused, his lips pinched together in consideration, then he jabbed Reuben in the arm hard.

"Hey!"

"Even if she was," Stanley repeated. "There's still nothing for it! That woman dumped you. Let her go."

"Lee ..." Reuben warned.

"No, you don't get to make the rules this time. You and your sissy obituary section—"

"How are obituaries sissy?"

"—are going to go right back upstairs and ask Miss Vine to dinner."

Reuben ducked around Stanley into the *Mid-Mississippi's* foyer. "No."

Stanley spun around, throwing an arm around Reuben's shoulders and nearly knocking him to his knees. "Come on, please? I'll ask Luella. We can double to the picture show. It's dark in there." He winked. "Think what a delight that'll be."

With two fingers, Reuben picked up Stanley's hand and threw him off. It was one thing to smooth-talk the girls at the newspaper and quite another to actually pursue his flirtation outside the *Mid-Mississippi*'s red brick walls. His head was still cloudy from being with Maggie and his heart was wounded from her betrayal. Not all women were so selfish, he knew this, but it had only been three months. He wasn't ready to open himself up to someone again so soon.

He was halfway to refusing again, when Stanley's low whistle slowed him to a halt. "Forget Luella. Who's this beauty?"

Dressed head to toe in mourning black, the young woman spoke softly with Miss Newton, her hands clenched around a white canvas bag bearing a red number 322.

"Tena?"

She turned at his voice and Stanley grinned like a jackshaw. He clapped Reuben on the shoulder, bending close to whisper in his ear. "Is that your foul little vixen? Because, seriously, why'd you ever let that sweet thing go?"

"Not exactly," murmured Reuben. "This one's with someone else."

Stanley stepped away and crossed his arms. "Who? Because I bet you could duel him for her."

Reuben eyed Tena. Her eyes were hollow, their usual golden sheen dull and bitter. Where there usually lived a vibrant fire was now nothing except burnt embers. For months they had smoldered, losing heat a bit at a time until now something had finally smothered them. What was in the bag she carried?

Did he really need to ask?

No. He already knew. They had been waiting for this since *Titanic* sank.

"She's my best mate's fiancée. His is the next obituary I have to write."

"Oh," said Stanley.

Reuben grimaced. "Yeah."

~ ~ ~

Hours later, Tena clutched the canvas bag to her chest outside the Kischs' home. She stared at the brown door, its little brass knocker, and the latch waiting for her to lift it.

She didn't flinch when an arm slid around her waist. After all, she had waited for him to join her. "Ready?" she asked Reuben.

He leaned down to kiss her temple. "I'll never be ready."

Five minutes later around a fully loaded dining room table, Elsa wept in Karl's arms, grief wrought anew for the son they lost. Tena wove her trembling fingers through Reuben's and watched as her heart broke all over again.

FOUR

TOSSING HER HAT AND ITS PINS onto the dressing table, Maggie flopped onto her back across the bed with a groan. Unfastening the row of buttons at her neck, she fanned the material and sighed as cool air hit her damp skin.

The walk from St. Francis de Sales had been sweltering, especially since Mrs. Kisch insisted that they dress completely medieval for Charles's funeral. After two hours in full black crepe with a high starched collar and heavy woolen stockings barely able to wrap around her swollen calves, Maggie had suspicions Elsa had intent to kill her. To make matters worse, she lingered too long in the vestibule before mass sneaking bits of bread from her handbag to fight off her ever-present nausea and missed the family's escort to their pew. As a result, she was forced to walk up the aisle during the opening hymn, a hundred Latin voices pacing her stride. Her face on fire, she slipped into the second pew beside Winnie and didn't shift her eyes from the priest's back the entire time.

Downstairs the Kischs' doorbell rang, startling Maggie from the memory of her embarrassment. Reaching through the bed's wrought iron headboard, she lifted the window curtain. Besides the Kischs' Rambler and their neighbor's Model T, there weren't any other new vehicles parked out front, which meant their visitor either walked or caught the streetcar. The front stoop wasn't visible from her low angle on the bed, but she assumed it was more of the same riffraff that crowded the funeral pews. Probably another *Titanic* thrill seeker who hadn't received their fill from the newspapers. There were hundreds of strangers outside the church happy to intrude on the Kischs' private time of grief. Only Karl's firm insistence blocked them from trailing back to the house in search of a free meal. Maggie found it all utterly disgraceful.

She dropped the curtain, craning her neck around as Winnie's bright blonde hair flew past the open bedroom door yelling, "I'll get the door!"

"Winnie!" Elsa shouted back as her youngest child clomped down the stairs. "Ladies do not shout."

Karl's matching German accent followed. "Elsa, *meine liebe*, you are not exactly being quiet."

"Emil," Winnie whined, "I said I was gonna answer it!"

"Too slow, little sis, too slow." Unlike their parents and older brothers, Emil and Winnie spent the majority of their lives in England. As a result, their strong British accents now bared little resemblance to their birth country.

Tena hurried in, tossed her hat, gloves, and handbag on the bed and without a glance at her sister, turned on her heel to disappear into the hall. Footsteps echoed on the stairs.

Maggie silently rolled her eyes. She would have to deal with Tena's silent treatment eventually. After their trip to the Botanical Gardens, it had been only three-word questions and one-word responses, usually with Tena only responding if directly spoken to. It had become no better when Maggie insisted that her days of unabashed intimacy were behind her.

"I didn't run off with anyone, if that's what you're assuming," Maggie told her when she had finally made it home.

"Coming to your senses at last, are you?" Tena had shoved a basket of dirty linens into Maggie's arms. "Well good, you can use all that unreleased passion on the laundry."

Under her black gloves, Maggie's hands still stung from the lye. So much good the moral high ground had done for her. Perhaps she should have actually slept with twenty men instead of simply telling radical stories about them. It certainly would have been more fun.

And yet, she no longer believed the stranger in the garden maintained interest of a carnal nature. The intensity of his stare and the way he followed her into the Herbarium—assuming he *had* followed her, and not ended up there by coincidence—suggested another reason for his observation. Maggie knew so few people in St. Louis. What reason could a stranger have for making her acquaintance if his intentions were pure? Perhaps she reminded him of someone, and upon discovering she was not his intended, he fled. Yes, that explanation made the most sense. Better than dwelling over something sinister.

Hefting herself onto her elbows, she pushed to standing and buttoned her collar, the heat already closing in again. She fought off the usual dizziness and made her way downstairs, surprised to find a pair of photographers setting up in the living room. Unkempt crimson hair, the brightest shade she had ever seen, drew her eye to the man at the room's center. Certainly not taller than an inch above her five-foot-three, he hefted a sizable black camera from an even larger case and attached it to a three-legged wooden stand. As he adjusted it, the frayed hem of his charcoal trousers hitched upward, revealing mismatched socks in scuffed boots with a patched tear along the toe line.

He swiveled the camera to face the living room sofa, twisting knobs on either side of the device presumably to lock it in place. An utterly demure woman helped him at the task, her muted brown hair peppered with silver strands and shackled to her scalp in a rigid bun. With her attention focused on the task at hand, neither of them noticed Maggie watching.

"What's this?" Maggie asked. The man turned at her question, ran all ten fingers through his hair in a failed attempt to tame it, and approached with hand outstretched. Although his feet shuffled nervously, the crooked smile behind his crimson goatee was as pleasant as the emerald eyes above it, like two bright frogs in a pond.

"Hello, ma'am. I'm Hugo Frye." He delivered a surprisingly disengaged handshake that didn't match the warmth of his smile and gestured to the woman. "My sister, Damaris. We're the photographers."

"I'm Maggie Archer."

"I only wish I could say it was a pleasure, Miss Archer."

She released his hand. "What do you mean by *that*?"

Mr. Frye's fingers were back in his hair. He stared somewhere past her shoulder for an amount of time long enough to cause her to turn towards the empty hall. When she did, he spoke to her back. "I only meant that a loss like yours isn't the ideal method of meeting."

Facing him again, she folded her arms over her chest and managed not to cringe with the pressure upon tender breasts. "It's not my loss. Mr. Kisch was engaged to my sister, not me."

The man seemed out of responses. His feet continued to shuffle absently while he eyed Damaris who made no effort to engage in the slightest.

"Do you speak?" Maggie asked Damaris. The woman's eyes settled into a scowl, her lips turning down in a hard grimace. She sniffed and moved away to adjust the window hangings.

Mr. Frye's right hand smoothed across his scalp, leaving the remainder of his hair sticking up like a half-burnt fireplace. "I should apologize. My sister's an incredible assistant, although she can be somewhat off-putting around others."

"Somewhat?" Maggie said. "The word, Mr. Frye, is rude."

Karl and Elsa pushed through the dining room door with Reuben on their heels, sporting polite if not forced smiles for their guests. Mr. Frye shifted his attention from Maggie and offered condolences to them both in turn.

"Mr. Kisch," Hugo said, pumping Karl's hand with far more vigor than he had shown Maggie. "Thank you for the invitation. I'm sorry it needed to be under these circumstances."

"Nonsense, young man. I am only sorry that we did not think to photograph our family sooner. We are supremely grateful you could accommodate us."

Elsa nestled Mr. Frye within her pudgy arms, bending low to press her cheek against his. "Handshakes are for my husband's business associates. I want you to feel like family." It was almost comical watching his arms tentatively embrace a woman six inches taller while her husband stood another six inches above that. Like a small boy trapped in a man's body.

Releasing their guest, Elsa dragged her husband towards Damaris who hovered near the window. "Who do we have here, my dear?" she asked, tackling the woman in a hug as Damaris attempted to shoo her away.

"Will she manage?" Maggie asked Mr. Frye as his sister responded to Karl's questions with one-word answers and cast sour looks at her brother.

Mr. Frye rubbed a hand along the back of his neck. "Oh assured. She's tougher than she appears." He turned his attention to Reuben, although he continued to glance at Damaris every few seconds.

Reuben grinned. "Nice seeing you outside of the *Mid-Mississippi*, Mr. Frye. Smithson couldn't have been more impressed with the work you sent on Friday."

The photographer offered Reuben the same relaxed smile he had bestowed on Maggie coupled with a much firmer handshake. "I've read your obituaries. Never read anything like them." He spit out a dry laugh. "You should write mine when I'm six feet under."

"Yes, well ..." Reuben fixed Maggie with those chocolate eyes that almost made her lose herself once. "Dead or alive, we all deserve a good story, do we not?"

She had said the same words to him the day they met about people in the cemetery and the extraordinary lives they might have led. Then two years passed, and she discovered womanhood far quicker than perhaps she should have. She fought the urge to press a hand to her abdomen.

"We should take the photograph," she murmured. "Isn't that what Mr. Frye's here for?"

Reuben broke his stare. "Of course. I'll find the others." He hurried from the room as though wild horses drove him there.

"Is everything all right? You're pale." Mr. Frye eyed her warily, as though she might combust before his eyes, and he would need to devise an alibi. The thought surprisingly brought a chuckle past her lips.

"Haven't your parents taught you it's of the utmost rudeness to comment on a lady's poor complexion?" She floated to a spot behind the sofa where the light would accent all her best features. "Better, Mr. Frye?"

"Much. You hardly appear ill at all."

Her rebuttal, and their exchange, were effectively silenced as Elsa and Karl relieved Damaris and settled themselves onto the sofa. Winnie bounced down beside her parents while Fred and Emil stepped into place behind them. With their sun-streaked blond hair, the Kisch family made a perfect summer's picture. When Reuben and Tena entered the room a moment later, Maggie's sister immediately claimed the seat beside Elsa, leaving Reuben to stand next to Maggie.

"Did I hear Mr. Frye say you're ill?" he whispered as he moved into place beside her.

"Why is everyone always asking me that?" she hissed.

Reuben shrugged. "You do appear fatigued."

"I'm perfectly well, thank you." Her eyes narrowed at the photographer rather than look at Reuben. Now positioned behind the larger camera on the tripod, Mr. Frye craned his neck around the box and gestured for Fred to shift slightly right.

"Are these photographs not usually completed with the deceased in the room?" Fred asked with his usual haughty air that made even the most tolerant person want to throttle him. "The *Fontaine Gazette* featured it once."

"Fred?" Emil spoke up. "Can I see your spectacles? I think there's dirt on them."

Fred carefully removed his glasses, holding them up to the light. "I do not see anything."

Leaning into his brother's personal space, Emil tilted his head in an effort to see better. He nodded. "My mistake, Freddie. It wasn't dirt. That was just you being a pompous fiddlehead."

"Emil!" Karl growled. Emil smirked, but conceded to silence.

With a frown, Fred returned his spectacles to his face. "Mr. Frye, am I not correct? The body is usually in the room for these sessions?"

The photographer dipped his head and twisted another knob on the camera. His hand slipped twice before he succeeded. "Um, yes, that's correct."

"Where is Charles's body?" Winnie asked her mother. "We had the funeral at the church, but when will we see him?"

Silence filled the room and everyone looked around at no one in particular. Damaris backed so far against the dining room wall that she might have melted straight through it if physics allowed. Mr. Frye tapped the edge of his camera as though it actually required adjustment. Rather than spare a glance at anyone else, Maggie's eyes cast down at the top of Tena's head while her sister stared resolutely into her lap.

Karl applied a gentle kiss to his daughter's brow. "There is no body, *liebe*. They buried your brother at sea."

"Why?"

"Sometimes that is what they must do with those who die in the ocean. They allow them to rest right where they were."

"Oh." Winnie nodded, resting her head against her father's arm. "It's awful when you don't see the body, Papa."

"It's still as awful when you do," Tena whispered.

Reaching across his wife to pat Tena's arm, Karl cleared his throat with a nod to Mr. Frye. "Please proceed, sir. Pretend we are any other family you might photograph."

Maggie stared directly into the polished circle in the front of the camera, ignoring the outsider watching her "family" from the other side. The Archers had no photographs together. If they took one at her father's funeral, neither Tena nor her mother ever mentioned it, and it wouldn't have mattered. Maggie wasn't there. She had nothing to remember him by.

Nothing except the untold secrets Laurence Archer left her.

The man with the blazing hair held up a hand to count down the time remaining. She gripped the cream upholstered sofa with both hands, and not one of them smiled.

"It'll be fine, Maggie," Reuben whispered through his teeth. "We'll all be fine again someday." His foot nudged hers, invisible from the camera, yet sending her into a spiraling breakdown. Moisture burned her eyes, but she forced herself not to move, lest she blur the photograph.

Mr. Frye's pinky folded into his fist. "All finished," he said. Reuben quickly shifted away.

Karl leapt off the sofa with a clap of his hands. "Enough somberness. Let us get to the *Zuckerkuchen*." He nodded to Mr. Frye and Damaris in turn. "You are most welcome to stay for the meal."

The photographer nodded despite the greenish tint his sister's face had taken on. "We would be delighted. Thank you, Mr. Kisch."

"Cake before the meal, Papa?" Winnie asked hopefully.

Elsa accepted her husband's hand as he helped her from the sofa. "Only this once, Winnie."

Winnie cheered at the same time Emil did. She fought her brother to be first into the dining room and ultimately lost.

"Close, but no cigar, little sister!" Emil cried.

"Yuck!" Winnie grimaced. "You can keep the cigar. I'll help myself to your share of the cake."

Fred rolled his eyes. "I am supremely thankful I do not live here every day."

"Not as glad as we are!" Emil called from the dining room. "I'm eating your piece too, Freddie!"

Reuben palmed the door, pushing past Fred. "Not if I eat it first."

"We raised a pack of wolves," Karl commented to his wife as they followed the rowdy bunch, the door swinging shut behind them. Not even Tena lingered.

Exhaustion struck Maggie to the sofa as though she hadn't slept for nine hours the previous night. She flipped her legs up, stretching out into the corner to rest her forearm across her eyes, effectively able to dry her tears without Mr. Frye or his sister noticing.

"Hugh, must we stay for lunch?" Damaris asked.

"I figured so," returned Mr. Frye. "You go on. I'll finish packing this up." Her severe footsteps moved away and the living room momentarily flooded with noisy table chatter as Damaris entered the dining room.

Maggie didn't move. She closed her eyes beneath the warm skin of her forearm and tried to imagine herself where she most desired to be—lounging in the cool shade of their garden in Fontaine, softly blowing steam from a cup of Earl Grey while she and Tena enjoyed an idle Sunday afternoon. Not speaking, but not because they were on the outs. It would be a comfortable silence, content merely to be in the other's presence. How long would it take to find that comfort again?

"*Zuckerkuchen?*" Mr. Frye's voice emerged from somewhere near the center of the room, successfully dislodging her daydream.

"God bless you. Do trouble Mr. Kisch for a handkerchief."

"*Zuckerkuchen* is German funeral cake," he explained. Amusement lined his tone, and she could hear his smile when he added, "If you were curious."

"My curiosity of the German tongue does not extend that far." Nudging her arm above her eyes, she caught him staring down into a small rectangular black box she could only assume was another camera. "Are you German too?" she asked. "I swear everyone I meet lately is German."

He flipped a lever on the box and it clicked. He looked up at her through paper thin lashes. "I don't rightly know. Aren't we all Americans anyway? What good is causing division?"

"Then how do you know about zuckercaak?"

"*Zuckerkuchen,*" he corrected. He placed the lid on the larger of the two camera cases and nudged it against the wall with his foot. "When you photograph enough funerals in a city ripe with Germans, you learn things."

She lowered her arm from her face. "Well, I say offer me a fine Brit any day."

"They certainly do speak prettier."

Mr. Frye's eyes were back on the small camera held against his stomach. He flipped the lever again, and from her current angle, she could see the metal plates inside spiral open then closed. "Are you taking photographs of me, Mr. Frye?"

"What do you know about cameras?"

"Nothing."

A smile edged his lips. The metal plates irised again. "Then no."

FIVE

HALFWAY THROUGH REUBEN'S *ZUCKERKUCHEN*, Maggie and Hugo finally joined them in the dining room. Despite bloodshot eyes and her earlier anxious bout during the photographs, she seemed to have returned to her old self, chin held high and fighting a smile at something Hugo must have also found highly amusing. His low chuckle carried as they took the two adjoining seats between Damaris and Elsa and across from Tena and himself. Damaris leaned over to whisper something in her brother's ear, and he adamantly shook his head.

Today hadn't been anything like either of Reuben's parents' funerals. When his mother died, no one attended except for Reuben, his father, Tena, and the Kischs. By that point, everyone else had heard of his mother's affliction and few seemed to understand that madness couldn't be caught as easily as the flu. Instead, they spied on the funeral procession through cracked doorways, and Reuben's father barely spoke even to his son. When Harris Radford died two months later, Reuben sat with Charles afterwards in near silence.

But here the atmosphere seemed light, almost cheery. Elsa served the cake, Tena assisted with the mid-day meal, and everyone ate until they were stuffed full. Still, there were leftovers for the icebox. This camaraderie was exactly what the family needed.

When the last fork settled on the table, Tena's head drooped against Reuben's shoulder. "I don't think I've ever been this tuckered out, and it's only two in the afternoon. You'll either need to carry me upstairs or stretch me out across the table and throw a blanket over me."

"You'll make a lovely centerpiece," Reuben said as her eyes closed.

Emil reached over him to poke Tena in the forehead. "You can sleep when you're old."

Tena groaned. She flicked his hand away and didn't bother opening her eyes. "I feel old already."

"No sleeping yet, Tena girl," Karl soothed. He made for the sideboard, extracted a bottle of Port wine from the lower cabinet, then transferred nine small glasses to the table as he spoke. "None of us would consider Charles fond of spirits, and I am thankful my son was wise in that respect; however, by the same token I doubt he would reprimand any of us for having a drink or two today."

Uncorking the bottle, he poured an ample amount into each glass and passed them around the table. Reuben took two, then nudged Tena until she sat up straight and reached for the drink.

Elsa declined when her husband attempted to fill her glass last. "I have not drank alcohol since we left Bayern, Karl. I am not about to begin now." Karl nodded, setting the bottle onto the table to pick up his own glass.

With a sigh, Emil reached across the table to nick the bottle and poured a shot into the last glass. He slid it towards his mother's clasped hands. "Do it for Charles, Mama. Just this once."

Her fingers lingered against the glass as she stared down into the dark liquid then nodded resolutely. Standing beside her husband, she raised her glass to the group. "For Charles. Just this once." Then she downed the glass with barely a flinch at the taste.

"For Charles," came the resounding reply as the rest of the circle, minus Winnie, emptied their glasses.

"But not just this once," Emil murmured to Reuben, elbowing him in the ribs.

Reuben held his glass out for Karl to refill. "Charles and I really were a wonderful influence on you, weren't we?"

Emil laid a hand over his heart. "Corrupting the innocent youth. It was a raw task, but someone had to do it."

Winnie nearly bounced out of her chair. "When do I get corrupted? Emil, tell Papa to let me have a drink."

Karl narrowed his eyes at his daughter. "Winifred, I told you no this morning and your mother agreed."

"But I'm halfway through eleven. Emil was probably younger than me when he had his first drink!"

"That's accurate," Emil admitted. "I was nine. Smoked cigars too."

"Emil!" Elsa gasped at the same time Winnie's face lit up. "See! See! Now let me have some."

"Really, Mama," said Emil, "you didn't know what we boys were up to when we stayed up late? Charles was five years older than me. Seriously, who do you think taught me how to distinguish the good cigars from the lousy ones? Sorry, mum, but your precious Charles corrupted us all."

"Not me," Fred stated with head held high.

"Of course, not you." With an exaggerated eye roll at his brother, Emil slid his near-empty glass towards Winnie. "Here you go, sis. Enjoy."

Karl snatched the glass from Winnie's reaching fingers and set it on the sideboard. "Winifred, have you finished your meal?"

"Yes, Papa, but—"

"Then you are dismissed."

"But, Papa!"

"Winifred."

"Fine." Winnie stood with a huff. "I always miss all the fun." The door banged against the wall as she pushed through it.

Fred tapped his fingers against his still nearly full glass. "You do know she will ask Emil for some later, right?"

"Way to throw me under the trolley, Freddie," Emil muttered. He rocked his chair back so he could make a rude gesture under the table.

Reuben stifled his laughter before Karl's stern expression could swing in his direction. He tapped his glass towards Fred. "Why don't you say a few words about Charles, Fred? Then we can go around the table."

Fred stood up and for once didn't maintain his usual obnoxious swagger. He adjusted his spectacles and barely managed to lift his glass without it slipping back to the table. His thumbs tapped nervously against the side. "I am not one for sentimentality. It is no secret that my brother and I were not close." He took another sip, swallowing twice. "He should not be forced to provide false compliments were I the one lost, so I think it best if I do him the same honor."

Emil leaned over to Reuben and made another rude gesture. "Leave it to Freddie to be boorish towards the dead." He snorted mid drink, inhaling his alcohol and being reduced to a coughing fit.

Throwing a deep scowl in Emil's direction, Fred set his drink down without finishing it and moved between his parents, wrapping an arm around each of them. "I believe it is time for me to leave. I will ring when I make it back." He bent down to kiss his mother. "*Ich hab' dich lieb*, Mama."

"We love you too, son. Be safe."

"I will." With a final nod to the room and a glance that didn't quite reach his brother, Fred extracted himself from the house through the front door.

Emil leapt up, holding his glass high like he won a first prize trophy. "Well, it's my turn and we all know I am by far the wittiest one here. So, now that Herr Killjoy has left the premises, can I just say on my brother's behalf that Charles was friggin' brilliant?"

"Language, Emil," Elsa cautioned, but her reprimand was only half forced.

"As I said," Emil continued, "Charles was a superior brother. He stuck up for me when Freddie thought a nine-year-old shouldn't smoke or drink—"

"Which one should not," Karl growled. "Had I known..."

"We would have done it anyway, Pop." Emil continued, "But Charles also taught me what it means to—" His voice caught and he took a drink to steady himself. He turned misty eyes on Tena. "He taught me what it means to love someone, Tena. Charles died for you, and I can think of no one more deserving." He raised his glass in her direction. "To Tena, for being the best thing my brother ever had and the only thing he ever wanted."

Six voices chimed in, "To Tena," and Elsa finished with, "Thank you, dear, for making my son the happiest he ever was." For a woman who never drank, she finished the rest of hers in record speed and doled out another round. "Reuben, please say something before I become emotional."

Reuben reached for his glass only to find his arm trapped beneath the table, locked inside Tena's firm grasp. She gripped his forearm, knuckles as white against his shirt as the sleeve itself and only a touch lighter than the complexion she now wore. Twisting his wrist, he slipped his fingers between hers, using his opposite hand to lift the glass to his lips.

"What's the matter?" he whispered around the rim. "Should we go somewhere else?"

Tena gave a thin shake of her head, her lips pressed together as though opening them would release the seven levels of Hades. Reuben suspected that was the answer to both his questions. He stayed in his chair, uncertain how to proceed.

In the silence, Hugo stood, garnering everyone's attention. He paused, napkin in hand, as he realized they expected him to express a sentiment. "Oh, no. I couldn't say anything. I'm sure he was a wonderful person, and Miss Archer, you do seem lovely, but I couldn't … I really just needed to use the lavatory."

"Mr. Frye?" Maggie smiled up at him, holding out her empty water glass. "Would you mind terribly finding me a dyspepsia tablet on your way back? I do believe the *Zuckerkuchen* has settled as well as its name sounds."

Relieved to answer a question not involving a eulogy, he snatched her glass. "Let's fix you up then. Mrs. Kisch, do you have any?"

Elsa gestured upward. "In the upstairs bathroom. Second door on the right. Brown bottle."

"I'll return straight away." He darted into the hallway, a man on a mission. A minute later his firm footfalls trudged up the stairs.

Reuben downed his drink without saying anything and ignored the raised eyebrows and confused looks of everyone in the room. He had been wrong about this funeral. Laughing with the Kischs wasn't the same without Charles. It was infinitely worse.

Charles had been cheated out of everything he wanted, everything that should have been. Reuben came to America for his friend, and now he would live Charles's life without him. He spent the last three days writing obituaries and made Tena read every single one. He saw the tears well up in her eyes every single time and heard her lips say, "It's perfect," even when her voice told him it never could be. Seeing Charles's name in print beside the words, "went to God" only made reality bite like a bitter dose of castor oil. So he quit and asked Stanley to write it. It burned that Reuben could write line upon line of beautiful stories for complete strangers, but when it came to the most important person in his life, the pages were completely empty.

"Reuben?" Karl said. "Would you like to say anything?"

Maggie leapt from her chair before Reuben could. "I'd like to say something." She smoothed her skirt and clasped her hands over her stomach, indeed looking a bit off color. "I know I haven't been easy to live with lately."

"An understatement," Emil muttered.

"But," Maggie continued louder, "Charles personally invited me to join you here. He knew that if there was one person my sister always needed it would be me. Tena, Charles loved you, but I do too, and I'm still here. So please, don't shut me out."

Squeezing Reuben's fingers until her engagement band dug into his skin, Tena stood with a troubled expression, still holding onto her empty glass and his hand. Karl's eyebrows hit the sky; however, he didn't comment which was a relief. Or would have been if Tena hadn't chosen that moment to yank her hand free and push past him into the hallway, the door swinging behind her.

Reuben laid his napkin on the table with every intention of following; however, Maggie's voice stopped him halfway out of his seat. "You *would* be so bold right now, wouldn't you?"

She stood straight and assured across the table from him, her blue-grey eyes brooding. Even her face couldn't help him fathom where she was going with this abrupt mood swing. Reuben eyed her then the door Tena exited out of, anxious to talk to the sane sister no matter how distraught she might be.

"Bold to leave this room?" he asked. "It doesn't take bravery to steer clear of your path of destruction."

Maggie pointed at the door. "Tena is still my sister. She is vulnerable and depressed right now."

Emil reached for his glass and upon seeing it empty, took a swig directly from the bottle. "Holy smokes, Maggie, we don't need a dramatic buildup. This isn't the theatre. Get to the point."

Maggie hesitated. She worried her lip and slid her hands to her hips then to the table, trying to find a stance that met whatever she was formulating. Her tone calmed significantly. "I simply would like Reuben to remember that Tena's in love with Charles. She doesn't need to question that right now."

Karl and Elsa both eyed first Maggie then Reuben and finally each other. Elsa placed a gentle hand on Maggie's wrist. "Of course he does. What exactly are you implying?"

A warm pain flooded Reuben similar to when he and Maggie stood on the platform at Grand Central Station. He seriously hoped she wasn't suggesting what he thought she was, except he knew her better than that. He was more intimately connected to her than anyone else in that room and wished so badly that he wasn't. He met Maggie's gaze and ignored all others pointed in his direction. "We need to talk. Now."

He trudged out to the front garden, knowing full well she would follow him. The door barely banged shut when it opened again behind him. He focused on the house across the cobbled street and pinched the bridge of his nose, exhaling. "Why do you always make me fight you, Maggie? You know I have aggressive tendencies, so why must you always bring them out in spades?"

"I don't want to fight, either, Reuben."

Reuben turned, her strained face flooding his vision. She seemed to have simultaneously aged ten years and yet looked like a child. Her arms wrapped her middle, clutching into her sides like she might be sick at any moment. "Then why are we standing out here about to have an argument?"

He didn't want to battle with her again. Whenever they fought, it renewed emotions he had spent the last two months burying. If his feelings stayed in darkness long enough then hopefully, like a plant, they would wither and die.

Her lips opened, a deep breath emanating from somewhere deep within. "I want to be the one to help my sister. Can't you let me have that this once?"

She turned those stormy blue eyes on him and the breath sucked from his lungs. That wasn't anger he saw. It was fear.

"What the devil is wrong with you?" Emil stalked across the lawn towards them. "Between you two and Tena, it's like the trio of houseguests from hell."

Maggie swept a loose hair away from her face. Something flickered and whatever Reuben thought he saw was gone. "It wouldn't be if Reuben would stay away from Tena."

Reuben's hands dropped to his hips. "Why would I need to do that?"

Maggie glowered. "The long evening walks alone, helping in the kitchen, buying her books ... you fall all over her."

"Of course. Because reading is a sign of amorous passion now."

"If so, then Freddie's really a closet lothario," Emil chuckled. He tapped a finger to his chin. "Does it count if you make love to a legal text?"

Maggie pushed Emil out of the way. "You think I don't see what you're doing, Reuben? Charles is gone, and you think you can move right in."

"Like you allow every man in America to move right in?"

"Stop it." Emil threw a hand against Reuben's chest before he could do more than ball his fingers at his sides. "Only one funeral per day. You can kill each other tomorrow."

Reuben pressed against Emil's hand, ignoring his friend's words. "Maggie, how could you even think that? Do you honestly believe me so shallow as to see an opening and step in where I don't belong? Charles was my best mate—"

"But he invited *me*!" Maggie shot back. "He didn't buy you a ticket to America; he bought it for me. You're here of your own accord. I'm Tena's sister; what are you? Nothing."

Emil's hand dropped an inch, his face as stunned as Reuben felt. "Incredible. You actually just said that, didn't you?"

Maggie stared him down. "My sister's heart is broken. I won't allow your friend to play her for a fool."

Reuben dug the toes of his brown loafers into the grass, fighting to maintain his composure. "Love is more than conquering someone on an impulse or manipulating their weakest points. I would never take advantage of Tena, and I didn't take advantage of you." He dropped his voice to a mere whisper. "Is that what this is actually about? You think you were just one night's lust for me?"

He waited for her response, and when there was none, Emil's eyes widened. "Blimey, you don't think that, do you?"

Maggie bit her lip and with head held high, remained silent.

Reuben gave a garbled choke. "If you still can't recognize how much I loved you, Maggie, then you're right, I'm nothing to you."

"Reuben," Emil cut in quietly, his eyes darting towards the house. "Let's go somewhere else with this."

Reuben ignored him. He folded his arms and stepped far away from her, too far to reach if he suddenly felt out of character and decked her like she so dearly deserved. It was exactly the type of thing to do if he was the louse she thought he was. "Since I'm such a scoundrel, Tena should be thankful you stopped me from chasing after her. You should talk to her, not me, because you obviously know her better than I do."

Maggie startled, her brow pinching in confusion, then she released a tiny breath and allowed a smile to light on her lips. "Really? Thank you, Reuben."

With a stiff nod, he unhooked one hand from the crook of his arm to wave towards the house. She glided away as effortlessly as she had asked Mr. Frye for a glass of water and some medicine.

Emil slicked his sun-bleached hair back, drawing the sweat dotting his brow. He gave a low whistle and slapped a hand on Reuben's back. "Well, that was something. I have to hand it to you for not becoming violent. Because if she said some of that to me—"

"Am I still insane, Emil?"

Emil frowned. "There is no positive way for me to respond to that."

"Because," Reuben continued, his heart heavy, "If I was sane, I wouldn't keep doing this to myself."

"She doesn't, you know," Emil said. "Know Tena better than you do. If that's what you're thinking, you're wrong. You were the one who was there for her through everything. Her courtship with Charles, her father's death ... blimey, you even convinced Charles to marry her. You think blood should automatically win over friendship, but why? When it comes to Miss High and Mighty, why do you always lie down like a dog?"

"So your answer is, yes, I'm still insane."

"No, my question is why do you act like you are?"

"I don't know." Reuben imagined Tena in the kitchen right now scouring dirty pans with a vengeance, struggling to keep her mind off the one person who would never be there. Denial was a beautiful thing when it worked. He should know, he was able to pretend all sorts of things to suit his needs. He could pretend his departed sister returned to harass him; he could even act like he deserved to be treated like rubbish by a woman who would never honestly share his affection. But perhaps it wasn't his affection he should have been most adamant about her returning when there was always someone more needy of her attentions. What a selfish, blind fool he had been.

He slammed his fist into his palm. "Maggie doesn't know Tena like I do, and that's the problem, isn't it?" He stalked towards the house, anxious to take to his room and leave this wretched day behind him. "I'm through talking."

Throwing a hand to his shoulder, Emil pulled him back mid-step, but Reuben pushed him back, nearly toppling Emil onto the grass. "Get out of my way."

Emil righted himself, clasping both hands onto Reuben's shoulders. "Don't walk away."

"Don't make me clock you."

Emil lifted his chin and pointed at his teeth. "Go on then. Right here'll do nicely. Knock a couple of them out. Fewer to rot later." Emil laughed. "Come on and clobber me if it'll make you feel better." He flinched as Reuben wrenched his arm back then let it fall to his side. Emil's haughty grin slid to confusion.

"Aren't you going to hit me?" he asked. "I mean, I have it coming, don't I?"

Reuben rubbed his knuckles along the ever fading scar lines from his duel with Lloyd Halverson—the night he almost died, the night Tena's memory saved him, the night he lost Maggie forever. "There is nothing I want more than to beat something until my fingers break. But what good would it do? Charles would still be dead. And everything else would still be broken."

He slammed the front door open, pushing past Hugo in the hallway and nearly spilling the drinks the photographer carried. "Excuse me," Reuben muttered gruffly.

Hugo stared at Emil frozen in silence in the doorway. "I've missed something, haven't I?"

SIX

"I SHOULD HAVE FIGURED I would find you in the kitchen."

Watching her sister labor over a sink full of dirty dishes, Maggie leaned against the counter and plucked a piece of leftover *Zuckerkuchen* from the platter. She popped it into her mouth and licked her lips. "I'm not sure why I'm eating this. It didn't sit well the first time around."

Her sleeves rolled up to the elbows, Tena continued to scour the skillet in her hand without comment.

"That's cast iron," Maggie noted as she nibbled another bite. "It doesn't need cleaning—"

"As if you would know. You can barely poach an egg." Tena dropped the pan into the sink and water poured over the side to soak the rug under her feet. With a sigh, she reached for a towel to mop up the soapy mess. She flung the now soaking towel across the kitchen where it slapped Mr. Frye's chest as he walked through the door.

Hugo eyed the watermark on his jacket and held up two glasses. "At least I didn't spill the drinks."

"That would be alcohol abuse." Emil edged into the room behind Mr. Frye, tossed Maggie a scowl she knew she deserved, then climbed onto the counter to scavenge the top shelf. "They think they can hide the good stuff from me, but are you too clever, Emil? Why yes, yes, you are." Pumping his fist, he slid out a bottle of gin and hopped off the counter. He tapped the bottle in Mr. Frye's direction. "Hey, photo man, want to toss back a few on the porch?"

"Here you are." Mr. Frye held a full water glass out to Maggie, unclasping his hand to drop a tablet into her palm. "Is my sister out there?" he asked.

Emil fished in another cabinet, propping the gin bottle under one arm to juggle two glasses in each hand. "I think she's still in the dining room with my parents."

"I should stick with her, I think." Hugo backtracked to the wet towel on the floor, tossing it to Tena as he left.

Emil held up the bottle to Tena and Maggie and raised his eyebrows.

Tena returned to the sink to wring out the wet towel. "I already had two during lunch. This isn't an occasion to be swept completely under the table."

Maggie popped the tablet into her mouth and nearly drowned herself with the full glass of water, her silence eliciting Emil's deep frown. "Not even you, Miss High and Mighty?" With a huff, he returned all the glasses to the cabinet and the gin to its hiding place. "Fine. Both of you are boring sods. Tee, tell Mama and Papa I'm down the street at Terry and Jakob's. I'll be home by dinner." He hopped through the door, whistling.

Without Emil's presence, the room's silence was unnerving. Tena popped the plug from the sink while Maggie filled the tea kettle and set it on the stove to warm. "Are you still upset with me?" she asked.

Tena watched dirty dishwater swirl down the drain. "No."

Surprisingly, even considering the past few days, her tone seemed genuine. But Maggie knew something bothered her. Was it only related to Charles's death? Or could it be more than that? Maggie begrudgingly admitted that Reuben would have known right off.

She located two teacups and filled them with a plentiful helping of tea leaves, enough that the brew would be good and strong ... and hopefully jolt her enough to fight through the next bout of pregnancy-induced symptoms.

Reuben had been right. Why did she always look for a row with him? She didn't want to, but she also didn't know how to stop herself anymore. Whenever they were together, the words just came out—the hurt, the accusations ... they fell from her lips as punishment he didn't deserve. He would never take advantage of Tena; he wasn't crass enough to force something that so clearly wasn't the least thought on his mind. But still ... Maggie was a woman spurned, and it grated her last nerve that he understood her sister so well while Maggie felt like she roomed with a stranger. Seeing their closeness right there in front of her nose, day in and day out, and neither making any attempt to hide it, hurt Maggie more than she would ever admit aloud. It was like being a child again when, as all seven-year-olds' forever friendships do, her best friend, Elsie, told Maggie she wasn't going to play with her anymore. She found someone new to share her skipping rope with.

The kettle's shrill whistle blew through her memories, causing both girls to jump. Maggie snatched it from the stove and turned down the fire to pour hot water into the waiting cups. She offered one to Tena who wiped her damp hands on her skirt before accepting. "Thank you," she whispered.

"Shall we go out back?" Maggie asked. "There's a perfectly good settee and no one to occupy it."

Tena shook her head. "Front garden. Everyone else is in the dining room. With the windows open, they'll hear every word."

Lifting her teacup, Maggie's first sip scalded her mouth along with her taste buds. She choked as the hot bitter brew slid down her throat. "Lead the way."

With shaking hands, Tena carried her tea outside, lifting her skirt to sink onto the grass underneath the study windows. Cloud cover had moved in, allowing some reprieve from the July sun, but no comfort from the humidity. At least a breeze was blowing, Maggie thought, already feeling sweat peak upon her neck. She arranged herself as best she could beside her sister and pressed a hand where her corset ground against the tender flesh. Between the corset, the heat, and her far-too-potent brew, she was likely to expel everything onto her sister's lap.

"Honestly," Tena said, an eyebrow raised at her sister's discomfort. "This stomach trouble has gone on long enough. You must see a doctor. You could have worms."

Knowing it wasn't any more serious than a person growing inside her, Maggie forced a smile. "I assure you I do not."

"Influenza then."

"I have a flu that lasts weeks and doesn't infect anyone else? Am I reverse Typhoid Mary?"

Tena chuckled. "Goodness. I certainly hope not." She tentatively brought her tea to her lips, jolting at the taste. "My word, how many leaves did you put in this?"

Maggie smiled. "Enough."

Tena drank another sip. "It's potent. If I'm awake all night, I'm poking you in the ribs until you stay up with me." Her smile fell and she laced her fingers around the cup, her eyes drawn out somewhere far beyond them. "I should have stayed with him."

"Who?" Maggie asked. Tena's eyes glimmered with tears. "Charles? Oh, no, Tena—"

Tena turned, eyes—and heart no doubt—full of sorrow. "Do you know what one of the last things Charles said to me was?" she asked. Her tone took on an edge of annoyance. "'I will find you.' I believed he would. I believed he could have ripped the world apart to return to me. Why wouldn't I do the same?"

"You didn't know. You thought everyone would be safe. Lots of ships are towed after wrecking. You thought that's all it was."

"Charles knew it wasn't. That's why I'm so spitting mad at him. He should have told me. Moreover, I should have figured it out. I should have stayed."

"You would have died."

"Then I died. He did. We can't live forever anyway. I would rather be loved so completely for a little while than live long remembering how it felt."

"You'll find it again. Maybe there's someone out there for both of us." It was a lie. Of course it was. Tena saw straight through it.

"Oh, Maggie, please. You don't believe that. You never have. Why would you start now?"

"Because you believe it, and heaven forbid, I try to be supportive."

"I would rather you be honest."

"Oh, blast it all. I doubt that's truly what you want."

"Maggie, don't you treat me like a child too. All of them have been walking eggshells around me since I arrived. Acting like I can't deal with reality. Emil's the only one who treats me like a normal person, but he's Emil so ..." She drew another sip of her drink and winced. "My word, that's strong!" Yet she took another without hesitation. "Be my sister, please. Not my parent."

Maggie adjusted herself on the grass, cold sweat trapped between her undergarments and her skin, her discomfort as invisible as the baby trapped inside her. Despite what she said, Tena didn't need the truth. She needed an illusion as much as Maggie needed one, probably more.

"Tena, I wish we still understood each other like we used to. As though the last year never happened. Charles tried to see something in me that's simply not there. He invited me here, at least in part, because he thought we were alike. Only I'm *not* like you, and I don't want to be. I'm selfish and cynical and I can't love anyone ... at least not the way they deserve. That's the ugly truth you ask for. You and Charles were willing to give your entire lives for each other. That kind of sacrifice is beyond my realm of understanding."

"I know it is. You live life with logic and my reasoning is illogical."

"So, by your reasoning," Maggie countered, "you would run into a burning building when there was little hope of escape?"

"Of course not."

"My point is proven."

"But one day, Maggie, I think *you* will." Tena set her teacup on the grass and scooted closer, until their knees touched like little girls whispering secrets. "I think one day you'll surprise *everyone*. You might not believe it now, but someday you will."

Maggie opened her mouth to argue until Tena cut her off. "Let's not beat a dead horse."

With a minuscule smile, she tilted back to stare into the clouds, shining brilliance laughing back in random formations. She released a dry bitter laugh, a noise that sounded much too old to be connected with her youthful features. "Besides, that belief sounds crazy even for myself. Right now in this moment, even though I know the truth, the notion is impossible to hold onto. Like dandelion seeds in the wind.

You can see them, you know they exist, and you know you could grow a new life if only you could catch them." She stretched forward to pluck a puffy white dandelion from the grass, fingering the soft cotton seeds. With a flick of her wrist, they came apart and floated away on the wind. "That's how I feel right now. Like I'm standing in a field watching the seeds of my future blow away, and I can't run fast enough to catch them."

Slowly, she twisted her engagement band. "I thought I could prove to Mother that it was possible. For two people to be together not for any socially contrived reason, but simply because they loved each other. My children would have freedoms we didn't, and I wouldn't disown them if they chose a different path. I planned to write Mother hundreds of letters about every way she was wrong and end them all with, 'I told you so.' I didn't want a life like Edith or Bianca or any other girl in Fontaine. Everything would be different. But in truth, nothing changed. At least nothing except me."

Maggie tugged another dandelion from the ground, this one soft and golden. The pollen smeared her fingertips. "I'm sorry, Tena."

"Honestly, what else could you have to be sorry for?"

If only you knew, Maggie thought, but that was for another day.

"If I hadn't met Reuben in that cemetery, if I'd only gone to the May Day festival with you as planned, none of this would have happened. If I never met Reuben, you would never have met Charles, and I would have been there with you when Father died. We never would have left Fontaine. I probably would have married Lloyd."

Every part of Maggie clenched, a dull pain enveloping her middle. If she never met Reuben, she never would have gone to London to escape him. In the end, she would have done what was expected of her if for no other reason than to please her father. Lloyd would be her husband now. She could very well still be expecting, and there would be no question as to whom the father was. No disparaging looks when the news was revealed. Only joy from her mother and pride from her father. She had fought marriage tooth and nail, but maybe it would have been better than what she chose instead. Maybe it would be better than the life she was living.

Maggie extended both her palms up in offering and willed her voice to remain as strong as she wanted to be. "If I never met Reuben, if you never met Charles, we would have been different people, and I think we could both do with being someone else right now."

"Oh, Maggie, I wish that too." Laying her hands upon her sister's, Tena stared into the clouds as though the heavens could divine all her answers. "Sometimes I wish we never met them. Does that make me horribly wretched?"

Maggie followed her gaze into the afternoon sky. "Wishing for a better life doesn't make you wretched, Tena. It makes you human."

SEVEN

REUBEN STARED UP AT THE SIGN for the *Mid-Mississippi* shining in the late afternoon sunlight and clutched his traveling case tighter. This is what life had come to, literally running away from home, or at least what had served as a home for the past few months. Sneaking out through the back alleyway, he walked for over two hours, until his heels pinched from rising blisters and his muscles ached.

He shouldn't have left them how he did. He shouldn't have deserted without so much as a proper goodbye or any explanation. Heaven help him, he *should* go back. He should, but he wouldn't. He couldn't.

The scent of soot and horse manure—the stink of the city—flowed through his nostrils. It swirled in his brain, and the only sound able to slip through was Tena's voice. It had been so broken, so helpless, so full of anguish and resentment, and all directed at him and Charles.

"I wish we'd never met them."

He had listened to the sisters' entire conversation from his upstairs bedroom window. He went there to be alone after his argument with Maggie and received an earful instead. He was the cause of all their problems. They were better off without him. If not for him, Maggie would have married Lloyd.

Reuben's fingers curled until they formed white-knuckled fists, thoroughly primed for ruining an enemy's face—or the brick wall in front of him—but he did neither. He pushed his way through the *Mid-*

Mississippi's revolving door, unable to conceal his scowl even for Miss Newton. He lowered his eyes and trudged up twenty-seven stairs, each step carrying a mule's weight, each one pressing him closer to the ground.

The day he arrived in St. Louis, he promised Tena he would stay for her. He promised he could overlook what Maggie did, accept Charles's death, and stay for her alone. God help him, but he couldn't bear to see her crumble when he broke that promise.

He was a coward. She was better off. With time, so would he be.

Rolling his shoulders, he paused on the third floor landing to plaster a convincing smile on his face and walked into the typists' room with head held high.

"Good afternoon, Mr. Radford," came the usual calls.

He tapped two fingers to his hat, sliding them across the brim and off the other side. "Afternoon, ladies."

Hazel Vine's grin spread ear to ear, cheeks flushed under his glance. "Have a fascinatin' day, sir!"

With a silent nod, Reuben shifted his traveling case to his left hand and pushed open the newsroom door, saying a silent prayer that Smithson had already departed for the day, and thanking the good Lord when the editor's office window lay dark.

He lumbered across the room to topple into his desk chair, grateful that the newsroom was relatively empty for a Monday afternoon.

After stowing his traveling case under the desk, there was precious little room remaining for his legs, but it was better than overtly advertising his extended stay. He removed his notepad and pencil from his satchel, then slung the bag over the chair back.

"Thought you had the day off?"

Pencil in hand, Reuben glanced up from Widow Claremore's obituary notes to find Stanley standing over him with hands folded around a steaming mug of coffee. Reuben cast his eyes back to the notes and pressed pencil lead to paper. "Change in plans."

"How was the funeral?"

"It was a funeral. How would you suppose it was?"

Taking a swig of coffee, Stanley set the mug on his desktop and rummaged through the top drawer, retrieving a folded up sheet of paper. He opened it then smoothed it out on the already cluttered desk. "I finished Charles's obituary. Do you want to read it?"

No, thought Reuben. *No, no, no. Definitely no.* Reading the obituary about his dead friend that he failed to write himself was very near the bottom of his list, right below "Contract dysentery" and a step above "Eat a salad of arsenic and straight razors."

Yet, he held his hand out for the paper anyway. And wouldn't you know, it was faultless. Without even having met Charles, Stanley's words captured Reuben's best mate to a tee.

Slowly, he folded the sheet up. "It's perfect, Lee. You sure can write. Keep that up and you'll put me out of a job."

"No thanks, I'll stick to murders and mayhem." Stanley set his latest article next to a blank sheet of paper and began copying without the scratch marks and squiggling marginalia. He swallowed another heavy dose of coffee. "That said, if you ever need another one—I hope you don't—but if you do, I'll happily oblige."

"Thanks, Lee. You're a real friend. It seems I don't have many of those these days." Before Stanley could do more than look up and open his mouth, Reuben filled in the gap. "Any more of that coffee left downstairs?"

"Should be. Miss Newton made a fresh pot about fifteen minutes ago."

Snatching up Charles's obituary, Reuben spun his chair and headed from the newsroom, making a brief stop to lay the paper in Hazel Vine's inbox. "This needs transcription today, Miss Vine. For tomorrow's edition."

Her fingers slid from her typewriter keys to examine the sheet, eyes swiveling to meet his with a frown. "But it doesn't have approval." She flipped the sheet over. "No, see, it doesn't have a signature."

He snatched the pencil from her desk and scrawled his initials on the top right corner of the page. "It does now. Type it, Miss Vine, and send it to the paste room. If Smithson doesn't like it, he can flay my hide, not yours." He tossed the pencil back on the desk and swept from the room. Then he climbed the last flight of stairs to the roof landing and lost control of everything.

The exterior door released a dull groan as he fell against it, one fist pounding frustration out against his thigh. For the first time since his arrival in America, he wept for Charles and the friendship they lost. His friend's absence was like a daily gut-wrenching punch, worse than anything he felt when Lloyd left him battered on the *Höllenfeuer*, more painful than the deaths of all his family combined.

He scrunched his eyes tight until colors spiraled behind them. He could taste salt in the corners of his lips.

"Mr. Radford?"

Reuben jerked upright at the sound of Hazel Vine's voice. Blue embroidered handkerchief extended, she stood slightly behind him with the most brilliant smile; its kindness reached all the way from her lips to her eyes. He found it incredible how she could maintain a presence like that while a fully grown man stood before her bawling his eyes out like an infant. He couldn't care less; he was out of cares to give today.

"I know it's thoughtless to intrude," she said softly, "But I read the obituary. I heard he was your friend, and I wondered, well, might you prefer a shoulder to cry on instead of a door?"

Reuben ignored her outstretched handkerchief to retrieve his own from his jacket. He blew his nose and blinked through lingering tears. "Did Mr. Leonard send you up here?"

She blushed as she folded her handkerchief and slid it up her blouse cuff. "You've caught me. He did. But that don't change my sincerity."

He didn't even consider it. He didn't know her well, and he certainly didn't feel like discussing his problems with a near stranger, no matter how many times they flirted. Besides, she already read the obituary. He didn't need to spell it out for her. "I'm sorry, Miss Vine, but I don't think so. It wouldn't be professional."

She nodded, that wide smile never faltering. "I understand, Mr. Radford. Still's though, a group of us are planning to have a bite at the Nightingale after we're done for the day. Mr. Leonard says he'll come if you do. Perhaps you'd be free to join us?" Clasping her hands, she rocked back on her heels with the sweetest little giggle he had ever heard. "My treat."

A faint smile hit his lips, and he wiped his eyes on his shirt sleeve. *Do it*, something whispered.

"You know what, Miss Vine? I won't allow you to pay, but all the same, I think I'd like that."

EIGHT

THE CLOCK IN THE KISCHS' HALL chimed five in the afternoon as Tena marched down the stairs ready to strike wrath into her sister.

Twenty minutes ago, she felt like a new woman. Although emotional, her conversation with Maggie also brought new insight into the situation. After a strained couple of days, they were finally on speaking terms and sharing stories of father and Charles and dreaming of better times. Tena finally pictured their lives in St. Louis as a possible opportunity rather than an interruption.

When Elsa called them for tea on the porch, Tena skipped upstairs to freshen her makeup and rejoin the family as a civilized human being. She sat down at the dressing table, barely recognizing her own smile as she swiped rouge across her lips, and noticed a scrap of paper wedged between the mirror and the vanity frame. Setting down her lipstick, she dislodged the parchment and unfolded it to familiar masculine penmanship.

Tena, forgive me for what you're about to read ...

Twenty minutes later, she pushed open the rear screen door and paused, her flushed cheeks and heaving chest a radical difference to the merry group situated at the other end of the porch. Karl and Elsa now occupied the settee at the end of the porch, Karl's muscular arm wrapped around his wife's plump shoulders while she fanned herself with a folded sheet of newsprint. Maggie, Mr. Frye, and Damaris occupied three of the four chairs now pulled away from the tea service on the wooden table. In the yard, Emil tossed a cricket ball with Jakob and Terry Schneider, the curly haired teenage boys from down the street.

Pull yourself together, Tena, she thought, managing to draw deep breaths and lower her heart rate. *No one will thank you for causing a scene after all that has already transpired today.*

"Three questions, you say?" Mr. Frye asked Maggie as he sipped a bottle of beer, his left leg crossed over his right. He had shed his jacket, his distressed charcoal vest now visible over shirt sleeves rolled past the elbow.

"That's what Father always said." Maggie settled back in her chair, fanning herself even as a breeze whistled across the porch. "Heavens, it is sweltering out here." She reached for her water and finding the glass empty, swiped Mr. Frye's beer instead. "Ah, that is delightful. Where have we been hiding this?" She attempted to give it back to Mr. Frye who gently nudged her hand away.

"No, thanks. You finish it."

"You know, Maggie dear," Elsa said, her newsprint flapping away, "If your stomach's been bothering you, alcohol may not be the best solution."

Maggie frowned at the bottle, then turned and shoved it into Damaris's empty hands. "You haven't said a word all afternoon, Miss Frye. Drink this and loosen up."

Neck muscles tensing, Damaris handed the bottle to Hugo who reached behind him to set it on the table. "So, those questions?" he asked.

"Why did you become a photographer?" Maggie asked, eyeing the beer as though she might climb over Mr. Frye to get to it. She was the only person Tena knew where one was always one too many.

Mr. Frye ran a hand through his hair, and it slicked back with sweat. "That question is oddly specific for something he would ask anyone."

"He wouldn't." Maggie looked down at her nails. "Two of the questions are determined by the requester. It's only the third question that remains the same."

Tena's anger flared again at the mention of their father's favorite game, and she took another deep breath to calm her tone. It would never do to have an all-out brawl in front of everyone. "Maggie," she said sweetly. "May I have your assistance with something inside, please?"

Ten eyes swiveled towards her. Karl rested his own beer on his knee. "Feeling any better?"

"Oh, much. I think soon I'll be better even still." She threw them all a broad smile to mask the pain crushing her chest. "We won't be long, I promise."

Maggie stood, flattened her damp hair back, and pointed at Mr. Frye. "I'll want your answer when I return." Her finger swiveled in Damaris's direction. "Yours too." She pushed herself out of the chair.

Tena ushered her sister through the back door, but Maggie continued into the kitchen. "Allow me one minute," she told Tena. "I need some water, then I'll help you." There was a clinking of glasses, and the sink turned on.

Tena wasted no time. Her nerves sizzled with anger from Reuben's note and the last two months of living under the same roof as a sister who cared for nothing and no one but herself. Their earlier conversation seemed like a turning point, as though Maggie understood a fraction of the pain Tena bottled up inside, but had been simply more of the same old deception.

Picking up the traveling case Tena left in the hallway, she slammed it against her sister as she emerged from the kitchen. Maggie barely managed to hold onto her full water glass as she shifted the case against her chest.

She stared at Tena over the buckles. "What are you doing?"

"Get out," Tena spat. She pointed towards the front door. "You're all packed. Take your things and be gone."

Maggie's eyebrow quirked upward. "Excuse me?"

"You're not deaf." Tena slapped her hand against the case. "I told you to leave. Take your bag and go away. I can't stand to share a house with you."

Maggie lowered the case and her water glass to the floor, knelt to throw open the latches, and drew in a breath when she saw that it was indeed full of her belongings. Her eyes lifted in shock. "What did I do?"

"Reuben said—"

"Listen, Tena, I know you have a soft spot for him," Maggie said. "But even you know his propensity to exaggerate a situation. If he told you about our argument, it was only a simple disagreement."

"It was a pretty big row. I saw it."

Both girls jumped as Emil sauntered between them into the kitchen. Bending into the icebox, he snatched two beer bottles and an opener from the drawer and popped the caps onto the counter. He returned to prop a shoulder against the doorframe. "What's the rumpus, ladies?"

"Aren't you supposed to be at the Schneiders', not the other way around?" Tena asked.

Maggie eyed his beer. "Don't you feel you've had enough today?"

"First," Emil said, "Jakob and Terry are here because their uncle, whom they live with, is out of sorts. Secondly, these beers aren't for me. They're for my father, who is plenty old enough, and for Mr. Frye, who claims you tainted his first bottle." He drew a swig and chuckled. "And now I've tainted his second."

"Emil!" Tena cried. "Either go outside or go to your room."

"My room?" Emil pressed further into the doorframe. "Thanks, Mum, but I'm not five. Regardless, I'm still going to listen behind the door."

Tena glared at him, then kicked Maggie's traveling case. "Fine. Stay. I don't have time to argue with you. Help me toss Maggie out on her rump."

"Harsh, Tee. What'd she do?"

"Reuben's moved out, and Maggie's to blame."

Maggie closed the suitcase lid. "He did?"

"Yes." She handed Emil Reuben's note. "I went to your room, and all of his things are gone."

"But why?" Maggie asked. "I know I haven't been very polite to him. We may have quarreled once or twice, but I never told him to leave."

"You didn't need to." Tena pressed the back of her fingers to her forehead. "It's all in the note. He said he was coming between us.

'Blood before friendship,' he said. You before him." She drew a shaky breath, rereading Reuben's words in her mind's eye and struggling not to scream.

Tena,

Forgive me for what you're about to read. I wish I could express my feelings in person, but we would quarrel, and I would fold like I always do. I can't change my mind this time. Trust that I'm in the right this once.

I cannot stay with the Kischs anymore. I'm becoming the wedge in your relationship with Maggie, and we both know there's only room for one of us in your life. It should be her, not me. Blood before friendship.

Forgive me for breaking my promise.

Yours,
Reuben

Another wash of anger soaked through her mourning dress, pressing her towards the floor. Her eyes flashed, and she hoped they were the color of fire. "Whatever you said made him leave." She bent to latch the traveling case and hefted it off the floor. Stalking to the front door, she opened it and tossed the case onto the front lawn. "I want you out now, Maggie."

Emil stood frozen in the kitchen doorway. "You can't throw her out," he said. "Where would she go tonight? To the poorhouse?"

"Thank you," Maggie whispered.

Emil glared at her. "I didn't say I agreed with you." He pushed off the wall and walked to the back door, throwing it open with his standard playful grin. "Hey, Pops," he called. "Still thirsty?" A minute later, he sidled back in sans beers, his glare refocusing on Maggie as he closed it behind him. "Does a week sound fair?"

Maggie stood, leaning backwards rather awkwardly as she did so. "A week for what?"

"Find a job, what else?" Emil retrieved Maggie's case from the yard, setting it on the stairs behind Tena. He lowered his voice, his gaze softening like the brother he had always been to her. "Listen, Tee, I know you're mad at her. I am too. But kicking her out when she has nowhere to go will only make you feel worse. St. Louis isn't Fontaine. It isn't as happy-go-lucky here. One street is kind and another might be overrun with gangs."

"Gangs?" Tena breathed.

"Not near us," he quickly amended, "But yes, they exist. Don't make this a rushed decision. Give her a week to find a new place. Once she leaves, we'll try to convince Reuben to come back."

Maggie propped a hand to either hip and strode towards them, some of her fire returning. "Why are you both so wrung out about him leaving? For pity's sake, we're adults. We can't all live here forever anyway."

"You don't understand," Emil said.

"Of course I do," Maggie huffed. "I'll admit it's been close quarters with all of us under one roof, and I certainly didn't want to be around him. But you'll still see him whether I live here or not."

Emil shook his head, blazing blond locks flying. "I've known him since I was five. This is what Reuben does. He disappears. You go to another city to escape; he stays exactly where he is and hides all the same. After Mira died, we barely saw him. He sat in that cemetery and didn't talk to anyone. He couldn't. Then he met you, Maggie, and suddenly he seemed better. Then you moved away, his parents died, and Tena said he vanished for over a month. That, Maggie, is how he is. It's what he does. He ferments in his turmoil like a dead rat on the cobblestones. You think that you alone wronged him, so why should the rest of us take it so personally? Except you've hurt everyone, Maggie. I have a little sister, and for all my jokes, I'm serious about protecting her. You are not the kind of woman I want her to become."

Maggie's arms folded defensively. "What about when I arrived? Tena, you said we were sisters no matter what." She eyed her suitcase then shook her head. "All those times we were apart before, I know you missed me."

Tena had missed her. She yearned for her sister more than anything those months alone in Fontaine, hiding her relationship with Charles, caring for their ailing father, and engaging in screaming matches with their mother. The world fell down around her while Maggie rubbed elbows with the London aristocracy and seduced her charming footman, Derby. Tena cried far too often praying for Maggie's return.

She turned eyes stained with memory to lock onto her sister. "Did you know Reuben's my dearest friend? It *was* you, of course. Blood over friendship, exactly as he said. Except that's not how it is for either of us anymore, is it, Maggie?"

"Tena—"

"Let me finish!" she shouted, something much stronger than anger coursing through her, something that made even Emil step back from her reaction.

"Were you aware that Reuben sent Mother flowers the day after Father died?" Tena asked, her voice eerily calm again.

"No," Maggie said. "I bet Mother hated it."

"She did." Tena could recall the day the courier showed up at their door with a dozen lilac sprigs, so fragrant they filled the entryway with the most wonderful odor. Their mother threw them into the hearth without so much as a second glance, but even in their destruction, the scent was heavenly.

"Or," continued Tena, "did you know that at the Winchesters' last Christmas party, while you were in London, Reuben never danced? He didn't even ask anyone. Instead, he diverted Mother from the ballroom while I danced with Charles." *And whispered witty comments in my ear about the other insufferable men on my dance card*, she thought before pressing on to the next thought, each memory coming quicker than the last. "He found Charles and I a secluded corner by the post office to meet in passing. He kept me going, kept me fighting to keep our secret. He listened to me blabber like an idiot when six months passed and you still sent no word. He said something must have happened to make you stay away. Reuben was the one I confided in about Charles, about you, about everything."

Tena lowered herself onto the staircase, her elbows on her knees and head cradled in her hands. "Did you know all that, Maggie?" she breathed. "No, of course you didn't. Because you were never there. Now Reuben won't be either."

Maggie sat beside her and didn't answer. She probably still assumed Tena would do what she always did—be cross for a few days then forgive and forget. Only nothing was so easily forgiven anymore.

"Here's what we'll do," Emil said. He squatted before Tena and carefully removed her hands from her eyes. "We're not going to breathe a word of this yet. Papa would overreact, and I am not nearly responsible enough to become man of the family when he has a heart attack. Instead, we'll tell everyone the newspaper called Reuben out of town on emergency assignment." He shifted his attention back to Maggie. "You will find another place to live within one week, else I will tell my parents every last snide remark you've made behind their backs, and they'll know how you were responsible for driving their fourth son away."

"I don't think your mother will toss me out even then. She said I was welcome as long as I liked."

Emil's vision narrowed, not even a hint of his usual comedic manner lighting through. "Shall we try it?" He paced towards the back door.

"No, wait!" Maggie jumped off the step and immediately swayed. She grabbed the banister to brace herself. "Blasted summer heat," she growled. "I'm nauseous *and* lightheaded."

Tena rose to face her. "Don't play ill, Maggie. You're not seven trying to get out of lessons with Miss Beue."

Maggie clasped one hand to her stomach, the other still firmly on the banister. "I think I'm going to throw up," she gasped. Sweat beaded her forehead and panic shimmered over her usually so perfectly determined features. "You can't throw me out," she cried again, pleading between her sister and Emil even from her doubled over state. "Don't you know what I gave up for you? I'm here because you wanted me here. I gave up England for you."

Tena's vision blurred, everything she was now forgetting everything she used to be. Charles had admired her reserved nature, that she loved her sister unwaveringly and forgave so easily. He agreed those were qualities any person should strive to acquire. It was why he had wanted to marry her. But right now admirable qualities were as far removed from her current emotional state as the Mississippi River was from the Thames.

"What you gave up for *me*?" she exclaimed, her voice growing more frenzied with each syllable. "What about what I've given up for you?" She stepped forward with fingers clenched, one step shy of knocking her sister into the wall. "You didn't lose anything! I waited for you to come home from London before Charles and I left England. He wanted to take an earlier passage, and I made him wait for you. You're the reason he's dead, and you're the reason Reuben's gone. That's what *I* gave up, and I'll never forgive you."

Tena raised a trembling hand, fully determined to slap the astonishment off her sister's face, when Emil grabbed her wrists and hauled her up the stairs. "Let me go!" she screamed, wrenching against his grip and only hurting herself further. "I hate her! And I hate you! Let me go!"

But Emil wouldn't relent. He dragged her down the hall into the room he used to share with Reuben and occasionally with Friedrich, and kicked the door shut, blocking them into blessed silence. Releasing her, he backed himself against the door like an armed guard. "Sit," he commanded.

"I'm too upset to sit." But one glance at the empty closet she had flung wide open searching for any remaining trace of Reuben, and she sank onto the bed as ordered.

Emil sat beside her, wrapping one arm around her shoulders to direct her head onto his own. "Stay here tonight. Dream about something brilliant, for instance; how smashingly handsome I am."

Tena drew a deep breath then another and against her wants, expelled a laugh. "You're smashingly ridiculous, is what you are. Perhaps I'll dream about someone knocking you from your high horse."

"Dare not, woman! That would break my beauty."

Tena laughed into Emil's chest, and he pulled away with a silly grin. "The fellow who makes you smile can't be all bad, now can he?" He studied her serious face. "Stop your worrying. We'll get him back. It'll be better tomorrow."

"I know you don't believe that, but thank you, Emil."

Emil nodded. "I love you, Tee. That's what brothers are for."

She waited until he exited the room then, despite the hour barely having turned past five o'clock, she drew the curtains. She slid from her dress and corset in the near darkness and removed the combs from her hair, dropping everything to the floor in a heap. Then she slipped into bed, her cotton chemise too warm for a summer's night beneath the covers. Even so, she drew the quilted spread up to her neck and closed her eyes, inhaling the familiar scent within the coverlet.

Everyone has one scent that describes them, yet can never quite be described. Charles was the heady breath of autumn if autumn could have a scent. And Reuben's was this—cigars and parchment and something unreadable—his own unique essence. To her, his was the scent of safety.

She burrowed under the blankets to allow the aroma to surround her, almost as though he was laying beside her. With anyone else, she would feel too exposed. Not with him. He wrapped his arms around her and held her close, chest to chest, her heart beating where his belonged. "Why is your pulse racing?" he whispered. "What is there to be afraid of?"

Tena closed her eyes, her cheek resting against his imaginary chest, so she could hold him to her heart the way she wanted to hold onto any of the pieces that were quickly slipping away.

"Say you're my friend whether Charles is here or not," she begged him on May Day. "Tell me you can overlook what Maggie did. I want to hear that you'll stay." Her fingertips traced the mauve scrapes from his battle with Lloyd, painful reminders of how much he had endured. She never wanted him to feel that way again.

On that day, her heart swelled with gratitude to a God who would save Reuben from certain death on *Titanic*, even when He had not saved Charles. They still had each other, and together they would heal.

"I'm not leaving, Tena," he told her then, molding his hand into hers. "That much I can always promise."

The cozy warmth of Reuben's imaginary arms dissolved into the lukewarm sheets of Midwest July heat. "You still did," she whispered. "You left just like Maggie and my father ..."

Just like Charles.

Palms pressed to her mouth, she stifled a scream into the pillow.

NINE

"WAKE UP."

Reuben's chair swiveled, startling him from sleep. He slid off the seat onto the floor of the *Mid-Mississippi* with a groan. Stanley stared down at him. "Man, you can't continue sleeping here. Smithson's gonna find out and boot you outta a job."

"Blimey, you worry too much. Maybe he'll assume I'm extremely dedicated and promote me." Reuben hefted himself off the floor, pushing into his lower back until his spine cracked. A dull pain pulled at his neck and his cheek felt warm from where it had rested against the desktop. A week's worth of sleeping at—or sometimes under—his desk meant he was worse for wear. He initially looked into some of the local boarding houses within walking distance of the newspaper, but they were all too expensive for his current savings. Any private boarders were too costly. Still, once he saved up enough money, he would find something. He simply needed to convince Smithson to promote him to a real beat and provide a raise along with it. At least the nearby bathhouse ensured his stench didn't match the ugly sleeplessness which left his eyes sunken like the deceased he wrote about.

Rubbing his eyes, Reuben leaned back in his chair. "Besides, I

71

leave for a few hours in the evening to maintain appearances, and I'm always awake before Smithson is in."

Lee thumbed over his shoulder towards the editor's office. "Check your watch, friend. Smithson's already here."

"What? I look like misery personified!" Reuben fumbled his arms into his jacket and combed fingers through his mussed hair as best he could. But when he glanced at the editor's door, the glass lay dark. He glowered at Stanley, even though fatigue surely made his expression more pitiful than intimidating. "You bloomin' well hate me, don't you?"

"Mmm, I do enjoy the way you British swear." Stanley slid his chair into his desk and after retrieving a stack of papers, flung his satchel strap over the chair back. He raised an eyebrow. "Do you know who else enjoys—pardon, takes a fancy to—your accent?"

"I truly have no interest this early in the morning." Cumulatively Reuben had only slept twenty-four hours in the past week, and his brain felt trapped in an endless hangover.

Stanley's resulting laugh reverberated around Reuben's skull. "It is never too early to discuss women. When are you going to ask out Miss Vine?"

"This again, Lee?" Reuben scooped up his notes and shoved them into his satchel. "How about finding me a cheap place to live—that isn't a prison or a brothel—and then I might consider it."

Stanley's eyes lit up like Christmas. "Interesting you should say that. I actually know of a place, and I'd bet you wouldn't pay hardly anything."

Reuben looped his satchel strap over his head. "Brilliant, Lee. Move me in. Now, excuse me. I have an appointment with a deceased Mr. Hilton."

Stanley shouted after him. "See if he has a widow!"

Reuben shook his head. Stanley's advice was a far cry from the solid counsel Charles used to provide. But then again, Charles had never been nearly as entertaining.

Taking the stairs two at a time, he emerged from the stairwell only to stop dead in his tracks. *Please let her be a figment of my imagination*, he pleaded. *God, if you like me at all, please have me start hallucinating again.*

But blast it all, God must have been a jokester worse than Emil because Maggie stood in the foyer, one elbow propped on the reception desk as she openly flirted with Elias Swanson, one of the political reporters. Reuben pressed his thumbs to his temples and rotated them against his hairline. *I do not have the energy to deal with this right now.* He walked straight for the exit, praying to hit sunlight without her intercepting him.

"Mr. Radford!" called Miss Newton as his hand landed on the glass of the revolving door. Blast, so close. He turned without removing his palm from the glass. "I'm on my way to an interview, Miss Newton; can it wait?"

The receptionist nodded in Maggie's direction. "You have a visitor."

Struggling to fashion an apologetic expression while his teeth ground, Reuben tapped two fingers to the brim of his hat. "I'm sorry, Miss Archer; however, I am quite busy this morning. Off to an interview. Perhaps Swanson here can assist you."

"Of course," Elias jumped in, looking ecstatic. *Good*, thought Reuben as he pushed the door around. *Maggie can't seem to resist anyone of the male gender these days. That should keep her occupied.*

But apparently it couldn't. When he re-entered the *Mid-Mississippi* four hours later, she waited on the only chair in the room. Drawing a deep breath, he looked heavenward and approached. "Why are you here? If you need an article transcribed, Mr. Swanson's a seasoned reporter. He should prove more than capable."

"Not with this." Maggie stood, smoothing the wrinkles out of her ebony suit skirt. She rubbed the small of her back. "Can we take lunch? It's urgent that I speak with you."

"I already took my lunch," he said, although he hadn't.

"Please, it's important."

"I'm not paying for your meal."

She tapped her handbag. "I have my own money."

"You won't leave until I agree, will you?"

"No."

"Fine then. I guess let's go."

They walked in silence to the Nightingale, a restaurant one block from the *Mid-Mississippi* that he never noticed until Hazel invited him there the previous week. The few times Reuben did leave the paper for a bite, he usually grabbed something from a street vendor.

The establishment was busy at this hour, nearly full with ladies out to luncheon, couples, and businessmen from surrounding offices. Reuben and Maggie were seated in the middle of the restaurant at one of the few remaining tables and handed menus.

"Good day, miss, sir," the waitress greeted them, her burnished brown hair pinned in wide curls against her scalp. "Tea? Or would you prefer coffee?"

"Tea only," Maggie replied.

"Iced, please. For both of us," Reuben told her. Maggie's eyebrow hitched up at him from behind her menu. "They like cold drinks here. Try something new."

"Addy," Another waitress called from the kitchen door, swiveling their waitress's head. "Help me with somethin', will ya?"

"Pardon me. I'll fetch those refreshments and be right back." Addy scampered away after the other woman.

"Cold tea seems unnatural," Maggie supplied, reading through the menu options. "How do they brew it with cold water?"

Reuben stared down at his menu. "I suspect that's what the ice is for. Brew it hot, then cool it down."

"Bizarre Americans."

"That they are."

Minutes later, Addy set two glasses of iced tea in front of them, took their orders, and scurried back to the kitchen. Maggie took a tentative sip and smiled. "That's delicious, actually. Fine choice."

"Occasionally I do make one." A strange silence fell across the table. Reuben sipped his tea while he reviewed notes from his morning interview of Marissa Winters. Maggie stared out the window and shifted silently in her chair.

"You needed to tell me something important?" he asked, eyes still on his notes. "Everything well with Tena?"

"Not exactly." He looked up, and Maggie's hand slid to her

stomach. She took a large gulp of her tea and drew a deep breath. "Tena's tossed me out."

"She's done what? Why?"

"Because of you, actually. She faulted me with your departure."

"She wasn't supposed to do that." Laying his notes aside, Reuben reached across the table to cover her opposite hand with his. She blinked in surprise. "I left so you wouldn't have to."

"She's not doing well without Charles," Maggie admitted. "She's so spiteful now. I preferred it when she pretended nothing was the matter." She flipped her hand underneath his so their palms touched. "No one wants me, Reuben. I have nowhere to live."

"Oh, Maggie ..." His fingers wrapped around hers. After all her deceit, he couldn't believe he felt sorry for her. But this wasn't her fault; it was his. His departure threw Tena into a downward spiral. He had wanted to restore their sisterhood and only damaged it further. "I'll speak to Tena. I'll insist she bring you home. She'll listen to me."

"No, she won't. I already asked her exactly that. She's upset with both of us. You for leaving and me for compelling you to do so." Maggie's eyes shifted to the window again, their blue haze vibrant against the deep ebony she wore. "Reuben, I'm sorry for my behavior after the funeral and what I said about you taking advantage of our night together. It was my doing; we both recognize that. You were good to me, and I'm sorry I wasn't the same to you."

Reuben's breath stilled. Apologies? From Maggie Archer? Was the world about to implode upon itself? "What else?" he asked.

"What do you mean?" Maggie moistened her lips and returned his gaze. He would rather she didn't. It was too unnerving to see those eyes drinking him in and suddenly doubt why he gave them up.

"I mean, what else are your intentions? It's never black and white with you, Maggie. Everything you say has nuance. You need something from me, don't you?"

"Here we are." The waitress plopped down two plates of chicken in front of them and flounced away. Reuben flipped open his napkin and laid it in his lap, taking a substantial bite.

Maggie folded her hands on the edge of the table, not even glancing at her food. "I want a second chance," she said firmly, "to marry you."

Coughing, Reuben lunged for his water glass as chicken bits clogged his esophagus. "Are you bloomin' mental?" he gasped. "I might care about you, but there is no way I'll marry you."

"Why not?" Maggie picked up her fork, nibbling at a piece of chicken. "Because I made a few mistakes? Told a couple lies? It's not like you didn't lie to me once or twice."

Reuben speared another piece of chicken, waving it in the air. "I *omitted* what happened between Lloyd and I. I'll admit my part in that. It was a mistake, but it wasn't a lie. What I did was nothing compared to your indiscretions. You slept with someone else when we were together then lied about how it happened."

"Oh, posh, let it be, Reuben. I apologized several times."

"No, actually, you never did. Just the once."

"Well, then, my apologies again." She folded her hands on the table. "Now, about my proposal. I've had some more time to think on it, and I can forgive you for abandoning me at Grand Central Station. I think marriage would suit us, and I'm willing to take you back."

"Oh, you're willing are you? What about my will?"

"But you said you still cared."

"As much as I might still feel for you, we can't go back to the way we were."

"Not even if I'm having your child?"

Reuben dropped his fork on the plate. This was too much. "No, you're not."

Maggie's hands moved to her middle. "I am."

"No," he repeated. "You're not." He grabbed for his tea and chugged. They didn't need anyone staring when this descended into another shouting match. With great effort, he set his empty glass down and managed a steady tone. "This charade is unnecessary. Your quarrel with Tena will right itself, and she'll welcome you back. You don't need to spin extraordinary lies."

"Please." She stretched for his fingers across the table, her voice pleading as her other hand clenched the fabric against her stomach. "It isn't a lie. There's a baby coming and I think it should have a father, don't you?"

Reuben removed his hand from her reaching fingers. "I think you should stop this right now and go home." He retrieved his wallet from his jacket to pitch money on the table. Coins bounced to the floor. "This is low, even for you."

Maggie sprang from her chair. So much for not making a scene. "Don't you think I'd know if I'm expecting? Why would I lie about this?"

"Everything you say is laced with dishonesty. This is simply the fancy icing on top of the cake." He stooped for the change and smacked it onto the table. "I'm sorry you're fighting with Tena and that she finally called a spade a spade. I'm sorry for her, not for you. You're a shrewd little vixen, and I'm not helping you out of this."

He grabbed his notepad and satchel and headed for the door, throwing his last words over his shoulder. "Why not ask Halverson? He accommodated your requests so easily before."

~ ~ ~

A blast of blistering air from the city sidewalks sizzled through the restaurant as the door slammed. Maggie stared blankly at Reuben's retreating form, her cheeks burning while an eerie silence indicated fifty sets of eyes pronouncing silent judgment. She sank back into her chair and returned her napkin to her lap, barely managing to keep from openly weeping. Gradually the tinkling of china and silverware indicated a return of nearby diners to their meals, and Maggie managed to pick up her own fork.

Somehow she finished her meal, each morsel scratchy as sawdust as she realized that she was out of valid options. Proposing to Reuben had been at the bottom of a brief list she wrote the night Tena evicted her and a solution she never intended to pursue. Laying her pitiful case at his feet revealed a desperation she never should have succumbed to; however, there had been little choice after every possible employment opportunity fell through.

Buried deep, she understood that even if she secured a position, it wouldn't be for long. The same fate would befall her as surely as all working girls who landed in a delicate condition, the same tragedy that befell Rita Martin. After only three months as a lady's maid,

Maggie witnessed Lord Alexander physically toss the poor scullery maid out of the servants' quarters into the dirt. Seventeen years old and six months pregnant, Rita became an example to the rest of the staff of what consequences resulted from extracurricular dalliances. Months later, Derby shared the dreadful news; Rita's body was found in Whitechapel, frozen to death as she clutched her newborn son beneath a threadbare coat. It was the way of women. Find a husband or be left to die.

Maggie had never been that type of woman. Until today.

Laying her payment on the table, she clasped her handbag and forced her feet to the door, each restaurant patron swiveling to follow her path. Still, somehow her chin remained high as she emerged onto the hectic street, streetcar bells and motorcar horns clanging an oppressive beat to match the press of July humidity and crowds jostling her for space on the sidewalk. Her legs pushed her past the stench of alley garbage, as rancid as a young woman's desperate plea and the rejection she so rightly deserved.

Despite she and Reuben being completely unsuitable for one another, when she grew large enough, he would return to her. Out of obligation, he would grit his teeth and live a lie that would bring neither of them happiness nor even contentment. But she wouldn't let him. Not with a child who may or may not be his, not when he so vehemently detested her, when he left her alone in a restaurant because of how he felt. She would no sooner let him save her now than she would slink back to her mother for help.

She was still the invincible Maggie Archer, and she would do what she had always done. She would save herself.

TEN

"HOLD TIGHT. FAST STOP."

Dust kicked up with the squeal of streetcar brakes as the Southern Electric Railway car came to a halt. Dropping her fare into the till, Maggie hitched her suit skirt upward an inch to descend the steps. Pausing halfway up the walk, she stared upon the Frye home.

This is where she would gain employment and with it hopefully find this country's so-called "American Dream."

The red-brick house stood on a cliff face overlooking the Mississippi River with the main level sporting wide bay windows on both sides and three dormers indicating a functional attic space. Impressive hundred-year-old elms offered privacy from the street and shaded the property with blessed coolness. To the right, the dirt packed drive wound to a sizable carriage house tucked nearly out of sight. Lifting the door's brass knocker, Maggie stared up at the covered entrance and wondered what type of man could afford to construct such a lovely home, yet fail to own a suit without frayed edges. It would be one of many questions to ask once she secured a position.

The door was opened by a middle-aged woman, a day hat pressed low upon her silver hair and a deep frown no doubt as a result of the massive chaos ensuing behind her.

A tiny girl with bouncing auburn curls, perhaps no more than three years old, ran circles with an energy most likely prompted by the handful of cookies she carried and the resulting chocolate stains on her pinafore. At the end of the wood-planked hallway stood a ginger-haired boy with hands buried in his trouser pockets and a scowl growing firmer by the moment.

"Sweet sassafras, Henry, we're only home ten minutes, and I already have to deal with more of your antics?" scolded Mr. Frye, one hand to his temple as he shook his head in frustration.

Henry gave a half shrug and dug his toe into the floorboard. "Why don't you get rid of me? I can go live with the newsies."

Mr. Frye exhaled. "Henry, go to your room."

"But, Dad!"

"Please, just go, before I lose my patience." He slipped past his son into the kitchen and Henry stomped up the stairs. On his way, he shoved his curly-haired sister to the floor then slammed his door with enough force to rattle the wall framings.

The little girl released a shrill wail and the woman scooped her up, rubbing the child's back as she crumbled her cookies into dust. "Oh, Miss Isa," the woman scolded. "Such a mess, child." With an exasperated scowl, she acknowledged Maggie at last. "What now can I help you with, Miss?" Her tone indicated her to be anything except accommodating.

Around the corner from the living room peeked a third crimson haired girl, clutching a kindergarten primer to her chest as prim and proper as Maggie's childhood, if only she hadn't also been completely barefoot and stocking free. All Maggie could think to herself in shock was, *Heavens, he has three children? No wonder his appearance is so frazzled.* One more look at Isa's tearstained face and chocolate covered hands and that thought was quickly followed by, *I'm going to have one of those too? I can never manage this on my own.*

Only she swallowed her shock, along with the nearly ever-present taste of bile, and extended a tender smile towards the woman before her. "You must forgive me, ma'am. I visited Mr. Frye's studio not but an hour ago, only no one was in, so I employed the city directory to locate him here. I wish to inquire about a position."

"Fat likelihood of that," snorted the woman. She jostled Isa to her hip. "I should caution you to turn right around and find yourself another establishment. Which is what I'm likin' to do soon myself."

"Mrs. Humes, are you threatening to jump train on me again?" Hugo Frye appeared from the kitchen. He had removed his jacket, and his tan trousers—similar to the ones he wore to Charles's funeral luncheon—were frayed and deeply worn around each cuff. Once again it struck Maggie the way he stood eye to eye with her, his brow a full three inches shorter than the woman holding his daughter.

He plucked Isa from Mrs. Humes and with a kiss to the child's head, set her to her feet. He wiggled a finger at the other little girl lingering in the living room doorway. "Molly? Take Isa to your room to play. Grown-ups need to talk."

"'Course, Daddy," Molly said. She clasped Isa's tiny hand in the one not holding her primer and together they climbed the stairs one at a time, Molly humming all the way.

"They're sweet children," Maggie managed, still floored by the idea of this reserved man as a father of three.

"The girls are," Mr. Frye said, eyes still focused on the stairs. "But Henry? Of course my only boy would have to be my handful."

"How old are they?"

"Six, five, and three. Although, if you ask me, Henry's six going on whatever age will be my end."

Mrs. Humes blew out a breath that ruffled her bangs against her hat brim. "I want payment, Mr. Frye."

"Next week. You have my word, Mrs. Humes."

"Your word is for the birds. You're already three weeks behind."

He folded his arms with an attempt at assertiveness that fell flat within his weary gaze. "This time I mean it. I have sessions arranged every day this week. You'll have your pay Friday afternoon."

"*Hmph.* You had better, or you'll find yourself a new nanny who will work for free." She flipped her handbag from the rack beside the door. "Girl's here for a job. Come Friday, she can have mine." With a huff, she shuffled down the entry steps to the drive.

Mr. Frye pushed the door closed with a none too subtle exhale and still managed to throw Maggie a half-lipped smile. "I'm sorry, Miss Archer, I've had a difficult day today. I was called away from the studio mid-session due to an incident with Henry and ... bah, this doesn't interest you." He rubbed the back of his neck with a shy grin. "You're honestly here about employment? I couldn't persuade you to leave right now and save me the trouble of sending you away?"

Somewhere between his boyish smile and his unease, her own discomfort began to dissipate. "I'm afraid not; however, you could brew some tea while I convince you to hire me."

His smile wavered. "Well, then it seems I will be the cause of many disappointments today. There's not a tea leaf to be found here. Although I can offer coffee."

No tea? Maggie wondered at the strangeness of it all. Telling someone in Fontaine that the house was void of tea was close to saying that the Pope was Protestant. Although she supposed it wasn't any stranger than she, the perpetual spinster, expecting a child. "Certainly," she said. "When in America, one does as Americans do."

His frown quickly flipped back to a grin, his bottle green eyes lighter. "Precisely, Miss Margaret. Have a seat. I won't be long."

"Oh, no, my name's not—" she began, but he had already disappeared into the kitchen. With a sigh, she wandered into the living room, claiming one of two fireside chairs tucked between matching sofas all surrounding a slightly distressed coffee table. As she allowed her gaze to wander the room, she noticed that, similar to its master, everything in the house was a little tattered. Not dirty exactly, but not the pristine finish of her parents' home. The Archers' housemaid, Olivia, had been meticulous in her daily cleaning habits, ensuring no upholstery patch remained visible and no floor scuffs unattended. The checkerboard cluttering the Fryes' side table would be removed and the little woven basket of blocks on the window seat stowed neatly out of sight.

How lovely, she breathed when her eyes fell upon the floor to ceiling shelves flanking the stone fireplace, each case containing four silver-framed photographs for every one trinket or vase and not a single book in sight. Cream tintypes propped up in cardboard folders stood beside black and white petite individual portraits, group poses of the children, and stunning architecture. The walls were decorated similarly, each frame containing magnificent landscapes from parts of the country she couldn't even guess at. Each one suggested unimaginable adventure. What might her own childhood have been like in a home like his, without a constant barrage of her mother's rules and stringent expectations?

Hands smoothed against her traveling suit, the same outfit she wore the day she left England, she felt a stirring deep within that had nothing to do with either morning sickness or a baby not yet large enough to feel. She ached for her father and a desire for his gentle strength beside her.

"You can do this, little girl," he would say. "You will be a good mother."

"But how, Father?" she replied. "How can I be a mother when I've had no mother to guide me?"

With a kiss to her brow, he would smile. "Never say that. Always be thankful for your mother, even if all she taught you was who not to be."

The robust scent of percolating coffee drifted in from the kitchen, its unfamiliar aroma in line with everything she felt about becoming a mother. The fear of becoming *her* mother.

"Napping, are we, Miss Margaret? It seems you need this coffee more than I do."

Maggie's eyes flew open, unaware she had even lowered her lids. Hugo set a silver tray onto the coffee table containing a dented coffee pot and two mugs already steaming with dark brown brew. With a shake of her head, she accepted the mug he offered her as he claimed the chair across from hers. "Nonsense, Mr. Frye. I was only thinking."

Cautiously, she sipped the coffee, amazed to find it pleasant. While it certainly had a bite compared to her usual tea selection, the drink was also delightfully warm with a hint of orange zest and was that ... "Molasses?"

Hugo nodded, raising his own mug. "My mother's addition. Too sweet?"

"Not at all. Actually, it's surprisingly appealing." She folded her hands around her mug and nodded towards the shelves. "Mr. Frye, why did you become a photographer?"

He studied the many framed photographs while he sipped his coffee. "My father was a photographer during the War of the

Rebellion. He captured the most incredible scenes; everyone clamored for them. After the war, he married my mother, then made the five of us faster than the Mississippi runs." Hugo pointed to a photograph of a handsome couple surrounded by three beautiful dark-haired teenage girls, a much plainer Damaris, and a boy of perhaps ten who mirrored Henry. "I was the youngest," he acknowledged, "but as the only son, I could apprentice under my father while my sisters remained home. I was only fifteen when the three middle girls married and moved to California."

He returned his gaze to hers, thumb running absently along the lip of his coffee mug as he spoke. "My father was celebrated for his work. Even so, it wasn't the money or the notoriety which drew me to the camera. I merely wanted to be like him. To see what he saw. Not only what the lens captured, but something deeper."

"You must miss him."

"How do you know he's gone?"

Maggie's eyes held his in one sympathetic moment of understanding. "Because my father's passed too."

"My sympathies." He quickly turned his attention into his coffee. "Tell me about your employment situation, Miss Archer."

"To put it plainly, Mr. Frye, I have been up and down this city searching the agencies and the newspaper ads; however, opportunities have simply not opened up. I need a position quickly or I will be in an unfortunate predicament."

His thumb stopped its pace around the mug rim. "How unfortunate?"

"On the street unfortunate."

"But the Kischs surely wouldn't—"

"There was a quarrel with my sister, Mr. Frye. I'm afraid I've done irreparable damage."

"I see." With another sip of his coffee, he placed the mug on the tray and moved to steal the chair directly beside her. "I want to help you. I do. Only I don't see how I can."

"Do as I asked. Offer me a position." Not allowing him to open his lips more than a centimeter in remark, she forged on. "I know you haven't much money, but I don't need much. Only enough for the cheapest room this city has. I can be your assistant. Or a secretary. I'm not overly fond of reading, but I can transcribe well enough. I spent nearly a year as a lady's maid in London, so you can count on my professionalism. If you require a reference, my former mistress would write one."

"Please, Miss Archer, you're making this terribly difficult for me." His fingers splayed, gripping palms down upon his knees. "My sister already assists me in my studio, and I have no need for a secretary. As you could probably gather from Mrs. Humes, I can't afford the nanny I have, much less a housemaid."

The clock in the hall chimed out the hour in two long mournful tones, as though the timepiece itself could feel its master's sympathy.

"What I don't understand," he continued when the tones had lulled, "is how you are experiencing any complication securing employment." As he spoke, he refilled his mug along with her own. Fresh steam billowed under his chin. "You have service experience which is desirable. You appear intelligent, are undeniably eye-catching, and young—far younger than I am anyway. They ought to line up to hire you. If I had the funds, believe me, *I* would."

Choosing to ignore his comment on her attractiveness, she focused instead on the mention of his age. Despite the tinge of grey in his goatee, which was only visible when she inspected closely, he didn't have a strand on his head. Originally she assumed he was perhaps only five years older than herself, but could his baby face and short stature have disguised an extra ten or fifteen years? He certainly didn't speak like her father's colleagues back in Fontaine. "What is your age?" she asked.

She knew she was already pressing her luck; she should ask him for a reference and leave. Instead, she had probably just insulted him.

Surprisingly, Hugo actually chuckled. "Why is it rude for a man to ask a lady that question, but not the other way around? There is a serious double standard at play here."

She breathed an inward sigh of relief. She could still remedy this. "So you're old then? Because only an old man would refuse to give his real age." She sipped her coffee with a smile as sweet as the molasses it contained. "Shall I guess? Fifty? Fifty-five?"

"Good grief, Miss Margaret," Hugo spluttered. "You're off by nearly twenty years."

Maggie gasped, lowering her mug in order to fan herself unnecessarily. "Heavens, surely not seventy? My friend, Bianca, would adore you."

With a roll of his eyes, he took a long swig of his coffee with only the slightest wince at its heat. "I'm thirty-three, thank you. How young are you exactly?"

She grinned. "I thought you said it was impolite to ask?"

"Don't care." He leaned in, green eyes tinged with mischief. "I'm asking anyway."

"Hugh!"

They both startled as a door slammed and Hugo's sister burst into the living room in a disheveled flurry. She peeled off her hat with abandon, sending her mousy hair flying.

"Miss Archer, you remember my sister, Damaris?" He raised a brow. "Where's the fire, Mare?"

Drawing the curtains on every window, she turned on her brother with troubled eyes. "Donovan came by the studio again. Banging on the front door and yelling such profanities. I snuck out the alleyway, but I think he'll come here next." She stole Hugo's coffee from his hand and drained it, breathing heavily when she finished the cup.

So, Maggie thought, *the timid mouse has finally found her voice.*

"You're probably mistaken," she said. "That was me knocking earlier. I promise I wasn't swearing though."

Only then did Damaris acknowledge Maggie's presence. Her face scrunched as though a stagnant pond had appeared in the room with them. "What is *she* doing here?"

"Employment interview."

Damaris swore, her brown eyes furious. "How in Pete's name are you planning to hire someone else? You don't even pay me full wages!"

Hugo ignored her question. He walked to the window, drawing the curtain back an inch. "Donovan's coming here?"

Damaris nodded, then pointed at Maggie. "This child—whom you are *not* hiring—showed up shortly after you'd gone. I was filing paperwork and didn't bother answering what I assumed to be another sales call. About an hour later, Donovan arrived with his usual threats. Only I believe he's serious this time."

Her brother's face paled and he dropped the curtain. "Well, that *is* a problem."

"Who is Donovan?" Maggie asked.

His eyes met hers briefly before shooting back to Damaris. "Get the children," he said urgently. "We'll call a taxi from the Kincades'. Beats me if I know where we're going after that, but we can't stay here."

"California?" Damaris asked hopefully.

Maggie sprang from her seat, nudging the coffee table and rattling the china. "Are you involved in illegal work?" Her arm flung in the direction of the shelves. "Is this *supposed* photography studio all a facade?"

"This would be a pretty elaborate facade, don't you think?" Damaris snorted. "Honestly, Hugh, this is the type of simpleton you hope to employ?"

"Excuse me?" Maggie spat. "Who's simple?"

A stiff knock on the entry door startled all three into silence. "Mr. Frye?" came a gruff call. "I know you're in there."

"Now, who is Donovan?" Maggie whispered.

Hugo watched the door. "The landlord. He's come for the rent on my studio, and he's the sort of fellow who will respond to an unsatisfactory answer with ... let's call it one step shy of my demise."

Maggie rounded the chair to face him. "Then pay him the rent!"

"I can't because I don't exactly have it at the moment."

"Frye?" Donovan called, and Maggie could imagine the man's face simmering red from neck to brow. "You're three months past due. I want my money today or you're booted!" The inflection on booted implied a more literal violence that merely throwing possessions into the street.

Upstairs the children were oddly quiet. "Shall I assume this isn't the first time he's visited?" Maggie asked.

Hugo rounded the room, tugging at his hair with both hands. "What am I going to do? I can't lose my studio. I suppose I could move everything home, but where would I fit it all? The study isn't large enough. In the dining room? The bedroom? Isa could crawl into it. Henry would break it. Beans and Bacon!"

"You're hungry?"

"No, sometimes I yell random food words so my children don't become vile gutter-mouths before they're seven."

"Hugh?" Damaris's voice strangled.

"Mr. Frye—" Maggie began, and he held up a hand.

"Listen, not to be insensitive, Miss Archer, but you need to wait. My problem is a touch more imminent than your employment situation right now."

"Maybe I can help."

"How could you help? I can't hire you! I can't pay you!" Hugo tugged at his hair again, the strands sticking up like a blazing fire. "I'm purging my finances to keep a nanny when I should just quit and stay home with my children. Only if I stay home, I can't work, and I can't take them with me to do my job, and I don't have room for a studio here, so you see how we go round and round again!"

"Frye!" Donovan's voice echoed.

"Baloney!" Hugo tugged his fingers through his hair again, staring at Maggie like he didn't know what to do with her. "Why am I telling you all this? I don't even know you!"

The sound of a fist slammed against the front door. "Frye, I'll break this door down, I swear I will."

Dread rolled off Hugo in waves. Maggie saw it building in the shallow nature of his breath and knew he was only a few minutes from a full-blown mental breakdown. She watched it happen to Reuben on the *Höllenfeuer*. Certain desperate acts couldn't be reversed.

Maggie splayed a hand on her own breastbone. "Slow breaths, Mr. Frye. We need you calm."

"No," he gasped. "Can't. All is lost."

"The situation is not so desperate as all that. Trust me. I've been attacked by a man before and that time my friend nearly died. This is not nearly so dire."

His breath hitched. "Attacked? Why did a man attack you?"

"Too extensive a story for today, I'm afraid. Come with me." Hands pressed to his shoulder blades, Maggie steered Hugo across the room into his study, ignoring his sister's suspicious expression.

Damaris lurched to grab her brother's sleeve. "Hugh, now is not the time for dalliances with some half-purchased secretary."

His neck swiveled from Damaris to Maggie and back again, eyes wide and breath barely slowing. "Please," he pleaded with Maggie. "Wait in my study." He slid the pocket doors closed, encasing her in darkness.

"This is ridiculous, Hugo!" Damaris's shout filtered through the door, her voice barely muffled behind its thickness. Cautious to keep the door from shifting in its frame, Maggie gently pressed her ear to the wood.

"We're ruined," Hugo choked. "That man is going to kill me."

"Not if you weren't acting the part of the city idiot," Damaris spat. "I managed a satisfactory haul at the Thompson funeral, not to mention what I collected from the Kischs. We sell what I stole and we have all the funds we need."

"Damaris!" he hissed. "I told you to return those."

"You refuse to charge for postmortem photos. Consider it our payment and clear your conscience."

"You'd have me take advantage of their grief, Mare?"

"Precisely, I would. Especially when we have Donovan on our doorstep. Every other penny we make goes to that nanny of yours. What would *you* have us do? Starve?"

Maggie's ears rang with the silence. She could picture him slicing through his hair in angst before eventually releasing a weary sigh. "The devil's reserved a special room for us. I hope you know that."

"Well, if you were open to any of my other suggestions, I wouldn't have to thieve."

His voice quieted, steps marching across the room. "What suggestions?"

Heels clacked across the floor, and Maggie gently slid the doors apart a crack. A cool draft whistled against her ear, and she edged them another centimeter. They now stood before the fireplace, Hugo's appearance all the more childlike beneath his sister's extra inches.

"I've said it before, Hugh. Henry's already six. Send him for a job."

"Don't you mean he's *only* six?" Hugo argued. "How long would he last in a factory or selling on the street? We see those kids walk past our studio; by gum, we've bought their sweet potatoes and newspapers. It won't come to that for my children."

Damaris remained impassive. "The house then."

"This was our father's house. My house with Emma. I can't sell it."

"Fine then. What if you dropped the children in an orphanage?" Her annoyance was so thick Maggie could hear the eye roll.

"What if I dropped you in the river?"

"More like you would hire someone to end me for you." Hugo turned away and her voice finally softened. "Please, Hugh. I know how much you love them, but Donovan's literally breaking down your door. Send them away for a little while—a few months, maybe a year. We travel again and sell our photographs. Once our debts are settled, we return to them safe and sound. You wouldn't be the first father to do it."

"No." Hugo shook his head. "They already lost their mother; I can't put them through that again."

Another slam reverberated the front door, vibrating into Maggie's fingertips against the study door. Then another followed. Glass clinked somewhere beyond the wall.

"Fine, Frye!" Donovan blasted. "Choose the hard way. I'll be back in one hour—with Marty—and so help me, you had better have a satisfactory answer when I return."

Maggie pushed away from the door, spinning in search of a lamp and settled on opening the window hangings. A harsh blast of light blinded her in the instant before the study door opened and slid shut again.

Hugo stood with his back butted against the doors, gripping the handles behind him. "You said you can help? How?"

Maggie stepped away from the window, still blinking. When she first offered to help, she hadn't a clue how she actually could. All she wanted was to calm a kind man enough so he could think rationally. At least, that was until she listened to Hugo's exchange with Damaris and formed a solution for both their circumstances.

"Allow me to pay the rent," she said.

He uttered a throaty laugh. "No."

"I have a bit of money. Allow me to help you."

"That only transfers my debt to you."

Maggie shrugged. "Very well. Would you prefer we open those doors right now, you can receive a thorough thrashing by Donovan, and then we'll all go to the police together? I'm certain they would enjoy hearing how Damaris thieves at funeral luncheons."

Hugo paled. "You heard?"

"I did."

"So this is blackmail? I can't offer you anything in return."

"I believe you can. You can return what you stole—"

"Done." He bolted for the far corner of the room where he dumped the contents of a satchel onto the floor. Retrieving a silver candlestick and a decorated cigar case, he thrust them into her hands. "There," he gasped, desperation clinging to his words like a wet sponge. "Now the money, please."

"It's in the bank. I certainly don't carry that much on my person."

"But I—" Apparently whatever Hugo was about to say he dismissed in his next breath. His eyes widened. "Wait. How does a woman who needs employment so badly she'll be on the street also have enough to pay my rent? Pigs feet, you called my sister a criminal? What did you do?"

"Nothing illegal. Unethical, perhaps, but—" Maggie dropped the stolen items on the desktop, her fingers leaping to cover her lips as nausea suddenly kicked against her stomach. The thought of her scandalous deal with Lloyd Halverson and the possibility of now being saddled with his child caused a heat wave to break across her skin. July sunlight blasted through the open window, turning the room into an oven. *Please no*, she thought. She pressed her other fist to her middle as her stomach churned harder. N*ot now, you annoying child!*

She ducked in search of a wastebasket and finding none, promptly vomited in the only empty camera case she could find. With a groan, she dropped to her knees on the worn parquet and wiped the back of her mouth with her dress sleeve before dry heaving one last time. "I'm sorry," she gasped, staring at the vile mess. "I'll replace this."

From the corner of her eye, she caught Mr. Frye peering over the desk in silent observation. Not once did he move towards her or ask on her welfare. Neither did he rail about a near stranger ruining his camera case when he quite clearly had no funds to replace it. She expected he would have at least demanded a thorough explanation before the landlord returned to thrash them all.

Reuben would have. He would have wrapped her in his arms, kissed her hair, and made certain she was well. Then he would throw open the front door and knock Donovan's teeth out before anyone was hurt. Only then would he demand her to explain. She missed that way about him. Or perhaps she simply missed *him*. The last two months, she played a woman scorned when she should have mended the broken bridge between them. Only now that bridge was instead a fence twelve feet tall and new rails were nailed higher every day.

A soft knock tapped against the study door. "Hugh?" came Damaris's voice. "Donovan left. What are you doing in there?"

"We're just ..." He turned from Maggie's hunched form to the door. "... discussing our options." Although he stared at the closed door a minute longer, he didn't make a move towards it. Instead, he knelt to clean up the items he dumped from his satchel. "So will you loan me the money? Because if not, then please go. My family needs to hightail it out of here."

Maggie inhaled deeply then released the breath then twice more, finding the next stage of her plan difficult. *This is not a desperate act,* she reminded herself. *This is a conscious decision. The best decision and one you should have considered all along.* Except she never expected him to make it so easy to ask or so difficult not to.

She closed the lid of the rancid case and rose. "I will certainly provide the money if you marry me."

Hugo dropped everything he was holding, littering the floor again with photography instruments. His neck swiveled back to gape at her. "Excuse me, what?"

"We should marry."

"That's what I thought you said." He swept the bits and pieces back into his satchel, slung it over his shoulder and began packing camera equipment into the remaining non-soiled cases. "You're out of your mind."

She could turn around right now, return to the Kischs' and leave Mr. Frye to his own troubles. She had enough funds left to last four months. And then what? Eight months pregnant, out of money, and frozen in an alley like Rita Martin?

Ask Tena's forgiveness, some annoying voice nagged. *No*, she argued. Not while she still maintained an ounce of pride. *This isn't desperation*, she repeated. *This is security*.

She straightened up, gliding towards Hugo with all the airs of confidence she could muster. "Marriage will solve both our troubles, Mr. Frye. You cannot argue with that."

Hugo stacked what appeared to be glass panes between pieces of cloth. He lowered them into a sturdy wooden box. "I had a wife once," he said softly. "I don't want another."

"As my mother once told me, 'There are many sound reasons for marriage, none of them involving what we want.'" Maggie returned to the desk, lowered herself into the wooden chair, and propped her elbows upon the surface as though it were hers to command. She had anticipated his refusal, but if there was anything gained from her sordid deal with Lloyd Halverson, it was the knowledge that everything could be negotiated.

She gestured to the chair across from her. "Please take a seat, Mr. Frye."

Still clasping the camera case to his chest as though it would offer him protection from her, he positioned himself on the edge of the opposite chair in tight-lipped silence. And to his credit, he remained so throughout Maggie's proposal. She was amazed at how steady her voice performed compared to the erratic pounding of her heart and how emotionless she sounded compared to the gripping peril she actually felt inside.

"This is a business deal, Mr. Frye, nothing more. I will be honest; you should expect no affection from me as I require none from you. I'm rubbish at emotions and the tough decisions. I can't form a well-rounded relationship to save my life. Marriage—a loving marriage anyway, if there is such a notion—is terribly difficult. It requires commitment and sacrifice. It requires two people willing to stand together in fair weather and storms. I'm beginning to understand though that marriage is also incredibly similar to a business dealing. In both instances, two parties sign a contract to abide by a certain set of terms for a set length of time. I may be terrible with love, Mr. Frye, but business is an art I believe I could be rather adept at."

She folded her hands, pressing her forearms to the desktop. "Here is what I propose. Seven years. Henry will be grown at thirteen, allowing me to acquire employment of my own at that time. Once said position has been achieved, we will divorce and separate our monetary assets into forty percent for myself and sixty percent for you. The house and all its belongings, minus any personal items of mine purchased during the seven-year term, will remain in your possession. A secondary agreement will then be signed indicating that both parties are satisfied with the conclusion of our original contract and expect no further commitment. I admit that in any other situation I would be a poor choice of wife; however, will you not admit that I could be an agreeable business partner?"

Lips parted in disbelief, he stared unmoving, those green eyes finally blinking only when his sister's voice reached through the door again. "Hugh? I really think you should open the door now."

"One minute!" Hugo yelped. The door flew open anyway. Damaris framed the doorway with one angry hand on her hip.

"Seriously, what are you doing in here, Hugo?" she hissed. "Enough delays."

Ripping his attention from Maggie, Hugo set the camera case and satchel on his desk and made his way to his sister. He gripped her hand between his. "Take the children to your apartment. I'll get the money, pay Donovan, and meet you there."

"You have the money?"

"I'm working on it. You need to trust me."

"Like I trusted you when you found your way into this mess with that wife of yours?"

"Mare," he scolded. "Just take them to your apartment, will you?"

She twisted out of his grip. "I'm not a wet nurse, Hugh."

His tone softened as his arms hung loosely at his sides. "No, but

I'm your brother. Please do as I ask."

"Fine," she sniffed. "But I won't smile about it."

The faintest smile found his lips instead. "You never do."

Sliding the door closed, Damaris stomped up the stairs calling for the children. Mr. Frye pressed his forehead against the wooden door, palm braced flat against the surface as though either attempting to keep evil spirits at bay or deciding to release them. His voice cracked when he spoke. "Why do you need this?"

"I'm with child."

Hugo released a low whistle, backing away from the door to drop back into his chair. "Well, that *is* a reason. Who's the father?"

Maggie shrugged. "If you marry me, then you are."

"The real father. Unless I was with you in my dreams before we met—which I seriously doubt would result in a baby—there's another man out there who might want to know about his child."

"I don't know who the father is. It could be a few men."

His face went slack. "Wow ... you certainly are honest, aren't you?"

"With you, it seems I have to be."

"Why choose me?"

"Why not you? You have a need; I have a need. The end result is all the same. What does it matter how we arrive there?"

He tapped his chin as though he were actually considering her idea. "So, I marry you, make your baby legitimate, give it my last name—the whole works—and in exchange, you'll be my unpaid maid and nanny and pay my studio rent for seven years?"

"I'll pay your studio rent for three months. Otherwise, you've caught the idea."

"May I ask you a personal question?"

"You may ask. I may not answer."

He slid to the edge of his chair, considering her face, reaching into her eyes with those vivid green ones, the irises ringed with a hazel trim. "These men who you were with before? The potential fathers. Did you love any of them?"

"No." Maggie admitted, only surprised by how easily she could admit it. "Not even the one I might have married."

"Did he love you?"

"Yes, I'm sorry to say he did."

Hugo's eyes shifted to a standing silver frame, the only photograph on his desk. In it stood a beautiful woman with a glowing smile and tiny waist, her hair meticulously pinned upon her head. Beside her stood a younger Molly with long tight curls and a tiny Henry with close cut hair, clutching his mother's hand and a teddy bear at his side. In the woman's other arm was the tiniest newborn Isa dressed all in white with sweet eyes closed.

"That's the wife you lost. You loved her, didn't you?"

Hugo wrenched away, reaching to turn the frame facedown on the desk. "With everything I had."

"And she loved you as much?"

"You said it yourself, Miss Archer. Marriage is terribly difficult. As in business, some of us are willing to work harder than others."

Three questions, her father always said. *That's how you know the worth of a man. But there's only one question that matters.* Maggie didn't need to ask Mr. Frye which day he would redo. The answer was visible in his face and the photograph on his desk.

Hugo stood slowly, his right hand extended. "I am amicable to the proposed terms of our contract. If you will pay my rent today, I suggest we marry four weeks from tomorrow. No woman knows she's expecting after one afternoon. If we are to sell the ruse that I am your child's father, the timeline must be believable."

"That's hardly necessary. I'll concoct a believable backstory. No one will question it." Standing, she clasped his hand. "Let's marry this Friday."

His fingers twitched. "That's in four days."

"Exactly, Mr. Frye. I'm three months along. I can't conceal it another month. Plus, after that I have nowhere to live." She squeezed his hand with a lighthearted grin in an attempt to alleviate the mood and her pounding heart. Maggie Archer was getting married. A week ago, even she herself wouldn't have believed it. "Imagine how surprised my sister will be when she hears. Back home they called me the perpetual spinster."

"We're not telling anyone about this yet. We'll tell them on Thursday."

She frowned. "Even the children?"

"Even the children, Miss Archer." He released her hand without so much as a hint of amusement. "Fetch the rent money and return here immediately. My lawyer will draw up the contract and forward it to you for signature. We'll verify everything at the courthouse over the noon hour on the nineteenth, wedding at one."

ELEVEN

FOR THREE DAYS, MAGGIE STRUGGLED to maintain her composure. Every time someone passed by, her heart raced, and she feared there was a tell written across her face, screaming, "I have a secret, whatever could it be?"

Secrets, secrets are no fun ...

Oh, shove off, she told herself. One more sleep. One more night of tossing and turning and she would be packed up and moved into the Frye home. Packed and moved and married.

Married.

The word, however silent in her head, still lodged in her throat like a walnut. The situation terrified her. She didn't want to be married. Not to Hugo Frye. Not to Reuben Radford. Not to anyone.

What the blazes was she doing?

Maggie's stomach turned over and she lunged for the powder room and the blessed relief of the toilet. She knelt on the floor and lost her stomach for the fourth time in two days, gripping the edge of the seat as she retched.

Oh yes, she remembered. *That* was why she was doing this. For her blasted baby and for herself. For Mr. Frye and his children too, she supposed. They would no doubt benefit from this marriage. At least she was doing a bit of good for someone else for once. She could do this. She had to do this.

Rinsing her mouth in the sink, she patted her face dry with the towel and made her way back down the hallway to the living room, where she was met by the curious eyes of every member of the Kisch family, minus Fred, and Winnie who preferred lounging on the back porch even after dark. Tena fought not to raise her eyes above the pages of her book, but still did the faintest amount.

Elsa struggled from her seat as Maggie entered, pressing the back of her hand to Maggie's cheek. "Goodness, child, you're pale as a specter." Wrapping a pudgy arm around Maggie's waist, she directed her to the sofa and forced Maggie down beside her. "There's no use pretending we haven't all seen the toll these weeks have taken on you, dear. Silent as the grave—"

"Except for when she's retching—"

"Emil!" Elsa admonished.

Emil closed his own book. "What? It's true. She's been like this every day for weeks. If I get sick and die, you'll all be sorry. You know I'm the only one around here who's any fun."

"Emil," shot Karl. "Apologize to your mother for your rudeness."

Elsa gave her husband a thin smile. "No, it is fine, Karl. Emil is correct. Someone in our family must be able to laugh in times like these." Karl frowned, then shook out the daily edition of the *Mid-Mississippi* and continued reading. Elsa redirected her attention to Maggie. "You must allow us to take you to a physician tomorrow."

Maggie shook her head fervently. "It's only nervous tension. I don't require a doctor."

"Nerves?" Emil scoffed. He flipped another page in his book and whistled. "If you ask me, I'd say you're on your way out."

"No one asked you, Emil," Maggie spat back. "If you must know, I'm nervous because I'm getting married tomorrow."

A room couldn't be any more silent if it was buried ten feet underground, filled floor to ceiling with mud, and sealed with cement. Elsa and Karl stared like she grew an extra appendage, and Maggie rubbed her neck to make sure there wasn't something amiss. One head, two hands ... not counting the ones belonging to the creature slowly invading her body. No, everything seemed in order. Minus Tena, whose fingers clenched her book's edges.

Finally, Emil tossed his book in the air, allowing it to clatter to the floor. "Are you kidding me?" He jumped up, ran into the kitchen and returned with a bottle of cooking sherry, popping the top open and taking a hearty swig.

"Emil Kisch!" Elsa leapt from the sofa, the flab on her arms swinging as she yanked the bottle out of his hands. "That is not for drinking."

"Aw, seriously, Mama. After the funeral, Papa banned me from the good stuff." He gestured flat palmed at Maggie still sitting on the sofa. "Maggie's getting married. Aren't we supposed to celebrate?"

"What are we celebrating?" Winnie asked as she entered the room, drawing notebook tucked under her arm and pencils in hand. She flipped her blonde braid off her shoulder and plopped down on the sofa in Emil's vacated seat.

Emil jabbed a thumb at Maggie. "Her wedding."

Winnie's jaw literally dropped a full inch. She hopped back up and threw her arms around Maggie, dropping to the sofa beside her with a squeal. "How brilliant! Who stole your heart?"

Maggie swallowed hard. Well, she *had* lit the explosive, she may as well distribute the shrapnel accordingly. "Hugo Frye."

Karl folded his paper. "The photographer? Did you not meet him only last week?"

Maggie bit her lip and with a talent that came as naturally as breathing, began weaving her tale. "Last month actually. I went to the *Mid-Mississippi* to speak with Reuben about ... well, everything that has happened. To apologize. Mr. Frye was dropping off some photographs. He invited me to luncheon, and he was such a lovely man that I accepted. We've been courting ever since."

"Oh, how lovely!" Winnie gushed. "Why didn't you tell us?"

"Yes, why?" Tena's voice made Maggie wince even though she had barely raised her tone. Yet even in the silence, her accusation was deafening.

"We're in mourning," Maggie explained. "Mr. Frye suggested it might be inappropriate to announce a courtship given the circumstances."

Elsa crushed her then in another embrace so her soft cheek effectively cut off Maggie's view of Tena's response. "Oh, my dear, I am pleased for you. It is wonderful to be a wife." She sniffed hard, reaching up to wipe a tear from her eye. "Oh, *mir leid*. It is almost as though my own daughter is marrying."

Karl pulled her away. "For goodness sakes, *liebe*. It is not as though she is off to war." He rested a hand on Elsa's shoulder with a frown. "I do not care for the hasty manner of this marriage, Maggie. Still, I am not your father. If you have set your mind upon it, there is little I can say to delay you."

The usual tears spurred at mention of her father. Even for a marriage of convenience, Maggie would have given anything for Laurence Archer to give her away. She stared Mr. Kisch down. "No, sir. I'm afraid Mr. Frye and I are in agreement."

With only the briefest nod, Karl turned back to his wife. "Elsa, fetch a bottle of the good wine from the stash. Our son said we should celebrate, so we shall."

Emil crossed his arms with a haughty grin and dropped himself backwards across the other sofa. "I'm sorry, Pop. Can you repeat that? I believe you actually agreed with me."

Karl pointed towards the kitchen. "Emil, make yourself useful and serve up some of your mother's leftover cake."

"We can serve it." Tena stood with a warm smile. "Come along, Maggie." Unable to maintain premise, Maggie followed.

Retrieving a server from the drawer near the sink, Tena moved the leftover *Zuckerkuchen* to the table and began slicing.

"We're celebrating my upcoming wedding with funeral cake?" Maggie exclaimed. Appropriate, she thought, but still ... a bit macabre. She lifted a stack of plates from the cabinet and set them on the table.

"Actually," Tena explained, "Germans serve it for both occasions. Joy and Sorrow Cake, they call it." She cast a glance over her shoulder. "Close the door."

Maggie swung the kitchen door shut and rejoined her sister after retrieving a stack of forks from the drawer. Visible tension lined Tena's jaw as she sliced through the cake. "Spill, Tena. Something's bothering you."

Tena set the server down and took a measured breath. "Tell me something truthfully. Is Mr. Frye the first man you've entertained since the *Höllenfeuer*? No others?"

"Of course." Maggie frowned. "You don't believe me though."

"I'm not sure what to believe. As long as I've known you, you never wanted to be a wife. You mocked me for wanting it. And now ... well, I can't say I'm not pleased to hear you weren't with half the city after all, except you've only just met Mr. Frye. What do you even know about him?"

"I know that he seems kind and he manages his own business. His photographs are beautiful. He's attractive—"

Tena's eyebrows shot into her hairline. "If you're going to lie about anything, don't lie about that. His crimson hair, attractive? It's always a mess. He doesn't exactly keep his clothing in tip-top shape. And my word, is he petite."

"Not terribly so." Although a blush rose in her cheeks knowing that she had thought all the same things about him. "He has kind eyes." There, she thought, that much was true.

Tena's own eyes widened. "At the funeral he mentioned children to me. Did you even consider that you'll be their stepmother now?"

"Don't say the word *stepmother* as if I fit in some fairy tale." Maggie roiled. "He may not be what you expected, but he'll take care of me."

"Since when do you need someone else to take care of you? You've always done that on your own. What happened to independent Maggie? Fierce Maggie?"

"Sometimes people change, Tena. Sometimes they have to."

"Why do you have to? You hide your relationship for a month, and then suddenly you're married? It's suspicious."

"How is it any different than what you did to me?"

"What are you talking about?" Tena jammed the server into the cake, sliced it lengthwise, and removed another sliver.

"Charles courted you for over a year and you hid it from everyone including me."

Tena waved the server in Maggie's face. "That is not the same at all. Mother stole my letters to you. If you had received them, they would have explained everything." She served another piece of cake, stabbing it with the fork that lay beside it. "Besides, how do you think this makes me feel, you married instead of me?"

"I didn't mean it as a snub."

Tena slammed the server on the table and pressed her palms to the wood breathlessly. "Tell me what Father wrote to you."

Maggie stepped back. "Pardon?"

Tena kept her palms to the table and her gaze on the cake. "You've kept his letter to yourself since April. I thought if I brought the letter to you unopened as a gesture of good faith then surely you would allow me to read it. You still haven't."

Maggie retreated another step as though her sister would grab the server and stab her with it. "Tena, what's this really about?"

"You swore before we came here that the secrecy would end. You promised."

"I've been honest! I told you what happened with Reuben and even with Lloyd. I didn't want to share that with you, but I did."

"I know you did. And as difficult as it was to hear, I was glad for the truth. But with this engagement, I can't help but feel that the story wasn't fully told. So tell me, Maggie, what was in the letter?"

"That's private." Maggie couldn't tell her. Tena would insist they write to Mother and further alter their lives all for the sake of integrity. Sometimes the appearance of truth was more important than the truth itself.

"I was the only one who didn't receive some special parting words. Father spoke to Reuben in person and he wrote to you. What did he give me?"

"Tena, you know Father loved you. You were with him in the end; you were everything he needed." Cautiously, she slid her arm around her sister's shoulders.

Tena quieted then. "He preferred you."

"Playing favorites?" Maggie turned Tena by the shoulders, only her sister refused to meet her gaze. "Father would never do that. If one of us was the disappointment to him, it was me. You did everything our parents ever asked of you, minus Charles, but even Father would have been proud to call him a son."

Tears sprang to Tena's eyes. She shook her head and jerked away from Maggie, grabbing the server, and dropping it. It clattered off the table edge onto the floor. She bent for it, but Maggie wrapped her arms around Tena and everything dissolved in that embrace. Her sister wanted to remain angry; she wanted to scream and yell and stomp her feet. Anger comforted more than despair. There were so few mistakes in Maggie's life she had ever truly felt remorse over, but every one involved her sister.

Maggie wanted Tena to slap her across the face, so hard her ears rang, but knew she wouldn't. Instead, tears washed down Tena's cheeks. She buried her face in her sister's shoulder and didn't say any of the hateful things Maggie deserved.

"Don't go," Tena sobbed. "Please don't marry him. You can continue seeing him, but please don't marry him yet. Not now. I need you."

"You tossed me out of the house."

"I didn't mean it. You know I never mean half of what I say when I'm cross. I forgive too easily. I thought you left me alone when Father died, and I still took you back."

Maggie's hand paused halfway through stroking Tena's hair. Hope surged anew. Tena forgave her. Tena needed her, and she needed Tena. Together, they could manage. If there was ever a time to tell the truth it was now.

"Tena?"

"Yes?"

"I'm having a baby."

A sob escaped her sister, muffled against Maggie's shoulder. "You are?" she whispered.

"I am."

"So, the sickness makes sense now." It wasn't a heartfelt congratulations, but this wasn't exactly a situation to be proud of. Yet at least, unlike Reuben, Tena actually believed her. That was really all she could hope for until the shock wore off.

Maggie exhaled, squeezing Tena tightly. "You can't fathom how glad I am that you finally know." Tena remained silent for a moment so long Maggie finally pulled away. Her sister's golden eyes smoldered.

She wrenched out of Maggie's grip. "Marry him tomorrow," she spat.

"But you said—"

"Forget what I said. If you're having his child, you should marry him."

"But I don't want to. I'll stay with you. You need me. We need each other."

Snatching the server up, Tena washed it off in the sink, spraying the counter with water. Groaning, she dropped the server into a drawer and vigorously attacked the counter with a hand towel. "You don't need me."

Maggie turned off the water and braced a hip against the sink. "Yes, I do. You're my sister."

Tena threw the damp towel on the counter where it landed with a sharp thwack. "When we were children perhaps, but not anymore."

"That's not true. I'm here, aren't I? I came to St. Louis because your fiancé asked me to."

"No one makes your decisions for you. You decided to go to London without telling me and you left me on *Titanic*. Go anywhere you want, Maggie. Be with any man or as many men as you desire. I doubt marriage will stop you from throwing it around."

"How could you suggest that? I would never be unfaithful to my husband."

"In the way you weren't unfaithful to Reuben?"

"He wasn't my husband."

Tena's hands sank to her hips, water dripping down her skirt. "Do whatever you want, Maggie. It's what you've always done. But please, don't bother telling me anymore when you do it."

Maggie stepped forward, thunderstruck, her entire body shaking. "I said I was sorry for not being there when Father died. I meant it. How long are you going to lord my mistakes over me?"

Tena's eyes darkened. "Until you stop making them."

Juggling dessert plates, she stalked into the living room where she laid them across the coffee table. Ignoring the stares of everyone, she walked upstairs and slammed her bedroom door.

It felt like the door had been closed on Maggie's heart.

~ ~ ~

Tena stared at the bedroom ceiling, unable to sleep, roiling with a heat so intense her ears literally burned from it. At least she had maintained her temper since opening that vile canvas bag. Anger was a constant these days.

She squeezed her eyes closed as the bedroom door slowly opened and someone walked in. Maggie, judging by the soft footsteps. Winnie was not nearly so polite with her eleven-year-old horse hooves. Then again, polite wasn't usually the word to describe Maggie either.

When the steps came to rest beside the bed, Tena involuntarily stiffened, wishing she hadn't moved back in with Maggie after only two nights with Emil. Her sister had shared a room with her long enough to know when Tena was feigning sleep, but she didn't say anything or nudge Tena's shoulder with her palm. When they were children, Maggie would throw pillows at Tena's face then jump on her bed, bouncing the mattress and screaming, "Wake up! Wake up! Breakfast is ready!" But breakfast was never ready when Tena bounded from bed. Disappointment with Maggie began at a young age.

But tonight there was no palmed shoulder, no bouncing bed, and no merciless squeals. The footsteps moved away followed by the scraping of a traveling case against the wooden floorboards. Maggie filled it with the few belongings she had and sighed. With a click of the latches and a final click of the door latch, Tena released a breath and opened her eyes, the now empty room swimming around her. On her pillow lay a handwritten note.

Maggie's going to be a mother, she thought. *She's going to become round and plump and beautiful with baby. A baby that looks like her, like me, like our parents. And like Mr. Frye. Maggie's husband.*

Maggie has a husband. Could the world be any more unfair?

Tena leapt from bed, snatching the note from the coverlet as she stalked to the window and without reading a word, shredded the contents.

Of all the secrets her sister could keep, of all the things she could have said, of all the dreams Maggie could steal from her, this was the absolute worst. Tena silenced her thoughts before she could change her mind and talk reason into herself. She had lost her fiancé, her best friend, and the future she planned on for so long. Maggie stole it all in order to keep it for herself. She held everything Tena wanted in her perfect little hands, held it aloft so there was no way Tena could ever hope to reach it. All she could do was watch her sister enjoy everything she didn't deserve.

Tena would rather have no sister at all.

She threw up the sash, where it slammed against the top pane with a satisfying crash. Palm extended, she blew the torn scraps from her fingers into the night. They swirled on the breeze, over the front garden and the black taxi Maggie stepped into. Slamming the window, Tena returned to the comfort of her bedcovers, not bothering to watch her sister ride out of sight.

Out of sight and out of her life.

TWELVE

MAGGIE JOINED THE FLOW of people through the front doors of the courthouse, one hand clinging to her traveling case and the other to her handbag with none left to hold her independence. In a little over an hour, she would enter into a business arrangement for seven years, and she must continue to view it as such. It was a marriage, yes, but how was a marriage defined, truly? By definition, a marriage was simply a formal agreement legally binding the assets of two parties together, blending two ways of thinking for the collective benefit of both. It was hardly different from the agreement Mr. Frye entered into when he established his studio with Damaris, two parties working towards a shared goal.

She supposed it would be a never-ending battle now between her and Damaris. What Maggie did to earn the woman's disdain after saving her from Donovan's fists was anybody's guess. Betrothal to her brother must have been enough.

The night before, unable to face the Kischs once Tena told them about the baby, Maggie rang Hugo. Without any questions, he summoned a taxi with instructions for her to stay the night at Damaris's apartment and that there would be no issues.

Except that when Maggie stepped into the third floor corridor of Damaris's building, the woman was on the telephone in heated discussion with her brother. "I'll do it for you, Hugo," she rasped into the mouthpiece, "but you're running out of favors." There was a long pause before spitting back, "I don't care if tomorrow is your wedding day or your funeral—frankly with that girl it's one and the same ... Don't argue with me, Hugh. You're thirty-three. She's practically a baby."

Damaris turned her back on Maggie in a failed attempt to stand closer to the mouthpiece. "You owe me, Hugo. Between Emma and now this ... You owe me more than you know." Dropping the receiver back into the cradle, she sauntered to the second door on the left and waved an arm in the air. "You get one night here, sweet-cheeks. Tomorrow you'd better marry my brother or find yourself another place to squat."

Maggie entered the apartment's perfectly arranged living room only to receive a slam in her face from the bedroom door.

Now standing in the center of the courthouse rotunda with people spilling into and out of its four identical exits, she stared straight up into the room's massive dome. Four floors above, the mid-day sun fell from the lone window at the dome's center, pouring around her in a perfect circle as though she stood at the bottom of a well too slick to climb and too deep to be heard.

"Miss Archer?"

Maggie blinked away sunspots to reveal Howard Reed, the assistant counsel to Mr. Frye's lawyer. The young man tugged one shaky hand against his suit lapel while the other awkwardly smoothed his scalp. Probably no more than a few years older than herself and completely wet behind the ears, it would be difficult for her to imagine this man as ever capable enough to argue a case even after ten years in the courtroom.

Luckily Mr. Reed's superior, Gerard Huppert, had been most efficient in drawing up the marriage details Maggie and Hugo agreed upon on Monday in his study. So efficient was he that Mr. Huppert sent his assistant to Damaris's apartment yesterday evening with the documents for Maggie to sign. For legal reasons, the marriage stipulations needed to be drawn as a prenuptial agreement, but Mr. Reed assured her she had no need to worry. Not convinced by the boy's stuttering assurances, she read through every word of the document's five pages of legal speak, although from what she could decipher everything appeared to be exactly as requested. Damaris had already witnessed for her brother earlier in the day, so Maggie was left asking Damaris's half-blind neighbor to sign.

"Mr. Reed," Maggie smiled. "It is lovely to see you. If my hands were not otherwise occupied, I would offer you mine."

The young man's face flushed the same as it had every time she spoke the previous evening. Exactly as so many men had been captured by her so many times. *Until one finally captured me*, she thought dismally.

"No matter, Miss Archer," Mr. Reed squeaked. "Might I assist with your luggage?"

"That is hardly necessary. We both know why I'm here so let us skip the remaining formalities, why don't we, and head to the judge?"

He pulled at his tie then, as though the material were choking him. "Ah yes, the judge. Unfortunately, your appointment is not until one, and the hour now is not much past noon. Allow me to direct you to a waiting area."

Leading her to the left, he circled into an alcove, up an impressive curved staircase, then proceeded down another hallway before stopping at one of several stained oak doors. He gestured to an upholstered bench situated against the wall. "Please wait here, Miss Archer. Mr. Huppert needs to finalize an additional transaction with Mr. Frye, and then he will call you in."

"Transaction?" Maggie asked. "Isn't everything in order? I thought the lot were signed yesterday."

Mr. Reed coughed. His eyes flitted to the office door and back again. "Of course, Miss Archer, they were, except for one other technicality to be addressed."

"Which technicality is that?"

He again nodded to the bench. "Please, miss, do take a seat. Mr. Frye informed us that you are in a most delicate condition—"

Maggie slapped her handbag against her thigh. "I'll show you how delicate I am if you don't answer my question. Which technicality?"

He eyed the fist clamped around her handbag handle. "I assure you it will not affect his decision to marry you in the slightest."

"Because that certainly has me convinced." Ignoring Mr. Reed's feeble protests, Maggie shoved past him to throw open the office door.

Inside the already cramped space sat a substantially sized desk surrounded by filing cabinets and bookcases, every one stacked full to overflowing. Several drawers couldn't close fully. The desk itself, buried underneath a mountain of paperwork, left Maggie wondering how the man in the rumpled suit behind the desk could possibly be the same lawyer to draw up such detailed contracts.

In one of two chairs opposite, Hugo Frye hunched over a thin stack of papers, one elbow propped up on the desk. His fingers tapped against his forehead, clearly itching to slide back through hair heavily slicked with brilliantine into a dark ochre sheen. A drop of the oil had fallen on the same charcoal suit he wore to Charles's funeral, marring the left lapel.

"Howard?" Mr. Huppert called, not bothering to raise his eyes from his paperwork. His assistant hovered in the doorway. "I thought I instructed you to keep Miss Archer occupied."

"I—I tried, sir," Mr. Reed stammered. "She forced her way in."

"She's here?" Hugo lowered his hand to regard Maggie with a heavy expression. He rubbed his eyes with the back of his cuff. "Oh, Miss Margaret. I'm so sorry. Is it time already?"

"You *have* been here nearly two hours," the lawyer commented as he casually licked his finger and flipped another page.

"Is this about Donovan?" Maggie asked. "I already paid him for three months. What more could he need?"

Mr. Huppert regarded her curiously. "Who's Donovan? Is that *your* prior husband?"

"Pardon me?" Maggie replied. "Why would you assume this isn't my first marriage?"

He shrugged and turned back to his work.

"I'm sorry, Mr. Huppert," Hugo said. "Another minute and I'll have this signed." Jaw grinding, he placed pen tip to paper and ... paused. Black ink pooled upon the empty line. He dropped the pen and leaned both elbows on the desk to cover his eyes in defeat. "God help me, I can't do it."

Mr. Huppert tapped his papers on the desk to align the edges before tossing the entire group onto an already teetering pile. He slid an unsigned marriage license closer to Mr. Frye, Hugo's name written in tight script beside Maggie's. "Well, you can't very well sign this one until you sign that one. Marriages of that nature aren't even allowed in Utah anymore."

Maggie lowered herself onto the chair beside Hugo and slid the mystery document closer. She needed only to read the title. "Divorce?" she gasped. "Whatever for? Isn't your wife deceased?"

Hugo shook his head miserably and buried his face deeper into his hands. Maggie's heart beat clear up into her throat where it met with her anger. He was still married? How could he allow her to assume he was a widower? She had given him all her money to save his studio, offered him everything she had, and for what? So he could finally drop his first wife and take up with her instead? She should have left him to Donovan.

"She's not dead?" Maggie spat. "Then where is she?"

"I don't know." He spoke into his fingers. "She left three years ago and I can't find her. I don't know what to do."

Oh, my, thought Maggie as her anger fizzled. *It's me who's the fool, isn't it?*

"Mr. Huppert?" she asked. "Would you mind affording a moment alone for my fiancé and I?" The lawyer raised a brow and she threw him her most convincing smile. "I promise all this will be resolved quickly."

"Eh, sure thing, doll. Though married or not, I'll still expect payment." Mr. Huppert snatched his jacket off the coat rack, pulling it on as he made his way to the door. "Excuse me, gotta bust on my assistant for incompetence." He gripped a pale-faced Mr. Reed by the shoulder and yanked the door closed behind them.

Maggie leaned back in her chair, absently rubbing a hand across her stomach. "So, Mr. Frye, any more skeletons you care to remove from the cupboard?"

Rubbing his face, Hugo finally straightened up. "I assumed it would be easy, divorcing my wife. She found it effortless enough to leave; why couldn't it be the same for me?"

"It was easy enough to keep from your *next* wife. You would have me believe she died?"

"No. I would have told you." His gaze shifted back to the divorce document still awaiting his signature and released a weary sigh. "You're right. I wouldn't have. What husband wants to admit he failed?"

There was such pain on his face, such heartbreak in his voice, that Maggie's heart went out to him. She wasn't familiar with him at all, this broken man who in a few short minutes would become her husband. She didn't know his birth date or the names of his parents. She didn't know how he felt when he held his children for the first time. All she saw was someone uncertain of the future and terrified of facing it alone. In that respect, they understood each other perfectly.

"What happened to her?" Maggie asked softly.

"I told you, she left. Didn't even say goodbye. Two months after Isa was born, Damaris and I planned a trip to Seattle for the 1909 Alaska-Yukon-Pacific Exposition. That was our specialty, world's fairs. All that excitement meant people threw money at you for a portrait as a souvenir. Not to mention the panoramas we brought home. Local folks lined up in droves to buy them. I was right in my father's footsteps, on my way to the top just like him."

Hugo sank into the chair and unable to stop himself, ran shaky fingers through his hair, grimacing when his hand came back as slick as fish scales. He retrieved a handkerchief from his jacket pocket to wipe away the mess, although there was no fixing the loose tufts of hair. "Emma told me she understood. 'It will only be two months,' she said. I didn't know that was code for, 'The minute you step through that door, I'll hightail it out of town.'"

"And she left no indication why?"

"Falutin' if I know. I guess she was unhappy." Hugo paused and released a tremendous exhale. If it was possible, he sank even lower into the chair, his thumbs pressed to a forehead now resting a full foot below Maggie's shoulder. "I'm sorry, I won't lie to you again. I *knew* she was unhappy. All her friends knew. Even Damaris saw it. Three children under four years old, and Isa hardly slept and ate like a racehorse; of course Emma was overwhelmed. Damaris pushed me to it, but the truth is I was itching to escape sleepless nights as much as my wife. So when Emma told me to go, I listened."

Standing abruptly, he pushed his chair back and edged around a half-open filing cabinet to face the window with folded arms. His tight features reflected back in the glass juxtaposed upon the stone and brick buildings of the city. "Emma wept every day for two months, and I still went on that train. The night I left, she tucked the children into bed and disappeared. Thankfully, our neighbor, Mrs. Kincade, visited the following day; otherwise, I can't bear to imagine what might have happened."

Oh, Mr. Frye, Maggie breathed. For those children to be so young and have their mother desert them, then to live for months without knowing what happened to their parents or if they would return ... the thought was utterly heartbreaking. True, Maggie's own mother had been an unloving one, but Beatrix Archer for all her faults never abandoned them.

Hugo turned, backing against the window ledge. "I always hoped she would come back, and we could start over. What if she does and I'm married to you?"

"What if she does?" Maggie asked gently. "She abandoned you and your children. Is she really the type of mother you want for them?"

"Are you?"

She felt the accusation of his question pelt like icy sleet in the dead of winter. Her reputation preceded her and she made him aware of enough for him to know she was possibly the least worthy person to care for his children. For pity's sake, she couldn't even name her unborn baby's father with absolute certainty.

"No," she whispered. "I'm not."

Hugo didn't love her. He never would. But she wasn't upset by that. In fact, she welcomed it. This was business, pure and simple, and the only way she could ever abide a marriage. No emotion. Nothing personal.

"Beans and bacon." Running all ten fingers through his hair, Hugo abandoned all pretense to appear presentable. He ruffled his hair until it stood on end in every direction imaginable and some that didn't seem to be so before collapsing into the chair beside her. "Forgive me, Miss Archer. I'm a man who has suffered a great hurt and has done his fair share of hurting in return. Even so, I still believe in the ability to work through anything. I want Emma to come back if only so I can finally know why she didn't."

Maggie clasped her hands tightly over her stomach, struggling to decipher her complicated emotions. She could scheme her way into his affections like she had done with so many men before, through deceit and a healthy dose of seduction. In his fragile state, she could slice through his insecurities like butter and remove all thought of Emma from his mind. Instead, she stared at her lap where in a few short months a rotund belly would protrude and said, "You don't have to marry me."

"What?" Hugo gasped. "But your baby—"

Hands pressed to her middle, Maggie offered him a simple smile. "I'll be fine. I always am one way or another."

"I'm sure you will be." Hugo lowered his eyes to the divorce papers, and his fingers edged towards the pen. "Only I'm a selfish man, Miss Archer. I'm out of money, and I still need someone to care for my children. Your idea was the most sensible one. I need to divorce my wife so I can marry someone else to care for them. Whether she's you or not, it doesn't change the fact of the matter."

"Maybe there's another option. I'm waiting on my grievance claim to be resolved from *Titanic*. I've been told it could take years, but when it arrives, I'll loan you money to hire an investigator to search for her."

"Don't you think I've tried that?" Hugo huffed, tapping the edge of the pen against the desk. "I have. Three investigators if we're counting. Even with all the money I paid, none of them could come up with so much as a whiff of Emma's whereabouts. Not a glance. She must have changed her name, bought a wig, ate half a cow and gained forty pounds to be unrecognizable. She doesn't want to be found." He touched the pen tip to the empty line set before him. "If she wanted to be with me, she would be here."

With broad strokes, Hugo scratched his name and finalized his divorce at last. The pen fell to the desk with a thud that sounded in the small room. Maggie couldn't steal her eyes away from his signature, two words so beautiful she wanted to cry. Selfish reasons or not, he forsook the possibility of a reunion with his beloved wife for a life with her. To help her baby, his own children, and himself.

A clock chimed somewhere to her left, buried under papers a mile high as it clanged out the hour. Hugo's head swiveled in its direction. "One o'clock. So, Miss Margaret, what do you say? Will you still marry me after this? A man divorces his wife and remarries within the hour? Most would brand me with a big red X."

Burying her emotion, Maggie replaced it with a sly smile. "Nonsense. I have a red X of my own. So you see, we're a perfect match."

Hugo only managed a crooked smile in return. "I have a feeling there's more about you I have yet to learn."

She stood, adjusting her hat as she picked up her traveling case. "Well, luckily for you we have seven years together. You may just learn a few things about me yet." A laugh bubbled from her throat as she took in Hugo's utterly ruined hair, brilliantine streaked locks standing straight up, flattened straight down, and curled every direction in between. Add an impish frown and a smear of dirt on his face—perhaps an adorable pair of knickerbockers—and Hugo was the spitting older version of his mischievous son.

"One request?" she asked.

Hugo raised a brow only a shade lighter than the hair above it. "What's that?"

"Wash that ridiculous mess out of your hair," she laughed. "Whatever were you thinking?"

He rose, removing her traveling case from her hands and reached to tip her hat brim away from her eyes. "I was thinking that I always look like I recently rolled out of bed. For once I wanted to appear respectable."

Her eyes traced the thin hazel line that surrounded his emerald irises. "I would rather my business partner be himself, respectable or no." She reached up to scruff at his hair. "But I refuse to marry you wearing that muck. Agreed?"

Finally, he grinned. "Agreed."

With a rattle of the knob, the door flung open and Mr. Huppert sauntered in, a cigarette propped behind his ear and a relative ashen scent entering with him. With a glance from them to the signed divorce document, he scooped everything off his desk and reversed for the door. "I don't know how you convinced him, Miss Archer, but who cares. Let's get you two hitched."

~~~

Maggie never pictured her wedding quite like this.

She always assumed she would wear an elaborate, white, seven-layered gown, hand selected by her mother and pieced together by their personal seamstress, with a flowing veil and train behind her. There would be a ceremony in St. James's Church in Fontaine and a formal reception attended by her father's banking partners and her mother's chattering friends. Instead, she wore black in a courthouse without either of her parents. There would be no formal reception; there would be no celebration of any sort.

Deep inside, in some place she locked away even from herself, she was actually envious of her sister's belief in love. Tena hoped for a real honest to goodness marriage with a man who would choose to love her, never lose her trust, and accept her for who she was. One who would provide her with the family they never had and the life they always wanted but been denied. If a man like that existed, Maggie thought, oh what an unusual man he would have to be. The kind of man Charles probably would have been.

Except for today it was Charles's family standing witness over Maggie's marriage instead, and their joyful presence couldn't erase the pain of Tena's absence.

Maggie's eyes shifted to Hugo as he slid a ring on her left hand. Dark tendrils fell across his forehead, damp from rinsing his hair in the washroom sink immediately before the ceremony. He did exactly as she requested, removing every last trace of brilliantine, which left him a dripping disheveled mess.

"Oh, Hugh, what a disaster," Damaris grimaced when they walked through the judge's chamber doors, but in that same moment two wild girls broke free of their aunt and leapt into their father's arms.

"Why are you wet?" Isa giggled.

Hugo rubbed his damp hair against her cheek, eliciting another round of toddler laughter. "Miss Margaret made me take a bath." He edged his lips close to his daughter's ear, whispering loud enough for Maggie to hear. "She said I smell."

"Oh, Daddy, she did not," Molly cajoled. "It's not nice to lie."

The guilt nearly tore Maggie up that she was lying to them, that after seven short years another mother would be gone. Then she caught a glimpse of Damaris and Henry's identical incensed expressions and suppressed any further guilt. Hugo was doing this for them. She needed to do this for her child. Success in this life wasn't about affection; it was about strength.

"Miss Archer, your ring."

Maggie accepted the solid gold band from the judge and quickly slid it onto Mr. Frye's left ring finger. Its simplicity paired nicely against the diamond in her own ring.

Diamond? She ogled the ring on her finger—a modest diamond flanked by two molded flowers and vines etched around the gold band. Heavens, it was breathtaking ... and assuredly too expensive.

Her eyes flitted to his. "You don't have the money for this."

Something tender flickered across his features and as quickly vanished. "I promise you," he whispered, "it didn't cost me a dime." But how could he say so? Even if Damaris stole it from another of her funeral pillages, marrying Maggie would still cost him dearly.

The judge placed his hand on top of their joined ones. "By the powers invested in me by the state of Missouri, I declare you husband and wife. It is your privilege to kiss the bride."

Before she could protest, Hugo pressed a gentle kiss to her cheek. "Business partners," he whispered in her ear. "Nothing more."

"Thank goodness," she breathed. She had done more too many times before.

THIRTEEN

"Mr. Radford? Excuse me, but are you busy?"

Polishing off the last line of Mrs. Hardwick's obituary, Reuben settled his pencil and looked up. Hugo Frye stood over him, the man's hair and expression more disorderly than Reuben had ever seen it. He tipped back on his heels, a blush seeping up his neck. "If you have time," he said, "I could use a favor."

"Afternoon, Mr. Frye." Reuben rested an arm on his chair back. "How'd you get past the warden? Miss Newton doesn't allow visitors up here without sounding an alarm."

The rouge of his neck spread to his ears. "I offered to photograph her family at no charge."

"Wow," Stanley interjected, his nose buried in an article behind a wall of books and news clippings. "Wish that cheapskate Smithson paid *me* enough to do side jobs for free."

"Ignore him," Reuben said. "What can I help you with?"

Just like that, Hugo's entire face matched the shade of his hair. Cheeks on fire, he extracted a folded sheet from his jacket pocket and handed it to Reuben. "I tried to write it, but I'm not any good with words. Could you make it better?"

Unfolding the paper, Reuben smoothed it out on the desk and reached for his coffee as he read the first line.

Hugo Denton Frye and Maggie Elaine Archer announce their marriage—

Coffee spewed from Reuben's mouth, spraying everything within three feet including the front of Stanley's desk. His friend leapt forward, handkerchief flying from his pocket to blot the sheets. "Reuben, you lout," he frowned. "Drown your own work, not mine." He held up a sheet between two fingers, words blurred on the page. "Thanks a lot. Now I have to recopy this."

"Sorry," Reuben croaked. "Hot. Burnt my mouth." Claustrophobia settled across his back from Hugo's presence at his shoulder, his mind unable to wrap itself around what he was reading. Maggie *married*? To *Hugo*? When she proposed to *him* only four days ago? Bracing his chin in his hands, he pressed his fingers to his temples and continued reading.

Hugo Denton Frye and Maggie Elaine Archer announce their marriage on July 19, 1912. Mr. Frye is the only son of the late photographer, Henry Frye and Malina Denton, and a native of St. Louis. The new Mrs. Frye comes from England—

"Wait." Reuben backtracked across the page. He lowered his hands from his face. "Did you come here from the courthouse?"

"Um ... yes."

Reuben's eyes flicked in shock to the gold band on Hugo's finger. "Didn't you just meet Maggie at the funeral?"

Hugo's voice sank. "We met the month before. We didn't want anyone to know." He butted against the desk with another sweep of fingers through his tousled hair. "Mr. Radford, it's difficult for a man my age to find a decent woman willing to care for his children, and I have three."

"Maggie with children?" Reuben tapped the announcement. "We aren't referring to the same Maggie Archer, are we?" A tick pulsed in his left eye. "Is she waiting for you downstairs?"

"No." Hugo gave Reuben what failed to pass for a smile. "I have a few other matters to attend to at the studio, so I sent her home with the children. Three clients to photograph this afternoon, then paperwork to keep me busy until after dinner I dare say. Speaking of which, I should get to it." Hugo pushed off of the desk, burying his hands in his pockets. "How much will it be for the rewrite? I can send payment early next week."

Knowing the *Mid-Mississippi* already didn't pay Hugo Frye what he deserved, and barely able to manage the calculations in his head besides, Reuben said the only thing fitting the situation. "No need. Consider it a wedding present from the newspaper." A present he would have to compensate.

Hugo grinned, pumping Reuben's hand in gratitude. "Thanks, Mr. Radford. I sure appreciate it." With a new skip in his step, he exited the newsroom.

Expelling a burst of air, Reuben pulled a new sheet from his desk drawer, squared it up beside the marriage announcement, and started writing. He only half paid attention to the lead strokes on the page, preferring to switch his personal opinions off while he penned the lines proving Maggie had managed to con another unsuspecting soul.

He slid the finished announcement into a folder with a stack of completed obituaries and slammed it onto Smithson's desk as the clock struck five.

Stanley waited for him when he returned, his bag slung over his shoulder. "Get stiffed by a girl? I could hear you lay those papers down from here."

"Yeah, you could say it like that." With a hard look, Reuben loosened his tie before crumpling it and his jacket into his satchel. He tossed his notepad onto the pile and swung the bag across his chest.

Stanley grinned. "You finally gonna let me meet this girl who wrecked you?"

Reuben slapped a hand to Stanley's shoulder. "Yes, Lee, I certainly am. I need you to keep me from killing her."

"Leonard!"

Smithson stood in his office doorway appearing to have recently sucked a few too many lemons. "Where do you think you're going, Leonard?"

Stanley pointed at the wall clock which now read five minutes after five. "It's five o'clock, sir."

"What, you think the news waits on your delicate schedule?" Smithson stalked across the room and slapped a note sheet to Stanley's chest. "Shooting on Third. Get down there and bring me the scoop tonight."

Stanley gave a sympathetic shrug at Reuben who sensed his visit to Maggie becoming a one-man show which made him cringe. Smithson caught their silent exchange. "You got a flirtation going with Radford, Leonard?"

"No, I promised him I'd take care of something with him."

"Ya did? Fine, Radford, if you're so anxious to spend time with Leonard, you can go with him. I want an article from both of you and we'll see who lines the more gruesome mockup." He shifted to smack the paper against Reuben's chest instead, and Reuben snatched it before it fluttered to the floor. "Stealing your fellow reporter's byline?" Smithson cackled, heading back to his office. "Radford, you just may have enough gumption for your own beat after all."

~ ~ ~

"This is what you see every day?"

That afternoon's coffee bubbled in Reuben's gut as he stared at the body face up on Third Street, blood pooling into the cobblestone cracks from the man's empty eye socket. Even from thirty feet away and surrounded by dark clothed police officers, the sight of brain matter was enough to entice Reuben's gag reflex. There was a day not too many months before when he had almost ended his life in the same manner, staying his hand right before Tena walked through the door. He had understood his death would have been gruesome, but seeing it up close was an entirely different cricket match. Witnessing what a horror he almost left behind, compounded by the stifling summer's heat and an unappealing afternoon in the newsroom, roiled his nerves along with his stomach.

"Not every day," Stanley replied. He bit his lip and continued to furiously scribble on his notepad. "But you'll need a stronger disposition if you want to report on this beat."

"I don't want to write on this beat," Reuben griped as another of the many reporters attempted to edge closer and was knocked back by an officer's club. "Smithson made me join you."

Stanley's lips rose in a sneaky grin. "Fine, then. Why don't you go do what we planned on?"

"Alone?" Reuben chanced another glance at the body now being loaded into a black police ambulance. The corpse's head lolled to the side to fix him with an empty gaze and caused an involuntarily shiver despite the eighty-degree evening. "Without you there, Lee, I'll be as dead as that corpse there."

"Women will do that to you. Oh, gee, time to throw on the interrogation hat!" Stanley flipped to the next page, his pen flying as fast as his feet to where a group of five reporters bull-rushed a nearby shopkeeper.

Jumping out of the way of traffic as the street opened up again, Reuben slumped against a storefront window, silently cursing himself for ever being polite to Hugo Frye that afternoon. He rested his head back against the window and closed his eyes, silently counting the tidy sum that marriage announcement would now cost him. And all due to a woman who couldn't care one lick about him. Honestly, what was he doing with his life?

"You're sleeping at a *crime scene*?"

Knocked from his memories by Stanley's punch to his shoulder, Reuben opened his eyes to glower at his friend. "I'm not *sleeping*," he growled. "I'm considering what a terrible idea it is for me to see her tonight."

Stanley seized Reuben's shirt collar with a firm shake. "Don't be a collypoddle, Reuben. You need to face this girl or you're going to be a sniveling mess forever and never make headway with Hazel."

"Has it ever occurred to your one track mind that maybe I don't want to make headway with her?"

Stanley thumbed the inside of his lip. "Sure, and that's the reason why you've been out with her the last four out of five nights this week. Seriously, if you lie this bad, how did you ever get this old flame into bed with you?"

"Sod off, Lee. If you've forgotten, I've also been out with Luella, Phoebe, Rosalea and their friends, not to mention *you* every night this week."

"Yes, but you don't live with any of those other women or me, now do you?"

Blood rushed to Reuben's face, almost certainly as red as Hugo's hair. Leave it to Stanley to set everything up so conveniently. He had already known all about Mr. Vine's posting for a boarder when he blindsided Reuben into handing the reins over on his living situation. Reuben returned from his disastrous lunch with Maggie to a note on his desk in Hazel's precise script, and Stanley's smirk was the last thing he wanted to endure after an hour being lied to and manipulated by his former flame.

He had wanted to slam the note and his fist into Stanley's smug face and would have if Stanley hadn't actually done him a favor. Reuben needed somewhere to sleep besides the newsroom, and both Mr. Vine's monetary rate and personal expectations were more than reasonable.

"I have but one rule," Mr. Vine said as Reuben stood in the entryway to their three-story brownstone. "If my daughter needs an escort to one of her dag blam girlish functions, you'll take her, understood? Her Mama won't let her go unattended, and I've got no patience for that argument."

"But-but," Reuben stammered, "Your daughter and I—we're not—I mean, I don't intend to—"

"Don't look so darned frightened, boy," Mr. Vine chuckled. "Whether you do or you don't with Hazel, well, that's Hazel's decision. Call me a progressive parent—and I right well am—" He thumbed his chin with a shrug. "But better for something to happen—if it happens—where I can watch it unfold than off in your second-rate apartment."

Stanley yanked at the collar of Reuben's shirt, practically dragging him down the street. He flagged a taxi and shoved him across the seat inside before jumping in himself. "Give him the address, Reuben."

Reuben slouched in the seat. "I don't know the address."

"The name then."

"The *Mid-Mississippi Daily*. We need to give that article to Smithson on the double."

"Eric Smithson can wait an hour." Stanley lunged, both hands on Reuben's collar. "So help me, I will beat it out of you."

"Cor blimey, enough!" Reuben pushed his friend away. "It's Hugo Frye's place."

"The Fryes?" said the driver. He eased away from the curb into the evening traffic. "'Course I know the place. My pop was friends with old Henry Frye."

Stanley's smile was as jolly as his laugh, slapping the leather seat like he had heard the world's funniest joke. "That's the girl you're stuck on?" he howled. "Hugo Frye's new wife? She ditched you in exchange for *him*?" Releasing a final chuckle, he bent over the front seat. "By golly, step on it, sir. We've got some major damage control to perform."

FOURTEEN

MAGGIE'S WEDDING NIGHT WAS the opposite of a honeymoon. It began badly and only continued to grow worse as the evening wore on.

Fifteen minutes after signing the marriage license, Mr. Frye neatly situated her in a taxi with the children, instructing that bedtime was promptly at eight o'clock and "Don't wait up." He shut the car door on her mid-rebuttal and scuttled down the sidewalk faster than she could wrap her mind around being deserted on her own wedding day. The resulting ride home contained enough tension to cut through the butter that sat on the Fryes' dining room table at that evening's dinner.

And what an atrocious dinner it had been.

Between the icebox and the root cellar, she managed to create a meal of pan-fried ham—overcooked, chopped beets—undercooked, and eggs of a somewhat dubious nature. Fearing she would leave the children starving and her new husband embittered, she sliced a few apples and served everything promptly at seven o'clock.

"Right on time!" she exclaimed. She settled Isa into a chair on top of two pillows.

"On time would have been an hour ago," Henry sniped, eyeing his meal as if it were laced with poison. "That's when Dad serves it."

Maggie set to slicing Isa's ham into toddler-sized pieces. "In Fontaine, we always ate at this hour, often later."

"Daddy always apologizes because he can't cook like Mama could,"

Molly said. She took a bite of ham and soured, swallowing politely before choosing an apple slice instead. "He says Mama cooked as pretty as she was."

Isa's wide eyes turned up to Maggie. "Are you our mama now?"

Maggie's face burned as red as the bowl of beets on the table, both from the little girl's question and her own rising irritation at Hugo's continued absence. They were *his* children, for pity's sake. Similar to a lesson about the birds and the bees, such questions should be fielded by a parent, not a complete stranger.

"Don't be stupid, Isa," Henry scolded. "You only get one mama. Ours left." He stabbed his fork into a beet. "Because she didn't love you."

Isa's upper lip jutted out and two fat tears dripped down her cheeks before a series of wails erupted from her mouth.

"Henry!" Maggie exclaimed. She slapped her napkin on the table. "You apologize."

With a glare certain to steam frozen water, Henry picked up his plate. "I'd rather eat calf's liver," he snarled. Then in a single sweep, he upended his entire meal upon Isa's head.

Maggie now stood in the tiny bathroom built off the kitchen, her annoyance at the boy in the doorway actually overshadowing the pregnancy nausea. "Return to your room, Henry," she hissed. She plucked a dripping Isa from the bathtub and deposited her on the bathmat before wrapping a towel around her little frame and rubbing her hair dry.

"But I haven't brushed my teeth," Henry countered. He dashed around her to nab his toothbrush from the box.

Maggie dropped Isa's towel to wrestle it out of his hand. "And tonight you're not going to," she spat, pointing the brush in his face. "The dentist can yank them out one by one for all I care. That'll teach you to be nasty to your sister."

She replaced Henry's toothbrush in its box and yanked him from the room by the arm. Half dragging him down the hall, she deposited him at the foot of the staircase. "Go upstairs and change into your pajamas. And heaven help you when your father hears about everything that went on tonight."

"What'll it matter what *you* tell him?" Henry backed up three stairs so he matched her height, his little six-year-old arms folded across his chest. "You're not my Mama."

"I'm not, thank goodness. You are the last child I would want for a son."

The defiance died in Henry's eyes and then sparked ablaze anew. He stomped up the stairs and slammed his bedroom door behind him before belting out a muffled scream. She didn't care. Let him be furious with her. After all, he was only a child.

"Henry's a bad boy!" Isa cried, her little bare bottom streaking past Maggie up the stairs as the front knocker pounded.

"I am not in sound mind for this," she muttered then yelled up the stairs, "Molly, please ready your sister for bed!"

"I will, Miss Margaret!"

Unbolting the lock, she yanked open the front door and felt fresh waves of nausea. *And I am most certainly not in sound mind for this*, she thought.

With fingers predictably clenched around his satchel strap, Reuben regarded her with cold calculation and a tone to match. "Excuse me, ma'am. Is your husband home?"

Without reply, Maggie closed the door.

"Maggie," Reuben called. "For once, can't we be civilized?"

Another gruff voice laughed. "Man, Reuben, she is one *fine* lass. Seriously, how did you let her pick him over you?"

"Shut up, Lee." Reuben knocked on the door again. "Maggie, please? I only need five minutes."

"Who's with you?"

"Stanley Leonard, Mrs. Frye," called the second voice. He gave a great laugh as though the entire situation were merely a lark. "You're quite the curiosity to me, ma'am, what with all the grousing over you Reuben does."

"Blimey, Lee, this is your idea of helping?"

"I've been trying to convince him to see this other girl," Stanley continued. "Except he's stuck on you, you see. So please, won't you give him five minutes and he'll leave you alone? On my honor, ma'am."

And what was that worth? she wondered.

With a deep exhale sure to be the beginnings of regret, Maggie inched the door open to see a stout young man with dark curls tucked beneath his flat cap and a jubilant smile directed at her. The stranger—Stanley Leonard—stepped forward with a tip of his hat, and behind him, Reuben huffed impatiently. "Please, ma'am?" Mr. Leonard asked. Won't you help out my old boy here?"

"Old boy?" Reuben shoved the door open, backing Maggie into the foyer, and turned to slam the door in his friend's face. Ignoring Stanley's colorful expletives from the other side, he flipped the lock and rounded on her. "Your *husband's* not home yet, is he?" The tone of the word husband fell off his lips like profanity.

Maggie felt all the heat of her fight with Henry reignite. "Who told you I was married? It was Tena, wasn't it?"

"Your sister wouldn't give you away." His lip curled. "Mr. Frye came to see me at the paper. Bloomin' asked me to write your blasted marriage announcement."

"He did?"

Reuben clenched her shoulders, spinning to trap her between his body and the door. He pressed a finger in her face. "I'm here to ask you one simple question, Maggie. Why did you marry him?"

The firmness of the door pressed against her back, its sharp handle dug into her hip, and with a harsh realization, she understood that she had been in this situation before. Over a year ago, her mother backed her against their home's front door while she screamed in Maggie's face, demanding to know why her daughter chose to defile herself with Reuben. Maggie hadn't done anything of the sort, but her mother wouldn't believe her then, and judging by the rabid look in Reuben's eyes, he wouldn't believe her now.

She straightened up and squeezed the door handle at her side. "I love him."

"No, you don't. Agrh!" Reuben slapped his hand on the wall beside her shoulder. "That's not even what I'm asking." He gestured back towards the stairs. "Why did you marry *him*? Why Hugo Frye of all people? For all I know about you, he's so not your ideal man."

"I do not have an ideal man."

"You do too. It's me. It's Halverson. It's that Derby fellow you snagged in London. It's attractive men with clever comebacks and arrogant attitudes." He adjusted his satchel, gripping it with the same fervor he always did when he would rather punch something, but she was the only one in close range. "Frye's slight and oddly stocky and far more subdued than anyone else you've shown interest in. You enjoy a fine banter more than anyone I know. Where's the enjoyment in a man who doesn't fight back?"

"Perhaps I'd rather not argue so much anymore." At his snort, Maggie drew her teeth across her bottom lip. "What do you care? You had your chance with me."

"I know. Only-four-days-ago," Reuben ground out, fading scars standing out against knuckles now white upon his satchel strap. "Hugo Frye's a gentleman, Maggie. Don't toy with him like you did to me."

"Sometimes people change."

Reuben shook his head. "Not you. You're the amazing and voluptuous Maggie Archer. You're proud of who you are. Too proud. If Hugo can abide you in spite of your shrewish ways, well then God help him."

"So you don't love me anymore, easy as that? Your song was very different a few months ago."

"As you said, people change."

"Not you. You're the tortured and misunderstood Reuben Radford. As much as you think I hold onto who I am, so do you. Although I will agree, you've changed quite a bit since we were together." Maggie eyed the last lingering scar under his jawline, the one that wouldn't seem to let them forget that fateful night on the *Höllenfeuer*. "Why do you really find such issue with my marrying Mr. Frye?"

"He's not the right man for you."

"Rubbish. Who would be in your opinion? You?"

"Of course not. I never wanted—"

She pressed a hand to silence his lips and was shocked when he didn't push her away. "This was your choice, Reuben. You sent me away. I would have stayed. I would have married you." She stepped back, smoothing her dress taut so the now gentle swelling of her abdomen was obvious. His sight locked onto her middle, eyes widening as he took in the truth of her quiet whisper, "This baby could have been yours."

Stunned, Reuben reached a shaking hand towards her stomach, fingers brushing short when she stepped again out of his reach. He stared at her, lips parted, temporarily without words. "My, Reuben," Maggie smirked as she released the fabric to once again obscure her pregnancy. She unbolted the door. "It appears occasionally I do tell the truth." She swung the door open to Stanley's face inches from her own. "Mr. Leonard, please escort your friend home."

Reuben shook his head. "You may have been forthright about *this*, Maggie, but remember. One day Hugo will see you for what you are— 'an infinite and endless liar, an hourly promise breaker, and the owner of no one good quality.'"

Stanley stepped forward. "That's harsh, Reuben."

"I'm only quoting Shakespeare. You know the play, *All's Well that Ends Well*? But I doubt her marriage will."

Maggie pointed out the door. "Confound you and your literature, Reuben. Both of you out of my house."

"With pleasure. 'More of your conversation would infect my brain.'" He smirked. "Open a book once in a while, Maggie, and you might even figure out which piece that one's from." He stalked past her and the door slammed before he even stepped off the porch.

FIFTEEN

THE BURN OF REUBEN'S INSULTS sliding through her nerves, Maggie's feet remained plastered to the floor in the foyer, unable to move her towards the stairs.

Could it really be only four days since she last stood here proposing marriage to a desperate man while his landlord threatened to break down the door? Mr. Frye's cozy living room with its comfortable worn furniture and breathtaking photographs now ridiculed her as the woman who didn't belong and would never be respected, perhaps not by anyone. She feared the jury was still twelve moons out on that decision.

Mr. Frye didn't want this marriage any more than she did. She probably wasn't his type any more than he wasn't hers. Reuben had been correct on that account. In any other situation, she never would have sought Hugo out in a crowded room, much less pursued a relationship with him, business or otherwise. Back in Fontaine, he would have blended into the wallpaper to her like her sister blended in to all the other gentlemen that chased after Maggie. Then again, back in Fontaine, she and Hugo's opposite social standings would have never even offered a chance to cross paths, much less marry.

She twisted the wall switch, the lamps snuffing out in a blink, and made her way to the kitchen, desperate for some warm tea to calm her nerves and her ever irritated stomach. Water trickled into the copper kettle while she took in the view from the lone window, the last rays of daylight making way for starlit skies over the Mississippi River. In the morning, the sun would rise above its muddy embankment and up the thirty-foot cliff face at the edge of the Fryes' property. Around the river's bend, the edge of the city lay illuminated, gas lamps and electric lights twinkling through the ever-present haze of smokestacks and the chug of river ferries. Somewhere within rose the chimney of the house where Tena resided, a woman who would hold onto her pride rather than attend her own sister's wedding.

The gall of Reuben to berate her with his opinions on her life choices, as though he had authority to pass judgment. She prayed she would never see him again. Her baby's creator or not, if she had her way she never would.

She halted the stream of tap water when the entry door knocked shut. Heavy footfalls followed, a man's steps by the sound of it, at an intense pace towards the kitchen. Only one man could be so determined, the one she had just tossed from her home and not bothered to lock the door.

Maggie brought the kettle onto the burner and called, "You're truly going to walk back in here like you own the place?"

"I do own the place."

Tripping over her own breath, she found Hugo's inquiring stare observing her from the doorway. With a quirk of his brow, he set her traveling case on the kitchen chair, draped his jacket over it, and edged past her to retrieve a mug from the cabinet. Filling it with coffee from that morning's pot of now-cold brew, he drank several gulps and stared into the murky liquid rather than at her. "Were you expecting someone else?"

"Absolutely not." Certain her face betrayed her lie, Maggie began opening cabinets in a mad search for tea leaves, slamming one hard when she remembered she would find none. "I forgot you're a coffee only household."

"Not anymore." Setting his mug on the counter, he twisted around to retrieve an unlabeled tin box from the counter identical in size and shape to the one pasted with *Folgers Coffee*. Upon opening it, the deep scent of black tea emerged, swirling through her sinuses and finally calming her nerves. She stole the tin from his outstretched hand and placed the box directly under her nose to inhale with delight.

"You bought me tea?" she breathed. Excessive warmth spread to her cheeks, even more so than she felt at him depositing her in a taxi minutes after their wedding.

She glared at him through her lashes. "One kind gesture does not cancel an ill one. Do you honestly believe it appropriate to shove me in a taxi—"

"I'll carry your case upstairs," he interrupted. He drained his coffee mug, then set it in the sink before picking up her traveling case and slinging his jacket over his arm.

"Excuse me?" Maggie spat back. "We're in the midst of a conversation, *business partner.*"

Hugo nodded, tossing the barest of glances back over his shoulder on the way to the door, and continued speaking as though they were holding an entirely different conversation. "Good idea; finish your tea, and I'll check on the children. Come up to bed when you're ready."

"Bed?" she yelled at his retreating back. "Not while we're still arguing, Mr. Frye!" Torn between the luscious scent of tea and walloping Mr. Frye into next Tuesday, she looked longingly at the tin box, cursed ... twice, damped the stove fire, and sped up the stairs after him.

Reuben's words were a bitter pill to swallow. *You enjoy a fine banter more than anyone I know. Where's the enjoyment in a man who doesn't fight back?*

Blast that confounded man, she thought. He was right about all of it.

Stumbling up the last two stairs, she emerged in a darkened hallway lined with three closed doors and a fourth narrower one she assumed led to the attic. A stream of light shone from only one. Slapping it open, she first noticed the full sized bed situated in the center of the room covered with a red and blue quilt and several pillows stacked at the head. While Hugo wasn't there, his jacket lay crumpled at the bed's foot. Antique furniture pieces stood at either side of the single window: a sparse writing desk and a mahogany mirrored dresser topped with coins, wallet, and pocket watch. A wardrobe with brown loafers tossed beside it completed the only room in the house that, so far as she could tell, contained no photographs. The lack of photographs in the bedroom of a photographer unnerved her far less however than her traveling case waiting for her.

She inspected every corner before opening the wardrobe and each dresser drawer. Every one contained a man's clothing. Dread simmered an inch below the surface, waiting for her to release it into all-out panic.

What she wouldn't give to tie that man down and bestow upon him a piece of her mind and a generous slap. This wasn't a real marriage. Even her parents had been afforded the luxury of separate sleeping quarters.

A tiny mop of crimson hair peered around the doorway, Molly's eyes drooping as much as Maggie's were wide. "Miss Margaret?" the little girl asked sleepily. "Is Daddy home yet?"

"Right here, sweet girl." Strong arms hoisted the child up, burying her close to her father's chest as he kissed her brow. He looked to Maggie from the shadows of the doorway, only his eyes reflecting the light from the bedroom. "You found your belongings then?"

She nodded. "Yes, but you can't honestly expect—"

Hugo whisked the little girl out of sight before Maggie finished speaking. "Come on, Molly, let's get you tucked in."

"Two stories?"

"Oh, very well. Two stories."

Maggie dropped onto the writing desk chair, completely worn from the day. After Henry then Reuben and now Hugo, she couldn't take much more masculine aggravation tonight.

But honestly, to share a bed with *Hugo Frye*? She may have made a commitment, but she would be hung if she spent seven years sharing intimacies with a man she could never be attracted to.

Perhaps his intentions are innocent, she thought. But when had she ever met a man whose were?

Blast it all! She hadn't agreed to this, and her pregnancy-addled brain hadn't thought to even discuss it. If she had, she would have insisted they write conjugal visits, or lack thereof, into their contract. This was a business deal; sleeping together was a complete conflict of interest.

Yanking open one desk drawer then another, she pilfered a half-sharpened pencil and absolutely no parchment. *What fool doesn't store paper in his writing desk?* she wondered. *Apparently the kind of half-wit I married.*

But just when she thought she might have to pen their contract amendment straight onto the wallpaper, Hugo entered. His eyebrows raised when he noticed her hand poised upon the wall.

"What are you doing?" he asked as he closed the door.

"Nothing." *Merely defacing your property.* Her entire face burned as she lowered her hand. "There isn't any parchment in your writing desk."

"The desk was my mother's. I think the last letter written there was during the McKinley administration." He unbuttoned and slid out of his vest, loosening his tie to undo the top button of his wrinkled Oxford. He dropped the entire lot onto the desk chair. Without sparing her so much as a second glance, he made for the bed in only his undershirt and slacks.

Maggie froze. "Wait, shouldn't we discuss this?"

Hugo tugged off his shoes, tossing them towards the wardrobe. "Discuss what?"

Mouth agape, she dropped the pencil onto the desk and finally managed to regain her bearings. "Surely you're not that simple. If you wanted to avoid a row before, you probably shouldn't now expect honors you're not the least bit privy to."

"All I want tonight is sleep." With a grunt, he tugged a rather large drawer out from under the bed frame. Or rather, as it appeared she saw that it wasn't a drawer at all, but a sliding trundle bed, already made with freshly starched sheets and a pretty blue checkered quilt. He stole one of the bed pillows and turned those sad green eyes on her. The deep-seated pain within them played on memories of her father's own troubled stare the day he sent her off to London, containing all the emotions he would never tell.

"You can trust me, Miss Margaret," said Hugo, "to be true to my word. We're business partners, and that's all I ever want to be." Laying down on the trundle bed, he pulled the blankets over himself and closed his eyes. "Good night, Mrs. Frye. Please don't write on my wall."

Too stunned to reply and too relieved to think anymore on it, Maggie turned down the lamp, and despite her sore breasts aching against her corset and frustration still aching in her brain, she slid fully clothed into the bed and a terribly restless sleep.

SIXTEEN

REUBEN TOSSED HIS HURRIED ARTICLE on Smithson's desk and left Stanley in the near-empty newsroom, his thoughts as mangled as the dead man's face on Third Street. Kneading the back of his neck, he slung off his satchel and unlatched the front door of the Vine home.

"Good evenin' Mr. Radford," came the usual greeting of the *Mid-Mississippi*'s typists from the living room.

"Evening, ladies," he replied without any of his usual flirtation as he shrugged out of his jacket and hung it on the rack beside the door.

As Stanley so kindly reminded Reuben, he had gone out with Hazel's friends the last four nights in a row, first to dinner and drinks at the Nightingale, then to a concert, then a showing at the nickelodeon, and finally to Jonathan Earhart's for triple rounds of euchre and gin rummy until nearly midnight. Compounded by a hectic workweek and the blow Maggie Archer dealt this evening, he could have already slept straight until Sunday. Another night of revelry would only remove him from much sought time to wallow in self-pity and depredation.

In a flounce of emerald taffeta and bouncing coppery curls, Hazel met him in the doorway. "Reuben," she cried. Her rouged cheeks flushed even brighter with her excitement. "Rosalea's invited us all out dancin'!"

"Correction," Rosalea spoke up, her satin-trimmed body draped across the sofa as though she owned it. "Earhart invited us. I'm simply along for the ride, and his ride is ever so lovely."

"Must you flaunt it, Rose," Luella moaned with a pinch to her friend's cheek, "that your man is the only one of us with a motorcar?"

"Oh, don't be so green about it, Lu," Phoebe giggled. She adjusted wrist-length gloves the same shade as her peach dress. "We can smell your jealousy from here, and it stinks."

Rosalea stretched her arms wide. "My man truly is the best. You should *all* be jealous." Flipping onto her side, she laced Reuben with a sly smile. "Say, Mr. Radford, are you escorting our Hazel? You just know she'll find it—"

"Fascinatin'!" All three girls finished, breaking into a round of hysterical giggles.

"You all leave me be," Hazel frowned. With a gentle sway of her hips, she sashayed down the hall, calling over her shoulder, "I saved you dinner, Reuben. Mama's meatloaf and potatoes with special gravy."

Unable to ignore the rumble of his stomach, Reuben followed her, a silent grin the only bit of amusement he had felt that entire day. Hazel's friends' rendition of her favorite exclamation had actually been pretty spot-on, and their vocal impression eerily accurate, but their propensity to tease was not something he typically shared. Hazel's excessive use of her favorite adjective may have initially motivated him to purchase the thesaurus he *accidentally* left beside her typewriter, but it wasn't long before her little quirk became more than a repetitious word.

Not once in the last four days had Reuben eaten dinner with the Vines as his schedule never reflected theirs; however, that hadn't hindered Hazel from attending to his evening meals. Her petite elbows propped up on the table, she would ask for gossip from the newsroom. Her pretty little lips curled around her speech like silk, and Reuben learned how fascinating one simple word could be.

"Louisiana steamboat ran aground, caught on a sandbar."

"Fascinatin'."

"Samuel Jefferson keeled over Tuesday night. They're having an estate sale on Monday after the funeral."

"Fascinatin'."

"Double homicide on Cherokee Street. Twelve gunshots delivered."

"Fascinatin'."

Usually her interest with morbidity intrigued him, but not tonight.

Reuben exhaled, dropping his satchel to the kitchen floor and himself into a chair at the table. Tonight his brain was wrapped in more knots than a sailor could set. If any part of his brain *was* functioning, it pictured Maggie's round abdomen, wondering if he was responsible and spinning the statistical probability that it legitimately was Hugo's.

Bending low into the icebox, Hazel retrieved a made up dinner plate, spinning in a whirl of pale green skirts and burnished locks. Her heavily blackened lashes fluttered above lined lids, aging her eighteen years by many more than seemed appropriate. "My, I cannot wait to dance tonight," she breathed, her skirt swaying on the way back to the table. "Papa's never allowed me at Cave Hall before." A blithe little grin tugged at her lips. "'Course that was before I had my very own handsome escort."

"I'm not going." His grit startled Hazel into dropping the dinner plate the last inch onto the table. It landed with a sharp clatter, and a few peas rolled onto the wooden surface.

Hazel quickly returned them to the plate and slid it towards him. She lowered herself into the opposite chair. "Luella said there was a shooting. Did the story not go well?"

Reuben scooped a helping of peas into his mouth, talking around his fork. "Mmm, hmm. It was fine. Although, I think from now on I'll keep my hands out of Mr. Leonard's territory." He raised another bite to his lips, not exactly tasting anything.

Her lip jutted out, glazed with pale pink rouge. "You mad at me then? That why you don't want to go?"

"No, I—" He met her eyes and sighed at the disappointment there. "Forgive me, Miss Vine. I'm not quite myself tonight."

Hazel traced her finger along the wood grain, inching it closer to his own. "We all have our times. You come out with me tonight, and I'll make it all better."

Reuben shoveled more food into his mouth. He would need to be blind not to notice how she hung on his every word or how the cut of her gorgeous gown left him heated. He would be smart to just chuck caution to the wind and do as Stanley suggested, making this attraction between them official. Get lost in her attention for a night, a week, forever. But, blimey, if he couldn't push Maggie's last words from his mind.

This baby could have been yours.

His baby ... was it really, though?

He had been but one in a line of Maggie's suitors. Her child could as easily be anyone else's.

Chewing the final bite of his meal, Reuben swallowed hard. "I'm a terrible dancer."

"That don't matter." Hazel's fingertips brushed the edge of his hand and her lashes fluttered. "I'm not."

He stood without response, rinsing his plate in record time, so quickly they should have enrolled it as an Olympic sport. He pressed his palms against the edge of the sink, lost in thought.

A few months ago—before sailing on the *Höllenfeuer*, before Maggie's betrayal, before Charles died—he would have wallowed in his room, drawn the curtains and lain in his bed wondering why the blows kept coming and nothing was fair. His crazy delusions would appear in the guise of his departed sister, probably perched on top of the dresser, swinging her feet with a wicked smile.

"Feeling sorry for yourself, brother?" Mira would smirk. "Well, you should. You had Maggie in the palm of your hand and you walked away. And not even a week later, she's married anyway. Married and stuffed full with some child. Like a kick to the groin. Like a knife, she drove it in and twisted. Like a—"

"Enough! I get it," Reuben would yell back. "But it wasn't right, she and I. Even if we do have a baby, even if I married her, what then? Married bliss for twelve hours then the same carousel of bickering we've bandied about a million times before? I need someone who wants the same life as me. I don't even know what she wants."

With a toss of her hair, Mira would hop from the dresser. "Clearly not you."

Reuben stared into the etched glass of the Vines' kitchen window, analyzing his weary reflection. Mira wasn't there. She never had been. She was in his dreams, his memories, and he still missed the innocent girl who lived a life of laughter and music. His sister had loved to dance. So did Tena. He remembered when she swept Charles, Maggie, and him away to Southampton on May Day last year. Reuben danced with Tena for hours and never once did she complain how often he pinched her toes or asked her to lead. How he missed her now. And Emil. Karl and Elsa and Winnie. Even Fred.

Not the least of, he missed Charles. Always Charles. His best mate with the uncanny ability to dispense advice Reuben never wanted to hear and hardly ever followed. Yet he always listened. Halfway to death after falling in icy waters off the *Höllenfeuer*, Charles offered him a choice. To stay with the family Reuben lost or return to a life with the Kischs—a family he should be proud to call his own. So he went back because his friend asked him too. Because Charles couldn't.

In the sky outside, hovering directly above their neighbor's twin chimneys, the moon's glowing orb hung low. *Sometimes, Charles,* Reuben thought, *I wonder why you bothered to ask.* The moon didn't answer, but he could almost imagine the man there winking slyly.

"That's not an answer," Reuben grumbled.

"Reuben?" The soft voice at his elbow brought him away back to sweet dimples tucked beneath bright eyes and loose burnished curls. "I'm sorry I mentioned dancing," she said. "You're tired, and I should have thought first. We can stay home tonight."

This wasn't his home. It wasn't even close. Home was somewhere far removed from here, a place tucked deep inside a heart he emptied when he walked away from the Kischs. Except that lately the emptiness ached, longing for something fresh to replace everyone he removed from his heart.

Sweet, classy, and a touch naive, Hazel was of a different cut than everyone else in his cluttered past. At the newspaper, her fingers flew across the typewriter, eyes rising to greet him through fluttering lashes as he returned from an assignment and never indicating aloud her desire for more than friendship. In her father's house, she never once crossed any boundaries, and her parents thought Reuben the highest of gentlemen. With her glossy copper hair and eyes the same shade as her name, she had one important attribute no other woman in his life did, and it made all the difference.

"You fancy me, don't you, Miss Vine?" he asked gently.

Hazel's eyes flitted to his, her soft breath hitching. "Oh, yes, Reuben. I'd be lying if I said I didn't."

"Brilliant." With a tease of his fingers across her jawline, he softly brushed his lips across hers.

Her eyes widened and she threw her arms around his neck. "Oh, Reuben," she giggled, "Does this mean you'll finally call me Hazel?"

Reuben laughed, thinking how unusual her response was. When he kissed Maggie for the first time, she recoiled as if he struck her. Well, Maggie had been correct about one thing. He had held onto who he was for too long.

He drew Hazel close for another solid kiss. "Yes, Miss Vine. I'll most definitely call you Hazel."

Let his heart's emptiness be filled. Hazel Vine reminded him of no one else.

SEVENTEEN

"GOOD GRIEF," EARHART GRIPED. "Why do girls always need to primp and prod? We've only just arrived."

Jonathan Earhart and Jonathan Tyler—respectively known by their surnames within their circle—stood with Reuben outside Cave Hall's ladies' lounge waiting ... and waiting ... and waiting for their dancing partners so they could make their way into the main dance hall. Still filled with apprehension over the prior events of that evening, Reuben needed Hazel to emerge so he could claim security from her hand in his. If the giggles floating through the lounge door were any indication, he would have to wait a while longer.

Tyler unbuttoned and reclasped his suit jacket. "Phoebe's a fine dame, but fellas, in near about a minute, I'm apt to head into the hall for another."

Earhart flipped the watch from his jacket pocket, swinging the chain once around his finger before he opened it. "Ten o'clock. If they take much longer, we may as well."

"Good glory, Jon, put away your watch, else you'll find an engagement ring on your porch come morning." Rosalea tossed him a flirtatious smile as she and Luella approached from the lounge.

Luella pulled her gloves back on one finger at a time. "We had to freshen our faces."

"What could you possibly have to freshen before you've even danced?" Earhart scoffed.

Rosalea hooked the last tiny button on her glove with a shrug. "Your motorcar blew our hair all up and dust in our faces."

"You did insist on driving with the top open, Rosie dear."

"Well, we needed everyone to know it was us."

"With all the hootin' and hollerin' you were doing, dearheart, how could anyone miss ya?"

Rosalea pinched his chin between her thumb and forefinger. "No more than you were doing, sweetie."

Sidling away from the group, Reuben passed Phoebe and caught Hazel as she exited the lounge. He clasped her elbow and led her to the entry stairwell where the lighting was so dim as to be perfect. Two couples passed before he stole her against him. "There's my girl," he murmured. "How does it feel to be out tonight?"

"When you kiss me?" She raised her lips and he obliged, kissing her in a way even her "progressive" father might not approve of in public. Hazel grinned. "Utterly divine."

"I knew it!"

Reuben lifted his face at Stanley's boisterous shout. He bounded up the stairs from street level with a grin as smug as his usual crude humor. "I knew it," he repeated. He threw an arm around his friend's shoulders and yanked him closer to whisper, "All you needed was to get over that dame and you'd have Miss Vine in your dainty obit writing fingers." Stanley stepped back, flinging his coattails behind him with a flourish. "Who do you need to thank for that, I wonder?"

"Finished your column and ready to meddle in my business again? Smithson needs to work you harder." Reuben extended his arm to Hazel whose face still burned like the devil's fire. "Come on, Lee. A little bird told me Luella's already claimed you for her partner tonight."

Stanley licked his lips and followed Reuben and Hazel back through the entry hall. "And I don't mind claiming her right back. In fact, I might do well with seconds of that blonde-haired beauty."

"My sympathies to Luella." Laughing, Reuben spun Hazel into the main ballroom before Stanley could frame a proper rebuttal.

Located above a row of Olive Street shops, Cave Hall's wood-planked dance floor and extended ceiling encompassed most of the building's top two floors. From the raised stage at its farthest end, a mixed band led hundreds of couples to the rhythms of a fresh ragtime beat. Up above, a narrow balcony allowed space to observe the dancing or spend more intimate time in its dark corners. But it was on the hall's edges that the boisterous gaiety was at its most extreme. A nearby gentleman raised a hand and an excited shout towards a young couple entering. Trussed up ladies and their beaus shuffled together in merry conversation, often discussing nothing of more consequence than the latest twenty-minute nickelodeon film. They were out on the town; talk of employment and politics were serious topics for parlors and dining tables, not rebellious dance halls.

With the electricity in the lamps and in the air, Reuben felt an unfamiliar twitch spark the hairs on his neck. They didn't have dance halls in Fontaine, at least none like this. Parties back home were hosted by wealthy families in private ballrooms, all very regulated and posh. Here they were quite literally dancing like wild animals.

Hands bared high like claws, feet moved past faster than any dance Reuben would have dared. Joining them beside the dance floor, Earhart flung his arms wide. "Radford, I offer your British sensitivities Exhibit A of American Ragtime—the Grizzly Bear."

"Not to be bested by the Turkey Trot." Tyler spun Phoebe out then back into his arms. "All the rage and all the bother for our parents."

"Don't forget that uptight morality squad," Rosalea fussed. "I declare the fear of them is like having another Daddy."

"Well then, down with the morality squad!" shouted Earhart.

That comment sent up a rousing chorus of "Hear hear!" from their group and everyone in the vicinity.

"What's the morality squad?" Reuben asked as their group merged farther into the room. Hazel held tight to his arm, her eyes taking in the excitement and her flushed cheeks acknowledging how much she adored being out on her own.

"Who," Stanley corrected, Luella now safely situated on his arm. "The morality squad is a group of officers who charge into places like this—saloons, dance halls, and so forth—in an attempt to dismantle them. They believe dancing leads to impurity and alcohol is the devil's brew."

"A bunch of poppycock, of course," said Earhart, "because Cave Hall's always been one step ahead. With all those temperance crackpots on the loose, the owners, Cornelius Ahern and Herman Albers, just did the easy thing and don't serve spirits here. No alcohol, no worries."

"But what would you bet," Tyler chortled, "that every Monday night when the place is closed ole Ahern and Albers are sipping the ale like the rest of us corrupt youth?"

"Bless his soul! Bless his soul!" shouted the ladies.

"Down with the morality squad!" returned the men.

"Hear! Hear!"

The band threw up another lively tune, a violin and banjo joining the tinkling piano keys. These people were barking mad compared to what he left back in Fontaine; however, he was starting to enjoy it. Just so long as he didn't need to join in.

Hazel tugged him towards the enormous dance floor. "Come along, my British beau. Dance with me."

Reuben dug his heels in while Hazel continued to pull on his arm in vain. "Hazel, please. I am a frightful dancer. Any English lady would vouch for this."

"That's but your silly little nerves, Reuben," Hazel giggled. "All these dances are brand new. Why do ya think they offer lessons twice a week?"

"I thought this was your first time here? How have you had lessons?"

"Who says I have?" A teasing little smile crossed her face. "But in a place like this? You don't need to know nothin' to dance here."

With the touch of her lips to his, he finally relented. By this point, the floor was crowded with swaying bodies, moving to an unfamiliar song. They turned around the north side of the floor past a long line of windows now featuring the darkened city sky.

Reuben focused on Hazel's pleasant smile rather than the pinch of his toes upon hers. He joined in with her laughter and admired how her eyes sparkled right before she tripped and fell into his arms. She peered up at him like he was a summer's day she couldn't get enough of. In fact, his focus was so well placed, he didn't notice the other figure drawing near until Emil's tall frame knocked them from the dance floor.

"Oi," Emil fussed. "Did you not see me off yonder jigging like the bloomin' Irish the last five minutes? That is a bit of a disappointment. My jig is quite a sight to behold."

"Emil!" Reuben grinned. "Aren't *you* a sight to behold? Also a tad youthful to be in a place like this."

"You're only young if you look it. Luckily I appear twenty while my fick of a brother looks less than, and you blimey well know that fact doesn't get old."

"Fred's here too?"

"Hardly. I want to actually have an enjoyable time tonight."

Continuing this conversation went against Reuben's new rule to steer clear of the Kischs for a while, but it was only Emil. How much harm could the little jester cause? Ushering them over to the bar, he held up two fingers to the attendant and sighed when Emil's sly gaze observed Hazel firmly attached to Reuben's arm. Time to get the mocking over and done with and quickly.

"Emil Kisch, Miss Hazel Vine. Yes, she's with me, so tame your flirtations now."

Emil slammed a hand to his chest with jaw dropped. "Well bowl me over and call me Lucinda, Reuben, you found a lady. This calls for a drink." He held a finger up to the beverage attendant before narrowing his eyes at Reuben. "This one ain't mental, is she?"

"Opposite of." Reuben accepted two glasses of punch from the attendant and handed one to Hazel. She offered her other hand to Emil. "Pleasure to meet you, Mr. Kisch. I've heard wonderful stories about you."

"Reuben's a right fat liar then." Emil released her hand and tested his own glass of punch with a grimace. "I swear, if that law passes and I'm forced to drink this nonalcoholic filth every day, I'm brewing beer in the cellar."

"No one would doubt that." Reuben tasted the liquid and silently admitted Emil was right. He would much prefer a beer. "Are you out alone, Emil?"

"Nah, with Jakob and Terry. Oi, Jake!" Emil threw his hand up to flag down the skinny eighteen-year-old. He had snagged some pretty young red-head and was leading her out to the dance floor. "You gots yourself one heck of a crimson fox there!" Emil hollered.

"Yes, sir." Jakob thrust his index finger at Emil. "Get yourself onto the dance floor, *meine freund*, and with a dame who's not your sister."

"Shut it, Jake."

Reuben gave him the once over. "You brought Winnie here? Isn't she a bit young?" It was one thing that, with Emil's physique, he could probably charm the skirt off a woman five years his senior, but quite another to bring his kid sister along for the ride.

"Not *that* sister." Emil cuffed the back of his neck. "Tena. She's in the ladies' lounge."

"Oh." That certainly complicated the situation.

Wanting to make an uncomfortable situation fleeting and get Hazel back to the dance floor, Reuben swallowed the rest of his drink and swiped Hazel's empty glass. "Shall we dance again?"

"Hold up, mate," Emil cut in. "If you say she's your girl, then this next set has *my* name assigned to it. How else will I know if she meets the Emil Kisch stamp of approval?"

"Emil, there's no such thing."

"There is tonight." He turned to Hazel with an innocent grin. "Care to join me?"

She looked to Reuben, blackened lashes fluttering. "Would you mind terribly?"

"Course not. Long as you come back to *me*." Reuben threw Emil a threatening stare. "Don't you steal her away from me."

Emil wrapped Hazel's hand through his arm and patted Reuben's shoulder. "No promises, mate. Keep Tena occupied though, won't you?" With his usually saucy grin, Emil led Hazel away through the throngs as the band readied their instruments for the next rag.

Rather than allow himself to be taken off guard again, he ordered two fresh glasses of punch and stuck himself directly outside the ladies' lounge to wait.

The band had started on their second song and Reuben finished his drink by the time Tena finally emerged. He had expected the girl he used to live with—hair left long around her shoulders, bare feet poking out from beneath her skirt, and not a stitch of rouge or power. Instead, her hair was pinned up in curls and her eyelids painted the same mauve as a twilight sky.

He held up the punch glass, tossed on a smile, and approached her before she hit the main hall. "Evening, Tena. Refreshment?"

Tena twirled, her ebony dress ever so subtly flaring around her ankles. "Reuben!" She released a tiny gasp and upon bending nearer, he noticed her eyes were swollen and glassy.

"Were you crying in the lounge?"

"Goodness, no. I'm here to dance and forget all that other mess. Is that punch for me?"

He handed her the full glass. "Dancing? You've not even reached half mourning, have you?"

"Mourning or no, it doesn't change the state of affairs." She swallowed some punch and grimaced. "That's awful. Maggie married Hugo Frye today, did you know?"

"I did, and I would appreciate if this was the last we spoke of it." Reuben knew all too well about Maggie's current marital status, and he suspected Tena would be none too happy if she heard how he stormed the Frye house earlier that evening. Curse Ahern and Albers for maintaining a dry hall. He could use a drink and a cigar and the lips of his new pretty lady. Except Hazel was currently being squired by his sixteen-year-old annoyance of a friend. So, on second thought, curse that blasted Emil too.

"Of course," she agreed. "Would you care to dance instead?"

"Of course," his lips answered before his brain caught up. Even talking to her went against the carefully laid rules he set out for himself when he left the Kischs. But they were already here, weren't they? If one dance would make her happy ... "I'll dance with you, but," he amended, "your lips are sealed. You won't weave your magic and convince me to return to the Kischs."

"I know." Tena wrapped her fingers around his, her own eyes focused on the cinch of his tie. "I truly wasn't planning to say a word."

Ditching the glasses on a nearby table, Reuben directed Tena to one the few remaining spots at the edge of the wood-planked dance floor. Piano strains kicked off the quick beats of an American tune Reuben heard on the Vines' radio for the first time only two days before. Luckily for him, despite the song being new, the steps were not. Tugging Tena close, he led off into the dance, joining the flow of the crowd: one-two-two-one. With a startled laugh, she tightened her grip as he whisked her away, for once managing not to fall over himself in the process. That was until the music shifted to the first song he and Tena danced to that May Day in Southampton.

"So, it's a right awful thing when a man has to ask a woman this on the first time out," Reuben had admitted in an attempt to laugh off his mortification, "but do you know the steps?"

"You compliment me," Tena replied. "I dare say Charles would never have the courage to admit he didn't know."

"Then Charles is only as foolish as I am." He extended his hand to her with his usual winning smile. "Won't you lead me, m'lady?"

Laughing, she laid her hand in his. "Why yes, good sir."

The same recognizable melody played in Cave Hall was now paired with foreign steps even Tena didn't recognize. When he spun them to the right, the nearest couple spun left, slamming them off the edge of the dance floor. Somehow he managed to yank Tena back before she pitched over a man on his way to the balcony.

"Careful." Reuben helped her back onto the wooden planks where the other dancers made wide berth to avoid them.

"I believe it was supposed to be one left, two right," Tena commented. She watched the other couples as they turned. "Now we move forward one, forward two, back and turn—watch out!" She tugged Reuben in the opposite direction from the path he headed, narrowing avoiding another collision. "I had forgotten how sorry a dancer you were."

Reuben released her waist to press two fingers to her lips. "We're not talking, remember?" He tracked to the left, this time keeping in step with the room. Another pace across the floor and the song slowed to silence then raised the enthusiastic applause of the hall.

"How 'bout a lame duck?" The bandmaster called from the stage.

"I haven't the faintest idea what that means, but let's try it!" Tena cried. She squeezed his hand, and her lips eased up at the corners. "Shall we see how many more injuries we incur?"

"Ah ..." Reuben craned his neck to locate Hazel. She now stood near Emil, Luella, and Stanley, the former three dissolved into fits of laughter when Stanley whooped at something Emil said. Emil brushed his lapels with the most cocksure grin and bowed to Stanley. Still giggling, Hazel's eyes roamed the floor until they found Reuben. She extended her hand towards him with a playful wiggle.

Dropping Tena's grip, Reuben gestured towards the stage. "I've been summoned."

Tena followed the direction of his gaze. "Are you here with someone?" she asked in surprise.

Reuben nodded. So much for not talking. "That's Hazel. We've only been official for a few hours."

"Oh. Well, she's positively adorable." Then the band dropped a three-quarter beat and Emil tugged Hazel's outstretched hand back in line. She offered Reuben a helpless shrug and turned into the dance. Tena laid a gentle hand on his arm. "Perhaps you *should* worry about Emil stealing her from you?"

"Ha. Emil's not any more threat than you are."

With the upbeat, they were off again in the cacophony of swishing bodies and *Alexander's Ragtime Band*.

Turn, turn, twist. He spun Tena back in the flurry of dresses and tap of heels.

Twist, step, step. Her dress no longer fashioned the outfit of a near-widow, but the slimming cut of a seasoned debutante, igniting elegance at a ball like the one they met at two years ago.

Her back curve fit beneath his palm until he held her close like the day her father died. Those glimmering irises held his tonight just as they had then. And within their touch, they both forgot hurts they were supposed to hold onto.

"And now a waltz!" declared the bandmaster, motioning for the change.

Tena paused to catch her breath within the slower temple switch. "Reuben? This girl you're here with—"

152

"Hazel."

"Yes, Hazel. Are things quite serious?"

"I believe you agreed not to speak."

"I only promised no mention of the Kischs. So tell me, do you honestly fancy her?"

"'I profess not to know how women's hearts are wooed and won. To me they have always been matters of riddle and admiration.'" At her curious expression, he directed her to the floor's edge and struggled with something in his jacket pocket. He yanked at it until finally he produced a small bound volume, *The Legend of Sleepy Hollow*. "From my latest read. I literally came across that line just this morning. Interesting how there's a line for every occasion."

"But if everything you say is a line, what then can be believed?"

"To quote Aristotle?"

"No. Tena Archer original."

He wrestled the novel back into his pocket and returned them to the dance floor. "You never question my need to carry literature to unnecessary occasions. Tena, I do believe that might be your best trait."

"Reuben ..." She gave him that look when she knew he was stalling. What should he say about Hazel? He had avoided the topic with Tena nicely through three numbers. He hadn't tried to hide it but purposely hadn't flaunted it either as he might in front of Stanley or Earhart.

Did he fancy Hazel? There was certainly no doubt he enjoyed her presence in his life. She was simple and uncomplicated and his most enthusiastic fan in all things. Diligently, she read each of his obituaries before he sent them to print, marking up errors and commenting on what needed work. Like a true fanatic, she clipped each one for her family to read at breakfast. The day after he moved in, she baked him pie simply because he asked.

It was an incredible feeling, to be honestly attracted to someone, to consider what could happen if they stepped outside the bounds of friendship. After so much time caught in the Maggie Archer whirlwind, it felt freeing. He wanted to run across the dance floor and kiss Hazel. Not one hidden away in dark stairwells, but in front of everyone, to light a fire and leave them both breathless. Maybe even be arrested by the morality squad. If only to see what it would be like. To know that he wasn't making this up in his head like so many other things he once assumed were real.

If he considered it start to finish, someday she could make a charming wife.

Then why was he hesitant to tell Tena everything he told himself? Her funny little lip hitched up in that way it did when she doubted whatever he was about to say next. She always seemed to know when he was about to walk around the truth. Or dance around it. Or climb a tree, swing from a vine, and into a lake to avoid it.

What would hallucinatory Mira have said?

Nothing good. Don't even travel there, Reuben. That's why you care for Hazel. That's exactly the reason why.

"I do fancy her," he admitted cautiously. "Hazel helps me forget I have a past. She's not tied to my other life and if nothing else, in the time I'm with her we have an enjoyable time. I could become used to that again."

Tena's lip dropped back into place and at the same time, her eyes widened minutely, the golden shine flickering. Reuben loosened his grip, unaware he had been clutching her hand with such fervor. "I know you miss Charles, and I'm sorry if hearing this hurts you."

Shaking her head, she reached up to tease a loose strand of hair back into her bun. "It does a little. Except I understand how you feel. Everything reminds me of Charles. It would be nice to be with someone who doesn't." The warmth of her fingers squeezed his bicep, their touch as reassuring as her smile was heartbreaking.

The band's final note broke the spell to audience applause. From the corner of his eye, Reuben caught Earhart bend Rosalea low before swinging her up into his arms, both of their breaths tapered from the dance. With an equally difficult breath, Tena released Reuben's hand.

His hand cupped her cheek then, his thumb hesitating at the corner of her lip. "You'll find someone, Tena. Think about Maggie. No matter how hopeless it seems, we all find someone eventually."

Tena stepped out of his touch, her eyes seeking out his shoes instead. "I don't think we should do this again."

"Do what again?" Emil hustled over with Hazel, both bearing

sweat-glistened faces.

Tena regarded him with a well-recovered smile. "Dance. Reuben is still as lousy as ever. I'm not sure lessons will do him much good."

Hazel sidled up behind Reuben to slide her arm through his. She rested her cheek against his shoulder. "Oh, they'll have to!" she trilled. "Now that I've been here, I'm coming back with the girls every week." She thrust out her arm to clasp Tena's elbow with a quick giggle. "You-must-come-too! Every Friday."

Tena twisted the long strand of her necklace around her finger. "I'm not certain. You don't know me."

"We'll get to know you. Let's begin with me." She gestured to herself. "I'm Hazel and of course, Mr. Kisch has told me how you know Reuben." She waved to the rest of their group as they joined them. "Phoebe, Luella, Stanley, Tyler—"

"My, who's this pretty little thing?" Earhart asked as he approached with Rosalea on his arm.

"Not yours," Rosalea said.

With a swoop, Earhart palmed the small of her back and leaned in to kiss his fiancée's temple. "You're adorable when you haven't the foggiest notion what you're talking about." He smiled at Tena. "I'm Earhart, and this is my sensible fiancée, Rosalea."

Rosalea rolled her eyes, pushing him away to tilt her gloved hand against her hip. "Do join us, Tena. The good Lord knows we could use a few outsiders to even out the newspaper ladies in this group. Oh good, they're starting another set."

With a rap at the podium, the bandmaster called for the room's attention, announcing the evening's fourth dance set: a foxtrot, followed by a one-step, a waltz, and another swing at the new Grizzly. "So empty those drinks, gentlemen, and lead your sweetheart back to the floor."

Hazel's warm brown eyes rose to meet Reuben's through thick lashes, her voice sweet in his ear as she cast Tena a momentary sideways glance. "It don't matter what she says. I think you're a fine dancer, and I'm pleased as punch to have you lead me."

Tena turned to Emil, murmuring something about needing to cool her throat. Now in heated baseball discussion with Earhart, he waved her off with instructions to bring back two. She walked away without a backwards glance, retreating in the direction of the entry hall rather than the refreshment bar.

Don't go after her. Reuben ordered himself. He would speak to Emil instead. Explain how complicated the situation became by him bringing Tena here. Once he made his case ...

Slim fingers entwined with his. "What's the matter?" Hazel asked. "We've been havin' such fun, haven't we?"

Tena disappeared through the doorway. *Let her go. The Archer sisters can't be your concern anymore. Them or their children.*

He bent nearer Hazel, stealing her chin between his thumb and forefinger. "I've heard, my dear Hazel, that the morality squad is on the hunt for scandalous dancers. What should we do?"

Hazel giggled, "Oh, dear, I suppose then we shouldn't let them catch us." She tipped her chin to kiss him. "Down with the morality squad?"

"Hear, hear, Hazel," Reuben laughed. "Hear, hear."

With a final glance over his shoulder, he pulled Hazel close and retreated into her frivolous fantasy.

~~~

On Maggie's wedding night, she slept without her husband and dreamt of another man. The same man she glimpsed amidst the trees in Shaw's Garden. Someone in one way familiar, yet she could not place. So tall she could crane her neck and still he loomed above her—seven, perhaps eight feet at least. No normal man could be so tall.

His mustache was flecked with grey, but he was still obviously young, no more than thirty, with the most pleasant smile. Cupped in his hands lay a flower, a lush violet bloom she could not identify.

He offered it into her reaching grasp. "For you I name my most beautiful flower. My beautiful Magdalena."

EIGHTEEN

NOVEMBER 9, 1912 –
FOUR MONTHS LATER

SQUATTING AROUND HER EVER BURGEONING pregnancy, Maggie wiped the splattered egg from the kitchen floor then leveraged the sink's edge to heave herself back to standing. The window's afternoon sun drew the only warmth in a frigid house. Wringing the soiled towel out under the tap, she squared against the pain resting above her hips then recited her daily mantra for the past four months: "This life is not mine. It's all a dream. When I next blink, all will be upright again."

One hand instantly slid to her stomach. *It won't be there. It won't be there*, she repeated although she knew such an event defied plausibility. *Please*, she begged whoever or whatever might be listening. *Please, take me away from here.*

She silently screamed as a sharp kick jabbed in response. Her wedding band dug into the flesh of her swollen finger, and she longed to wash the metal down the sink or chuck it into the rushing river. In Mr. Frye's effort to maintain a peaceful household, he wouldn't dare confront her over its absence.

She pressed a hand to her forehead as, in a daze, she made her way back to the living room. Isa lay curled up asleep on the sofa, right where Maggie left her prior to Henry's egg rampage. She cradled the child into her arms, already breathless from the effort before she reached the stairs. When the front knocker sounded, she whispered a curse Molly could not possibly hear from her bedroom, then shuffled to the door and threw up the latch.

"Mrs. Kisch?"

Tears sprang to her eyes at the visage of Elsa upon the threshold. A ragged breath escaped as Maggie adjusted Isa's thirty-five pounds across her middle. She assumed the older woman hoped to talk sense into her, to convince her to return home and make nice with Tena, none of which she would consider. Yet seeing the face of the woman who had only showered her with kindness made Maggie's guard falter.

Worry etched into the age lines already embedded in Elsa's brow. "Oh my child, hand her to me before you drop on the stoop. Take this instead." She swept through the doorway and stole Isa from Maggie's arms in exchange for the basket she was carrying. With tender movements, Elsa kissed the little girl's brow and managed herself up the stairs, pausing against the railing for support.

"Do not fret," she called back. "I will put this little one to bed and join you in the kitchen. Fix us up a pot—whatever you have will do."

Ten minutes later, the two women sat across from each other at the small kitchen table, empty cups waiting while tea steeped in the kettle on the stove. Elsa clutched Maggie's hand across the table and extended her a generous smile. "It brings my heart such joy to see you well. We have missed you at home."

Maggie focused on the puckered skin around the woman's knuckles. Elsa's hands were worn from years of effort, weathered from household labor and caring for her children—from the strain of menial chores Maggie's mother never fussed over.

She had overheard Beatrix Archer talking to Mrs. Winchester one day two summers past. "Heaven knows why my husband amuses Tena by allowing her to cook," Beatrix said. "Ladies have no use for such domestic tasks. Why would God give us servants if not to use them?" As a result of such simple thinking, her eldest daughter couldn't even manage the simplest tasks now without defeat.

Maggie refocused on her visitor. "You must understand I'm married now. I cannot simply move back into your home."

Elsa's fingers squeezed around hers. "Of course Mr. Kisch and I understand that. Your place is with your new family." She tapped a finger against Maggie's ring. "May I ask how you are faring? Raising three children with another on the way ... it would be an adjustment for any woman."

How have I fared? Maggie thought. *To be truthful ...?*

In honesty, every day was more of the same torture. Wake up. Squeeze into increasingly tight clothes. Dress the children. Grow larger seemingly within hours. Send Henry and Molly to school with a poor breakfast in their bellies. Begin story time with Isa. Stop to change Isa's diaper because she still refused to use the toilet regularly. Continue reading. Stop reading to change Isa's soiled diaper again. Want to smack the smile off that little girl's face for laughing at the "smelly poo poo." Finally finish reading in time for lunch. Eat lunch as inadequately prepared as breakfast. Somehow Isa finds peaches in her hair. Want to slap Isa for giggling while Maggie toweled the mess away. Change the child into fresh clothes for a walk in the park. Open the door to smell that Isa's soiled herself again. Silently question how so small a person could contain such a large amount of excrement.

Finally arrive at the park only to be inquired upon by every other nanny and mother who knew the Fryes. Politely decline their many obligatory invitations to tea and ignore their gossipy whispers. Return home for tea alone while Isa napped. Henry and Molly return from school, both filthy. Scold Henry. Grind her teeth through another horrid dinner. Scold Henry. Pry buttons out of Isa's mouth that she found heaven knew where. Scold Henry. Tuck the children into bed. Get called back because she forgot to kiss Molly's doll goodnight, because Isa threw her bear on the floor, because Molly saw a weird shadow, because Isa threw her bear at Molly and hit her in the eye. Finally collapse on her own mattress, screaming into her pillow and wondering if she should smother herself with it. Sleep. Wake at one a.m. Go back to sleep. Wake up at three a.m. Go back to sleep. Wake up at four-thirty and claim sleep as futile.

Repeat it all again.

One might ask where Mr. Frye was throughout this nightmare? Well, that was a question long withstanding.

Before they married, she thought they had developed an

understanding. That between Charles's funeral and their wedding day, there were a few shared moments which lumped together added up to a sort of mutual respect. However, since that first night, Hugo had all but disappeared. He departed early in the morning to take photographs, returned for dinner, then retired into his study to do what heaven only knew until after Maggie dropped into bed exhausted. Some nights she was still awake when he nudged the bedroom door open. He would pad quietly across the room in an attempt to be considerate, thinking her asleep. She laid in the dark and watched his faint silhouette move about until it dropped to the trundle bed below her. Minutes later, soft breathing and the occasional snore would emerge, and she envied him for his ability to rest so easily when she could not.

She had never wanted children and now here she was raising three with another on the way and no one to help her. As her stomach increased in size, her mental fortitude slowly decreased until, by the birth in January, she might not even recognize herself.

"Maggie?" Elsa repeated. "Has it been difficult? Motherhood?"

She forced a smile. "Nothing I can't manage through." Shifting from her chair, she lifted the silver teapot from the shelf and filled it with dark tea from the kettle. Carefully, she returned to the table and palmed the lid to pour both cups.

Elsa shifted in her chair and stood, crossing to the counter to root through the basket she brought. She listed each item out, announcing their existence as though Maggie were unable to identify them for herself.

"Salt and bread, of course—the traditional housewarming gift— then there's potatoes and beans and these apples were picked from our neighbor's tree. Only one nearby and the best for cobbler. I have a recipe if you desire it."

"Thank you," Maggie managed even as her guilt threatened to swell over. It was a generous housewarming gift, one she didn't deserve after ignoring the Kischs ever since the wedding. She hadn't even posted a note of gratitude after Karl blessed her and Hugo with a ten dollar note at the ceremony. She focused on the ripples in her tea, each altering the somber woman reflected there. "How is Tena?"

"Tena?" Surprise laced Elsa's expression which was no wonder. Even Maggie hadn't planned to mention her sister. She assumed the conversation would steer in that direction eventually, but while she thought of Tena daily, she stopped herself just short of contact. Her sister created the chasm between them; it was her responsibility to fill it in.

But when Maggie saw herself in the murky liquid of her cup, Tena's features stared back. The curve of her eyes, the flow of her hair, the rise of cheekbones and the dead stare they both wore so often since *Titanic* ... Maggie blinked and her sister blinked back.

"I miss her," she whispered, watching as her reflection mouthed the same words in return.

"Oh, my dear..." Elsa waddled back to her chair, fingertips tightening against Maggie's shoulder. "She too misses you. You are her sister. Whatever may have been done, you must remember that."

"Family is not always forever. Tena believes I ruined her life, and she hates me for it. Just as my mother hated my father for ruining hers."

"Tena's life is not ruined, dear. Her life is different than she planned, than we all planned. Not ruined though. In time, she will see it too."

"How long? It's been months ... she will never forgive me, exactly as she said." Maggie swallowed her tea in four massive gulps rather than see her reflection any longer.

"She is not cross with you, dear." Elsa talked over Maggie as she started to refute. "She is not. Tena is angry with the world, with Charles, and with God. She has lost control of her life. Even in our house full of those who face the same losses, she feels alone without Charles. She is afraid to surrender that feeling."

"Why?" Maggie asked. "Why would anyone want to live that way? I hate that our father is gone. What good would it do for me to be consumed by it?"

The faintest of smiles tugged Elsa's lips, the expression of a mother who understood grief all too well. "For protection. Tena is afraid to lose you."

"Lose me? She tossed me out! She pushed me away!"

Elsa shook her head. "That's not how she sees it though. You must understand how Tena cares for you more than anyone else in this life. Except she has recently lost the only person she loved more than you. And this only weeks after your father passed and days after your mother sent you both away. Those were events out of her control, yes, but she felt the weight of them all the same." Elsa lowered herself into her chair. "When we are grieving, it is often impossible to see past it. We cannot think rationally because we do not wish to. To feel anything except despair would be a betrayal to the ones we lost."

"That doesn't mean I'm going to die too. Not right away. She won't lose me yet."

"There are many ways we can lose someone, dear. Death is but one. Tena assumes in one fashion or another, you too will abandon her again. So instead of waiting for the inevitable, she chose to let *you* go. It is far easier to say goodbye if you are the one doing the leaving."

Needing an excuse to busy her shaking fingers—whether from anger or hurt she couldn't tell—Maggie poured herself another cup of tea and neatly avoided eye contact with the surface. The steam rose off the liquid in tiny waves. "You may not believe this, Mrs. Kisch, but fear is one emotion I understand. I've spent most of my life avoiding attachments for that very reason."

"So you see, Maggie, give her space and give her time. You are her dearest friend. Soon she will remember it."

"I wish Father were here." Maggie couldn't form more words around her father without breaking down, and her pride wouldn't allow it. She wouldn't blubber so Elsa could use her emotional turmoil as leverage. Yet inside she was sobbing on the floor. Once she thought that if only she never met Reuben all her problems would have been solved—no baby, no marriage, no difficult choices. Except now she understood that it wasn't meeting Reuben which sent her off the proverbial cliff; it was losing her father. If her father were alive when Charles asked her to join them in America, she would never have left him, not even at the request of her sister. It was one reason why she refused to ask the secret of her mother; there wasn't a truth in the world she would allow to tarnish Laurence Archer's memory.

As though in response, a visible rippling of unborn limbs passed across her abdomen as though to say, "Give up what might have been. What would your father say about *this* life?"

What could he say, the man who always stifled his own wishes for his wife's, who allowed her to use him, who in his only act of defiance sent Maggie to London, hundreds of miles from home? He saved her from an unwanted marriage only for her to end up married to a petite, poor, standard package of a man with his fiery hair and opposite air of impassivity. What a laughing stock she would be if she brought Mr. Frye back to Fontaine.

"I worry, Mrs. Kisch, that I'll never live up to what my father believed to be in me." She laid her palm down on the table and pointed at her wedding ring. "Did you know I was engaged once before? For only a few days before it all fell apart." She shrugged. "It was my fault. I ruined it. I destroyed everything he wanted. I didn't love him, but I think I might have still been happier than I am now." Her hand felt for the little foot pressing outward from her stomach, possibly the only remaining remnant of Reuben's love for her. Outside the window, the navy sky enveloped the stains of the setting sun. "Yes," she repeated. "If I chose him, we might have all been happier."

"But if you didn't love him, in the end you could never have been truly happy." Elsa spoke slowly, carefully, tasting her next words before she said them. Her eyes followed the baby's fervent movements. "Besides, my dear, you married Mr. Frye. There must be something there for you to have chosen him in the end."

Maggie smoothed her hands over the stretched fabric. "I was with child. Sometimes there's no other reason than that."

A gentle cough drew both their eyes to the doorway and blood rushed to Maggie's face. She leapt from her seat, nearly toppling the teapot before Elsa slapped a swift hand to steady it. "Why Mr. Frye!" she exclaimed. "Forgive us women chattering. Have you been waiting long?"

"Not very." A camera case lodged under each arm and a satchel slung over his shoulder, Hugo's figure filled the kitchen doorway. Per the usual, his hair was untidy and dirt lined his trouser cuffs despite Maggie having laundered them only days ago. His knuckles clenched white around the cases, as pale as his expression. An unspoken hurt sagged the wrinkles around his eyes, and she knew he heard every word of their conversation.

But truly, what did he have to be wounded over? He knew this was purely business from the beginning, a fact he reinforced by his complete lack of association with her ever since.

Elsa pushed up from her chair. She bent to buss Maggie's cheek. "Have a lovely evening, dear. Do stop in for a visit sometime."

"Certainly," Maggie said, knowing full well she wouldn't do anything of the sort without Tena's prompting. "Thank you for coming."

Hugo stepped into the kitchen. "Do you need an escort home?"

"Goodness no, dear, the trolley stop is none too far. I will manage." With a gentle pat to his cheek, Elsa shuffled past into the hallway. A moment later the front door closed.

Collecting the empty teacups and pot, Maggie set them in the sink to wash. The sound of running water neatly masked any need to speak, and she jumped when Hugo appeared at her elbow with a towel. "Mind if I dry?"

She sank the tea kettle into the water, sliding a cloth around its inner rim. "You must have loads of work to finish."

"It can wait."

"How can that be?" she asked. Water dribbled off the kettle she held, streaking toward both wrists. Hugo quickly took it before her sleeves soaked.

"Slow week." He buffed the kettle and set it on the counter.

"A slow week when you've recorded more hours than any other? Where's Damaris?" Maggie propped a wet hand to her hip with brows raised.

Damaris used Saturday dinners as an invitation to belittle Maggie at every turn whether her brother's back was turned or not. Ever the coward, Hugo ignored the situation and instead addressed Maggie only in regard to the children. Rather than engage in an all-out row, she sat silently, inwardly seething and deeply resenting the fluttering in her abdomen.

Yet tonight he was alone.

Hugo mumbled something completely incoherent and folded the towel. "You're right. I should work."

"Too late, Mr. Frye." Maggie latched onto the sleeve of his jacket and jerked him back into the room. "What snipe did your sister give about me this time? I've heard them all now, I think."

"I need to change my jacket." He tugged against her grip where a damp patch had expanded around her fingers.

"You need to not change the topic." Maggie twisted her wrist to draw nearer. "Why must you insist that Damaris, the she-devil of St. Louis, can do no wrong, but when she condemns me for sins not even committed, you can't manage one word in my defense? Am I not even worth one word?"

Hugo carefully met her gaze. "Yes."

"Bully, you managed *one* word. My, you're well on the path to surpassing your words towards me in a single day! How do I know? Because I counted."

"You *counted*?"

Maggie's hands fell to her sides. Hot tears pricked her eyelids, but there would be no victory in him seeing her cry. "Of course I counted," she whispered fiercely. "Every word you said and especially the ones you didn't."

A sharp rap at the kitchen door jolted them both. Hugo lunged for the knob, his fingers struggling to tame his hair before he opened it. Spinning on her heel, Maggie toppled from her poor center of gravity and barely saved herself before landing on the floor. Tears sprung anew and she pressed the heel of her palms to her eyes, tears working past despite her efforts. Three months ago she was the queen of telling someone off; she could banter with the best of them, loud and long and without remorse. Now she was a bumbling mess. She rooted herself before the stove, distress streaking her cheeks, and for the twentieth time that day lamented her childbearing emotions.

Behind her, Hugo greeted Mrs. Kincade, the elderly neighbor she had heard about but never bothered to visit and didn't desire to initiate pleasantries now.

"Caught this one prying up the paving stones again," she grumbled. "Little beggar hid 'em and won't fess where." There was the sound of shuffled footsteps followed by Hugo's stern, "Henry, again?"

"Didn't mean nothin' by it," Henry mumbled. "Had to get away from *her*."

A deep silence issued where Maggie felt all eyes boring into her back. She fetched a utility knife and a potato from the counter and began chopping. She had planned to serve Elsa's housewarming dinner, but to retrieve it she would need to succumb to small talk.

"Is this the new Missus?" Mrs. Kincade asked followed by a brief pause. "I see. Well, I do hope she's better than the last one." Her volume raised, words directed at Maggie and tone clipped on each one. "Did you know that it was I who found those poor children left behind to starve? Never pictured Mrs. Frye'd go all half-cocked and leave 'em that way. You can bet your bottom dollar I won't make the same mistake again. You harm those babies and you'll have my husband's pistol to answer to."

Hugo coughed. "Mrs. Kincade, I assure you that will not be happening."

"Best not." Her voice swiveled away, now radically calmer. "Do be careful, Mr. Frye." Another movement and the door slammed.

"Upstairs," Hugo gruffed. Maggie tilted her head enough to see him yank Henry up by the elbow. With a firm grip to his son's collar, Hugo pushed Henry through the doorway. "Stay in your bedroom until you can remember to not take what isn't yours. Study your numbers while you're considering what punishments await thieves." After a few swipes through his hair in frustration, Hugo retrieved Elsa's basket and set it on the counter beside Maggie. His eyes studied her while hers studied the half-chopped potato in her hand.

"Are you all right?" he asked quietly.

"Perfectly." The word expelled with heat, but its force petered out as quickly as it emerged. She chopped through another potato. "As my mother would say, 'Never allow a man to see your tears. He'll lord it over you forever.'"

Hugo continued to observe her without further comment. He just stared without saying anything for the longest two minutes, enough time for their nearness to grow uncomfortable, enough time that Maggie finally set down her knife and turned her chin. Little crinkles tapered the corners of his attentive eyes, the brown specks emerging from the green, as though each contained a stagnant pond and she tossed a pebble in for the first time in ages. As if he wasn't seeing a different side of her so much as himself. Finally, he drew a handkerchief from his jacket's inner pocket and offered it to her. When she refused, he gently pressed it into her hand. "Please. Take it. It's because of me that you're miserable."

"I'm not miserable." But she blew her nose anyway and nearly lost her lunch all over the kitchen. The cloth was pungent, like fermented cheese hidden underneath a soup of turpentine. "Heavens, the smell." She flung the handkerchief and sidestepped him in haste to the adjacent bathroom. The horrid scent had leached onto her fingers and even a thorough soap scrub still left wisps behind. Thankfully it worked well enough, however, to restrain her lurching stomach.

Hugo remained where she left him. His hands had crept into his pockets where she assumed the foul handkerchief also disappeared to. "I'm that rank, am I, Miss Margaret? So dreadful women flee in my wake?" He watched her wipe still damp hands on her apron. "I'm aware that when a person marries typically it's no holds barred, although I didn't think brutal honesty applied to business partners. Should we pen a contract amendment?" The small attempt at wit didn't deliver well. Even so, the sparkle in his effervescent eyes brought a twitch to her lips.

"No," she said. "Your handkerchief smells exceedingly foul. Although I cannot place the odor."

"Chemicals from the studio. I use them in development, so by the end of the day, the smell ends up all over my fingers. Hence my hands now safely in my pockets." He shrugged, his trouser hems rising with the motion. "Not the most pleasant; still, it does the trick. Would you like to see the studio sometime?" He offered a crooked smile. "I can show you how it all works."

She returned to slicing potatoes with a noncommittal wave. "I've seen enough in your study."

"There's so much more to it than that. Imagine what I could teach you!" His hands whirled as he became lost in a tangent about frames and lenses, lighting styles and the way a camera could capture one's face like no other. "If you're my business partner, Miss Margaret, you need to learn the business."

Unable to stop herself, Maggie laughed, a deep sound that found its way to every muscle and left her stomach aching. He so reminded her of the excitement she and Tena shared on childhood Christmas mornings. Side by side, they laid with temples pressed together and arms linked as they whispered about all the wonderful presents they would receive that year. Now here she was with this little boy so excited to show her all his own special gadgets.

"Was Emma as invested in all this as you are?" she asked.

His smile died mid-laugh. "No. She did a marvelous job of listening to me squawk then pretending like she actually cared." He snapped his fingers and with it, his boyish attitude returned as quickly as it left. "The trick, Miss Margaret, is to act extremely enthused about whatever your husband is interested in. It makes him feel important, and as a bonus, he will reciprocate when you cluck on about knitting needles or whatever silly thing you women like these days."

"Certainly not knitting," Maggie scoffed. She reached into the lower cupboard for a stock pot. "Lady Alexander was lucky I could mend a fallen seam."

Taking the pot from her hands, Hugo tilted it under the sink tap. "We can change that. My sewing machine and I have taken up together quite nicely these past few years. But that lesson is for another day."

He stripped off his jacket, tossed it over the nearest chair, and gestured for the knife in her hand. "Tonight we at long last celebrate our partnership with a proper meal."

NINETEEN

"IF IT WASN'T SO AWFULLY COLD, we could take some outside," Hugo admonished for the fourth time that afternoon. He scrunched his brow and peered up at the studio's skylight. "A pleasant sun on a day this cold is flat out cruel."

"Stop your grousing. You wanted to show me the studio, didn't you?" Closing one eye, Maggie squinted into the small window on the back of Hugo's boxy camera, currently secured to the same wooden tripod he used for the Kischs' family photo. As he instructed, she analyzed the frame's width compared to the angle of late autumn sun through the second story skylights of Frye Photography.

The weather had turned cold last week, the collection of vibrant red and gold leaves along the Mississippi riverbank turned brown overnight. Even so, it hadn't been enough to dampen her spirits. Ever since the night she and Hugo finally celebrated their partnership, she had been able to sleep and able to smile. With their newfound understanding—and Hugo's assistance—meals were now edible and conversation no longer lacking. When she settled herself into bed, the baby's feet set to tapping their nightly dance, and she was actually glad to feel them.

"So I squeeze this and it releases the shutter?" Even though Hugo nodded, Maggie paused with her eye to the viewfinder and fingers around the bulb. "Won't this waste the film?"

"Only if you consider it a waste," Hugo said. "Others might consider it art."

"I consider it a photograph of an empty settee." She waved a hand above the camera. "Sit, please. You will be my first subject."

Hugo continued to hover near her elbow. "Now that *would* be a waste of film." He whistled to Molly and Isa sitting on the floor, currently deep into building their own contraption from a box of old camera parts. They had been more than enthusiastic to visit the studio while Henry, on the other hand, refused to ascend the studio stairs. After much fuss, Hugo finally relented to his son remaining in the downstairs parlor with Damaris.

"Girls," he called. "Come be in Miss Margaret's photograph." With a squeal, they ran over to plop themselves down on the sofa.

"And you too, Mr. Frye."

Tilting her face away from the viewfinder, Maggie fixed him with a cold stare. "You're always taking the photographs. How long has it been since you were in one?" She pointed again at the empty space between his daughters. "Sit, Mr. Frye." With a half-hearted grumble, he dropped onto the sofa and fixed the camera with a flat stare.

Turning her attention back to the viewfinder, she squeezed the bulb like he showed her and heard a click as the shutter collapsed upon itself. "Brilliant!" she squealed. "I did it, didn't I?" She reached for the back panel to retrieve the film slide.

"Leave that there!" Hugo leapt forward as she flipped the clips up and the back panel opened. He sighed. "That floods it with light and overexposes the film."

Maggie stared at the rectangular slide in her hand. It didn't look any different than when they inserted it. "Overexposure is bad, is it?"

"Not if you want your photographs undecipherable." He took the slide from her hand. "I'll find another, and you'll try again." Casting her a scowl that contradicted his smile, he headed behind the curtain that separated the workroom from the rest of the studio.

The second their father disappeared, Isa hopped feet first onto the settee. "Bounce!" she squealed as the sofa springs groaned under her enthusiasm. Maggie caught her mid-bounce, swinging the sprout onto her hip while at the same time her stomach visibly fluttered. Molly grinned and with light touches, prodded the baby until he—or she—returned another playful response. Entertaining their new sibling had become the girls' favorite game these last few weeks. Maggie knew she shouldn't indulge them, that attachment now would only make everything more difficult when it eventually came time to part ways. But Molly and Isa were the same tiny sprouts she and Tena started out as, wide-eyed and wondering, unable to believe their mother was anything but lovely. Molly splayed her fingers over her stepmother's stomach, her grin lighting a face as lovely as a sunrise. No one else looked at Maggie like those girls did.

It was only the pregnancy speaking, she reminded herself. Only two more months, then she wouldn't feel such sentiment at the slightest of things.

When the baby's little foot pressed against her palm, Molly gently nudged it back and held her breath until the tiny movement came again. She exhaled, finally bringing her gaze back to Maggie's. With a voice full of wonder, she whispered, "You must be Daddy's most special friend."

"I suppose that's an accurate descriptor." Most special friend was certainly more accurate than wife. Isa squirmed from Maggie's arms to land in a heap on the floor beside her sister. She used Maggie's leg to climb up where she could press an ear to her stepmother's middle. "Baby?" she whispered. "Hello, baby."

"You *are* special," Molly continued seriously. "Otherwise Daddy wouldn't bring you here. He never lets *us* come here neither."

"I don't hear anything," Isa pouted.

Molly poked Maggie and the baby let off a proud kick to Isa's face. "Ow!" Isa cried. Backing off, she wagged a finger at Maggie's stomach. "Bad baby! No hit!"

Lunging, Maggie snatched Isa around the waist, eliciting wild giggles as she tickled the child. "Never?" she asked Molly. It seemed impossible that a man so absorbed in family would refuse his children entrance into such an important piece of himself.

Molly shook her head, pretty crimson curls bobbing against her shoulders. "That's why Aunt Damaris was angry at dinner. This is her and Daddy's special secret place. Even Mama never saw it."

Never? Maggie dashed through the reasons Hugo may have invited her here and not Emma. Only one made the most sense. He hadn't. Molly was barely two when her mother left; the simple memories of children were not the complex truths of adults.

"A quid for your thoughts?" Hugo asked as he rejoined them. Thoughts still jumbled with Molly's innocent words, she stared at him too long without replying. He frowned. "Was that wrong? It's not a quid?"

Maggie flinched and her eyes finally focused. Hugo was holding the small black Brownie camera that he seemed to carry around everywhere. It was the same one he brought to Charles's funeral. He once told her it was so simple to use even Henry and Molly could do it. "Apologies," she said. "I'm afraid I wandered off for a minute."

"Is everything all right?"

She buried all further consideration within her smile. "Of course, but if the saying is 'a penny for your thoughts' then it wouldn't change when in England. A quid is most equivalent in nature to an American dollar." She laughed when his brow scrunched in confusion. "Just you wait, Mr. Frye. When you visit England someday and hear talk of florins and tuppence and groats, I dare say you'll be glad for the simplicity of American currency."

"At the rate I'm going, an overseas holiday will not be on the schedule for another two thousand years."

"Two thousand years? If you've discovered the secret to immortality, please do share with the rest of us."

"See, Mrs. Frye, you're more clever than you let on." With a wide grin, Hugo handed her the Brownie. "Let's try some with this one instead. Girls, back to the sofa, please."

He found her clever? she thought. Well, she had certainly been called worse. Rarely had she been called better.

Balancing the black Brownie on her swollen abdomen, she peered down into the viewfinder. Hugo's inverted appearance filled the glass, an arm around each of his daughters and the twinkle that seldom left his eyes these days.

With a smile, she lined up the frame and flipped the lever.

~ ~ ~

The next hour flew by and before Maggie knew it, she was able to capture photographs with nearly the same proficiency as either Henry or Molly—or at least so Hugo claimed. She returned the Brownie to its case and stepped downstairs in search of Henry. Damaris glowered at her from the swivel desk chair she occupied, brows nearly knit together. In one hand she held a camera casing, a dingy rag in the other, and an assortment of other bits and pieces sat upon a towel on the desktop. Grunting, she slid the rag along the edge of the camera with the precision of one cleaning a revolver and from her scowl, probably wishing it was one.

"Is my brother leaving soon?" she asked. "Sunday is supposed to be my day off."

"He's packing the cases as we speak."

"Good. No sense stuck in here when I could be outside with my camera."

"You're a photographer too?"

"What'd you think, stupid? I was just the hired help?" Seizing two unrecognizable camera parts, she slid one inside the other and flipped a latch back into place. "Let's get somethin' straight, sweet cheeks. I know this equipment better than my brother does and capture photographs a whole lot better too. For instance, that one's mine." She pointed at a framed landscape of spectacular white polished buildings set against a background of fir trees and white-capped mountains. The plate read *Alaska-Yukon-Pacific Exposition, 1909*.

"Lovely," Maggie admitted. Damaris obviously had inherited the same talent as her brother, although she suspected the woman rarely received the public accolades Hugo did. If that was the inherent reason for her bitterness, perhaps all Maggie need do was extend the olive branch. "Damaris, for your brother's sake, perhaps we could—"

"Listen, child," Damaris cut in. "We ain't family. At least not to me. So don't apologize for being who you are, because I certainly won't."

So much for the olive branch. The dove must have flown away from the ark and drowned itself. "Point noted," Maggie gritted. "Have you seen Henry?"

Damaris jerked her chin towards the rear office. "Alley."

"Thanks." She snatched her coat off the rack.

Judging from the shambled wreckage of Hugo's office, it became clear why he chose Mr. Huppert for his lawyer. Two overflowing filing cabinets stood against one wall, an unlit potbelly stove in the opposite corner, and between them, a table littered with coffee mugs and a half-filled percolator. Stacks of paper—including several old overdue notices from Donovan—occupied the desktop along with a pile of flat twine-and-paper wrapped commissions ready for delivery. On the wall behind the desk, two thin boards had been tacked together to create a makeshift shelf on which sat five framed photographs—Henry, Molly, Isa, and a glowing youthful Emma. The final photograph was of Hugo.

Barely out of his youth, Hugo stood on the sidewalk outside Frye Photography Studio, one hand propped to his hip as the other braced the camera standing at his side. With the faintest of smirks and his signature tousled locks, he stared the photographer down as though to say, *"I own this place and this camera, and with it, I can do anything."* He was pre-heartbreak, ready and waiting to conquer the world. In a way, his expression reminded her of Reuben; however, the similarities between her current partner and her old flame ended there.

Hugo's son on the other hand often reminded her all too much of a younger version of Reuben. When she opened the door to the alley, Henry's sullen stare and clenched fists folded across his chest ignited memories of the day she first interrupted Reuben mid-mourning in the cemetery. He had berated her cheerful attitude and for not considering the pain he endured through his sister's loss. Without intention, her smile drew him in like flies to honey, an attraction she couldn't recognize then and barely understood now—one day in many she would redo if she could.

"Henry," she said gently. "It's time to head home. Your father's waiting."

"So? I'm not going." Henry's voice could have been Reuben's. Cold, angry, distant—the sound of a child afraid of his feelings, afraid of what it could mean to share them. The gentle swell of her abdomen left her imagining what would be if this baby shared that same inner turmoil.

She carefully maneuvered the rickety stairs into the windswept alley and longed for the day when her coat could again button fully. "Henry, let's not have another squabble. Can't you at least try to be pleasant for your father's sake? He wants us to be a family."

Henry's eyelids narrowed to slits. "No, he doesn't." He kicked at the bottom step, running his shoe into the wood until a piece chipped away. Then he proceeded to do the same with the other foot.

"Your father would not approve of that behavior."

Another chunk of wood shot into the alley. His shoulders extended in the most minuscule of shrugs. "Aw, go on and let him scold me. I don't mind."

"You feel like you don't matter to him, don't you?"

Maggie knew she hit the mark. The little boy reared back and slammed his heel against the wood grain, splintering the end of the board. He glared up at her. "Dad won't care if I don't come home."

"That's not true." She remembered how fired up Hugo became when Damaris suggested sending the children to an orphanage. Those children seemed to be one of the only things he could break out of himself to fight for. "Think of the sacrifices your father makes for you."

"That's why I should run away. He wants to see places like before. When Mama was here, he would go away for months and never let us come." He threw another firm kick at the stairs. "Now he doesn't leave anymore, and he hates us. That's why Mama left. She didn't want us either."

How was she supposed to react to such words? A mother should probably respond with arms outstretched to offer hugs and kisses and pearls of wisdom. But, despite the child growing inside her, Maggie didn't feel like a mother. Among her parents' set, mothers were emotionally absent, their children more connected to their nannies and governesses than their own blood. Then one day every young lady woke up to receive a husband, breed babies, and treat her little ones in the same manner she had been treated. That was the golden rule, was it not?

Clasping her hands, Maggie templed two fingers, channeling her father's spirit instead. "Henry, sometimes adults do things children simply cannot understand. I felt like you do when I was little. My father often traveled to London, many miles away from our home, and he never brought me with him. Even so, I always knew in my heart that he loved me very much." That statement at least was truthful. Her father had never treated her like a commodity.

Henry frowned. He picked a rock from the ground and tossed it up in the air once ... twice. "Mine doesn't. I made Mama go away. Now he's got you. What does he need to love me for?" Winding back, he launched the rock against the brick of the opposite building and the mortar crumbled. Fat tears spilled out of his little hazel eyes, rolling down wind-chapped cheeks into his collar. With a yelp, he ran up the steps and disappeared inside.

Maggie stood shell-shocked in the alley unable to quite regain her bearings as Henry's accusation stabbed her senseless. She collapsed onto the stairs and cradled her head in her hands. His sisters never knew their mother like he did. They didn't understand what it meant to lose a mother or gain a new one. But to an adult, it spoke volumes when a woman voluntarily walked away from her husband and abandoned her children. That wasn't exactly a story for polite conversation with strangers or one any man would be proud to claim. Certainly most would blame Hugo for his wife's absence, just as he blamed himself. Like father like son, they were both trapped in their own personal torment.

Only when the wind whipped the first flakes of an oncoming snowfall through the alleyway did Maggie pry herself from the steps and re-enter the office. She paused on the other side, rubbing her hands together for warmth.

"I won't stand for it, Hugo," Damaris spat, her voice slipping through the cracked parlor door. Maggie stepped closer, edging behind the desk to listen. "You always behave poorly after a birth, and I won't be kept home for months because of *her*. Let's go before the next one gets here and you lose your head again. We leave Tuesday."

Maggie nudged the office door open an inch. Through the crack, the children were visible outside the front window. Molly and Isa danced in circles on the sidewalk, sticking their tongues out to capture falling snowflakes, while Henry sulked against the glass. Hugo watched them with his back to Maggie. "Thanksgiving is Thursday, Damaris."

"The girls won't notice," his sister insisted. "Maggie won't even care. She's British." She forced a wide envelope into Hugo's hands. "This might be your only chance. You can't argue that time is of the essence."

"Essence for what?" Maggie stepped into the room, drawing both their attentions. Hugo averted his eyes to the envelope clutched in his grip. Unfortunately not before Maggie saw the embarrassment on his face. His posture was quiet, as small as Isa's when she found herself in trouble she never intended.

"Come see for yourself," Damaris purred. A grin rivaling the Cheshire Cat's played across her lips. "The investigator found her. He found Emma."

TWENTY

NEITHER HUGO NOR MAGGIE spoke again of Emma's assumed discovery until they were home with the children tucked into bed and steaming coffee situated on the study desk between them. Neither reached for their mug nor could either entertain the other's gaze. All eyes stilled on the photographs Hugo slid from the investigator's envelope—hurriedly captured photographs of a slender waitress through a restaurant window, her slight face tilted half in shadow. Impossible to identify with any degree of certainty, the woman could be the former Mrs. Frye as easily as she could not.

Yet statistical probability mattered little when even the slightest *possibility* existed that Hugo could finally gain reparation for three years of life and love lost. He held the investigator's typed correspondence in a white-knuckled grip, reading again the words he spent every penny searching for.

Dear Mr. Frye ... pleased to inform you ... located your estranged wife ... Salt Lake City, Utah ... recommend immediate departure.

He would divorce Maggie as soon as he found his other wife. Of course he would. It was exactly what she would do if the roles were reversed.

With her usual haughty grin and a jar of molasses in her hand, Damaris floated into the room and perched upon the edge of the desk. She added a spoonful of the syrup to Hugo's mug then prepared her own and handed the jar to Maggie. After the surprise announcement at the studio, she insisted on joining them for dinner supposedly to finalize the details. Mostly Maggie suspected it was to ensure her brother agreed to her plan.

"We'll be off on the usual ten o'clock train Tuesday?"

Hugo stared at the letter without comment. Maggie sipped her coffee simply for something to do and waited.

"Tuesday, Hugh?" Damaris pressed. She snatched the correspondence from his hands and scanned the lines again, her grin expanding with every sweep of her eyes. "If they think they found her, we have to go." Her voice drew upward with a childlike ecstasy. "I've always wanted to see the red rocks of Utah. Ever since Papa told us about them all those years ago."

Hugo picked up the photographs. "Utah," he repeated.

Damaris stabbed a finger against the paper. "This even tells us the exact town and the boarding house she's staying in. She's listed under the name Adeline McClay."

Tossing the photos on the desktop, Hugo ran both hands through his hair and tilted back in the chair. He stared at the ceiling as though the plaster held the answers. "Adeline McClay." He closed his eyes. "Adeline McClay. My wife." The lilt made it a question rather than an assurance. Disbelief tinged with hope. Never had their age difference seemed more expansive to Maggie than it did now. Thirteen years seemed a lifetime. The day he married Emma, Maggie had only crossed into her twelfth year.

"You should go to her."

Hugo's eyes shot open with Maggie's command. His lips parted, ready to ask the question, only she ordered herself to answer first. "Because this is the day you've been waiting for."

"What if it's not? What if it isn't her?"

"Then you return home and try again."

He nodded, another question sealed within. *And what if it is? What happens then?*

Maggie patted her stomach gently. "All will be well. I've always managed before."

His fingers came to rest on Emma's image with a heavy exhale. "I don't deserve you."

Slowly, she swirled her coffee, a single thought breaking through the steam, *Does he mean her or me?*

"Absolutely true," Damaris snapped. She flung the letter towards her brother only to stop its flight with a nail tip to the desktop. The abrupt motion deflected Hugo's attention in her direction. "You don't deserve Maggie. You can do much better, and in fact have done. That's why you're taking this chance."

"Precisely," Maggie agreed, "and you'll bring Henry with you."

With chin squared, she rose from her seat in defiance against the unbelieving stares now focused on her. She folded her arms on her stomach. "That boy is longing for your attention, Mr. Frye. It's why he's acting out. Twice each year my father traveled to London, and he never once invited me along. Not even when I was all but grown. I never thought to question his reasons. I think now, like Henry, perhaps I should have."

"You couldn't," Damaris said. Bitterness punctuated her scowl, full of a deeper loathing than she had yet shown towards Maggie. "You were his eldest, entitled to everything if only you were a boy. Satisfied with a portion if you managed to marry well. But you were a plain insignificant little girl and unlike your sister, not destined for love. So you never traveled with your father, and you never questioned it, because what answer would he give? Surely not the truth?"

If any words should have sent Maggie clawing the volatile sneer from her sister-in-law's face it should have been the ones just spoken. Her skin warmed at the insinuation that Laurence Archer didn't love her how she believed, or that he never brought her to London because she was less than worthy of his attentions. It had never been so with her father. With every breath, every smile, every heartbeat, she trusted in him more than anything. He was the only man who loved her unconditionally, the only man who ever truly could.

Except even within his affection her father also held secrets, ones he refused to share even after death.

Damaris sneered. "Your father left you no inheritance, the same as me. I refuse to believe you lost everything on *Titanic*—a ship you never boarded. So tell me I'm mistaken."

She wasn't, Maggie admitted and questioned how she had the

ability to keep her head held so high when inside she was now crumbling. Laurence Archer's last will and testament left every monetary asset to Beatrix Archer, and their mother disowned them when her daughters chose Charles—chose America—over her. All their father bequeathed to Maggie was a letter, a letter he wouldn't even hand her himself.

"Go on," Damaris laughed. "Argue with me, Maggie. Tell me how your father loved you so much more than my father loved me."

She couldn't. Her tongue was heavy and her throat frozen. Had her entire life been merely a scream for attention? A little girl lashing out because deep down in some hollow part of her she craved a love she never fully received?

"Mare, enough." Hugo reached for his sister's hand. "Why are you so heated? You know Pop loved us all the same."

"No, Hugh. Papa loved *you*. You were the one who loved me." The danger in her eyes finally dimmed. She tapped the investigator's letter. "I refuse to agree with *her*, but let us take Henry. Have him appreciate the life girls like us aren't allowed."

Shoving her dark thoughts aside, Maggie focused on the issue at hand. There were only three things she could say with absolute certainty: Henry needed his father, Hugo needed his estranged wife, and unfathomably she and Damaris had pledged sister solidarity to the cause.

She yanked at her left hand until she could twist her wedding ring ever so painfully off her swollen finger and held it out to Hugo. "Give this to Emma."

He pushed back from the desk and shook his head. "That's yours."

"No," Maggie argued. She extended her reach, even as he retreated further against the bookshelves behind him. "It's *yours*. You need to offer her something when you find her. Don't assume she still has hers. If I ran away, that's the first thing I'd trade." She shook it fervently, wanting him to rid her of the thing.

The smoldering fireplace logs crackled into the silence while he argued with his eyes and the firm shake of his head. She knew what he wanted her to say. He was terrified of knowing and not knowing, of giving up a seven-year certainty—her—for a possible lifetime of doubt. Some unknowns were meant to stay buried, but this was not one of them.

"Take it, Mr. Frye. If Emma were here, she would insist."

"No, she wouldn't," he whispered. His broken eyes searched hers. "Because if Emma were here, you wouldn't be." Without a second glance, he swept the ring from her hand and escaped the room.

Once his footfalls ascended the stairs, Damaris hopped from the desk. "Thank you, dearie, for making that so very easy to accomplish." With a condescending pat to Maggie's head, she sauntered for the door.

Maggie whirled to snatch the older woman's arm, her fingernails digging into a surprisingly firm muscle. "This is all a contest to you, isn't it? Meddling with my emotions to win your brother's?"

"Of course it's a contest," Damaris twittered. "One I will win. Emma was no match for me, and neither are you."

"If you're planning some treachery to rid Mr. Frye of me, it won't work. If he can't convince Emma to return, he has to abide by the prenuptial agreement we signed."

"That agreement was no more based on nuptials than your child shares blood with my brother."

"You know nothing," she spat, although it was becoming increasingly clear that Damaris observed far more than they assumed. When the woman smoothed a single finger over Maggie's stomach, she flinched and slapped her hand away.

Damaris's smile broadened. "Oh, Miss Margaret—such a revolting pet name my brother has for you—I'm twenty-three years wiser than you. It hasn't been easy biding my time, but I knew luck would turn in my favor sooner or later. Before Emma left, our lives were about the rush of the journey, fairs and parties, something different and new and exciting every day. Now it's been three years of doldrums." She motioned to where the photographs of Emma's alter-ego, Adeline McClay, still lay face up. "Utah is everything I've waited for. Hugo will never stay put once he remembers that the road is where we truly belong."

"Once he finds Emma, he'll never leave her alone again. How foolish do you believe him to be?"

"Not a fool. It will be under my direction that he'll decide to bring all the devils with us." With a final snide smile, Damaris swayed to the door, pausing only once before she turned the knob. "Life is like a carnival game at the fair, dearie. The fact is when it comes to my brother's heart, Emma was the grand prize. You're merely a consolation and always will be."

"Do you think I mind? Emma can have his heart," Maggie returned vehemently as the door swung shut. She glazed her palm over her stomach, pausing at her baby's favorite spot beneath her left hip. Immediately came the return of a tiny jab. "We only need each other," she whispered.

Dropping another log into the flames, Maggie sat alone until long after midnight, able even in the fire's warmth to notice the chill on her barren finger and wonder why she felt it at all.

~~~

DECEMBER 15, 1912 –
THREE WEEKS LATER

Scouring her hands and the dinner dishes in the hottest water she could manage, Maggie listened to the wind howl outside the window, every so often shaking the glass above the kitchen sink. Sleet pelted the panes behind the curtain, closed in a feeble attempt to ward off December's cold. The garden lay as frozen as the ice floes bobbing in the Mississippi, and she prayed again for one of St. Louis's unpredictable spring days to appear.

For the hundredth time, Maggie glanced at the early Christmas card lying open on the counter from Amara Müller, her cabinmate on *Höllenfeuer*. She missed the young German girl's spunky attitude, as positive as the flowing script wishing *Gesundheit und Glück*—health and happiness—in the new year. Her letters were the solitary bright spot in what was an otherwise most depressing winter.

After Christmas, Maggie planned to pack her trunk. She had already located the women's home in the city directory and by New Year's Day, she would be gone from this place. She would bear another person into this world, and she refused to yet acknowledge her fear in doing it alone.

Pressing a hand to her heart, she yanked the plug from the sink. Hugo would have found Emma by this point. Had she agreed to return home or was he using this time to woo sense back into her? Would seeing her son be enough to convince her?

"Molly!" she called. She flipped a towel from the drawer. "Isa! Dishes to dry."

There was no response. No sound at all and now that she thought on it, hadn't been for a few minutes. She moved into the doorway. "Girls?"

A scream echoed and Maggie sprinted for the living room, both hands braced to support her burgeoning stomach. She skidded to a stop when Isa slammed against her, buckling Maggie's knees into the doorway. The little girl buried her face in her stepmother's skirt and pointed over her shoulder.

"Heavens, no ..." Maggie breathed. Shoving Isa to the side, she fell to her knees as panic seized.

Eyes rolled back beneath a face burning with fever, Molly convulsed upon the rug unable to respond while her stepmother cradled her body and helplessly called her name.

TWENTY-ONE

"RACE YOU TO THE BOTTOM!"

Hands snug inside Karl's woolen gloves, Tena clung to the red wooden sled, her knees hugged nearly to her chest and toes tingling against the rudder. Flying down the snowy hill, her heart sang as icy wind nipped her cheeks and laughter bubbled from her lips. With her only light from the waning moon and three glass lanterns perched at the slope's end, the world rushed by in the dark blur of the eleven o'clock hour, announced only minutes before by distant church bells. For all that mattered, it may as well be the middle of the day. Neither the hour nor how numb her feet became could end the joy of this night.

As she neared the end of the hill, she flung herself sideways into the snow inches from the edge of the frozen water. Situated at the bottom of what the locals referred to as Art Hill, the Grand Basin had been constructed for the 1904 World's Fair along with the magnificent Palace of Art on the hilltop above it. Even in the near darkness, the white columns of the city's art museum gleamed in the light flickering from their bonfire. She imagined its brilliance under the daytime sun must be even more spectacular.

Laughing, Hazel slid to a stop followed shortly by Rosalea, their hair billowing in wild tendrils beneath their woven caps. "Well, Tena, looks like you win again," Hazel sighed. "You're certain you've never been sleddin' before?"

"Certainly. My mother would faint if she caught me in such a state."

"Well," Rosalea countered. "Thank the stars your Mama isn't here then."

Tena linked her arm through both girls' and pulled them to their feet, shaking the snow off her coat and skirts before she popped her sled rudders from the snow. The movement sent a spray of moisture at the nearby lantern and it went out with a sizzle.

Hazel's tiny lips turned into a pout. "Oh folly, fire's gone out."

Tena pointed to the one farthest down the line. "That one too."

With an absent shrug, Rosalea tugged her own sled loose. "There's still one left. Leave those here. Earhart can bring his lighter on the way back down."

Luella and Phoebe trudged over from where their sled went off course. "I will never learn to steer this darned thing!" Luella cried.

Phoebe pinched her cheek. "I dare say it's the extra weight."

"What are you implying, Phoebe?"

"Ladies." Rosalea halted the argument with a flick of her wrist. "It's my birthday and there will be no squabbles. The night is young, there's another round of cake calling me quickly, and our men are looking very ample in the firelight." She frowned as she squinted towards the hilltop. "Oh dear, young Mr. Kisch has channeled the spirit of dear old Louie."

Barely more than a spot in the distance, the fire illuminated Emil galloping circles around the forty-foot bronze statue of St. Louis—also installed immediately following the World's Fair. Raising an imaginary sword to mimic the statue's stance, his voice carried over the others as he led his steed into battle. Stanley, Reuben, Tyler, and Earhart egged him on with a rousing rendition of the recent radio release, *Ragtime Cowboy Joe*.

"Come, come," Luella said. "The lads are having a better time than we, and that is simply not allowed." She started up the hill, high stepping her way through the snow.

They trudged up the rest of the rise, limbs finally rebelling against dragging sleds up the hill for the seventh climb that night. Unlike the rest, Tena couldn't complain. She cherished the burn in her muscles and the pinch of the cold on her skin. Being out late into the evening. Laughing about nothing. Living life. She reveled in the invigoration—and the unusual accent—of her new American friends and their clandestine ways.

Their frivolity made Tena remember Charles with every waking moment and deliberate how different life was from what he would have chosen for them. He had been surefooted and certain of what would meet them across the pond. Focused on home, marriage, family—always stretching towards the future while her new friends relished in the moment. If she returned to a life of similarity, the pain of living it without him would consume her heart.

So, after the third invitation and a helping of Emil's coercion, she accepted the typists' offer for evening tea every week like clockwork. Whether they met at Phoebe's intimate flat or Rosalea's three-story estate, they turned the radio on, kicked off their shoes, and laughed around several pots of tea until someone rang to discover one of their whereabouts.

On Friday nights at Cave Hall, she slid into a new deep-lilac dress with embroidered ochre flowers on the bodice and a hemline an inch above the ankle—the only gown of color in her current wardrobe. Within a month, she learned the steps to all the disreputable dances and could mock the morality squad with the best of them. She tried to partner with anyone besides Emil—pushed herself as far out of her comfort zone as propriety would allow—but no one made a suitable match. Only one man could make her feel as secure as Charles had. The problem was he avoided her eye at every glance and clung to Hazel like tree sap.

Only at night in the bed she should have shared with Charles did she encounter the terrible pang of longing for his arms and her sister's comfort. Even though thoughts of Maggie made hot tears sting Tena's eyes, she still prayed that in between all the lies her sister actually found happiness. She wished it with all she had, but her heart could not carry the weight of watching it come to pass.

Jovial male voices amplified as the girls dropped their sleds on the hilltop, the glowing bonfire and triple pillars of the Palace of Art a perfect backdrop for a birthday celebration. Laughing with Stanley, Reuben slapped Emil's back and ordered him to "Move that pony faster!" When he noticed her watching, he raised his hand in acknowledgment and caught her eye with an unexpected smile before turning away. Hazel giggled beside her. Of course, she thought, his glance was meant for her.

Earhart strode towards them with arms outstretched. "Ah, they return to us safe and sound!"

Spinning Rosalea into his chest, he planted a firm kiss on her cheek and whipped the cloche from her head so her hair flew wildly about her face. He pressed a palm to her flushed cheek. "My beautiful girl," he breathed then called to the group. "A toast to my Rosie! To her 21st year and the last before I call her my wife."

"*Prost!*" Emil shouted.

"Hear! Hear!" Tena laughed along with the rest as Rosalea pressed her lips to her beau's.

It was Earhart's third similar toast in the hour since they arrived. He had arranged the entire affair with glass lanterns arranged around the peak of the hill, simple hors d'oeuvres, cake, bottles of soda and beer for those who fancied it. There was some disagreement over whether they were allowed in the park at such a late hour, but Earhart insisted that his father had a friend who knew someone's brother who knew the chief of the Forest Park mounted patrol. There wouldn't be an issue.

Hazel slipped her arm through Tena's, pulling her towards the supply wagon parked behind the two motorcars that carried them there under Earhart's instructions. She pulled two Coca-Colas from a crate and popped the caps, handing one to Tena. "How are you enjoying Rosie's little party?"

Tena sipped the sugary beverage. "It's nothing like any birthday celebration we would have back home."

"Rosalea don't like to do anything the usual way. She's the worst of all of us. If it isn't fancy, it isn't Rosie."

"This isn't fancy. Fancy is what my life *was*. Gemstones and ballrooms, conversing in straight-backed chairs. *Very* straight-backed chairs. If my mother saw us at tea sitting on the floor like a gang of hobos, she would lose her mind."

Hazel giggled. "We must have come as a shock."

"A shock yes, a bit, but a good one. It's easier to overcome past times in the unfamiliar. I fear that having to deal with Charles's loss in a town where he had walked every step would have been far more difficult to accept. Anywhere I go here, I go alone."

"Oh." Hazel turned her attention to the dish of cookies, sticking one in her mouth before handing the other to Tena. For a minute they chewed in silence while they watched the others across the way. Emil, Tyler, Reuben, and Stanley had instigated a snowball fight against Luella and Phoebe, who were squealing as they attempted to hide behind the statue's concrete base. Stanley grabbed Luella around the waist and smashed snow against her back while off to the side Earhart had Rosalea in the makings of a rather intimate kiss.

"I must ask," Hazel whispered suddenly. "Was it so very wonderful? Being in love?"

Tena nibbled on her cookie then swallowed another long drink of her soda while she continued to watch the chaotic snowball fight unfold. She would have loved to participate, but not Charles. He may have taught his youngest brother how to drink and smoke in private, but in a public place, he had been all reservation and conformity.

"Wonderful," she said. "As wonderful as the smell of winter before it snows. Even when he leaves you, it doesn't change. It's impossible to forget." Beneath her glove, Charles's gold engagement band froze around her finger.

She flinched when Hazel touched her forearm. The girl offered her a timid smile. "What will you do at year's end?" Of course, thought Tena. Her year of mourning was already half past; in another few months, she would have needs to consider. What would she say when gentlemen came to call? Could she unwrap Elsa's white wedding satin and wear it for another man?

Her eyes flicked back to the fire. Earhart was now serenading Rosalea with a poor rendition of *Come Josephine in my Flying Machine*, having changed the title lady's name to Rosalea, and the snowball fight appeared to have concluded. Reuben and Emil stood shoulder to shoulder by the bonfire, their hands warming over the flames. "You're quite fond of him, aren't you?" she asked Hazel.

Even in the dim light, a pink blush prettied the other girl's cheeks and she gulped her soda pop, sputtering. She was an adorable girl, sweet as a button and a true delight. Naïve in some ways, but her innocence made her loyal to a fault. Able to be impetuous around her friends, but safe and secure. She would never betray Reuben; she would never hurt him as Maggie had. Tena understood why he was drawn to her over the other girls in their group.

"Well?" she smiled sweetly. "I need to know if my friend's heart is in good hands."

Hazel blinked then her face lit up. She set her soda pop on the wagon bed and clasped Tena's hands around her own bottle. "Oh, yes," she whispered. "His heart is very safe. As safe as mine must be with him."

The crunch of boots against snow brought them around to Earhart, Rosalea, and Reuben approaching. With a pinch to Tena's elbow, Hazel flung her arms around Reuben's neck. "Come to keep me warm?" she asked.

He tugged Hazel's hat nearer her ears and tucked copper strands back into the sides. "Precisely. Come stand by the fire with me."

Snatching Hazel's waist, Earhart pulled her out of Reuben's arms and close to his side. "Listen not to this man's outrageous request, Miss Vine. I have declared a race to end all races. A contest to circumvent all competitions. A triumph to outlast the glory of all other victories." He leaned in beside Tena, Rosalea shaking her head with a simple smile behind him. "Ladies," he hushed. "This will be the sled ride of a lifetime."

Rosalea swatted his hands away from her friends. "You are too dramatic, Jonathan."

Earhart captured her fingers before she could cast another blow and pressed them to his lips. "And you, future Mrs. Earhart, adore me because of it."

She giggled and tossed her head with emphasis. "He's right, ladies. I do."

"Oi!" Emil called. A snowball careened in their direction and landed short. "You ninnies afraid to lose another race? I'm four for four and planning to make it five."

"Fancy chance of that," Reuben shouted back. "We've gone easy on you, being the baby and all." He offered Hazel his right arm, then, to Tena's vast surprise, extended his left to her. "M'lady?"

"Are you sure?" she asked.

The edge of his lip quirked up. "Of course. Unless you'd rather not."

When he offered again, she threaded her arm gingerly through his, and the three of them followed Earhart and Rosalea back towards the fire.

"Did you really let him win, Reuben?" Hazel asked.

"No, and don't you ever tell him he's just that fine a sportsman. He'll become too egotistical to live with. Probably go to the Berlin Olympics and kill himself doing mother knows what."

"Sounds to me like we need to join forces and take down the buffoon," Tena said. Reuben's arm tensed against hers, and she worried that her jest had furthered the strange rift between them. Except when she lifted her eyes to check, the firelight caught his simple smile. Her toes felt warm again. It had been months since he paid her so much mind.

"What is this, Reuben?" Stanley gawked as the three of them approached. He slid an arm around Tena's shoulders with a sly smile. "You've already found yourself a lady friend. You can afford to give this one up."

"Cool it, Lee ole boy. Answer's the same as last time you asked."

"Mourning sure lasts a long time," Stanley muttered, but he removed his arm all the same. "Guess the best I can hope for is we take Kisch down."

"All of you against me?" Emil argued. He frowned with mittened hands tucked inside his armpits. "Hardly seems fair."

Earhart settled his sled on the hill's edge and ran the blades back and forth twice while Rosalea did the same beside him. "Time to receive your sweet comeuppance."

"Hey!" Emil glared. "You are all so secretly jealous of me that you must take such extremes?"

Tyler set his sled beside Rosalea and tugged Phoebe down in front of him. "'Course," she laughed. "It's so secret we didn't even tell ourselves."

Stanley slapped Emil's back on his way past, knocking off the boy's cap and nearly slicing his toes with the sled blades. "Eat crow, Kisch."

"Hear hear!" Hazel cried and claimed her spot beside Tyler followed by Luella and Tena.

At the end of the line, Reuben adjusted his sled. Situating his too large feet against the rudders, his knees pinned into his chest. Finally, begrudgingly Emil took the place beside him.

"At the ready, my good lads and ladies!" Earhart called. He raised his arm with a flourish. "On my mark of three, a race to—"

"Three!"

Emil's whoop sounded as he kicked off and sailed away down the hill, his hands waving above him. Shouting protests—and Earhart vowing revenge to all dirty cheats—the others followed close behind. Reuben's deep laughter escalated as he bent over his sled in pursuit, and the same delicious elation caught Tena even as her eyes watered and the wind blew the cap from her head. Her hair fell loose around her shoulders and whipped behind her. Her fingers twitched at the freedom of it. Itched to let go. But at their speed, and with the ice below, it would be far too dangerous. Charles would never have done it.

Charles would never have raced down the hill at all.

Reuben looked over when she called his name. Tena stretched her arms out like an eagle's wings if eagles could also throw mischievous smiles. "Let go!" she yelled.

"Seems reckless!" he countered but did so anyway, only to pull his arms back in the next second.

"Oi!" Emil shouted. "Roll off side!"

Reuben squinted forwards then thumbed sideways. "Into the snow!"

He flung himself off the opposite edge of his sled, and she whistled past him. She couldn't see what he had gone off about, until she realized that was the trouble. She couldn't see anything. The last of their safety lanterns had flickered out with barely a moon in the sky, leaving no indication where the snow ended as she rushed towards the water. Dark and still and for a split second—the time it took to soar through the air and crash onto the basin—there was naught but silence. The hush of an ocean after the loudest roar of voices. The emptiness of a thousand lives upturned.

The sled blades sliced through the ice and with a crack, it broke away in jagged edges. At first only her face stung with the bite of the cold then the water worked its way through the layers of her coat, her dress, her undergarments, and she finally understood how Charles died.

Like shackles chained to a cannonball, her sodden clothes dragged her into the inky blackness, and her shoes felt full of lead. Unaware which way led up and which would end her quicker, she drifted. Lost without a lifebelt to save her.

Except a lifebelt hadn't saved *him*.

Water roared in her ears, two thousand imaginary voices blending to form the shouted memories that haunted her nightmares. Those voices of *Titanic* looped together into a conversation that never made sense.

Running.

Frantic.

Hopeless.

She returned to that lifeboat with forty other women on a moonless night. All of them silent as the air around them shrieked for a savior. Mothers clasped their children. Fully matured women covered their ears. It made not a smidge of difference. Nothing was powerful enough to block out that sound. The women stared at each other or at the floor of the lifeboat, but hardly one looked towards the ocean. The sound was terrible enough.

The calm came on suddenly as though a dark beast moved through the water and swallowed those voices up. A few remained for another moment more—a frantic plea here, a whimpered cry there—and then they too went quiet. The officer in the lifeboat took up the oars and began rowing, to where Tena didn't know and she wagered neither did he. Simply away. Away from the other boats, away from the death, away from the guilt of survival at the cost of fellow human lives.

Man this boat, officer. She had heard the command given when the lifeboat first swung away from the davits, minutes before Charles's final farewell. The officer had only been following orders. So had she.

"Look!" one of the survivors cried as the sun rose hours later. She pointed into the open water, and the other women craned their necks. Far off bobbed hundreds of white objects, bursting above the water and down again with the waves, too distant to make out their exact shape. "Must be seagulls," Tena noted. "Curious to see so many this far out."

That was the beginning of the denial, the start of self-preservation.

Tena now hovered in the water of the Grand Basin, balanced between the world of the dead and the land of the living. Her lungs burned with the need for air and her limbs from the pain of frozen water. Charles felt it all. In terror, the last breath of air passed from his lungs. He knew no help was coming.

Once many years ago, she read a book in her father's collection that told of a man who bartered with the ancient gods. He asked for the life of his love and the gods granted it. It was not without great cost, but he would have paid any price.

Why not now? she thought. She raised her face in the direction she thought to be upwards. *Why can only the gods of old grant wishes? What could I have done to change it?*

Nothing, came the reply. *Trust me,* liebe, *there is nothing you could have done.*

Charles's face appeared above her, his dark dishwater blond hair floating around the eyes of an angel. Her angel.

His hand reached out and beckoned her up. It swirled through the water, and Tena raised her arm. Her fingers brushed his, but her gloves had fallen off on impact, leaving her bare skin too slick to hold on. A single bubble passed through her lips, the last bit of breath before she could bear it no longer. Clutching her chest, she kicked upwards with the last of her strength and Charles's face dissolved in a cloud of silt.

Panic fell as she grasped wildly for his hand. Her lungs were spent. This would be her end too, the same as him.

Charles, no, she pleaded. *Don't leave me. Please, save me one more time.*

And then her fingers landed again on his, and she was hauled from the lake, out onto the snow and into wind no warmer than the water she came from.

Tears clouded her vision and her lungs choked bitter air as she tumbled into Charles's arms. His ragged breath warmed her cheek, and she realized he was weeping as much as she. Was she dead? Or merely dreaming? If dead, then he was hers forever, and if a dream...? Well, she prayed she would never wake from it.

"You kept your promise," she whispered. *You found me.* Then, giving in to the closing darkness, she kissed him with everything he left behind.

For all the dreams they lost, the moments they would never share. For the second chances she didn't deserve and the remorse in her heart. She kissed him for all he was and would never be. This moment would never be enough to satisfy her.

She was either dead or dreaming. But she wouldn't wake up.

Not until she must.

TWENTY-TWO

WHEN TENA CRASHED THROUGH the Grand Basin, Reuben had felt the ice crack inside him as much as he heard the noise. Ten feet from his sled, he sat up in the snow and stared towards the Grand Basin. The water was only thirty feet in front of him; even so, he still couldn't tell what had caused that sound.

He quickly performed a count of the dim silhouettes scattered across the hillside. "Who's missing?" he called.

"Whatta you mean?" Earhart asked. The silhouette farthest on the left.

"I only see nine of us," Reuben returned. "Is someone missing?"

"Tena!" Emil shrieked—the silhouette closest to the ice.

No. Not her.

Abandoning his sled where it lay, Reuben stumbled down the hill and slid out to where Emil stood staring into a dark jagged hole. Space filled with perfectly calm water and no movement beneath it.

God, no, he prayed. *No. No. No. This cannot be happening.*

"Emil, help me." He drew himself onto the ice, Emil beside him, and both men lunged their arms into the frigid darkness.

"Fetch a lantern," Reuben shouted over his shoulder. "I can't see a blasted thing."

"Earhart's gone for one," Rosalea confirmed.

Frigid water displaced onto Reuben's chest and down his coat as his arms circled helplessly. He couldn't reach more than three or four feet and the basin had to be at least ten deep. Without Tena reaching for them, they would never save her.

"This is my fault," Emil said. He pulled his arms from the water and sank back on his heels. "Fred'll say it serves me right for cheating."

"This isn't your fault, and Fred's an imbecile." Reuben pulled himself up and forced his heart to keep beating normally. "She isn't gone."

He peeled off his sodden overcoat, tossing it towards the bank. His damp Oxford clung to his torso and the wind bit in a sensation too familiar to the night he fell off the *Höllenfeuer*. If Maggie hadn't been there then, he would have died. If Tena died tonight, he might as well have.

Appearing from nowhere, Stanley grabbed Reuben's wrist when he stooped to remove his shoes. The rest of their friends stood ten feet away at the edge of the ice. "Stop it, Reuben. You're not leaping in there. It's too dark; you'll never find her."

"I have to."

"What good will it do to drown yourself?"

Reuben yanked his wrist free. "Then I drown myself! I can't lose her, Lee. I can't."

"You're an idiot."

"Shut up!" Emil dove at Stanley and the latter, not expecting the gesture, fell flat onto the ice. Emil pointed a finger at him and leered. "You stand in the way of my sister's life again and someone will write a column about *your* demise."

"Emil, stop." Reuben pressed a hand to his friend's chest and stared down at Stanley. "Hold my feet then. Keep me from sliding in."

Stanley shook his head. "It's a lost idea, man. She could be anywhere under there, and you'd never find her." His voice was a mere shadow. "Don't you think if she was going to come up by now, she would have?"

Emil began sobbing then, terrible gut-wrenching cries that broke the night wide open while precious moments ticked away. The rest simply remained silent. Stanley on the ground. Earhart running down the hill with a brightly lit lantern. Tyler with his arms around Phoebe while the other girls huddled together.

Reuben turned towards the deep black abysmal pit that was stealing a piece of his soul.

"Reuben," Hazel breathed. "Don't." But he didn't look back.

He knew she didn't mean for him to leave Tena for dead. She just couldn't chance him doing something reckless when Plan A didn't succeed. Except Hazel didn't understand the ties that bound him and Tena together or his broken promises to Laurence to keep his daughter safe. Hazel could go on living without Tena. He couldn't. He had tried and apparently failed.

She was his light, his hope, this beautiful part of his life he could never put into words. What had he accomplished by distancing himself from her? Not a bloomin' thing.

He dropped to his chest, forearms suspended over the water. "Someone hold my feet or I'm going in the blasted lake." He drew in a deep breath then exhaled. Emil latched onto his ankles. He would save her. Or else he was dead.

"Please, God, if you never help me with anything, help me with this." Then he plunged his entire upper body into the water.

In a darkness so penetrating, he could only pray Tena would take hold of him. Once he thought he felt her, the ghost of an impression, but then the water swirled and anything he might have felt disappeared.

Seconds passed. Above him, a second set of hands clasped his ankles. He stretched until his shoulder tendons strained. *Please, Charles, help me find her.*

Miraculously his hands found hers. Her grip was weak, but he held on for her dear life as Emil, Stanley, and Earhart towed them from the water. In a heap on the ice, Reuben clung to her, crying as much as she was, while her hair froze around her shoulders and his own turned to ice against his scalp. Soaked through, the wind burned his skin, yet the comfort of her safety made it so he barely cared.

It startled him to the core when she caressed his face between her hands and whispered, "You kept your promise."

Before he could ask, "Which promise?" her lips met his with a passion he never imagined could come from her modest form. Call it relief over her safety, call it male stupidity, call it being a first-rate scoundrel when he was already more than spoken for, but he didn't immediately tear himself away. He kissed her back.

Blimey, did he ever.

And wouldn't he figure if that didn't open a whole new can of emotions. Ones he thought about before and a whole ball of ones he hadn't.

But somewhere between the cold of the water and the cold of the air, she hadn't seen Reuben, she saw Charles and that was who she kissed. He figured it out when she blacked out seconds later and asked where her fiancé was twice on the eternally long drive back to the Kischs'.

"He saved me," Tena whispered to Emil. Her head rested on his shoulder with her legs across Reuben's lap, and all three buried under a mess of blankets while Earhart sped them home. Tena's fingers played over her engagement band. "Charles saved me. Where did he go?"

Emil's eyes flashed at Reuben in steely silence, and Reuben had never felt like more of an idiot. He saved Tena's life, but at what other cost? Sitting in an icy puddle, the frost on their bodies crackling as he claimed a desire meant for someone else?

Whatever his feelings, Tena's were clear. If Reuben chose to think past his own nose, he would be competing with his best mate, and he wouldn't have done that in real life, much less with Charles's ghost.

Back at the Kischs', Reuben stepped from a tepid bath, water sluicing across the smooth tile floor. He yanked the plug and reached for the towel, quickly drying off before pulling on a set of Friedrich's spare clothes. It was strange being back in this place he used to call home. The scent of Elsa's soap emerged as he rubbed the soft towel over his damp hair. He missed this place. Even after so many months with the Vines—even after courting their daughter for almost as long—he still felt like a visitor there.

He hung up the towel and padded down the hallway, passing Tena's closed door on the way and forcing himself not to check on her. There would be time later.

Voices met him outside the door to his old room. Karl and Emil in tense discussion.

"He's a lousy cad," Emil spat.

"Language," Karl warned. "When someone in this family makes a mistake, you forgive them."

"He's still a cad," Emil shot back. "Charles is barely buried and—" His lips clamped when he noticed Reuben standing in the doorway. With a glare certain to burn bridges, he pushed past, banging into Reuben's shoulder on the way out.

"Need to warm up?" Karl held out a steaming mug to Reuben from where he perched on Emil's bed. The rich scent of coffee beckoned.

Reuben nodded in thanks, the warm liquid soothing to his soul. He wouldn't be able to sleep a wink after, but he probably wouldn't have slept much anyway.

"Emil's upset with me."

"Yes." Karl crossed his legs and rolled his hand across the air. "I want to bring it right to the point. I know what happened tonight and I have a few opinions on it." He held up a hand to deflect Reuben's interjection. "Drink your coffee, son. You will have your chance when I am through." Reuben nodded and remained silent.

"It does not take a learned man to see how you have carried a torch for Maggie as long as you have known her."

"What's Maggie to do with this?" Reuben interrupted. Karl shot him a glare. "Sorry."

"What I have not figured," he continued, "is what happened between the two of you on the *Höllenfeuer*—and I don't need to know. But you have allowed it to addle you too long. You have allowed your unresolved affections to latch onto someone else."

"No. I haven't. I'm still with Miss Vine."

Both of Karl's bushy blond brows raised. "I know. Who else would I mean?" He folded his hands on his round stomach and stared, his brows never lowering as they waited for a response.

"No one," Reuben coughed. The china mug was too warm in his hands. He would not initiate a conversation about Tena with her almost-father-in-law. The embarrassment would know no boundaries. *Bury it, Reuben.*

"I want to be happy, Mr. Kisch. Miss Vine makes me happy. Isn't that what we all want?"

Karl nodded. "It makes sense that you want to move on; however, taking up a home with your sweetheart, well, it is not right."

"I haven't 'taken up a home' with her ... well I suppose I have, but only in residence." Reuben squared his shoulders and faced Karl with a blaze of annoyance. "We don't have an intimate relationship, I don't intend to, and frankly I believe it isn't your business if I do."

Karl extended both hands towards Reuben. "Come home, son, please." His gesture pleaded more than his tone and both troubled Reuben. He removed himself a distance and gulped the remainder of his coffee.

Downstairs a telephone rang. Karl stood, then apparently thinking better of it, shook his head and lowered himself back to the bed. "Elsa is concerned about you and so am I. We worry that your life will pass by lost in wants while refusing to recognize what you truly need." He paused, eyeing Reuben carefully. "Or perhaps you have, but are too afraid to trust it?"

Reuben had trusted that Maggie's marriage to Hugo would free him from her betrayal, only it hadn't. He thought his relationship with Hazel would fix his feelings, except it didn't. He thought Tena was his friend and only that, but maybe she wasn't. Once people thought the world was flat and the sun revolved around the Earth. They believed Zeus threw lightning and the plague was punishment for sins. Until one day they knew better.

Afraid? he thought. He was bloomin' terrified.

He handed the mug back to Karl. "I should go. Thank you for the coffee."

"Reuben?" Karl's voice stopped him at the door. "Thank you for saving Tena."

He turned only to meet a gaze full of disappointment. Karl expected better from a man he called his son.

Reuben nodded. "I couldn't not."

Unfortunately, Emil blocked his path to a quick exit. He sat on the middle of the evergreen-wrapped staircase, twirling an unlit cigar between his hands. Hair still damp from his own plunge into the Grand Basin, Emil's usual platinum strands had darkened to nearly the coloring of his eldest brother's dishwater locks.

"Earhart rang," he said without looking up. His voice was gruff. "Everyone returned to his place after *the incident*. They're all in agreement. Given the circumstances, we won't tell Tena about the two of you canoodling. Let her think it was all a dream."

"Canoodling? Who says that?"

"Would you prefer we call it what it was? Having a poorly timed flirt with my brother's fiancée?"

Accurate, Reuben thought, but hearing his actions spelled out still stung. He sank to the stairs with his elbows on his knees and stared at the worn carpet runner. "I'm sorry. I wasn't thinking straight."

Emil continued to flip the cigar across his fingers. "Listen, I know I'm a jokester and usually I can't keep a serious face—frankly, why would I want to—but tonight was just so flipping unbelievable. All I wanted was my older brother, and that's when it hit me ... holy happy baby, Charles will *never* be here again. It's only me and Fred left. But, he's away at university and that's that. So I rail on you instead because really truly you're the only brother I've got left."

"You think of me as your brother?" Reuben had always considered the little troublemaker as his baby brother from that first day Charles injected him into the Kisch household. He watched Emil grow from an outrageous child to a wise-cracking young man and loved him as much as he had Mira. But he never assumed the reverse to be true. He always thought Emil viewed him as his eldest brother's friend and five years of difference.

Emil finally faced him. "'Course I do. You were best mates with my brother ergo you're my brother too. You sealed your fate the day you sidled up to Charles in the schoolyard." His lips curled with mischief. "My brother didn't speak English. You really should have messed with him more."

"I'm not a complete miscreant." Reuben tossed him a simple smile and ran his hands over his knees. "Thanks for making me face myself."

Emil laughed. "That is something you can always count on." He held up the cigar. "Want to join me for a late night smoke?"

"Emil." Elsa's quiet reprimand brought their heads around to the living room. Reuben paled at Hazel standing beside her.

Blimey! Hazel! In all the chaos that followed Tena's rescue, he had nearly forgotten about her. She stood mere feet away when Tena kissed him and had been only silent after. He already told her goodnight at Rosalea's auto, but she hadn't gone home; she was here waiting. Why? To ensure Tena was well? To be with him? To dump his sorry self out on the street?

The clock on the mantel read quarter after one in the morning.

With a low whistle, Emil slid the cigar into Reuben's front pocket then patted it for good measure. "I think you'll need this more than I will." A shudder tingled Reuben at the gesture. Charles had done the same once.

Elsa joined them on the stairs with an obviously forced smile. "Feeling better, Reuben?"

"Much, thank you."

"*Sehr gut.*" Her thick arms enveloped him and she pressed a kiss to his cheek. "*Gute nacht, liebe.* We will see you for Christmas, *ja?*"

"*Ja. Gute nacht.*"

Elsa clasped Emil's elbow, and without a word, the two disappeared up the staircase. Bedroom doors closed seconds later, leaving Reuben and Hazel to stare helplessly at one another. She was still buttoned into her winter coat, her knitted cap pulled low against her ears where windswept copper ringlets played over her left shoulder. Those hazel eyes, circled dark from crying, followed him as he walked down the stairs and claimed the space before her.

"I still cannot believe it of you," she cried. Her hands flew into the air, her intent as infuriated as it was disbelieving. "I've tried not to imagine your actions into something unpleasant, but how can I not?" She paused with a short gasp. "Please tell me you aren't having an affair."

"Never," Reuben barked.

Hazel frowned. "Your response was a little too quick."

"I've known Tena for years. She was engaged to my best mate; she's closer to being my sister. You know this."

"Egads, your sister? With a kiss like *that?*" Hazel snatched at her collar as though it might choke her. "You barely even kiss *me* like that."

"Hazel, someone almost died tonight. Can't you understand—"

"Why did you move to America? You never told me. Was it for her?"

"Technically, yes, she asked me. Oh Hazel, be reasonable!" With a clap of her wrist, he pulled her down to the sofa beside him. He needed to convince her as much as himself. He was not—could not be—attracted to Tena. "Hazel, Tena loves Charles, not me. That's who she thought I was tonight. I didn't ask for it; I didn't want it. People act strangely in the cold. When they grieve, sometimes things happen. It happens to us all."

"Certainly not to me. I don't dredge up dead people because I'm a little sad." Hazel rolled her eyes. "Have you ever heard of anything so ridiculous?"

Yes, Reuben thought. He was Exhibit A.

But instead, in response he tilted her chin and pressed a gentle kiss to her lips. "I can understand it, yes. But blimey, can't you believe I'm only with you?"

Hazel finally smiled and wrapped her arms around his neck. "You could charm anyone with that accent, you know?" She ran her fingers through his damp hair and curled a lock around her finger. "I think I might love you, Reuben Radford."

She kissed him then, but he barely felt it. His lips—and the rest of him—had grown cold with her words. She loved him. Sweet Hazel with her innocent smile and ability to be so wonderfully forgiving loved him. Finally, he had exactly what he always wanted.

Only heaven knew why he didn't say it back.

TWENTY-THREE

FOR THREE DAYS SNOW CONTINUED to fall. A thick blanket covered the yard and sparkling multi-dimensional ice crystals clung to the edges of every window while sharp icicles hung from the eaves. All the while Maggie's stomach twisted as the snow accumulated along with Molly's temperature. The road was inaccessible to all except the bravest traveler or one wealthy enough to own a sleigh; a physician would not be. Without transportation of her own, she only had her legs to carry her. There were too many miles between home and the hospital; it wasn't worth the risk of freezing in the snow.

For now, Maggie was alone.

She glanced from the storm outside the living room window to Molly asleep on the sofa. *Thank goodness she can finally find some rest in this*, Maggie thought. She herself hadn't slept well since the evening she found Molly writhing on the floor from fever seizure. The girl's slender limbs had flapped like a broken sparrow, and Maggie had never experienced such terror. Once the tremors dissipated, she was able to drag Molly the few feet across the room to the sofa, but no farther in her current condition. So she transformed the living room into a quarantine and confined Isa's playthings to the study. The younger child still seemed relatively ignorant of her sister's true condition and was currently sleeping soundly upstairs.

Ignorance, however, could prove fatal; even without medical training, Maggie knew Molly's temperature had been elevated too long. How many days were too many? she wondered. Four? Five? Was she already too late?

No. There must be a manageable solution if only she could discover it.

Except there appeared to be nothing left to try. Of the few home remedies she remembered, none lowered Molly's fever more than slightly or afforded her comfort. Most foods roiled the child's stomach. Too much water had the same effect. Maggie scrubbed every surface and washed each piece of linen twice in an effort to purge the house of disease, but even that proved disastrous.

Rather than create an ice slick by emptying the wash basin near the door, she dragged the full tub through the snow to the cliff's edge. The baby flipped over in protest, jutting against Maggie's pelvis and every nerve from hip to ankle. Crying out, her legs buckled, and her knees landed hard on frozen earth. At the same time, she dropped the washbasin. It clanged against the ground and rolled off the side of the ridge. Banging once upon the cliff face, she heard it splash into the river.

Tears stung while bitter wind cut her face and chapped hands, the promise of another winter's storm in the air. More snow. She finally knew how those flower girls in London felt, slowly freezing while they begged for a sale and knew no one would help. If she could go back to those days, she would buy them all. Every pound would go to help those children, and her room would be filled with beauty even in the dead of winter. Her own garden here was similarly lifeless now, barren beds surrounding the buckled patio blocks. With her luck, none of the bulbs would germinate come spring. It would be as hollow and desolate as she felt right now.

Drawing the curtains closed against the cold, she turned down the living room lights and closed the pocket doors to shut herself into Hugo's study alone. She settled herself behind his desk and swiveled to face the bookshelves. Interspersed between framed portraits, half-constructed cameras, and dated photo boxes sat a liberal number of books. Their layers of dust would have made her father shudder even more than his favorite volumes being lost on *Titanic*.

Hugo's collection differed from Laurence Archer's in every way it could. Not a single title or author could Maggie recognize. Stevenson, Twain, Hawthorne, Alcott. Multiple volumes on photography, a few related to the American Revolution and the War of the Rebellion, and a copy of the 1910 St. Louis City Directory. Not a single medical book.

But why would there be? Hugo was not a learned man; he told her once that his father whisked him away at the age of ten to be a photographer's assistant and that was when his schooling ended. Even so, he was terribly intelligent; she sensed it by the way he spoke. Life had been his teacher. He would have known enough not to let his daughter die.

She swept her arm along the shelf, spilling all the books onto the floor, and sighed. Now she would need to pick those up. As she bent, another group of novels caught her eye from the bottom shelf and she finally located what she hadn't even realized she should be searching for.

Stacking a fire in the hearth, she settled in to read while the wind whistled and snow drifts rolled across the garden. When she finished, she flipped to the beginning and began again. Those words passed night back into dawn and snow lay calm and sparkling in a new day's sun. She read until her eyes hurt. Reuben had believed this book held all the answers. He believed time had the power to change things. How desperately she needed an impossible change right now.

So she vowed to read it until she saw what Reuben did. She would read *The Time Machine* until either a miracle occurred or she died of fatigue.

~~~

Maggie woke to insistent knocking at the front door. The firebox lay cold, the room layered in late-evening's frozen darkness. She shivered and rubbed her arms to drive away the chill.

An unpleasant crick seared her neck. She hadn't meant to fall asleep, but after two full days without any, she supposed it had been inevitable. Her baby bounced with her awakening, throwing arms and legs against her mother's insides like a frolicking foal.

"Quiet, you pest," she scolded. Pushing herself up from the chair, she stepped her way through the trove of Isa's toys littering the study floor, checked Molly's forehead—still hot—and turned on the entry lamps. Immediately, the knocking ceased.

Her hand paused against the lock. Hugo wasn't due home until weeks after Christmas. He hadn't wanted to stay away so long, but she insisted.

"I'll only be away a few weeks," Hugo assured her as he packed his traveling case. He folded each item carefully, the crease between his eyes lengthening. "We'll return before Christmas."

Stooping to retrieve his boots from the floor, Maggie set them inside the open trunk. "No need. The baby has until January, so you may as well spend Christmas with your sisters. California is bound to be warmer than what we'll have here."

He turned mid-fold, pressing her with troubled eyes. "I *will* be home in time."

As much as she could force a smile with her fate hanging in the balance, she managed to offer him her best. "Do not surrender your commitment to Emma over an impetuous promise to me. Stay as long as it takes."

Emma. The woman who provided Maggie's baby a chance by her absence and would quite possibly ruin its only chance at legitimacy if she returned. Mr. Frye's kindness had made her forget she didn't belong and never would. She was merely filling in until Emma reclaimed her place. The hired help.

After all her careful planning, it was difficult to accept defeat.

This is why, she reminded herself, why she needed distance from love, from marriage, from additional children of her own creation. Spare herself the aggravation and the pain. For as afraid as she was of hurting someone she loved, she was equally afraid of being hurt. For two weeks, her heart had encouraged her to dismiss that fear until her head—that rascally devil of logic—smacked her with the sense that nothing was worth the pain Hugo endured. No one could take the ache away once it had been inflicted.

Securing the latches on the traveling case, Hugo picked up his Brownie from the writing desk and settled the case strap over his shoulder. "There's about twenty minutes of light left. I want to take a few before dark hits."

He slipped from the room, and his steps faded away on the stairs. A minute later the bang of the kitchen door followed. From their bedroom window, Maggie watched him at the river's edge, a silhouette against the eastern sky, his amber hair taking on the glow of smoldering irons as the sinking sun set it ablaze.

Not once did he reach for his camera.

TWENTY-FOUR

REUBEN COULD HAVE SAID HE had no inclination to visit the Fryes, only he would have been lying. After three days insisting to Hazel—and himself—that his mind wasn't a jumble of uncertainty, there had been only one person he believed could truly set everything straight. If Karl thought Maggie held the key to the chains that shackled him, then he needed to ask her to use it.

This feud between the sisters needed to end as much for their sake as his own. Once Reuben restored Tena and Maggie's friendship, he could cease worrying about them, focus on righting his relationship with Hazel, and drown that kiss in the Grand Basin where it came from.

Snow-soaked to his knees and damp socks frozen around his toes, his trouser cuffs dripped into a puddle on the Fryes' stoop. Another blizzard emerged the day after Rosalea's party and barely relented since. With the lesser used streetcar lines frozen and many roads still covered, he had to abandon city transportation at Broadway and Jefferson and walk over a mile through the drifts. Reporter attire was definitely not fashioned for such a trek.

Entry lamps suddenly illuminated, flooding the portico with light as the door eased open.

"Reuben?"

He wasn't prepared for the heavily pregnant woman who opened her front door to him on that cold snow-driven night in late

December. Even though he understood the mechanics of childbearing, he couldn't have primed himself for the extreme swell of her stomach, the quick movements nestled beneath it, or the alarming sensation rising within him. There was one thing for which Maggie genuinely hadn't lied.

"May I come in?"

"Please."

He stepped past her and hung his wet overcoat and hat on the entry rack. Dropping his satchel on the floor, he made for the living room without speaking. Something sharp had wedged in his throat. It grew thicker as he took in the feeble child asleep on the sofa before the dimming fire.

Maneuvering around the dish-cluttered coffee table, he moved the mending basket from the floor to kneel beside the little girl. The back of his knuckles barely made contact with her forehead before pulling back. The child simmered with fever. He eased the stack of blankets down, and she shivered when the cool air hit her sweat-soaked nightgown.

He pressed two fingers to Molly's wrist. Her pulse fluttered. "How long?" he asked.

"Three days. I tried to carry her upstairs, but that's not an option in my state."

"Why haven't you rang a doctor?"

"How would he find his way? The roads are impassable."

Reuben craned his neck to peer up at her. Her always impeccable brown locks hung in limp strands and deep purple rings stained her eyes as though she hadn't slept in days. "Maggie, it's ten at night. Where is your husband?"

"He's on a photography trip with his son in Utah." She raised a trembling hand to her lips, and he noticed a plain finger where a wedding band should be.

Following his gaze, she quickly wrapped her right hand around the left. "My fingers are too swollen to wear it," she explained, although her voice held an edge he had heard before. It contained a host of words she wouldn't say.

"Right, well let's get to work." He stripped off his jacket, wet shoes and socks and tossing the pile into the entryway, rolled his sleeves up. He nodded to Maggie. "What have you been using to reduce her temperature?"

"Snow from the yard and—"

"Too cold," Reuben interjected. "The fever's too high; we need to bring it down gradually. Do you have any apple cider vinegar?" When Maggie nodded, he rattled off an additional list of supplies. A few minutes later, she returned with a bowl of lukewarm water, clean washrags, and a round brown cider jug.

"Thanks." Pouring the cider until he thought the measurements were correct, he set down the jug and swirled the mixture together. Then he dipped the first washrag into the bowl and gently laid it across the child's forehead. Molly released a slight moan, and he gestured for Maggie to dim the lamps so only the low fire's light remained.

"Where did you learn this?" Maggie asked as she walked the room.

"It's what I did for my father—what the doctor told me to do—when he was sick." He dipped two more washrags, and easing the blankets from Molly's feet, wrapped one around each sole of her feet. "If this treatment is unsuccessful, we can try the same method again with garlic. Maybe a warm bath and some broth come morning." Although, judging from Molly's tapered breathing, he didn't know how much good it would actually do.

"You said 'try.' You think Molly might die then?"

Yes, he thought. Only a cruel world killed children right before their parents' eyes. Even after all the harm Maggie had done, he still couldn't wish that for her.

"Maybe not."

Maggie nodded and walked from the room. He heard water run and dishes rattle down the hall.

Reuben released the sigh he had been holding in. He had to follow her. He came here on a mission—to convince her to reconcile with Tena and in turn hopefully rid himself of any residual affection for either sister.

Rinsing the washrag, he resituated the cool cloth on Molly's forehead. Then, after he poked the last embers of the fire, he closed her into silence and carried the cider jug and washbowl to the kitchen. A kettle simmered on the stove while Maggie dispersed tea leaves into two saucered cups. She barely glanced up as he emptied the washbowl down the sink.

"Tell me how to believe the impossible," she whispered.

"What do you mean?" He reached around her for the drying towel.

Turning, she butted her hip against the counter. "*The Time Machine.* You told me that book made you believe in the impossible. Well, I read it, Reuben. Then I read it again. There is nothing in it to convince me anything will get better. If anything, it did quite the opposite." Her eyes lowered to her stomach then upwards through her lashes. "How did you survive it, Reuben? When your mother was sick then your father ...? I never realized how strong you were until now."

Reuben set the now-dry bowl on the counter. "You lost your father, too."

"I didn't feel it the same way. I loved my father, and I miss him every day, but Molly ... I can't describe it. She's different."

Tears fell then. They drew uneven lines through her usually flawless features and dotted the dark cotton of her mourning dress. She wiped at them furiously and only managed to create more. She wiped her nose with the back of her hand and turned back to the tea kettle.

Maggie is crying, he thought in shock. Maggie didn't cry. She was a fortress, and her unexpected emotion caused his own blockades to tremble. He needed to rectify the situation, and he needed to do it *now*. "No tears, Maggie. This isn't the end, you know. We'll see them again."

She spun, her bright blue eyes flashing dangerously. "Don't lecture me on heaven, Reuben Radford," she spat. Another solitary tear trickled down her cheek, and she swiped it away. "Nothing you say makes it any less unfair. Mr. Frye lost his wife while he was traveling. How can he lose Molly in the same way? He'll loathe me."

"Maybe he's the one who should think twice about leaving."

"You can't blame him. This time, I browbeat him into it."

"Why?" Reuben waited for her to expand on what reason she could possibly have for sending her husband away so close to the birth of her child. The decision was irresponsible, yet he supposed Maggie always had been too.

The tea kettle whistled. The shrill melody cut through the air, but neither of them moved to silence it. "How did you accept it when Mira died?" she asked quietly.

Reuben hesitated. In truth, he couldn't accept it then. He would have liked to sit in that cemetery forever, wasting his life away in mourning until the grass grew over his body and suffocated him. His heart raced with the memory of those eternal lonely days and the one that made time finally step forward again—when he met her.

She wanted an answer and he didn't have one that would help. He mustered the only semi-truth he could. "I don't know."

Maggie seized his shirt, wild as a hurricane while the tea kettle continued to wail. "Yes you do," she insisted. "Tell me. When Mira died, how did you accept it? How?"

"Would you silence that blasted thing?" He reached around her for the towel and slammed the kettle onto the side burner. "I don't know how I did it, Maggie. I just did. You think Molly's death will be unfair? That's how I felt with Mira, only worse. You have a chance to say goodbye. I didn't." He uncurled his fingers from where they were digging into her shoulder. He couldn't even remember placing them there.

"How did you manage with all that pain inside?"

Another loaded question. For Reuben, he resorted to a psychotic remnant of his sister's memory trapped inside him rather than lose her forever. It had driven him to madness, nearly to his own demise. Maggie had seen him in that weakness; she knew the cost. "I made my fair share of mistakes."

Her piercing gaze found his. "Was I a mistake?"

She was so dangerously near. *Hold it together, Reuben.* "Don't ask me that. You won't prefer the answer." He laid a firm hand on her arm. "Let's return to the living room before you make fools of us both."

"Don't patronize me, Reuben." Her fingers tightened around his shirt. "Your answer—was I a mistake?"

Don't answer. He could still remember the feel of her body beside him during their singular night together, when he wanted her more than anything in the world. He would have given anything to have her, even forget Mira. Even forget himself.

He exhaled. "Yes. I imagine you were."

Maggie didn't even hesitate. She pressed her body against him, and Reuben's brain momentarily short-circuited. Her lips parted, and all he could think was, *What about Tena?*

What do you mean, what about Tena? he admonished. *What about Hazel?*

Heaven help him; he had a monstrous problem.

Reuben stripped Maggie's hands away. "For king's sake, Maggie, we can't do this again."

"It doesn't need to mean anything."

"But it would. Why do you think we haven't spoken in five months?"

"Then why are you here now? Showing up in the night? That could only mean one request." Pulling her hands free, she ran her palms over his chest. "I'm not asking for anything except one moment to clear our heads. That was our original agreement, remember? One day, nothing more?"

Reuben held a hand to her lips. The fog was indeed clearing and underneath it ran a familiar rampant stench. "So per standard Maggie, you're using me to forget about your problems?"

Maggie rolled her eyes and slapped his hand away. "Confound it, Reuben. You do the same thing to deal with your issues. You admitted it—'I made my fair share of mistakes.' So let's make one more mistake together."

"We don't belong together."

"Does it matter?" She waved both hands towards the hallway. "If your brand of medical magic didn't work, there might be a dead child waiting for me in there. If I can have even one second of freedom of that—well, hate me if you want, but I'm going to take it."

The silence that followed couldn't have been thicker even if it were water from the Dead Sea itself. Incomprehensible, he thought. This conversation was completely unfathomable.

Reuben shoved past Maggie and cracked his fist on the kitchen table. "Your stepdaughter might be dying, and all you can think of is yourself?" His voice broke along with his heart. "You have a husband who loves you. He wants your baby. You received everything your sister should have and still your soul is black. Well, not with me."

Maggie shook her head. "Love is for the weak. My sister can have it for all the good it did her." China rattled as she moved to pour water into the teacups. "Pretend you weren't around in my moment of weakness. I promise I'll never fall so far again."

Reuben reached for his father's silver pocket watch, clutching it with such fervor that the winding knob cut into his palm. *Time always changes things,* he reminded himself. Except sometimes it didn't, no matter how many times you wound the knob.

"All this time and not a thing changed, did it, Maggie?" Releasing the watch, he gently took the tea kettle from her hands and set it on the stove. Try as he might to tilt her attention, she closed her eyes and refused to acknowledge him. "I know you, Maggie. You shared a piece of my heart once. You're still lying to everyone, but no one more than yourself. You pretend you're incapable of genuine feeling so you can believe your actions never have consequences."

"Reuben," she whispered. Her eyes scrunched with the strain of holding them closed. "Tell me one thing. Do you remember that girl you met in the cemetery on May Day two years ago?"

"How could I forget? *That* was the girl I fell in love with. She told me everyone has a beautiful story to tell."

"The stories aren't real, Reuben. That's why I told them. Everyone deserves a good story because there are no good stories. Not even mine. No matter what you might believe about Mr. Frye, he's fooled you."

That's when Reuben finally understood. This was how he would find his freedom. This was how he would unlock the chains.

"Maggie, I see Mr. Frye far more than is healthy given our relationship to you. I try to avoid him, but for a large city, St. Louis is terribly compact. The infernal man just won't go away. He attends half the funerals I write obituaries for, and I overhear him as he socializes. He tells everyone about you. He doesn't try to hide it. He tells them about the baby you're having together, and he's proud. He's proud, and I'm jealous."

Her eyes popped open, and he shook his head before she could speak. "No, not jealous because I want you to myself. Jealous because you never felt that way about me. Because I still don't believe why anyone ever should. Angry because he gets to be a father to the kid I could have had." Reuben sighed. "I was wrong. When I told you that he wasn't the right man for you, I was wrong."

He gestured out the kitchen window where the navy sky lay adorned with its glowing orb and her most favored gemstones. "Maggie, that man thinks the moon and the stars of you."

Maggie's eyes took in the sky while her right fingers slid to the absence on her left hand. "Even if that were true, the problem is that the moon and the stars are both beautiful, and yet completely unobtainable. What good is loving something if it's impossible to hold onto?"

TWENTY-FIVE

MOLLY'S FEVER FELL TWO DEGREES by the second night and another degree on the third day, all thanks to Reuben's continued presence. When he first suggested staying in Henry's room, Maggie argued like the dickens but eventually relented when she realized there was no other sane option. For three days, Reuben somehow managed to trudge through the snow-packed streets to the newspaper then returned to help her fix dinner. In between caring for Molly and inventing games with Isa, he took charge of the housework, and the house hadn't been so organized since the night Hugo left town.

On the fourth night, Maggie laid awake while her fingers followed the tiny footprints marching across her stomach and nearly screamed when a figure appeared at her bed well after two o'clock in the morning.

"Heavens, you gave me a fright, you oaf."

"I can't sleep either," Reuben whispered, even as he rubbed his eyes. Through the glint of moonlight between the window curtains, she could decipher his outline clothed in Hugo's pajamas. The pants held several inches above the floor. Underneath all his usual business attire, he was still the same boy from the cemetery, the one she laid beside on the *Höllenfeuer* and possibly made a baby with. The man she might have loved if those stars he spoke of aligned another way.

When she offered her hand, he grasped it without hesitation. She pulled it down to where a little unborn foot pressed against his palm.

He inhaled sharply as though it physically pained him to touch her, but then splayed both his hands upon her stomach, the thin nightgown seemingly invisible between their skin.

"That's the baby," he whispered with such emotion, Maggie felt her own begin to swell. As his eyes locked onto the ripples beneath her skin, he sighed. "I'm sorry I didn't believe you."

"What did I ever do to convince you that you should?"

Even in the near darkness, his eyes locked onto hers. "It's mine, isn't it?"

"I couldn't say for certain. But of the three possibilities, I want to believe it's yours. You're the only one who would make a good father."

"Hugo *is* a good father." Reuben continued to watch the tiny movements for another several minutes, and Maggie wished she could read all the intentions beneath his words. He sat beside her on the bed, quiet as the night. What would he do once the baby arrived and they knew the paternity for certain? Tonight he was playing the hero, sacrificing himself on the altar of Hugo Frye, but what about when he held the child in his arms? If it was his, would he still choose to be so noble?

"Reuben, why did you really come here the other night?"

"I think you should find peace with Tena."

"This is her fight. She needs to come to me."

"You're both being impossible, you know."

"Aren't we always?"

"Yes. It's a wonder I associate with either of you anymore."

"You probably shouldn't. Why don't you find yourself a nice lady and settle down?"

Reuben sank into silence. The baby jumped again under his fingers, and he laid his hands in his lap. "I've actually been seeing someone ... in a way."

"In a way?"

"It's become a delicate situation. Complicated, really. Still, she's sweet, clever, a brilliant dancer, overall a real fine girl. I do care about her. There just doesn't feel like there's enough substance beneath it, at least not on my part."

"Give it a chance. She may surprise you."

"Perhaps ... women do surprise me often."

He sank into silence again, his face turned away in shadow.

"Reuben?" she asked gently. "Is anything else the matter?"

"Other than watching a person squirm around inside you that I possibly made? Because, I'll be honest, that's kind of taking the cake right now." He poked her stomach for added emphasis, sending off a new round of frantic movements.

"For your information, that never stops being peculiar." Maggie circled her hands over her stomach. "But I meant anything else."

"Tena kissed me."

"What?" Maggie sputtered, sleep a thing long forgotten. She reached over to turn on the table lamp and slapped his knee in frustration. "Why didn't you lead with that four days ago?"

"She thought I was Charles."

"How, pray tell, did she confuse you with Charles, whom I hate to mention is no longer alive?"

"She fell in the lake when we went sledding. It was so cold, she became a bit addled and mistook me for him. You know me, Maggie; you know I'm no stranger to odd hallucinations. And no—" he countered at her look, "—I haven't had any of my own for a very long time, not since the *Höllenfeuer*. But sometimes I wish for them back, just to see my sister again. Despite the way she tortured me, I miss seeing her every day."

"That wasn't really her though." Maggie recalled how Reuben's eyes glazed over that night on the *Höllenfeuer*, how he lashed out at a being that wasn't there. In a fit of madness, he had nearly chosen death in order to escape.

"I know, but sometimes the worst of someone is better than nothing of them at all."

"So, do you love her?" she asked. "Tena, I mean."

Reuben ran a hand through his hair and lay back on the pillow, hands behind his head. "How do you know that you love anyone? I thought I loved you, but did I even understand what love was? I don't think it was that. If it was, how could I go from loving you to loving someone else in so short a time? How could I possibly have a baby with you and walk away?"

She rolled on her side to face him. They lay only a foot apart, her enormous stomach nearly touching his side, and it surprised her how natural it seemed. "I think you've always loved her, haven't you?"

Reuben didn't reply. He just stared at the ceiling, arms folded behind his head, and sighed.

TWENTY-SIX

REUBEN LEFT MAGGIE ON the 24th of December, six days after he arrived. He still felt uneasy leaving them alone but knew he had overstayed his welcome. Hugo would be home in another few weeks and by then Molly's health would no longer be in question. When Mr. Frye was good and settled in, Reuben would give that bloomin' idiot a piece of his mind for leaving his pregnant wife unattended, but for today he would leave it where it lay.

When he slid into the newsroom with a hearty, "Top o' the morning, Lee," Stanley didn't even look up from his writing. His voice was strangely aloof. "You sound refreshed."

"I'm having a splendid morning." Before he left, Molly had managed an entire meal on her own. Without his visit, she would assuredly be dead, but even with his assistance, her recovery could be considered nothing short of a miracle.

"'Bout time you're in high spirits again," Stanley said. He scratched out an entire line from his article. "You've patched everything up with Hazel, then?"

Reuben paused halfway through emptying his satchel, his mood suddenly soured. He stared at the notepad in his hand and tried to spin an acceptable response to Stanley's question. All he could come up with was, "Yes."

Stanley tapped his pencil against his chin. "Hmm, I do wonder if she would say the same." He crossed out another two sentences and jotted a note in the margin. "Because I know you haven't been sleeping at home."

Reuben didn't need to ask how Stanley gleaned that bit of information. He smoothed a blank sheet out on the desktop and tossing his satchel to the floor, silently rummaged in the top drawer for a pencil.

"Have you been staying here?" Stanley asked.

"No."

"Well, I know you haven't been home. Hazel finally spilled it to me this morning. Told me you've been missing for almost a week. That you've barely said two words to her since then. She's afraid you don't like her anymore."

"Hazel's nineteen. She worries too much for someone so young."

Stanley finally looked up, expression concerned and lips tight set. "Reuben, Hazel loves you." He glanced around the crowded newsroom. Harried reporters hid behind piles of paper, save a small contingent joking near the windows while they consumed their morning coffee. Eric Smithson's usual frustrated phone conversations floated through the crack in his office door. No one paid the two men a bit of mind.

Even so, Stanley lowered his voice. "Does this have something to do with ... you know, um ... the *kiss*?"

Reuben glowered, gripping his pencil just shy of snapping it. "No. The matter is that Christmas is tomorrow, and I'm drowning in a sea of unfinished obits. You should know, Lee; homicides have been up this month too. Being around the Vines' incessant holiday cheer wasn't helping my concentration so I went elsewhere." He returned to his article, jotting down details about the wife, eight children, and fifteen grandchildren that seventy-two-year-old Harold Dentsworth recently left behind. Fifty years and an entire family more than Charles had, he thought miserably.

"Listen, man," Stanley said gently. He laid his pencil down. "As your friend, I gotta say something. You're grumpy at the paper and boot outta here at the end of the day like the building's on fire. Except you clearly don't go home, and you don't return here. Not even on your day off. So where on God's green Earth are you?"

"With a friend."

"But not with the Kischs?"

"No, someone else."

"Who else? I've met all your other friends, and you didn't stay with any of them."

"Lay off, Lee." Reuben's hand slipped, his pencil lead driving a thick grey stain across the article. He crumpled the paper up and tossed it towards the already overflowing rubbish bin.

Stanley snatched Reuben's notepad before he could start over. "We went to Cave Hall on Friday and for the first time in months, you weren't with us. You want to know who else wasn't? Hazel. She stayed home wondering why you stood her up. So what gives, Radford?"

Reuben leaned in and pressed a finger to Stanley's desk. "I helped a friend whose child was sick. You don't know her. And I wish you would call off the guard about it."

Stanley's bushy brows shot up. "*Her*?"

"Yes. My friend has a daughter," Reuben clarified, accidentally stabbing his pencil lead clear through another sheet of paper. He tossed the instrument on the desk and buried his face in his hands. *And I might too,* he thought. *A daughter or a son.*

A deep groan escaped his friend. "You're gonna lose her, Reuben. You can't have it both ways. Whatever you got going on the side, I beg you, let it go. Because if you don't, you'll find yourself every bit a bachelor again. Is that what you want?"

It was the only time Reuben ever stormed out of the newsroom. Hazel met his eyes as he passed by and he held out a hand to her. "Come with me."

"Where are we going?"

"Anywhere. Out to lunch. On the train. To another state. I don't care. I just want to leave with you." He cared about Hazel. He knew that much at least. For now, knowing one thing with certainty was enough.

Hazel's eyes returned to the typewriter. She continued clacking away at the keys and slid the return back. "I can't leave now. I need to finish these sheets before five. Christmas is tomorrow. Or perhaps you've forgotten with how *busy* you are."

"I'm sorry I've been such a cur lately." Reuben hunched over her desk and his breath blew stray hairs from her face. He stilled her typing with the touch of his hand. "Let's go shopping. I'll buy you a Christmas gift you're worthy of."

Ever so slowly, she raised her eyes to meet his. "I don't want you to buy me anything. As long as you're at Christmas dinner with Mama and Papa, that's really all I want."

"I thought you were joining me at the Kischs'."

"You're still gonna go there?" she cried. "After what happened?" Her voice dropped to a low whisper. "It's because of Tena, isn't it? You said it didn't mean nothin'."

He slammed his hand on her desk, rattling the typewriter keys and causing Luella to jump in her seat. "No, Hazel. How many times do I have to tell you? It didn't."

Her fingers struck against the keys, a series of meaningless letters ruining the article she had nearly finished. "I did this then. I told you I loved you and I frightened you away."

The rest of the room stood silent, eight typists now openly staring. Rosalea stood with arms folded beside her desk, ready to pounce when signaled. Half a dozen reporters including Stanley crowded around the newsroom door.

Reuben rocked back on his heels, flexed his fingers around his satchel strap, and exhaled. He was making a scene. Well, who cared? It had been a hot minute since he made a scene and inside he was a balloon of unhampered emotion ready to burst.

He stepped around the desk, wrapped his hand behind Hazel's neck, and kissed her hard. To his right, someone gasped.

"Radford!"

He straightened up to find Smithson leering in the center of the doorway, eyebrows pressed together with a glare likely to burn that day's edition. When he released Hazel, she sank into her chair with a shudder, fingers typing furiously and face burning. All other eyes were on him.

"What in the blue blazes is wrong with you, Radford?" Smithson yelled, his face redder than Hazel's. "Are you drunk?"

"No, sir, Mr. Smithson, stone cold sober," Reuben asserted. "Give me my own beat. You know I can write as well as any of these half-wits."

"You'll get beat all right, but not with the paper. Get back to your desk before you don't have one to return to."

For once Reuben did as he was told.

~~~

Twelve hours later—long after every other reporter made for home and not one with a holiday greeting towards him—Reuben lingered in the shadowed newsroom with a cigar between his teeth and Geraldine Murphy's obituary on his desk.

That afternoon, while his thoughts were still wrapped up in Hazel, Reuben interviewed Geraldine's parents in their cottage outside the city. Having been deserted by her intended, their daughter suffered a nervous breakdown and threw herself into the Mississippi. A twenty-four-year-old girl dead three days before Christmas. The body still hadn't been recovered.

"She was attending St. Louis University," Her mother tearfully acknowledged. "Not many women are admitted. Why wasn't it enough?"

"She would have married eventually," her father said. "To think that she felt so alone ... it doesn't reason. She had us. She had her sisters. We loved her."

Reuben accepted the coffee mug they offered without drinking. "Grief can make it difficult to remember what you still have."

Her mother nodded. "You still grieve someone close to you?"

"Too many," he replied. "My parents. My sister. My best mate. ... far too many."

"Tell them you love them."

"Who?"

"Whoever you have left." Mrs. Murphy tapped a finger to her nose with a heartrending smile. "Tell them you love them. Make amends. Take it from a mother—there's no greater time to love than Christmas."

Tell them you love them.

Reuben hadn't told them often enough. Not his parents nor his sister when they were alive. He simply ran out of days. Proclaiming his love to their gravestone was not the final endearment they deserved.

Make amends.

How many did he need to ask for forgiveness from? How often had he made an unwise decision and hurt those he loved the most? Too often to count.

The newsroom clock read twenty past eleven. If he hurried, he could make it to St. Francis de Sales' Christmas mass by midnight. He wasn't exactly dressed in his Sunday best—his shoes were scuffed and his jacket didn't match his trousers—but it had also been months since he stepped foot in a church. He doubted God would mind what he wore.

He would do as Mr. Murphy asked. He would sleep in his own bed tonight and wake with the sun. He would make amends with those who needed it most and apologize to Hazel under the mistletoe come morning.

After all, there was no greater time to love again than Christmas.

TWENTY-SEVEN

MASSAGING DISCOMFORT FROM HER lower back, Maggie hefted herself up from the bedroom writing desk where she had finally finished penning a letter to Amara.

One toll of the clock. Half past eleven on Christmas Eve. Time to play Father Christmas then to blessed sleep. She would have settled down at the same hour as the girls but feared she wouldn't wake in time to play the red-suited hero. Molly and Isa would have scampered downstairs on Christmas morning to no presents and end Santa Claus fantasy at the tender ages of five and three. That would have only ruined the holiday.

Her outstretched fingers brushed the packages on the top shelf of the wardrobe when, in the upstairs hallway, a bedroom door closed and soft footsteps descended the stairs. *Those girls still believe they can outwit me*, she thought. They had begged her to sleep beside the Christmas tree until Maggie insisted they sleep in their own bed or Santa would never come. Although, she understood how they felt after the excitement of the day.

As though he hadn't already done enough, Reuben ordered a small Christmas tree to be delivered earlier that morning, and the girls whiled away the afternoon stringing popcorn and cranberry garland and singing carols. Afraid Molly might overexert herself, Maggie insisted the girls assemble from the security of the sofa and leave her to the actual trimming. When they were finished, the top listed slightly and the garland was haphazardly spaced, but its electric lights glowed against their grandmother's hand-painted ornaments and she found it beyond beautiful. With tender voices, her stepdaughters read the nativity story from their worn family Bible, and she tucked the carved baby Jesus in to sleep with Molly exactly as Tena had done for so many years. When they insisted on extra kisses, she obliged willingly. If this was to be the only Christmas she shared with those girls, she wanted it to be magical.

Nudging the presents back into their hiding place, Maggie tiptoed down the stairs, determined to catch the girls in the act. Halfway down she paused, confused by the gentle humming of *O Come All Ye Faithful* floating from the living room in a tenor too low for either Molly or Isa. Inside the front door set a stack of luggage and a familiar collection of camera cases.

Mr. Frye? she wondered. At this late hour? Had he brought Emma home? She gripped the banister for support as her pulse quickened and the baby flipped in her womb. With cautious steps, she descended the final five stairs and paused in the doorway.

Her eyes swiveled the room, reached into every darkened corner and behind every shadow, only there was no one else present. No one except the man stooping beneath the Christmas tree, five small presents in his arms, the lights of the tree casting a gentle glow upon his unkempt crimson locks. Hugo continued to hum the old-time carol, his heels bouncing with the rhythm.

Maggie's heart plummeted. To be so pleased, he must have reconciled with Emma. Although it appeared he had at least been delicate enough to keep the woman at a hotel until morning—when he could break the news to his second wife himself. She would at least thank him for that.

Straightening up, he stepped back to rake his gaze up and down the tree. "I never expected her to do something like this."

The baby pressed hard into Maggie's stomach at the same time something firm and terrible clenched inside her. It latched onto her breastbone and clawed its way up to settle behind her eyes. She had a dozen questions, likely more, only her voice wouldn't obey.

Hugo adjusted a fallen garland and caught sight of her lingering in the doorway. "Merry Christmas, Miss Margaret," he smiled. "The tree looks incredible."

His expression was nearly electric with excitement—so unlike any amount of happiness he had shown before—that Maggie lost every ounce of her reserve. In that tiny pocket of time while they stared at one another from across the room, she forgot to be steadfast in her strength. The fear of the last month enveloped her—the utter terror of Molly's illness, the anxiety of being overrun by Emma, and the overwhelming apprehension of bearing her child at the women's home alone. She pursed her lips around the admission that she invited another man into their home and he made a highly adequate substitute husband. With one exception—Reuben wasn't the man she pledged seven years of her life to. Now that man she had truly missed.

She *missed* Mr. Frye? Utter nonsense. She couldn't. He wasn't hers to yearn for.

Hugo cautiously stepped towards her. His smile wavered. Nervous fingers caught in his hair. "I'm sorry the hour is so late. The train was delayed, and I carried Henry up to bed first thing. Did we wake you?" When she didn't respond, his hand slipped into his pocket. It emerged holding a gold ring fashioned with a diamond and flowers on either side—her wedding ring. She puzzled why he hadn't given it to Emma.

Hugo blinked slowly, something undistinguishable hidden in his viridian stare. He drew a deep breath and offered her the ring. "I want another six years. Please."

Six years, she thought? But that was impossible.

Nothing is impossible, a voice ticked in her head. *Don't you understand, Maggie? There is no Emma. If you want to, you and your baby can stay.*

Tears cascaded down her cheeks and she hid her face behind her fingers, turning away to sob like a child. It didn't make anything better when Hugo's sturdy arms enclosed around her. He smelled of the stink of travel, like leather luggage, railway soot, and photography chemicals. Like someone who hadn't bathed in a week. He must have ridden for days on the train and paid extra in order to arrive before Christmas.

"Is it so terrible to see me?" he asked gently.

His warm breath brushed her ear, and Maggie shook her head, embarrassed as her untamed hair flew, for all she could do was cling to him and cry.

TWENTY-EIGHT

"*FRÖHLICHE WEIHNACHTEN, HERR KISCH*, and a merry Christmas."

"*Danke, Herr Rothschmitt. Fröhliche Weihnachten.*" Karl Kisch tipped his hat to the gentleman holding the door open to St. Francis de Sales Catholic Church. The clang of bells peeled in the tower above, announcing the final ten minutes before Midnight Mass would begin.

Heeling the snow from her boots, Tena followed the Kischs through the church's ornately carved double doors, all the while willing her tension to melt like the snow dripping from her shoes. After her unintended dip in the Grand Basin and the week that followed, she could certainly use a bit of spiritual intercession.

From what she had gathered from Emil's account, he, Stanley, and Reuben dragged her from the water, not Charles as she believed at the time. She had been delirious, talking nonsense the entire ride home. They could barely rouse her enough to ease her from Earhart's motorcar; however, after a bath, a warm blanket, and some chamomile tea, she slept peacefully through the night.

Being Emil—and always ready for an elaborate tale—the account also included one too many colorful phrases plus nonsense riddles with quite a few laughs for good measure. Only he could make her near demise sound a skit worthy of the theatre. Karl said the humor was because Emil had been scared out of his wits the entire time, and it only added to Tena's love for him.

For a week after, the family treated her like a delicate egg that could shatter at any moment. No one breathed a word about the incident or Charles or her father or Maggie or anything that had the slightest possibility to invoke negative emotions. The fewer questions the better. Simple replies were best. They hadn't acted so cautious since she arrived fresh off *Titanic*. But they also hadn't thought she was a hair's breadth away from doing herself in before, either.

Sliding into the narrow church pew, she settled herself between Friedrich and Emil and craned her neck to stare up at the dazzling cathedral ceiling. Decorated columns rose into intersecting arches between rose-shaded frescoes, everything leading her eye down to the main altar. Tucked on either side of the central worship space were smaller altars, one honoring the Blessed Virgin Mary and the other for St. Joseph, the Carpenter.

"Impressive, is it not?" Fred whispered. "Were you most aware that this church's construction was modeled after the tallest church in the world, Ulm Minster? In addition, the entrance portal is an exact replica of the one in Munich Cathedral." He pointed discreetly towards the altar's vibrant artwork. "All of the frescos were created by Fridolin Fuchs—ow!"

Friedrich rubbed his arm where Emil had reached across Tena to pinch him. He shot his brother a loathsome glare to which Emil merely grinned. "You're boring the lady with your history lesson, Professor."

"*Stille*, both of you," Elsa scolded. The pew returned to silence as organ strains beckoned the congregation rise for the processional.

The sweet perfume of incense rose as the processional passed, its aroma mixing with the lingering scent of four-year hewn timber and the slight must of hymnals. At this hour, only darkness lay beyond the stained glass, but Tena imagined how exquisite the space would shine with the sun. A thousand colorful rays of light would flow over the congregation, and even though the ceiling rose into shadow above them, not one person would feel small.

For far too many months, she had lived without faith in much of anything. Not since the Sunday evening service on *Titanic*—four hours before Charles handed her a book of poetry and kissed her goodbye forever. She read that one marked poem every night before she closed her eyes, the words now dedicated to memory. They played as sacred as a hymn, as though the words were written for the very melody played in the church loft above her.

Wait not the night for me / If the sun refuse to shine
If the grass does cease to grow / If the music loses rhyme

The glorious organ strains swirled deep inside, and in a place she had closed off from herself a door opened. Only a crack, the tiniest amount, but enough. Enough to pry open and free her weary heart.

Wait not the night for me / If my tomorrow never starts
If the dark goes on forever / If death has pierced my heart

Wait not the night for me / It wouldn't do you any good
To spend life waiting for my heart / When to have me you never
could

A week and a day ago, she was certain Charles was the only man she could ever love as she had, the only person to make her heart sing as he did. A week and a day ago, the pain of abandonment was still fresh as a new wound—from Charles, from her parents, from Maggie, even from God. She lived with only a toe grounded in truth and the others dangling over the edge. Then a week ago, she saw Charles under the Grand Basin's murky water, believed he saved her, and thought she kissed him. An illusion; however, an effective one. It planted all ten of her toes on the ground and slowly moved her forward for the first time since that dreaded day on *Titanic*.

Wait not the night for me / For when the day is done
To love you was to have loved you / And our hearts shall be
forever one.

Tena's heart soared, lighter than it had in years. She sang the Latin hymns and chanted the unfamiliar prayers and finally offered thanks for a night in a lifeboat and the man who forced her into it without him.

"There it is, Tena." Elbows propped on *Titanic*'s stern rail, Charles had pointed into the radiant brushstrokes of the ship's final setting sun. "Can you see it?" he urged.

Tena strained to locate anything in the open water. "What am I looking for?"

Charles grinned, his face alight like Emil's when he told a joke. "The future," he breathed. He kissed the back of her fingers and placed her hand in the crook of his arm. "*Our* future. It is as bright as the sun."

All Tena saw were the ripples of miles and miles of ocean waves. The future to her was still a world away. "When will it start?"

"Do you not know, *meine liebe*? It has already begun."

~~~

When mass concluded, Tena followed the Kischs down the expansive aisle and out into the cold December night. A full moon lit the church steps—and her future—with the same hope Charles must have felt staring into the setting sun on *Titanic*. The moon was but a reflection of the sun, a suggestion of all the joy her life might one day hold. There was eternal loveliness in her short time with Charles; she would carry its magic with her always. Then one blessed day, many miles down the road, perhaps God would shine that same enchantment with someone else.

Perhaps it was time to forgive God for how her life had altered. Maybe with His help, she could forgive everyone including herself.

She was halfway to Karl's motorcar when someone tapped her shoulder. "You were honestly going to walk right past me without so much as a 'Happy Christmas'?"

Tena spun with a smile, knowing she would see the familiar chocolate eyes that stared back at her now. "Reuben Radford," she cried. "Whyever are you here? You're not Catholic." Praise the heavens he was though. She hadn't yet had a chance to thank him for his part in her rescue.

"Neither are you," Reuben winked.

"You lousy bloke, what are you doing here?" Emil, having now noticed Tena lagging behind, walked up with Fred at the same time Winnie tackled into Reuben. Her skinny arms looped his waist with her enormous smile. "We missed you," she giggled.

"Some of us more than others," Emil said. "Twice in one week, mate? You might want to lower the frequency." He frowned, but then his upper lip lifted into a smirk. "Happy Christmas, mate."

Reuben reached around Winnie to clasp Emil's hand. "I had a few issues to get off my chest with the man upstairs. Besides, I wanted to be the first to wish your family *Fröhliche Weihnachten.*"

"Sorry, mate. Herr Rothschmitt claimed that honor at the door."

"Upstaged by a man thrice my age," Reuben declared with a shake of his head. "Winnie, between us, can we pretend I was first?"

"'Course." She motioned for him to bend closer. "Do you think Father Christmas will bring my presents here or take them to our old house in Fontaine? I wrote him a letter, but I'm still worried."

"My word, Winnie," Fred admonished. "You still believe in that old superstition?"

Winnie pressed a hand to either hip. "'Course I do. I bet Reuben does too."

Reuben threw Fred his fiercest scowl. "You bet your plum pudding I do. Don't listen to him, Winnie. Father Christmas knows exactly where to leave your presents."

Winnie stuck out her tongue at Fred and after giving Reuben another squeeze, skipped off to the waiting motorcar. She climbed in beside her mother while Karl leaned over the Rambler's hood, cranking it to life. When the engine caught, he straightened and caught sight of the others as they approached the auto.

"Well, I say, if it isn't the prodigal son returned! *Fröhliche Weihnachten.*" He and Reuben clasped hands with equal pleasure. "Wonderful to see you again, son. What brings you out this way at midnight?"

Reuben released Karl's hand and readjusted his satchel, an item Tena found odd he would carry to mass. Upon a quick visual check, she found his entire appearance a bit of a mystery. He owned more sophisticated suits, so why would he select such a poor one for church? It didn't even match. The newspaper must be running him ragged.

"I considered what you told me, Mr. Kisch," Reuben said. "You were correct about most of it, and a man doesn't appreciate being called out when he's foolish. So, I'm moving out of the Vines'."

Emil's jaw dropped. "You're ditching Hazel?"

"I am not," Reuben corrected. "I simply think your father was right. I shouldn't be living so close to her; it invokes temptation, and being alone will give me time to think things through."

Karl clasped Reuben's shoulder. "Good for you, son."

"Thanks for still thinking of me as your son. I've acted like a poor sod over the past months. I'd sorely like to make things right between us again."

"Christmas dinner." Karl nodded. "That will make it right."

Reuben shook his head. "I promised that to Miss Vine, and I think I should keep my promise."

"Breakfast then. Bring your *Fräulein* with you."

"That I believe I can do." Reuben approached Tena then, just as she had begun to wonder if the entire family had forgotten her existence. "Will you allow me to escort you home? Or would you prefer to take the auto and we'll speak tomorrow?"

Reuben held a hand out to her with the sorriest eyes she had ever seen. Or rather quite a lot sorrier than she had seen him since the night she found him huddled on the floor in the midst of a massive breakdown over her sister. With a face like that he could never keep her off for too long, especially if he succumbed to his usual chivalry.

She slipped her arm through his. "I believe I'll walk tonight."

"Oi, no," Emil groaned. He kicked the auto's rear wheel and pointed at Friedrich with a most inappropriate finger. "You are *not* sticking me with Mr. Killjoy on the ride home. I'm walking too."

Karl gripped his son's collar and pushed him towards the open motorcar. "Stop this nonsense. You are brothers. Find some common ground."

"Fat chance of that." Emil folded his arms with a scowl now directed back at Reuben. "It's awfully late to walk alone. What if you're mugged?"

"As if some scrawny kid like you could protect them," Fred scoffed. He gave a snort and squeezed himself into the back of the Rambler behind his mother and sister.

"Scrawny?" Emil yelped. "I'll show you who's scrawny. Get out here and back up your fat mouth."

"Emil, enough!" Karl shoved his youngest son towards the auto. "Inside now and not another word."

Fred scooted over to make room on the bench. "She's safe with Reuben. For pity's sake, Emil, cut your squirrelly nose out of their business."

Emil pointed a finger at Reuben as he stepped up into the motorcar. An odd warning poised in his gesture. "*Nothing* will happen."

Tena waited until the doors were secured to speak again. "I swear they are all acting stranger by the day. Completely overprotective of me."

"Is it so terrible to care?" Reuben asked.

"There is such a thing as caring too much."

They waved as the Kischs pulled away from the curb. The Rambler rounded the corner and disappeared. Alone at last, she thought, with the one person she hadn't been alone with in months. She savored the warmth emanating through Reuben's overcoat as they started down Lynch Street. "Karl and Elsa think I tried to do myself in at the Basin," she explained. "So they've decided to guard me like a porcelain statue. They think I'll break if they push too far too soon. I didn't want to take my own life, you know."

"I know."

They walked the next several blocks in silence. Between the moon and the street lamps, they had all the light they required. Their feet crunched in the packed snow on the walk while breath fogged around their faces.

"Well, Reuben," she said finally, as they turned onto Lemp Avenue. "Let's not pretend you didn't ask to walk me home for a reason."

"I want you to promise me that you won't linger too long over Charles."

"Reuben, what ...?"

He paused in the light of the next street lamp. "If you see Charles again like you did in the Grand Basin, promise you'll walk the other way. Don't keep him alive, not in that way. It isn't worth it." His eyes darted into the corners of the dark. He was scared; she could feel it.

"It won't happen to me how your sister did to you. I promise I won't see him again."

"You can't promise that. Madness isn't something you plan. It just happens."

Tena edged closer, gently prodding him on down the walk. She had heard the story of his affliction from Maggie at the same time her sister spilled every other one of his secrets. Owning those truths had led to many intimate conversations during the first months she and Reuben were in St. Louis and a deep-seated friendship she would never trade. One she hoped she now had back.

"Seeing Charles was a byproduct of the cold and lack of air. I was about to *drown*, Reuben. People see what they most want when they're on death's doorstep."

"That's what Charles said too."

She pulled to an abrupt stop. "Pardon me, but what did you say?"

Reuben ran a hand through his hair and urged her onwards, his pace speeding up with the rate of his words. "I promised myself I wouldn't tell you yet about the night Charles sent me back from my grave. That's how I learned he had died. He appeared in my dream limbo and sent me back for you. You were standing on a house porch, dressed all in black, but more beautiful than I had ever seen you. You told me then that I reminded you to have hope. I swore I'd wait to tell you until Charles's specter wasn't hanging over our heads, when you were no longer in mourning and finally able to wear the bright colors that lighten your hair and sparkle in your eyes. I guess I broke that promise, didn't I?"

"I had no idea," she whispered. Even in death, Charles was always looking out for them, saving them, telling them to hang on and have hope. The world hadn't stopped. The living world didn't end no matter how many times your personal world felt like it had.

She managed a half laugh. "We're so alike, aren't we? We both see Charles when we fall in freezing water."

He returned her nervous laughter, finally slowing his pace as they approached the Kischs'. She could have walked forever with him; there was so much more to say and far too long since they spoke so openly. She wouldn't force him, though. If this was the first step towards fully restoring their friendship, she wouldn't push him where he didn't yet wish to go.

Reuben released her arm and readjusted his satchel strap again. "Goodnight, Tena. I'll see you tomorrow for breakfast. If I'm lucky, Hazel will be with me."

Tena lifted her lip halfway in question. "Are you truly moving out of her home?"

"I think it's for the best, don't you? It'll provide some perspective. They tell me absence makes the heart grow fonder."

"Then you should have this." Before she could think twice, she reached behind her neck and unclasped a length of chain which she pulled from beneath her dress. A simple gold band slid off the end and she could almost hear Reuben's heart skip as she laid it in his hand. She couldn't worry about his discomfort. Her mind was made up. She had taken the first step to healing that evening at mass. The second step was letting go of Charles one small piece at a time. She just couldn't let the pieces go too far.

"Charles's wedding ring," she explained. He turned the ring over in his palm. "The Kischs never knew I had it. I never showed it to them. I think you should have it now though. I think that's what Charles would have wanted."

"What about Emil?" he stuttered. "Or Fred?"

"He didn't visit them in a dream, did he? He came back for you."

"You believe that it was really Charles then? Not my insane imagination?"

"Don't you?"

Reuben stared at the ring between his fingers and then ran the heel of his palm across his eyes.

"I want you to use it when you marry," Tena continued. "More so, I want you to know you have my blessing with Hazel. When you told me you were serious with her, at first it hurt terribly. The wound of Charles was still so fresh ... but the truth is I've always wanted every good thing for you. So, why not this, the happiest of all things? If you love Hazel and want to marry her, then you should. She's lovely, and I will be so very pleased if you do."

His eyes remained glued to the ring, "You would?"

"That girl is mad about you. The way she rants you'd think you had kisses made of pure gold." She chuckled. "Luella and Phoebe are beyond jealous." His eyes still hadn't raised and his frown only deepened at her words. "You needn't worry. Hazel's nothing like Maggie. There isn't a chance she'll say no."

Finally, he slid the band onto his right hand and lifted his gaze. "Can't have her thinking I'm assuming too much before I even ask, now can we?" He clasped her hands and then pressed them to his lips with a smile. "Thank you, Tena. Happy Christmas."

"For the man who helped save my life, it's the least I can do." His close proximity warmed the night, his breath smelling of tobacco and coffee. Tendrils of his russet hair fluttered in the breeze and she had never been more thankful to God and to Charles who would save this man so they could be together this Christmas. No parents for either of them and no siblings, but they had the Kischs and they had each other. Reuben returned to her exactly as Maggie said he would.

"Happy Christmas, Reuben," she said with a squeeze of his hands. "Promise you won't drift too far."

Beep, bee..bee, beep.

A black Model T pulled up to the curb, horn blasting despite the late hour. The driver reached across the seat and threw open the passenger side door, bracing his hand against the cushion. "Get in, Miss Archer," he called.

"Who in the world?" Reuben positioned himself in front of Tena and bent to catch the man's identity. A cool frown crossed his lips. "Mr. Frye? Are you not supposed to be in Utah?"

"*Hugo* Frye?" Tena leaned around Reuben, astonished when she saw Hugo's frazzled expression, his hair as rumpled as the pajama bottoms visible beneath his overcoat. "It's nearly three in the morning, Mr. Frye. Whatever are you doing here?"

"Whose vehicle is this?" Reuben bit out before the man could respond. "Last I checked you didn't have the funds for a new auto."

"I haven't time for inane questions," Hugo burst out. His fingers kneaded the passenger seat's supple leather. "I borrowed the motorcar from my neighbor and, not that it's your concern, but I *was* in Utah. Circumstances dictated I return early."

"What circumstances are those?"

"Reuben." Tena stepped between him and the open door, a warning in her gaze. He had his legs braced and hands clenched like he was ready to have a go at the poor man, and for what reason she couldn't fathom. "Go home, Reuben. I can handle this."

"No."

Tena blew out a hot breath and turned back to Hugo. Reuben lingered beyond her left shoulder. "My apologies, Mr. Frye. I'm afraid Mr. Radford is rather tired. We've only just returned from midnight mass and—"

"The baby is coming. Maggie asked for you."

She grabbed the edge of the door frame. "The baby? She has?"

Hugo shifted until his face was visible in the dim light from the street lamp. A five o'clock shadow wrapped his goatee and above that, his eyes swam with an anxious father's plea. "Yes. Of course she did."

Tena's heart pounded. She thought she had come to terms tonight at mass. She thought if she made peace with God then maybe she could forgive her sister. But she hadn't planned it would be tonight. She figured she would have days to perfect exactly what to say. Now here she was with only a stranger's word and no time left to prepare.

"I should send Elsa. She's done this before ..." Tena turned away, but Hugo caught her hand before she could remove it from the door frame.

"She asked for *you*."

"Are they in danger?" Reuben asked in alarm.

With a shudder, Hugo released Tena and moved back into his seat. "I haven't any idea. We can't afford a doctor."

Thoughts flooded Tena's mind, a jumble she couldn't untie without a proper night's sleep, and one that if she stepped in that motorcar, she wouldn't manage anytime soon. Seeing her sister after five months not speaking ... and in such a vulnerable state as childbirth ... with a new little niece or nephew to remind Tena again of lost dreams with Charles ... was now the right time to beg forgiveness or to give it? It was Christmas after all—the time for miracles.

A terrible realization lodged in her chest like a painful bout of heartburn. There was no wonder for the haggard appearance on Reuben's face, as though experiencing a nightmare when he wasn't even asleep. Surely he had already figured what she only now realized. If Maggie met Hugo in June, then the baby was early. Far too early. One miracle that wouldn't be.

Forget planning what she would say to her sister. She would become a master of improvisation.

She pressed a flustered kiss to Reuben's cheek. "Tell Karl and Elsa I'll ring when the baby's here." Without an answer, he pulled her into his arms and squeezed her to his chest. His lips found her temple twice before releasing her towards the auto.

Accepting Hugo's hand, Tena folded herself into the passenger seat and yanked the door closed.

TWENTY-NINE

THE FIRST LABOR PAIN FELT LIKE an awful intestinal cramp. In fact, that's what Maggie originally thought it was. She crept to the toilet an hour after falling asleep, tiptoeing around Hugo's sleeping form and down the stairs. After thirty minutes without relief, she brewed an extra dark pot of Earl Grey and drank three cups straight. By the time she finished the final one, she realized the horrible sensations were not from eating tainted beef and could barely see through tears of pain.

Returning to bed, she laid back while her insides ached and sweat soaked clear through her nightgown into the bedsheets. Her teeth clenched against a moan as every inch of her body tensed from ribcage to pelvis. *You musn't panic*, she repeated. *If Mother could do this, so can you.*

Another hour passed and still she couldn't force herself to wake Hugo. He slept so soundless, curled on his side like a little boy, one lock of hair flat across his forehead. But what was to be her other option? Give birth while he slept below her? She had no education on the process and what if the child was stillborn? It wasn't yet time, that much she knew even if she couldn't pinpoint the exact date to expect the child. A doctor could probably have calculated it down to the hour, if only she had bothered to visit one. If only she wasn't always so stubborn and careless.

At least the baby continued moving. Kicking so strong and so often that she wondered if her excessive tea intake was actually poison, and the child was slowly drowning in its own fluid.

In between painful fits she slept and in dreams waited the same mysterious stranger from Shaw's Garden.

He appeared in a prestigious townhouse which overlooked the entirety of London. The windows of a well-kept parlor opened onto a luscious park, vibrant trees of green rustling in the breeze while pedestrians prattled by. Maggie crouched within the room's cupboard, and when the doors flung open, she met blue eyes the color of the summer's sky. The stranger's hands reached down to guide her from her hiding place.

"Who are you?" she asked. "Why do I continue to dream of you?"

"Let me show you." In the squeeze of his hand, the room dissolved, melting like watercolors on a canvas. Hand in hand they traveled through the haze, nothing entirely distinguishable from anything else. With another wave of his hand, violet blossoms floated from above in a glorious display—the elongated petals of her mystery flower.

"Look at it, Magdalena." He spread a palm across the sky. "Look at this world I created for you exactly as you asked." A violet haze engulfed her, petals falling from the clouds to bury her beneath them. He held her in place even as she scrambled to escape.

"Please!" she screamed. "I'm not who you think. I'm not Magdalena!"

Her fingers stretched upward, grasping at empty air. She would suffocate in a sea of flowers and her child would never even experience its first breath. Moaning, she pressed a hand to her middle and came up empty. The fabric of her dress hung loose.

"Where is she?" she cried. "Where's my baby?" Her lips parted, only screaming required air of which she now had none. Only flowers. Flowers and the final words of a mysterious dark-haired visitor.

"You can't escape who you are, Magdalena. It's a part of you, the same as it was a part of me."

Maggie's eyes shot open, one hand at the collar of her damp nightgown. She stared at the ceiling, and the beat of her heart could have kept pace with the racehorses of Aintree. Logic told her dreams were no indication of reality, except that Reuben's dreams had been.

He learned of Charles's death when in an unconscious state and upon waking found it to be so.

She anxiously kneaded her stomach, certain the anonymous dream menace managed to kill her child while she slept. "Be there," she whispered. "Please kick me into next Friday."

And there it was—searing pain as a tiny foot collided with her prying hand. Her baby was alive. She slumped back against the pillows as the movement subsided, and a small laugh passed through her lips.

"Oh, wonderful, you have awoken. I'm drawing back the curtains, your husband's wishes be forgotten."

Maggie winced as the room flooded with morning light, revealing Mrs. Kincade's irritated form. She set a bowl of steaming water on the writing desk and positioned herself at the foot of the bed. The blankets had been completely stripped away, leaving Maggie in only a damp, now translucent nightgown and modesty every bit compromised.

"Let's have a look shall we?" Mrs. Kincade said.

Maggie kicked out as the unsightly woman moved to raise her nightgown, "Why-are-you-here?" she managed to snap. "Where-is-Mr.-Frye?" The trundle bed was currently hidden away from sight and Hugo's personal effects vacant from their usual nightly location atop the dresser. Had he sent for the neighbor and left? How did he even know she was in labor when she hadn't whispered a word? Heavens, had she said something in her sleep?

"Downstairs with the sister," Mrs. Kincade explained. "He borrowed my auto to retrieve her for you. She asked that I help you out, seeing as I did this for Emma too."

A hiss whistled past Maggie's lips with another fierce ache to her abdomen. Hugo invited Damaris? That witch *would* summon Emma's former midwife and assign her to oversee the delivery. Maggie pinched her eyes closed and breathed through another labor pain.

"Get out," she spat when her muscles finally loosened. "I'll not have the woman who touched Emma do the same for me. I'd rather bear this child forever."

"Don't be ridiculous, Mrs. Frye. 'Sides, I already checked you twice while you were out cold."

"How dare you." Maggie pressed her knees together, but in the same breath strained against further tightening around her middle and complied to the woman's examination.

"Well, I'd say we're nearly there, thank the Lord." Mrs. Kincade lowered Maggie's gown and wiped her hands on her apron. Maggie didn't want to think about what exactly would need wiping away while she gritted her teeth through the continued wave of discomfort.

She snapped towards the pile of discarded bedding. "Toss one of those over me," Maggie ordered, "then fetch Mr. Frye."

Stooping for the goldenrod quilt—fabric much too heavy in the already stifling room—Mrs. Kincade dropped it on Maggie's chest and yanked the door open. "Calm down or you'll overwork yourself and hurt the baby." She leaned into the hallway. "She's callin' for you."

"I heard."

Maggie drew the quilt over herself as Hugo hurried in, legitimate worry wrinkling his forehead more so than the pajama pants beneath his dressing gown. She jerked back when he reached for the damp hair plastered against her forehead. "Leave it."

All three children peered around the doorway. "Is it time for presents?" Isa asked.

Molly took in her stepmother's face scrunched with pain, and her innocent eyes grew round as dinner plates. "Daddy, is Miss Margaret ill?"

Mrs. Kincade ran over and nudged the door closed against their pleas. "Go downstairs with your aunt, children. Your stepmother is fine."

"But—" Henry cried, but the door had already swung closed. Mrs. Kincade twisted the lock. "Hey! Dad!" He extended a final futile bang on the door then stomped down the stairs. The patter of his sisters' feet followed.

Maggie breathed through the contraction as much as to breathe through the mess of emotions playing through her head. This wasn't how her first child's birth should be. She needed family nearby—real family, not one she had contracted. Her father more than any other. She longed to be seven again, dancing around his study while he read stories she never fully listened to at the time. She would sit for them now. She would curl up on the sofa beside him, rest her head against his shoulder, and listen to his soothing voice forever. He could hold her baby and laugh at how its little nose and perfect brow were an exact match to his.

Maggie turned to Hugo. "Send for Tena. When this is over, I need her forgiveness."

"I already went for Tena hours ago."

"Oh."

Of course. Tena wouldn't come. That was it. Maggie had stayed away too long and lost her sister for good. This was her fault as always. How could she have hoped to raise a baby without her sister? In the midst of her most terrible pain, she managed to feel even worse.

"Why so sad?" Hugo asked. "Tena's caring for the children. It was she who convinced me to retrieve Mrs. Kincade against my better judgment."

The midwife gave a mighty roll of her eyes and stepped behind Hugo, forcing him forward until his knees hit the bed. "We're a family," he continued, "unusual though we are, and we should begin acting like one. That family includes your sister." He reached up to scratch his temple, cheeks tinged with embarrassment. "For what it's worth, I told Tena you sent for her. But I don't regret the lie. I would have told her anything to get her here."

"Tena's here? Not Damaris?"

Hugo smiled gently. "Of course not Damaris. Wouldn't you think I know you better than that?"

Maggie shook her head in amazement. Tena was *here,* caring for her sister's stepchildren although she never met them, all because Hugo knew his wife better than she knew herself. Her passive partner finally found his voice, and he had found it for her.

Her stomach tightened, and through the haze, she heard the midwife say, "We're nearly there. Mr. Frye, out of the room."

Maggie lashed out for Hugo's wrist. "Don't leave," she breathed. "Please. I need you too."

He appeared suddenly terrified. "You want me to *stay*? But I've never done this before."

"Are you mental? Where'd you think the other three came from? Father Christmas?"

"I was always out there. She never let me watch."

"You're not watching. You're standing here next to me, reminding me to breathe, holding my hand, and oh my word, it hurts." Every muscle strained as the pain intensified, and a sob escaped unbidden. She had no idea it would feel like this. Those women who claimed the experience didn't hurt so much if you simply breathed through it? They were out of their minds.

Mrs. Kincade shoved a wet cloth into Hugo's free hand, water dripping across the floorboards. "If you're going to stay, for heaven's sake, be useful. Wipe her brow."

He did as he was told, eyes always on Maggie's face while he watched her labor a child who wasn't his. The first time he had ever seen someone give birth, and she wasn't even his real wife.

Another contraction squeezed her insides then another until it seemed she would tear apart and the agony would never end. Her nails left crescent moon marks on his hand. A dull throb sliced across her forehead.

"Breathe, Miss Margaret, don't forget."

She exhaled in a burst, the ache across her skull easing. "I can't do this," she gasped.

Without asking, he set the damp cloth in the basin and knelt to where his face was level with hers. Ever so gently, he smoothed back the matted hair from her face and whispered, "You *can* do this." His fingers gripped hers. "I will help you do this."

Through the next moments, whether they were but minutes or hours, Hugo never left Maggie's side. Before today, he had never seen this version of her—a fragile woman coated in sweat and crying for relief. She didn't feel strong or independent or alluring. Her body was out of control and her mind had forgotten every piece of herself. Something had broken, and try as she might, within the confines of such terrible pain she couldn't remember who she was or what she should be.

With a final strain, a cry erupted into the room, that first sound a newborn babe emits to stretch its lungs.

"You have a ruddy-faced little daughter!" Mrs. Kincade declared. She lifted the slight pink body all covered in mess. Those tiny fingers reached for something they didn't even know, so frightened to be out in the unknown. The midwife wiped the infant's face, gave a firm swat to her behind and back in turn, then laid the baby atop the quilt still draped across her mother's chest. Maggie shifted her free arm around the tiny body, encouraging warmth after being pulled into this cold cruel world. The child snuggled up, her cry bold and determined.

This miniature being shouldn't belong to her, Maggie decided. Surely fate made a mistake and would demand its ransom returned. There could not possibly be a book which listed her name underneath "competent women sanctioned for motherhood."

Hugo eased himself up onto the bed beside them, his eyes unable to leave this new incredible life. This child wasn't of his making; she would never look like him or share a drop of his blood. But sitting there on that bright and beautiful Christmas morning in nineteen hundred and twelve, watching his wife cradle their newborn daughter, heaven help her if Maggie didn't recognize how much he loved that little girl.

With something almost resembling a smile, Mrs. Kincade retrieved the now cooled water bowl and carried it towards the door. "I'll give you a minute with her. It'll provide me time to fetch some more water and clean linens."

The door closed and Maggie's eyes locked with Hugo's to find his emotion matched her own.

"I'm glad you're here," she rasped. "Thank you."

"I promised I would be home in time." He squeezed her hand, gently circling his thumb across her knuckles while his sights ventured somewhere far outside themselves. "Tena said I shouldn't tell you this, but for months I've been afraid of what I would feel right now. I never thought I could love someone who didn't even belong to me." He ran the side of his free hand down the baby's smooth cheek to the corner of her tiny lips where she turned to gum at his fingers. A whimper escaped, and Hugo's eyes welled with tears. He didn't bother to brush them away. "I marvel now at how wrong I was."

How could Maggie not forgive him for the same sins she herself was guilty of? She recalled now that first cool September day when the gentle butterfly wings inside her belly first turned to distinguishable kicks. Without her father or a legitimate husband to share it with, the concept that she had a person attacking her insides became a sudden disturbing reality, and she couldn't acknowledge it for the beauty that it was. She could only feel the movement inside her and curse what a crime it was that this child existed, what an injustice to be borne of Maggie's worst mistakes.

You are not a mistake, she thought now as she smoothed back her daughter's dark curls. *How could anyone so lovely ever be a mistake?*

Lashes fluttered as tiny eyelids eased apart. Round brown eyes stared out with such devotion and such ignorance as only a child could master. This baby didn't know the truth of who her mother was or the fiery temptress she once had been. She didn't know the lies her mother told, the people hurt, or the deals made on the path to becoming Mrs. Frye. This child loved Maggie unconditionally. She was the only person alive who did.

Maggie released Hugo's hand so she could offer their daughter into his arms. He cradled the child with nothing short of reverence. "Her name should be Abigail," she said. "It means 'My father is joyful.'"

"Abigail," Hugo agreed. He eased his lips to the baby's miniature brow. "Abigail Lorraine Frye. Now there's an American name if ever there was one." He laughed, and it was a sound more lovely than all the chimes of the world playing in harmony. "Abbie, my girl, your father could not be more joyful at your existence."

Claim your happiness, my little girl, Laurence Archer wrote in his final letter. *Love will find you one day.*

Don't worry, Father, Maggie thought. *Love has already found me. It's this. It's her.*

THIRTY

TENA STAYED ON WITH THE FRYES for thirteen weeks after Abigail was born, as much to assist Maggie with the new baby as to realign their sisterhood. Henry temporarily moved onto a pallet in the girls' room without fuss—or not much anyway—leaving Tena his bed while a cradle was assembled in the master bedroom. Hugo was careful to store the trundle bed before leaving the room each morning; it wouldn't do any good if they aroused suspicion. Even after so many months, they still hadn't spoken of Hugo's trip to Utah. He had offered to stay for the remainder of their contract; what good would it do to question the reason?

Twice each week brought visits from Winnie and Elsa. Winnie would play with the children in the living room while the older women chatted over tea and Elsa fawned over Abigail. She may not have been blood; however, a more loving substitute grandmother there could never be.

But today it was only the two sisters alone in the kitchen, Maggie slicing cherries while Tena cuddled Abigail against her shoulder. "Have you talked to Reuben lately?" she asked.

Tena traced Abigail's dark curls with her thumb. "Not since Christmas. I've been here helping you. When would I have the time?"

"I thought he might have rang. Perhaps one day while I was napping." Juicy cherry flesh splattered between her fingers. She scraped it into the bowl and wiped her hands on her apron.

252

"Not that I recall. Why do you ask?"

"You mentioned how he worried at Christmas. I assumed he would call before now."

In her sleep, Abigail whimpered, and Tena rubbed her back with a gentle sway. "Mrs. Kisch keeps him updated. I'm certain he feels visiting would only be a nuisance."

"I suppose." Maggie raised her hand to tuck a stray lock of hair back into her untamed coif and heard a sharp click behind her. She spun in her chair and tender muscles tugged along her side, a lingering reminder that three months ago she was round as a hot air balloon. Centered inside the doorway, Hugo stared into his black Brownie positioned against his stomach. She hadn't even noticed him steal it from the kitchen counter after breakfast.

Maggie frowned. "You've chosen this, of all times, to photograph me? My appearance resembles a wrecked barge on the Thames."

"I wouldn't know what that looks like." Hugo peered up through his lashes and flipped the lever on the little box. The shutter clicked open then closed again as it captured another frame. "Walter Persons has been making decent enough change with his works. We could use the money."

She sliced through another cherry and flicked the pit onto the pile. "You are not pedaling pictures of me."

"Yet. You wait; I'll convince you."

"Fair warning: If you continue to address me with such cheek, Mr. Frye, I'll ship you and Damaris off to California. You can both live with your sisters."

"I hope that's a promise and not a threat. Damaris would hold you in the highest regard." He swiped the cherry from her hand and popped it into his mouth. "Although the good Lord knows how I would miss changing diapers."

A slow smile met her lips. "Good. Why don't you carry Abigail upstairs and make a memory? She's soiled herself so much today I wish I hadn't bothered to dress her."

With a sweet, albeit sarcastic, smile, he stole the infant from Tena. He pressed a soft kiss to Abigail's forehead before planting her against his chest. "Don't you worry, Abbie girl. Daddy will take care of you. Woah!" he exclaimed as three children plowed through the door nearly bowling their father over. "Bacon and beans, where are you rushing to?"

Molly reached for Abigail. "Isa and I want to play tea party with the baby."

"But I want to take her outside," Henry whined. "This house is too prissy. Can't we have another boy?"

Hugo flushed as red as his hair. "Maybe your schoolmates could stop by one day instead."

"Ugh, not the same." Henry stomped his feet and muttered about unfairness all the way out into the backyard.

With a shake of his head, Hugo ushered his daughters towards the door. "Come help me with the baby, little ladies, and then we'll see what we might accomplish with that tea party." He crooked his chin back at Maggie. "Worry not, Mrs. Frye. I'll ensure all tea is drunk and diapers changed before I hop on the next train west."

Maggie rolled her eyes and shooed him away with her knife. She sliced through another cherry and deposited the pieces into the bowl before glancing once more at the doorway. "He's incorrigible sometimes."

With the scrape of chair legs against floorboards, Tena rounded the table and threw her arms around her sister's shoulders. "I'm so pleased you finally found your Charles, sister dear. Father would be so proud." She kissed Maggie's temple. "I am too."

"I wouldn't go so far as to compare him with Charles. He certainly doesn't squeeze my heart or flutter my innards. But he loves Abigail so I suppose that's enough for me."

"I still envy you Maggie, and that's a way I thought I'd never feel."

"Oh, Tena, don't envy me. Happiness isn't always so simple as it seems." Tena wanted Maggie to have a happy ending as terribly as she wanted one for herself. But what was the use in assuring her of something that simply wasn't? Endings nearly by definition were never happy. She couldn't fade into someone with too much heart and lose the solid-shouldered realist she prided herself in.

Maggie worried that her behavior during Abigail's birth had shifted—nay, complicated—the dynamic of her partnership with Mr.

Frye. Out of her mind with pain, she had said things she couldn't fully remember afterwards and didn't fully understand. He stayed beside her and she was grateful, but now weeks later she wondered if it hadn't been an awful mistake. They needed to remember what this marriage was and what it was not. She couldn't have him developing true affection for her, not when they still had so many years left together. Not when she had the looming problem of Abigail's paternity to worry about.

Tena still hadn't asked about Abigail's stature—slight, but not nearly enough so for any sane person to believe she was conceived in early June. Or how Maggie's blue-grey eyes and Hugo's green could never result in such a solid brown. Tena was either completely ignorant of such facts—unlikely—or choosing to play her hand as such. No, without solid proof, she would rather play the silent fool than chance another rift with her sister or her closest friend.

Maggie wouldn't be so lucky when it came to Reuben. He was a man of action and emotions worn securely on his sleeve. Once he saw Abigail, he would recognize the truth in a heartbeat, and everything was certain to come tumbling down. One day soon she would need to devise a plan to tell them, but perhaps the blow of Reuben's sudden fatherhood could best be broken after addressing more pressing matters?

Removing herself from Tena's embrace, Maggie silently walked upstairs, retrieved a certain worn envelope from the depths of her traveling case, and returned to the kitchen. She handed over Father's letter without explanation. None was needed. Her sister deserved to read it long ago, if only Maggie hadn't feared Tena would seek out explanation for their father's words.

There is a secret your mother holds, and once I am gone, she will not hesitate to tell you. I am sorry I cannot explain myself. It is her secret to reveal, although I fear she will attempt to destroy you with the truth.

It wasn't that Maggie shared the letter now because she was braver or wiser or anything more than she always had been. She wasn't. It was her small world which had expanded. Now there was someone more important than herself. Now there was Abigail.

Tena folded the letter and returned it to the envelope. Her expression lay far more stoic than Maggie expected. "Have you written to Mother?"

"No. I swore to kill my curiosity after how far I went with Lloyd. I promised myself I would never ask ... but that was before Abbie."

"And now?"

"Now I'm not certain of anything." Maggie tapped the letter. "Father believed Mother would tell us the truth, but she didn't. Why? It isn't like her to see an opportunity to hurt us and not use it." She seized Tena's wrist. "Come with me. I need to show you something."

They ran across the backyard, yanking open the carriage house door to slip into the chilly room. After Hugo sold his motorcar two years back, the building had stood empty except for a few miscellaneous gardening tools stored in the disused horse stalls, and a narrow wooden table against the far wall. Five vases lined the surface, each containing an assortment of purple flowers. Their aromatic fragrance filled the open space.

"I continue to dream about these," Maggie said by way of an explanation. Of course, that told Tena nothing, but there was so much to say and no good place to start. Her sister would surely think her explanation mad.

Tena approached the table. "You dream about *flowers*? Why only in shades of violet?"

"Have you heard of the Magdalena flower?"

"Was that variety in the Winchesters' gardens? They had so many. Something about the name sounds terribly familiar, like I should know but have forgotten."

Maggie breathed a sigh of relief. Good, she thought. She wasn't the only one then.

"The Winchesters didn't grow them; I knew those beds inside and out."

"Where then?"

"That is the question, isn't it? Shortly after Abigail's birth, I posted a letter to a horticulturist at Shaw's Garden inquiring into the

Magdalena's existence. Bully for me, he never heard of it. I then surmised that the dreams might be a lingering product of pregnancy, except they still haven't stopped." She nodded to the vases. "So I purchased every type of purple flower I could find and brought them here in hopes one might trigger something."

"All those *walks* alone this week to clear your head, get some fresh air and time away from the baby? You were visiting floral shops? How did you find so many?"

"It was no easy task, I assure you. I didn't want to bother you if my search came to naught, and according to everything I've found, it has. No florist ever heard of the Magdalena."

"Because you invented it."

Tena's condescending tone grated Maggie's nerves. "What if I didn't? What if everything is interrelated—Father's letter, my dreams, the man in shadow?"

"What man?" Tena's patronizing smile vanished. "Maggie, what affliction are you suffering from?"

"I'm in my right mind." Maggie ventured to the window where Henry tossed his baseball near the garden. "The day we visited Shaw's Garden, there was a man watching me. He followed us into the Herbarium, however, fled when I caught him staring. Before I could track him down, he vanished." She turned from the window, bathed half in sunlight and half in shadow. "He's in my dreams, Tena. He calls *me* Magdalena and says he created the flower especially for me. Only I can't recall ever being familiar with him or the flower."

Tena now appeared truly concerned. "It was a *dream*, Maggie, and a stranger in a garden who mistook you for someone else. Discomfiture caused him to flee. There isn't a conspiracy we need to solve."

Maggie pressed a hand to her forehead. It *was* all connected. She couldn't shake the feeling; the more she tried to stave it off, the worse it became. Returning to the table, she focused on the flowers until her vision blurred into a sea of violet. She knew each of their names and had always loved them, even the ones with thorns, even those deemed unlovable. Exactly how she always believed her father felt about her until Damaris planted the seed of doubt with her own father's indifference. Hugo's absence on his quest for Emma only made that seed sprout, and Abigail's birth made it flower.

"Tena, can you recall what our life was like before Fontaine? Mother and Father never once spoke of it. They never mentioned what he did before Fontaine or why he return traveled to London after."

"He went on business."

"Except that could mean so much! Personal business, banker's business, secret trysts with a lover, obscene dark alley deals with unseemly characters. Who was he meeting? Why did he always leave us behind? Why didn't we ask? There are so many more questions within this letter than the one he mentioned."

As expected, Tena stared as though Maggie had misplaced the last of her shooting marbles. "Do you truly believe Father capable of such a deal? Or taking an extraneous mistress? He loved Mother."

"Mother never loved him back. He knew that—heavens, we all knew that."

"But do you believe him capable of such behavior?"

"No. Father was a man among men. It's impossible to fathom him locked in deceit."

Tena folded her arms and sat back against the table. "So, there. Do you see? You've built a dramatic exchange inside your mind that could never be."

Maggie wanted to shake her. This wasn't nothing. Perhaps she overreacted about the stranger, but she hadn't invented Father's letter or his words of warning. She breathed out then in then out again. "I have Abigail to protect now. What if the truth involves some*one* who could place her in danger when I'm not around? Can I leave so much open to chance? I'm willing to risk my own future, my happiness, my everything to never know, but am I truly willing to risk hers?" She lighted a hand on Tena's arm. "I have an accursed past already, Tena. Isn't it better that we know the battle we have in store?"

Tena glared at her. "I already know the battle in store. To find out the facts, Father's sent us to a woman who would rather toss her daughters to the lions than overcome her prejudices. I won't go back there."

Still clutching Father's letter, Tena unlatched the carriage house door and began at a rapid pace across the yard. Maggie gave chase, quickly winded post-pregnancy, but managing to stay near enough. "Wait, Tena," she called.

Tena didn't slow. "Leave me alone, Maggie. We're on good terms, lest you say something stupid and ruin it."

"It's been a year. Perhaps Mother will be reasonable after a year."

Tena stopped in her tracks but didn't turn. "Because of Mother our father never knew about the most important pieces of me. Often I wonder how glad might he have been if I spoke up?" Tena shook her head. "Then I realize I'm fooling myself. Look how Mother reacted when we did tell her. She disowned us. If she knew all along, those months with Charles very well would have never been." She passed the letter back to Maggie. "A year or ten, I can't speak to her. If I do, she'll feel the palm of my hand and never hear an apology. So let the past die."

She rounded the house, Maggie on her heels, and nearly plowed into a man coming up the walk. He wore a freshly pressed suit with attaché in hand and a grim smile. "Do excuse me, ladies, but are you the misses Archer?"

"Yes, sir." Tena didn't accept the hand he extended to her. "What is your business here?"

"My name is Alfred Goodfellow." He shuffled through his attaché and removed a long packet closed with an indigo seal. "I carry a matter of importance concerning Laurence Archer's final will and testament."

"You must have the wrong misses Archer," Tena said. "Our father's will was resolved over a year hence." She pointed down the street, one arm straight as an arrow and her face as firm. "If you insist otherwise, you're a fraud and you can peddle your deceit elsewhere."

"Tena." Maggie gently nudged her sister's arm back in place. "Sir, can you provide evidence of this supposed will?" Mr. Goodfellow offered her the thin envelope which, upon opening, contained three second class steamship vouchers and a typewritten letter from the Weston Law Offices of London requesting the sisters' presence on or before the twentieth of April. Sure enough, Mr. Goodfellow had told the truth.

"How were you able to locate us?" Maggie asked. "Our decision to leave England occurred well after Father's passing."

"Why, via your very own marriage announcement, Mrs. Frye."

Of course, she thought, nothing nefarious about that. She handed the packet to Tena. "Our father arranged this, you say?"

"Yes." Mr. Goodfellow nodded. "A summons to be delivered one year, one month, and one day following his death. Passage prepaid by my office from his assets with return fare to follow discussion with our London associates and acceptance of all terms."

"What terms?" Tena asked as her eyes scanned the letter.

"It is all explained in the will. The London office is prohibited from forwarding a copy per your father's request."

Ah, so they would have to go to London or else forfeit their right to whatever further assets Laurence Archer left behind. How maddeningly inconvenient. Maggie peered over her sister's shoulder in order to see whom the third steamship ticket was assigned to and laughed out loud. Of course it would be Reuben. Somehow that confounded man managed to follow them everywhere. Like a bad penny ... or an impending paternity conversation she would rather avoid awhile longer.

"Listen, sir," Maggie said. "Ensuring access to a proper travel companion seems the exact situation my father would arrange." She smiled. "Protective of us to the last. However, I have a husband now who is entitled to a portion of my interests. He will be enough of an escort to satisfy my father's worries."

Mr. Goodfellow frowned. "I'm afraid that will not be acceptable. The stipulations of your father's will are quite clear. All three of you in attendance." He narrowed his eyes over his glasses. "Or none at all."

With a look sure to sear flesh, Tena shoved the summons into Maggie's hands. "Well, sister dear, it appears you may receive those answers after all. I hope you realize the trouble this could cause."

Me too, sister dear, Maggie thought. *Me too.*

PART TWO

~~~

Undertow

THIRTY-ONE

LIKE A DOG CAGED INSIDE on a sunny day, Reuben paced before the closed window. His fingers tapped against his right hip while he held a mug of coffee in his left. Anxiety clung to him like a second skin, as though his entire body were wired with an electrical current. It made him want to scream, slam a fist into the lawyer's office wall, and leap out the third floor window.

Only fifteen minutes ago, Maggie, Hugo, Tena, and Reuben were shown into Robert Weston's spacious Bedford Park office. He greeted them like old friends while offering them substandard coffee and condolences on Laurence Archer's passing.

"He was a true man of vision," Mr. Weston mourned. "He enlisted my services for fifteen years and will be sincerely missed."

Lips pressed tight, Maggie sat where directed with Hugo and Tena on either side. In her arms lay a sleeping Abigail whose tiny fist curled beside her cheek. Mr. Frye left Damaris with the other three children, but it was impossible to leave the still-nursing baby behind.

In fact, Hugo planned every detail of the trip. He exchanged their vouchers for passage, secured lodging, and looked into the process of exchanging their American currency for British pounds. His efficiency removed all admissible excuses for Reuben not to travel, including one of the most important—the fear of returning to sudden harsh unemployment.

The only way Smithson allowed him to leave at all was by demanding he return with a story better than every other put together. Without a single notion how to accomplish that, he figured the day he returned to St. Louis, Smithson would brush his hands and gleefully show his obit writer the door. Reuben's only possible salvation lay in Hugo's hands when the man suggested they submit a piece together highlighting the voyage. He would provide photographs if Reuben wrote the words.

"Photographs complete the piece," Hugo told him. "They bring all the details together."

Reuben's fingers tightened against his hip. How long could he work beside Hugo and maintain such elaborate pretense? He had known he couldn't avoid Abigail forever. But he hadn't anticipated Hugo would bring her to the newspaper with him either.

One look at Abigail and he gladly offered Hugo his second class passage to purchase himself a week alone in third.

It would be simple enough to hide the truth. Anyone who was to look on her assumed she received her dark hair from her mother and that Hugo passed along something more abstract like his gentle demeanor or his photographic eye, skills to be revealed with time. Only Reuben knew better. That child was as certainly his as the air in his lungs and the shoes on his feet. One look and there could be no doubt.

He needed to share this with Tena. She had always been his rock, his voice of reason, the gentle influence that literally stilled his hand when he once held a revolver to his skull. He doubted Maggie told her Abigail's paternity—for pity's sake, she hadn't even officially informed him yet—but Tena would reason it out soon enough. Of any of them, she should have suspected it first, and she would feel it more if he remained quiet than if he came clean. He used to trust her implicitly ... when had that stopped?

His fingernail absently tapped the window sill. Tap...tap...tap...tap, tap, tap, taptaptaptap. He sipped his coffee and grimaced. Too dark, too bitter.

"Please take a seat, Mr. Radford."

He lowered himself onto the hard wooden chair beside Tena. Why had he stood in the first place?

"I assumed Father's assets were long since reconciled," Maggie argued.

Oh yes, Reuben thought, they were here to settle Laurence Archer's second mysterious will. Mr. Weston barely made it through the first two sentences before Reuben's nerves had set him to pacing. The coffee only enhanced his jittering, and after listening to an entire page of legal gibberish, he still hadn't sorted why the third summons belonged to him.

Mr. Weston folded his hands over the short stack of perhaps only four or five papers. "Actually, Miss Archer—"

"Mrs. Frye," Hugo corrected.

"My apologies, Mrs. Frye. As I was saying, your father maintained significant investments divided into a number of accounts. He was quite the affluent man and regulated his spending so both of you and your mother would be provided for. The will paid out upon his death was only one of two he created. The second, given his explicit instructions, your mother was to remain blind to."

Maggie visibly relaxed. "How clever. All this time, Tena, we believed he left us nothing. What a relief to know our fears were unfounded."

"Hmm. Quite interesting you should assume such." Mr. Weston removed the second sheet from the stack. He looked to Reuben. "Mr. Radford?"

"What?" Reuben folded his arms with a scowl. He couldn't even say why he was irritated. Too much coffee, probably. He shifted his chair back a few inches, and Abigail disappeared behind Tena's shoulder.

"According to my notes, Laurence Archer believes you can learn more about a man in his response to but one inquiry. Are you familiar with this principle?"

"Yes." He repeated Mr. Archer's words, "'Given any day of your life, which one would you redo?' What of it?"

"Mr. Archer's instructions are clear. You must answer that question correctly and answer without assistance."

"If I refuse?"

"The proceedings will end."

Well, bugger. All eyes fell to Reuben. He swallowed hard.

If he declined to answer—or failed to answer correctly—then the Archer sisters would never receive their inheritance. No pressure, he thought grimly.

Of all the possible days, all Reuben's mistakes, which ones did Laurence even know about? How could he possibly discern which he was supposed to choose? The response he provided at Laurence's bedside had been honorable and truthful—any day that saved him for his daughters—but he always felt it wasn't the one Mr. Archer had hoped for. Until Reuben was forced to stare at this cryptic will, Laurence never seemed like one to speak in riddles.

On his deathbed, their father told Reuben, "Sometimes even old men make mistakes." So then, what would have been Laurence Archer's gravest mistake? Marrying his wife? Sending Maggie away? Not being enough to Tena? What did he regret? Which day would *he* redo? Was it actually Laurence's response, not Reuben's, that was required?

That's the answer, thought Reuben. He sat up straighter, the electric charge humming in his fingertips. Perhaps the correct response wasn't the truth, but the ideal. Laurence died with regrets, but he also died wishing he didn't have any.

"None of them," Reuben said with confidence. "If I could redo any day in my life, I wouldn't change a bloomin' thing."

Mr. Weston folded his hands upon the desk and smiled. "Excellent work, Mr. Radford. You are now the sole heir to Laurence Archer's remaining assets."

THIRTY-TWO

THOSE FIVE WORDS—*You are the sole heir*—felt like a horse hoof to Reuben's temple. A kick from a dark steed that strongly resembled the phantom from *The Legend of Sleepy Hollow* yet somehow retained the essence of Laurence Archer. He should stop reading New England folk stories. They were no less disturbing than his boyhood penny dreadfuls.

"This is absurd!" Maggie cried, "Father only met Reuben twice."

"Most importantly, he's not even Mr. Archer's child," Hugo stated.

Mr. Weston narrowed his eyes at him. "Neither are you, sir. Need I remind you, Mr. Frye, that your involvement is by invitation of your wife. So I suggest you remain quiet else you and your daughter may wait in the corridor."

Hugo's daughter, Reuben thought. *My daughter too.*

His spine found the curve of the chair and sank into it until his shoulders butted against the wood. Another figurative horse galloped by with another kick to the skull for good measure. He didn't know how much longer he could sit in this room without hitting something.

Tena's fingers squeezed over his with her usual gentle smile as though she could understand every cause for his current temperament. *I'm here*, her eyes seemed to say. Then they refocused on her sister, and her touch disappeared as quickly as it had come. Reuben exhaled and pushed himself upright.

"It makes sense, doesn't it?" Tena said. "Father needed assurance that his assets would be divided fairly. So he listed Reuben as his heir—a neutral third party."

Maggie's hand rapidly circled her daughter's back. "He didn't trust us."

Tena shook her head. "No, he didn't trust Mother. What if the secret he spoke of is as simple as her disdain for us? She had no intention of providing us with our rightful inheritance after father's death. That's why he drafted two wills. She would believe she still retained power over us."

"Even if that were true," Maggie said, "that doesn't explain why he left everything to Reuben. After a year, Mother would never suspect there to be more money. I certainly won't tell her and I know you won't."

"You're forgetting something though. Mother was bound and determined to have us both wed and wed well." Tena said excitedly. "Perhaps that was the secret. Mother chose husbands for us that fit her bill, but not ours. Father knew we wouldn't take to them, that we would rebel when forced. When we refused, he knew she would disown us. Father couldn't risk us never receiving the money or having it fall into the hands of an ill-chosen husband."

Nestling Abigail closer, Maggie overtly avoided looking at Hugo. "So as I said, Father didn't trust us."

Reuben returned to the window. Just as many people traveled the dreary streets, automobile horns honked, and yet something had changed—him. He now possessed power. Thousands of pounds in his waiting grip to be doled out as he saw fit. Abigail was *his* daughter. He could provide for her now. Claim her as his own. He had leverage to inflict vengeance on Maggie and earn Tena's disgust with the wave of his billfold.

What a despicable thought; he couldn't believe he even allowed it to surface.

He ground the heels of his palms into his eyeballs until colors spotted his vision. Turning, he butted against the window ledge. His eyes narrowed at Mr. Weston while his vision gradually cleared.

"So, I'm the heir, am I?" When the lawyer nodded, Reuben did the same. "Very well, then I relinquish my right to the Archer fortune.

Mrs. Frye is correct; I'm not their brother, and I shouldn't be entitled to what isn't mine."

Mr. Weston leaned forward, his slender fingers nearly reaching the desk's edge. "Would it make a difference if you heard Mr. Archer's opinion on the matter?"

"Not likely."

The lawyer withdrew an additional parchment from the file anyway filled with lines of tight erratic script. Holding it up, he cleared his throat and began to read.

"My girls, Laurence wrote, First, do not punish my memory too severely for the plans laid before you. The decisions of my youth were not easy ones, and I fear that the choices of manhood were more difficult still. Although I hope perhaps, I made them with a touch more wisdom than I possessed at twenty-five. I pray you can understand why I withheld so much from you during my lifetime and why there are one or two items more to reveal."

"More?" Maggie asked. "What else could there be? I thought this was all, isn't it? The terrible secret? The—"

Abigail's hollow wail pierced her argument and Maggie gently rocked her daughter against her chest. The shrieks descended with each sway of her mother's arms and Reuben saw a vision of himself accepting Maggie's proposal in the café. He would have held Abigail in his arms the day she was born and never had to hide a thing from her. Instead, he made Laurence Archer's same decision, lying to his daughter until death claimed him.

He rolled his fingers at Mr. Weston and snapped, "Get on with it then."

Mr. Weston shook out the letter.

"To Mr. Radford," he continued tersely, "I must acknowledge this. You may believe you have erred in ways you cannot redeem; however, what you do not realize is you were forgiven long ago. The sins of your life were made known to me long before you met my daughters. Desperate to save you from arrest after assailing Lloyd Halverson, your father approached my bank for a loan. Hush money. For a few thousand pounds, he could make all litigation against you disappear. But paying the money brought your father such shame. He desired punishment for Mr. Halverson, not reward, but it was more important to protect you. 'I won't see my son in prison for attempted murder,' he told me. 'My children's word against a shipping magnate? If Reuben stands before a judge, he will lose.'

"I barely knew your father—in fact, our paths didn't cross again after that day—but mine did cross with yours. When it came to my daughters, I was grateful they made acquaintance with someone who would protect them, a man I could trust."

Trust? Reuben forced his expression to remain passive while his fingers clenched his forearms so tightly against his chest that the inside of his elbows went numb. None of this made sense. His *father* first believing in him as he rarely expressed when alive, then pouring his life story out to a complete stranger, and Reuben consequently earning Laurence Archer's confidence through an act of violence. Some, including Tena, called his attack on Lloyd Halverson an act of bravery, loyalty, and love for his sister. It seemed Laurence Archer would say the same. But if he had known the things Reuben did on the *Höllenfeuer*, how he saddled Maggie with a child, or every argument with her since, there wasn't a chance Mr. Archer would have trusted Reuben—and not a bone in him left unbroken.

"Shall I continue, Mr. Radford?"

The room's unusually hushed tone indicated it had been at that volume some time now. Everyone stared. Tena's brow furrowed and Reuben relaxed his own.

"Yes, sir, no need to pause on my account."

Mr. Weston continued. "It is unconventional, but I place my wealth in your hands. Divide the assets amongst my daughters as you see fit. Take care of them. It is all I will mind when the end of my life draws near. I cannot see them taken advantage of by their mother; I cannot bear them hearing only her version of my life. Lastly, I offer you the only item you ever asked of me. I leave you my blessing. I couldn't provide it before and I still believe it was right not to do so. But one day you will find a woman worthy of the kindness, compassion, and love that you have shown both my daughters.

"For you see, I have always seen the truth you try to hide. The fear of losing everything you love is justified; allow no one to convince you otherwise. I have been that afraid for half my life. Even so, if you are reading this letter, the time for even that is at an end. Call it cowardice to die without seeing the aftermath; however, I would rather die with my daughters beside me than die alone. Sincerely, LKA."

"Dying alone," Maggie said dully. She pushed herself from the chair, Abigail still cradled to her chest. "Excuse me, please." With one hand to her forehead, she exited the room.

This is wrong, Reuben thought. It was inconceivable that they sat here reliving pains—and guilt—from over a year past. Quite far from offering Reuben comfort that Laurence always stood in his wheelhouse, it made him seethe. Who was Mr. Archer to withhold his confidence all those years when it might have made a difference? He had the power to possibly save Reuben from Mira's sick mind games, and the infernal man held it to himself. Now he had the audacity to once again demand the burden of his daughters' safety while granting Reuben his blessing? Too little too late.

"There must be more," Hugo said. "You left a document in the file when you removed the will. What does it say?"

Reuben hadn't even noticed. Given the circumstances, he was bewildered he still stood straight.

"That, Mr. Frye," Mr. Weston said, "is none of your concern. That amendment has already been directed to the applicable party and resolved many months past."

"Resolved by whom?"

"Mr. Frye," Tena hissed. "If Mr. Weston says we are not to bother, then we should leave it be."

Hugo eyed her carefully. "How can it not matter to you when it means so much to your sister?"

"My sister's actions might not carry the same weight if you truly knew her."

"I believe I do."

"Your belief has been misplaced then." Tena clasped her handbag and stood, holding a gloved hand out to Mr. Weston. "Thank you, sir. I trust you will make arrangements to secure the funds in Reuben's account?"

"No," Reuben spat. He crossed the room to glower at the man behind the desk. "I still refuse my share." His fist slammed against the wood before he could stop it. His fingers stung.

"One more outburst, Mr. Radford, and there will be no share for you to refuse."

"There will be if Mr. Archer has paid you in advance to do so." When all eyes turned on Hugo, he guiltily waved a hand and fell silent.

"As I was saying," Reuben continued. "You will split the assets thirty percent each between the Archer sisters. The remaining forty belongs to Abigail Frye for her dowry."

Hugo shot from his chair. "That's too much," he sputtered.

"It's what her grandfather would have wanted."

What I want, Reuben amended. He couldn't give a two pence what Laurence Archer wanted anymore. From his vantage point, all Mr. Archer seemed to want was to craft the story of his life how he saw fit, to reveal or disguise truths when they seemed to suit him best. It was little wonder now where Maggie received her own manipulative antics from. Yes, Laurence may have believed that Beatrix disowning her daughters was the worst thing that could happen after his demise, but he should have trusted in *their* strength as much as the credit he gave Reuben. Those sisters were tough as nails. Together, doubly so.

Blood pounding in his ears, he strode from the room and slammed the door behind him. Maggie waited in the hallway with Abigail.

"Come with me," Reuben said. Not waiting for her response, he marched to the end of the corridor. A window overlooked another street that stretched uninterrupted to the bank of the River Thames. Maggie followed in silence while Abigail babbled her incoherent language and latched tiny fingers onto Reuben's coat sleeve.

"Would you like to hold her?" Maggie asked quietly.

"No." He jerked his sleeve out of the child's grip.

"You act like she's going to give you the plague." She paused. "Wait. You're afraid of her, aren't you?"

"Yes. I am. Keep her away from me." Reuben stepped back and repeated more firmly. "I never want to hold her. If I hold her, I'll ..." *never want to let her go*, he finished. If he touched her, she would imprint on his core, and he would lose a bit more of himself every time he handed her back to Hugo. "I can't."

"She looks like you, don't you think so?" Maggie slipped her finger into Abigail's waiting grip, and the baby flexed her fingers repeatedly. "She has your eyes."

"Radford eyes." Reuben cuffed his neck. "Maggie, why are you doing this to me now?"

"Because I'm afraid to say it anywhere else." There was a lengthy pause, broken only by soft cooing. It was strange to be back in England with her, a woman he once maintained stalwart affection for, an attraction he now found shallow. A woman and her child who belonged to another. Promises to her father he no longer knew if he should keep.

His lips formed the words he needed to ask, *What does this mean for us?*, but his throat wouldn't release them. Whatever it meant for them, it meant for Tena and Hugo as well. Whatever decisions they made about their relationship with Abigail affected their relationships with each other. This was a choice he needed free of their influence.

"Mr. Radford! Mrs. Frye!" Mr. Weston called from his office door, impatience prominent in his tone. "Do come back. I need your signatures." Plastering on apologies, Reuben and Maggie returned to the office.

Two hours passed while Mr. Weston obtained the necessary details related to division of assets until finally only one empty line remained. If Reuben signed, everything would happen exactly as he asked—four-tenths of Laurence Archer's inheritance would go to Abigail Lorraine Frye's dowry with the remainder split evenly between her mother and her aunt.

Reuben's headache only grew. It took all his effort to ignore Abigail's incessant noise and focus on the document. So he signed the line and hoped he interpreted all he read correctly. Hugo returned to the office for Maggie's forgotten handbag and within ten minutes, they clamored into a waiting taxi. Hugo, Maggie, Tena, and Abigail shared the rear while Reuben rode in the passenger seat.

"The Royal Botanic Gardens, please," Hugo told the driver.

"Very good, sir." Glancing over his shoulder, he shifted the car into the flow of traffic.

Tena's hand shot against the front seat. "Wait a moment, please. At the street side there, yes, that will do nicely. Mr. Frye, why do you want to go there?"

"How do you even know of it besides?" Maggie blustered.

"Your father's will." Hugo lifted Abigail from Maggie's arms, and with a kiss to her cheek, set her against his shoulder. Reuben averted his gaze out the front windshield. "That is what you wanted," Hugo asked, "when you *pretended* to leave your handbag behind? To know what was in the half of the will Mr. Weston left in the folder?"

Silence followed, and Reuben imagined Hugo's arched eyebrows and Maggie's flushed cheeks in response.

"He would never have left you alone in his office. Your expression had ill intent all over it."

"You know me too well," Maggie huffed. Hugo gave a throaty chuckle as though to say, *See, Tena, I do know your sister better than you thought.* Reuben supposed that was as close as the man could come to actually gloating.

"The Royal Botanic Gardens were mentioned on the first page," Hugo continued. "Your father bestowed a sum of money towards research and maintenance at the Palm House paid out every six months over three years."

"Why?" Tena asked.

"I'm not sure. I only had time to skim. Your father often visited London; maybe he just enjoyed the gardens while he was here."

"I don't think so," Maggie said. "Father was a man of books and letters. Floral arrangements and frippery didn't appeal to him. That was more or less Mother's interest. Not once did he mention visiting either."

"One's interests can evolve over time," Reuben said, still adamantly refusing to turn around, the street lamp outside his window suddenly fascinating. "Fascinatin'," as Hazel would say. He breathed a silent tortured breath. "You can fancy something one day that you never understood an admiration for. Then lose it as quickly the next."

He felt Maggie's eyes on him from the rear seat and pictured her sly smirk in his mind's eye. There were several things she could accuse him of in that area. But thankfully all she said in front of Tena was, "I suppose that could be true."

"Where am I off to, Miss?" the driver asked impatiently.

Tena sighed. "To the Botanic Gardens then. I won't wait to be defeated when it's clearly three against one. Let's solve the confounded mystery."

THIRTY-THREE

"THIS WOULD HAVE BEEN FAR easier if Father simply wrote everything into the letter," Maggie said. Their feet crunched against the damp gravel path as the group wound around puddles from that morning's rain shower. Drops lay like jewels on every flowerbed they passed, many of the plants still fighting to break their way through the soil. Beside her, Hugo focused on their steps rather than her ongoing disagreement with Tena.

"He would have told us if he ever intended us to know, which he didn't," Tena countered. "It's not too late to respect his wishes and go home."

Reuben flipped open his pocket watch, holding it out for both sisters to see. "It's been fifteen minutes of squabble, ladies. Can't we bring this to a close?"

Maggie ignored him. "You know I won't leave, Tena, and you know why. This affects you too, so why won't you help me?" When would her sister wake up and understand that they couldn't bury their heads anymore? She may believe that they had already ousted the family secret with Reuben's inheritance, but the picture was only partially developed. Maggie wasn't naïve enough to believe their ending up at another garden was a coincidence. Not when the man with the purple flowers continued to plague her nightmares.

"What do you think I'm doing? I'm here, am I not?" Tena jerked the pram handle to a stop, her very pointed glare focused on her sister. "Would you rather I wasn't?"

"Of course not." She wanted Tena beside her on this. If it came down to brass tacks, Maggie would continue the search on her own, but better if she could convince Tena to help her. The last time Tena stormed out in anger, they hadn't spoken for five months.

"Fine," Maggie amended. "We learn why Father donated money to the gardens and then I promise I'll concede. Is that acceptable?"

Tena searched her sister's face for any trace of deception, then finally nodded. "I think I can agree to that."

Up ahead, the path curved towards a round pool reflecting the vast building beyond. Made of glass, its curved walls rose three layers high with intersecting panels like a dramatic enclosed bird cage. Beside her, Hugo inhaled sharply.

"Mr. Frye?" Reuben asked. "Anything the matter?"

Hugo shook his head. "Don't trouble yourself over me." He lifted his Brownie from his shoulder, released the case and turned to capture the Palm House in its lens. "The light today is intriguing. Mr. Radford, why don't you continue on with Miss Archer? We'll be along in a minute." He flipped the camera lever and the shutter snapped.

Maggie watched Reuben and Tena walk away, fading into a sky painted with retreating thunderclouds. Soon enough their voices became incoherent hums amongst the bird songs and wind whistles. Somewhere nearby the gentle scent of violets stirred with the breeze, not so very different from the day Reuben stole her umbrella and kissed her beneath a pouring sky. Not her first kiss, but the first one that truly mattered.

Click. Hugo stood off the other side of the path with her neatly in his camera's sights. A sly smile crossed his face. "The frame seemed ideal. I believe I can sell that one easy."

She scowled at him. "Stop kidding about that. No one is buying photographs of me. I hope you're burning them instead."

"Could be," he said. "It seems more fun to keep you guessing."

"Oh, what did I do to deserve such an exasperating partner?"

"Something very rotten, I'd bet." He grinned, eyes glittering like Henry elbow deep in a candy barrel, and Maggie itched to finish this business quickly.

She took hold of the pram handle again. "Shall we continue on?"

Hugo returned the camera to its case and slung the entire apparatus over his shoulder once again. It tapped against his back as they continued down the path. He pointed to the Palm House in the distance. "That building reminds me of the flight cage at the St. Louis World's Fair. Had all sorts of birds in it. It's still in Forest Park. The cage, not the birds. Those were sold." Hugo shrugged. "I try not to visit it anymore."

On the hill above, Tena and Reuben waited near the entrance to the glass building, still far enough away not to overhear them, but Hugo's eyes were focused somewhere far beyond any of them.

"Many things happened at the fair. It was a photographer's paradise. Every surface shone, white and dazzling. Rolled up waffles filled with ice cream, glasses of fresh ice tea, and the most enormous Ferris wheel. Plus the palaces of industry and art and electricity. Sure, I'd seen fairs before—Chicago, Buffalo, Charleston—but this time I was home. For four years, I hadn't stayed in St. Louis more than a few weeks at a time, and now I had reason to be grounded for nearly a year. I had such pride for our city, and I thought, this is where I want to be buried."

Maggie smiled at the light in his eyes. "Then what made you decide to leave again?"

"Ultimately Damaris. She's not one to sit still, especially after I ruined our constant travels by falling in love." His lips hitched up, his eyes lost far away in memories of Emma, and all at once, Maggie felt like an intruder. She pushed the pram a little faster.

Hugo skipped to keep up. "I met Emma near the flight cage. This girl taps me on the shoulder and says, 'Pardon, sir, could I trouble you for a photograph?' She was beautiful, the most beautiful woman I had ever beheld to that point. Hair like mine; not since my mother had I seen the same shade. She was barely eighteen, and I was twenty-five, but she seemed older. She was a full seven inches above me, like peering up at an Amazon warrior. She twitched her nose and popped her hip with her parasol for me to photograph.

"And I did. Over and over. I used the remainder of my film for the day. Half the photographs didn't even turn out; I was so nervous when I developed them, aching to see her face again. Her family stayed the length of the fair, all the way until December, and we married the week before it closed. It was bitterly cold, but there was more warmth between us to start a blaze in every fireplace. I think now it was probably very impetuous for a man of my age to be attracted to someone so youthful."

There had been only seven years between Hugo and his first wife. Seven, Maggie thought, not thirteen.

A shrill wail erupted from Abigail and Hugo moved to the pram. Stealing it from her hands, he gently pushed it back and forth until the baby quieted.

"Back then," he said slowly, "as things were only beginning, I would never have wagered in a hundred lifetimes, that it wouldn't always be that way. I wouldn't have believed that five years later Emma would choose another life. Or that the one she chose wouldn't include me. Sometimes we'll never find out the answer to our whys, but in your case, Miss Margaret, you can. Don't concede to Tena if you don't have to. Don't spend life like me, an old man wondering."

"Thirty-four is not old. I wouldn't marry an old man."

"Thirty-four is not twenty. Your life is only beginning."

They stopped a few paces from where Tena and Reuben stood shoulder to shoulder. He had divined a copy of *The War of the Worlds* from somewhere and held it up for both of them to read. Every few lines, Tena would comment and Reuben would shake his head. If the two of them didn't acknowledge their implicit attraction soon, Maggie would need to do so lest it eventually implode upon them all. But first, she had Hugo to deal with. He was scorching her with his troubled eyes and wounded soul and she hadn't any indication of how to help.

Fortunately, he spoke before she figured it out. "I'm sorry, Miss Margaret. It's this place. It reminds me of another time and things I once wanted." He tucked his chin and smiled up at her. "Don't worry about me. Today the focus is on you."

Today *was* about her: discovering her family's secrets and securing Abigail's future along with her own. Hugo had given her leave to be selfish, but suddenly she found it didn't thrill her as it should.

When Abigail cried out again, Maggie reached for her, but Hugo nudged her hand away with a firm shake of his head. "I'll handle her. You go on in with Tena and find your answers."

"What will you do?"

Bending low, he lifted Abigail from the pram and with a kiss to her curls, snuggled her against his chest. This time, he didn't meet Maggie's eyes. "I'll do what I always do. Wait for my wife to come back to me."

~~~

Walking into the Palm House was like experiencing a city summer in St. Louis—hot, humid, and packed into close quarters. The brick-laid path wove between thick layers of lush tropical green so dense that Maggie and Tena could only see around the path's curve and no farther. Above them, the sun shone through the glass dome, but at points struggled to break through the foliage. To the left, a white wrought-iron spiral staircase led to an elevated walkway over thirty feet above.

"What made you change your mind?" Tena asked as they walked. She pushed back a tropical frond, allowing Maggie to walk past before letting it slap back in place.

"I don't want to spoil this again." She gestured between them. "Us as sisters. And I think that there should be some give as well as take." *Although*, Maggie thought, *if you don't give, then I'm going to have to take anyway*. She really, truly, didn't want to harm their friendship again, but what else could she do if Tena didn't agree? Let the past lie? But what if someone found it later and used it when she wasn't looking?

"Reuben had me consider something else," Tena said. She stared down at Maggie as they ascended the staircase.

Maggie rolled her eyes with an unladylike grunt. "He did? I suppose it placed the chips firmly out of my favor then?

"Actually, he reminded me that you're as much an Archer as I am. He reasoned that maybe you shouldn't be the only one forced to make concessions."

"He did?" Maggie repeated. "He took *my* side?"

"I believe his point, Maggie, was that we should be on the *same* side." From this high, they could now see the entirety of the central room. Tena raised her hand to flag down a gardener as he entered. "Assistance, sir?" she called. She turned back to Maggie as the man made his way to the staircase. "I'm willing to take this to the end, wherever it goes or whatever we may find out. But you must promise me one thing."

Maggie nodded. This was working in her favor, she thought with excitement. Perhaps, everything could work out. Perhaps once in awhile, there was a happy ending.

"You must agree to never leave me again, Maggie." The wrought-iron creaked as the gardener ascended the staircase, but Tena's eyes never strayed from Maggie's. She laced her arms behind her back and Maggie pictured two little girls in white dresses dancing around the maypole on the day declared just for them. Until the year the elder sister walked out in the night and never said goodbye.

"Promised," she swore. "I'll never leave again, and don't you ever ask me."

"Never fear, because I never will." Tena tugged Maggie into her arms with a squeeze. "Even if I certainly feel like it."

Both women grabbed the railing as the walkway shifted under the gardener's weight as he strode towards them. Slipping off his cap, he smoothed back hair glistening with sweat from the tropical environment. "Afternoon, ladies. 'Fraid I've had my hands in the soil otherwise I'd extend one in greeting." He grinned, revealing one crooked tooth in the center of his smile. "Could I help you locate a particular botanical variety?"

"Are you familiar with a donor by the name of Laurence Archer?" Maggie asked. "If he had any long-term connection to the Palm House?"

The gardener scratched his head. "Can't say I know of a *Laurence Archer*, although, there is a man who goes simply by L. He's been one of our most magnanimous donors for—what has it been?—about fourteen or fifteen years now? Taller bloke, fair hair, smart dresser."

"That could be him."

"Or it could be anyone," Tena muttered.

"Real decent mate, I tell you, ladies. He came around 'bout twice a year, checking on the houses, I suppose to make certain he had his farthing's worth."

"He invested the most in the Palm House?" Maggie asked.

"Yes, miss, on any project in which Dr. Schweitzer had a vested interest."

"Dr. Schweitzer?"

The gardener stared. "Blimey, you mean to say tell you've never heard of Dr. Alois Schweitzer, the celebrated botanist?" Both girls glanced at each other and shook their heads. His eyes widened. "Are you quite certain?"

Tena shook her head. "No, sir. Should we have?"

He released a low whistle. "Well, I should say so. The bloke towers over you, commands a room he does. You're not likely to forget him once you've met. He's at the South London Botanical Institute now, so unfortunately we don't see him as often anymore."

"How did Dr. Schweitzer meet Mr. Archer?"

He thumbed his chin. "You know, I don't rightly know. I was only a lad then, didn't get my post in the Palm House 'till ought-five. Also, do you know those women?"

Maggie and Tena turned in the direction he nodded to see two familiar faces energetically waving up at them from the path below. The twins matched head to toe, from their navy day suits to blonde hair coiffed under hat feathers lying limp in the humidity. Edith and Bianca Winchester—now Mrs. Christopher Hartnell and Mrs. Colin Smith after their whirlwind marriages last year—were the thorns Maggie yanked from her side and tossed off in Fontaine. If not for the Winchesters, she wouldn't have won the May Queen crown two years past and never been sentenced to the tumultuous path she ended up on. If given the option, she would now walk away without a word.

Unfortunately, the only way back to the ground deposited them directly at the Winchesters' feet.

"Oi, Maggie, Tena!" Bianca called. "We have missed you, darlings."

"It has been too long!" Edith echoed. "What are the odds that the exact time I visit my sister, you both come to stay?"

In a flash they rattled the stairs to join Maggie and Tena on the walkway, kisses pressed to both cheeks in greeting. The gardener wisely slipped back down to his plants.

Edith playfully shoved Tena's shoulder. "Too long!" she repeated. "Not even a letter in all this time. Christopher and I must have you both back here for the Christmas holiday, no arguments."

"Where are your children?" Maggie asked. Both women had been expecting when the Archer sisters left Fontaine. Their babies would be a few months older than Abigail.

Bianca rolled her eyes with an exaggerated sigh. "They're with the nanny, thank goodness. It would be simply dreadful to cart those little things all over." She reached into her handbag, removing a white card with a flourish, and held it out to Tena. "I'm hosting a small soiree tonight. Details are written here, and you simply must attend. We so missed you at the Christmas party. Oh! Did I also hear tell about the perpetual spinster making a baby?" Bianca raised a hand to her lips and whispered, "What's the name of the little baseborn thing?"

Maggie pressed a hand to either hip lest they lash out and strike Bianca's perfectly powdered face. "I-am-mar-ried," she ground out one sticky syllable at a time. "Abigail is as legitimate as you are. How did you even learn about her?" There had been a newspaper announcement for the wedding, but nothing regarding Abbie's birth. Tena appeared as baffled as she did.

Bianca offered her a cool smile. "Oh, darling, we have our ways."

I'll bet, Maggie thought.

Leaning over the railing, Edith traced the pathways with her eyes. "Where is that husband of yours?" She threw a sly smile over her shoulder. "He must be quite the catch to have caught *you*. Don't tell me you snagged a Vanderbilt, or I will never forgive you."

"Family name doesn't buy importance," Tena interjected. "The heat in here was simply too intense, so Mr. Frye kept the baby outside with Mr. Radford."

"*Reuben* Radford?" Bianca smirked. She exchanged a sly look with her sister. "My, whose skirt has he been ruffling these days?"

Before they could set in on their own special brand of harassment, Tena silenced them. "Before you think it, you couldn't be more mistaken. Mr. Radford has a beau of nearly nine months now, and I

am quite pleased to stand my own ground for the moment besides."
She pushed past Bianca with gentle force. "Do excuse us. We really
must attend to some pressing matters."

"Oh darling, you've always been so sensitive," Bianca scoffed.
"Whether some man's titillating you or not, you've already come an
ocean's length. What's one little night out of your schedule to spend
with old friends?"

Friend was not the word Maggie would have used.

"Maggie hasn't anyone to tend to Abigail," Tena argued.

"Nonsense!" Edith exclaimed. "You must bring her with you.
Bianca's nanny is the finest money can buy, and you know her Colin,
so money can buy them quite a bit. Your Abigail will stay in the
nursery with my Dina and Bianca's Tilly." She emitted a tiny squeal
and slipped an arm around Maggie and Tena, squeezing them close.
"Why, you both should stay with us for the duration of your trip.
We've plenty of space!"

Maggie wriggled out of her grasp. "That's not necessary. We've
rooms at the Sentinel."

Bianca's nose wrinkled. "An inn? Heavens, what has American life
done to you?"

"No, no," Edith chuckled. "That place is ghastly. We insist you stay
at the estate in Chiswick."

Bianca grinned evilly. "It's all settled then. I'll send the driver to
collect you and your belongings at six sharp. Wear your best! Tata!"
With a final waggle of their fingers and matching giggles, the twins
scampered down the staircase and disappeared into the foliage.

"I'm not certain my best will impress them anymore," Tena said,
her face as dumbfounded as Maggie felt.

In her mind's eye, she conjured an image of Hugo working in his
photography studio. His suit was old, the hems frayed, and his hair
stuck up in directions that shouldn't be physically possible. Never
once in his life would she wager he stepped foot in a ballroom nor
owned a set of proper tails. He wouldn't be able to list the duties of a
valet or express the difference between a first and second footman.
Could he even forge a waltz if pressed?

"No, Tena," Maggie said. "I'm afraid our best doesn't even come close."

THIRTY-FOUR

"STOP FIDGETING," TENA SCOLDED. "You're wringing my nerves dry."

Maggie forced her limbs to stillness. "I can't help it," she whispered. Shifting Abigail into the crook of her arm, she accepted Hugo's help from the motorcar. Under the overcast navy sky, the massive three-story grey-stone was illuminated from only its windows and low-hanging electric lamps secured beneath the luxurious portico. Not since her service to Lady Alexander had she been within ten miles of a home so superior. It made the Fryes' riverside dwelling akin to a hovel.

Hugo stole Reuben away to address a servant's question regarding their luggage, leaving Maggie alone with Tena. "This house holds an uncanny resemblance to the one I served in," she whispered. "I half expect Derby himself to open the door to us."

Her stomach churned. Given an acceptable reference, it wasn't unusual to encounter servants who moved position from time to time. She had shared a good many firsts with Derby, and despite his womanizer ways, there would always be a soft spot in her heart for him. He was there for her the night she learned her father died and kissed her goodbye the day she returned to Fontaine. He hadn't loved her, and she never expected him to, but it was hard to forget the butterflies he once moved inside her.

She breathed easier when the deep oak-paneled door opened and a footman bearing no resemblance to Derby ushered them into the foyer. Maggie barely crossed the threshold before a robust nanny appeared to wrangle Abigail into her waiting arms.

"You will care for her properly, won't you?" Reuben asked as he jogged up behind them. Maggie looked for Hugo, but he was still outside fighting to secure a trunk latch which a nearby footman insisted he could handle instead. Another one of many societal differences she hadn't any chance to explain beforehand.

"'Course I will, sir," the nanny asserted. She gave a rapid series of nods with an energetic smile. "Excites me to no end to have three babies in the house. No need to worry 'bout this one. She'll be safe with the others."

Reuben folded his arms, his brows wedged against the top of his nose. "You had better."

"Oh, Mr. Radford, always running away with your emotions. You're worse than my mother," Bianca reprimanded as she and Edith floated into the foyer, chiffon gowns swishing. Their necklines teased low with long strands of onyx beads to lead the eye exactly where they desired it. Not the type of evening attire usually worn for a simple soiree between friends.

Bianca extended her hand to Reuben. He made no move to acknowledge her gesture, or her plunging neckline, in any way. With a flirty pout, Bianca turned instead to Maggie and pressed a kiss to her cheek while Edith did the same to Tena.

"Where is Mr. Smith?" Maggie asked.

"The gentlemen have gone to the country for the hunt," Edith explained. She embraced Maggie and quickly released her. "The husbands are away so the ladies may play." She pinched her sister's elbow. "Bianca finds herself in disastrous trouble whenever I leave her on her own."

"And well I know it! Oh, Rookwood?" Bianca addressed the footman who had welcomed them at the door. "Do show Mr. Radford into the sitting room. We ladies will meet the others for dinner at eight."

With that they grabbed hold of Maggie and Tena, ushering them through the entryway and up the wide wood-planked and red-carpeted staircase. Even the delicate carpet pattern reminded Maggie of her time with Lady Alexander, although as a servant her presence upon the grand staircase was usually forbidden. She did remember racing down them the afternoon Reuben appeared out of the blue, a solemn force ready to crush her with news of her father's death and then leave her broken in the cold.

As they tugged her across the gallery, she caught a final glimpse of Hugo standing alone in the entryway, then Bianca pushed her into an upstairs room and closed the door.

Quite clearly Bianca's personal accommodations, the suite's private sitting room was adorned with lush fabrics, feminine pastels, and prettily drawn paintings with a gilded mirror above the fireplace mantel. A low fire burned in the hearth, affording enough warmth to temper the cool breeze blowing through the adjacent bedroom's high windows. Beyond that, a third doorway revealed the edge of a porcelain bathtub. The suite was alive with fragrance from gilded floral vases in varying colors and varieties. None of the purple flowers matched the Magdalena.

"Now, darlings," Bianca said. She pulled twice on the rope that rang for her lady's maid, then threw open the doors to one of two wardrobes. There were gowns in nearly every color in sheens of satin and lace, the lamplight glittering off their silky folds. Tena sighed and Maggie for once understood. Although she had fought suitors tooth and nail, there was still a certain flattering joy in wearing such attire. It was nice to be fawned over and adored.

Maybe someday someone would again, she thought. Maybe someday she would let them like she used to. But one glance at herself in the dressing table mirror and she dismissed the thought. Grey rings lined her eyes from an infant stealing her sleep and her cheeks appeared sunken without any rouge. She hadn't fixed herself up in any way for too many months. Worse, she hadn't noticed. Two months shy of twenty-one, and already her vixen days were far behind her.

Although, Maggie reasoned as Bianca forced her into a sapphire gown too tight in the waist and revealing more of her milk-swelled breasts than was appropriate, perhaps for tonight she could imagine herself to still be a tiny bit coquettish.

"That simply won't do," Tena declared, shifting Maggie's attention away from her own reflection. "If it's not plum or at the very least lavender, I'm not wearing it."

"Whyever for?" Edith asked. She held up a scarlet gown with a pale lace overlay. "This one would be striking on you."

"Because I'm in mourning, that's why. Have some decency, Edith."

"This is 1913, Tena, not 1892. Stick with those outdated Victorian traditions if you'd like, but not on our watch. It's been well past a year since your father died; you deserve a little enjoyment."

Maggie stole the dress from Edith and held it against her sister. After over a year in simple black garments, the stunning gown accentuated Tena's golden eyes and added color to her static pallor. "It's only a dress color, Tena," she said gently, "and you would only break mourning one day early. What does one day matter?"

"You of all people should know what difference a day makes," Tena said softly, but she accepted the dress from Maggie and allowed Edith to help her into it. When the final button was looped, she was exquisite. If Maggie was correct about Reuben's affections, that gown would leave him speechless.

"Tena, I will never understand how I had all the suitors when you are clearly the pretty one."

Tena stared at the ground, a pale blush rising into her cheeks. "The shoes don't fit."

"Wear your own. Trust me, sister dear, no one will care about your feet."

"Rella, Irene," Bianca snapped at the two maids quietly waiting near the door. "Make our friends the fiercest beauties at dinner tonight." The maid Maggie thought to be Irene, although Bianca hadn't distinguished, gave a curt nod and immediately directed Tena to the dressing table. The one she had decided to call Rella settled Maggie on a second stool and began unpinning her hair with vigor.

"How do you expect to woo your man looking half dead?" Bianca tsked. In the mirror, Maggie watched her scrutiny from over Rella's shoulder. "No man will want another baby with you looking like this."

"I don't want another baby," Maggie said, although now that she considered it that might not be entirely true. Abigail *was* adorable, and she had come to love Hugo's children like her own. She even found herself missing them in the week she and Hugo had been away. Maybe one day she *would* want another. After her contract was complete, perhaps then she would consider adopting and form her own family. She squinted as Rella brushed shadow across her lids, shocked at the direction her thoughts had wandered.

"Moreover," Maggie asserted, "I assure you that will never be a consideration for Mr. Frye."

In the mirror, Edith and Bianca exchanged a sympathetic glance. "Post-baby woes?" Edith asked. She nodded to Bianca. "We've both been there. You try everything to entice him, but with a baby around men run scared. All the crying and no sleep at all. Even with a nanny, it's such a challenge. They would rather sleep down the hall than risk another go at it." She pushed up on her cheeks, examining her features from either side in the mirror. "It took pots of cream to fix the mess motherhood made of me. I don't blame Christopher. I truly was a sight."

"I wasn't," said Bianca. "Colin was simply too fickle. Either that or he couldn't understand what I was asking for. Use these." She handed Rella a strand of pearls for Maggie's neck. "The alternative was—well, I'm twenty, ladies. When you're twenty and outshine a room simply by walking into it, I dare say the alternatives simply line up at your bedroom door."

"Bianca!" Tena exclaimed. "I swear, you never learned the meaning of modesty."

"I've learned how to take care of my own needs. Women do have them, you know."

"But you're married."

"And you're not, so please darling, don't advise my life. I leave yours be, don't I?"

"No."

Bianca burst into a fit of giggles. "Too true! Why else do you think I invited you both tonight? Exciting one's flirtations through friends is the next best thing to being saucy oneself."

Tena winced as Irene tugged another curl into place beneath a pearled comb. "I don't need your favors, Bianca. I had a splendidly clever fiancé and enticed him all on my own."

"What fiancé?" Bianca turned to Edith. "Edie, do you recall our Tena being engaged? I believe we would have caught that in the society papers."

Tena's grinding teeth were audible. "It wasn't in the papers. I wrote you last year about my engagement to Charles Kisch. Both your heads are so full of your own demands you couldn't even spare a moment to remember my letter, could you?" Tena attempted to stand, but Irene held her hair in a vice. She sank back onto the stool with folded arms.

"Oh, darling, we get so many admiring letters, you can't expect us to remember every detail. But, Charles Kisch, you say?" Bianca looked upwards, clearly injuring herself with the thought process. "No, I'm sorry, but his name doesn't come to mind tied to yours. Of course, I do remember him from all those lovely Christmas parties. An excellent dancer, wasn't he, Edie?"

Edith gave a shy smile and nodded. "He was by far my favorite. Never would have pictured him with you though, Tena, especially given your mother's prejudices."

"True, yes," Bianca agreed. "Mrs. Archer was always so vocal about those German instigators, wasn't she? I do wonder why. She never would tell the story there, but you know it had to be succulent." She clucked at Rella who had begun painting Maggie's lips a tint of light rose. "No, no, Rella, must I instruct you in everything? The brighter the better. That one." With a smile that didn't reach halfway to her eyes, the maid exchanged the rose color for the vibrant crimson Bianca indicated.

"That color's for a trollop," Tena contended as Rella swathed the color across Maggie's lips. "Besides, Maggie's married. Who does she need to win?"

Edith laughed, edging her way beside Irene to clasp a white sapphire pendant around Tena's neck. "She's winning back her husband. After tonight, he wouldn't dare leave her wanting."

Bianca laid slender fingers on Maggie's shoulder, displaying a clear shot down her ample bosom. "But if he does," Bianca whispered, "I've conveniently placed Lloyd Halverson in the room adjacent your suite."

"What?" Maggie gasped, but before she could give the severity of the situation any attention, Bianca dragged her up by the arm.

"Come, come dears, our admirers await!"

THIRTY-FIVE

DESCENDING THE STAIRS ONE step at a time, her arm linked through Tena's, Maggie's inner turmoil quickly shifted to an unusual sense of girlish pride. Hugo waited at the foot of the staircase, watching—no, correction, staring at their approach. He smiled at her and in that honest expression, Lloyd Halverson's suite adjacent was momentarily forgotten.

I have a husband now, she reminded herself, her wedding ring firmly situated under her elbow length white gloves. Hopefully that would be enough of a deterrent from Lloyd's advances.

"Like what you see, Mr. Frye?" Tena laughed. She nudged Maggie's ribcage with her elbow.

Hugo shrugged, although there was a noticeable rosiness to the space between his white collar and crimson hair. Someone—probably Reuben—must have insisted he wash up before dinner. Maggie hadn't seen his cheeks so smooth or his goatee trimmed with such precision since their visit to the photography studio in November. He had smoothed back his hair, thankfully not as grotesque as on their wedding day, however, enough to tame it into something resembling manageability. Even with his threadbare suit and scuffed oxfords, he was handsome. How queer that she never noticed before.

Maggie removed her arm from Tena's and pressed both palms to her stomach. Her corset stays must be drawn too tightly. Perhaps the house fires burned too hot, but heavens was she warm.

Instead of answering Tena's question, Hugo shifted his attention towards the twins. He gave a slight wave, uncertain whom of the identical women to address. "Good evening, ladies. Hugo Frye. I would like to thank you for your kind invitation tonight."

"My word indeed, would you listen to that accent, Edie?" Bianca splayed her fingers against her bosom. "When we caught sight of you out on the drive earlier, I said to Edith, 'Why Edie, our girls brought their own traveling footman.' You must forgive us, Mr. Frye, for mistaking your unrefined apparel for servant's garb." She stretched her dainty fingers outward. "Mrs. Bianca Smith. It's your pleasure, I'm certain."

Hugo bestowed her waiting hand with a limp shake rather than a low bow as was customary, and Maggie hid her smile by scratching her nose. Bianca must be seething inside. It served her right to meet a man unwilling to fall at her feet.

After Edith introduced herself with the good sense to offer a handshake, the twins led the way to the dining room. The butler announced their entrance with unnecessary enthusiasm and noted where each guest was assigned seating during dinner. Tena had been placed between Reuben and young Matthew Troughton whom she had noted as a rather fine dancer at the Winchesters' Christmas party. Her sister gave a pretty smile and an even more becoming blush when Mr. Troughton not only gave a low bow, but also a kiss to her hand. Reuben stood behind his chair and glowered unnecessarily.

The final seat on the nearer side of the table was occupied by one of Maggie's holiday dance partners, Peter McCoy. Across from him, conveniently separating her assigned place from Hugo's was Mr. McCoy's new bride, Vivian, and beside her as promised sat the grey-eyed, dusty-haired, self-serving grin of Lloyd Halverson.

Ah, thought Maggie, so that was the true reason why Reuben's hand currently clenched as though he held a dagger shaft. Honestly, after all that had been done, who was to blame him?

Hugo held out Maggie's chair for her, unaware that it was polite to stand until the hostess was seated or that half the room silently judged him for not doing so.

Bianca sniggered. Very well, perhaps one not so silently.

Maggie's heart burned for her partner. She walked behind Bianca's chair and fought the urge to kick it as she passed. Across the table, Reuben's grimace turned even lower. With the insatiable stare of a wild dog, Lloyd followed her path until she stood beside him with what she hoped was a smile directed only at Mr. Frye, yet the effort left her face oddly contorted.

Finally, Edith and Bianca accepted their places at either end of the table and welcomed everyone to sit. Easing Maggie's chair in, Hugo claimed his seat between Mrs. McCoy and Edith. Rookwood gestured to the footmen, and the first course, an asparagus cream soup, was served followed by a second of boiled salmon in hollandaise.

By the fifth course—roast lamb forequarter—most of the table was engaged in a conversation surrounding suffragette Emmeline Pankhurst's recent sentence, and Maggie could finally address Lloyd. "You're unaccompanied this evening."

He chewed his lamb. "Unfortunately, yes."

"Couldn't find anyone who would have you?"

"You should know well that plenty of women will have me, Maggie. But I'm afraid no one ever captured my attentions quite like you did." Her head whipped up when the back of his fingers slid along the outside of her thigh. Annoyance flaring, she found only an invitation in those eyes that often mirrored the color of her own. She grabbed his hand, intending to throw off his prying fingers. It would have worked if he hadn't locked his pinky around her own. Without a care what anyone else in the room assumed, he pressed closer until his forehead rested mere inches from hers. "Mrs. Smith was kind enough to allow me to remain the night. The bed is far more comfortable than the one we shared, although there are some other details from that night I wouldn't mind repeating exactly as they were."

Thank heaven and the saints and all the stars above that Abigail wasn't his. It would be unbearable to find her own child so repugnant.

"Stop this, Mr. Halverson," she hissed, loathing him so completely and wishing she could find some ammunition to burn a man who was so completely unbreakable. "I'm married."

After a long moment, he shifted back in his chair. "Tell me why *that* matters to *you*?"

The question gave her pause. Given the unusual nature of her marriage, indulging in another man's affections shouldn't bother her. Yet, somehow it did.

"Photography does sound interesting, Mr. Frye," Mrs. McCoy said then from Maggie's other side. "Have you traveled far for your photographs?"

Hugo set his wine glass down and dabbed his mouth with the napkin. "Here and there across the States. Several World's Fairs. This is my first visit to Europe though."

"Sounds too base for my tastes," Bianca said. She delicately sipped her own wine. "I simply cannot envision life without the occasional jaunt to Paris. Mr. Smith does so love to spoil me. Maggie, darling, please tell me you haven't grown accustomed to such mediocrity."

Throwing her focus off of Lloyd, Maggie tossed Hugo a smile. The gesture seemed to surprise him. "Mr. Frye is a fine man," she told Bianca as much for herself as anyone else in the room. "I'm lucky to have him."

Lloyd's fingers tightened against her thigh. "Yes, my dear, you may have him," he whispered in her ear. "But do you find it most pleasurable when you do?"

She jerked, her plate sliding into her wine glass which toppled. Maroon liquid pooled across the white linen. Rookwood appeared in an instant, mopping up the mess while Maggie apologized profusely. Shortly after, the butler returned with a clean napkin and a fresh wine decanter, refilling her glass with more than was required.

"Maggie," Tena asked. "Are you well? You seem pale."

Maggie shoved a bit of potato into her mouth and chewed sourly. With a hard swallow, she choked it down and nodded. Hugo stared at her with such concern, her fingers slipped on the way to her wine, nearly felling another glass. She steadied it with her other hand. "My apologies, friends. I need to check on my child. I've never been away from her for so long. Please excuse me."

"Do sit down, Maggie," Bianca chastised. "She's perfectly cared for, I assure you."

"Thank you; however, I will feel much better if I judge for myself."

"You seem shaken, Miss Archer," Lloyd commented. "Would you

allow me to escort you upstairs?"

Silverware clattered against china and all eyes swiveled to Maggie's left. Hugo stood alone, stunned to find himself the source of attention. He timidly folded his arms across his chest. "If anyone is escorting *Mrs. Frye* from the table, shouldn't it be me?"

Lloyd chuckled. He held up his glass to Hugo as though in toast. "Yes, and a hearty many congratulations to you, sir, for managing to win this beauty. Many have tried, you know, and just as many have failed." He lowered his glass to his lips. "Many are sitting in this very room."

Reuben threw his napkin on the table. "Sod off, Halverson."

Eyes glittering in amusement, Lloyd drew a triangle in the air between the three men. "You're coming to this guy's rescue, Radford? You do understand the irony here, don't you?"

Maggie was on her feet and out the door before the remaining gentlemen could so much as push back their chairs.

THIRTY-SIX

EVEN AT FULL HEIGHT, HUGO couldn't be said to tower over anyone. The top of Lloyd's scalp while sitting shared the same plane with Hugo's chin as he stood. Now the center of attention in a silent room, he focused on Lloyd, then Reuben, then at the half-eaten plate below him. After what appeared to be much consideration, he sat, picked up his fork, then set it back down and carefully folded his napkin. "A delicious meal, Mrs. Smith," he said without looking up from his plate. "I'm sorry to leave before dessert." Then he stood, pushed in his chair, and walked from the room with complete composure.

"I'll take dessert on the veranda, Rookwood," Reuben said and stalked from the room.

Tena couldn't blame either of them leaving. Frankly, she would rather not be there either. But it would have been the height of impropriety for her to follow Reuben, even if only to talk. The next morning, Edith and Bianca would give her nothing but grief about it and assume, as anyone else would, that something nefarious occurred during the night. Although honestly, after the past few days, she didn't even think Reuben would open the door.

He was avoiding something. It hadn't been hard to surmise after he exchanged his steamship passage to travel third class alone. Their walk through the Royal Botanic Gardens had been too cordial, and when she finally brought up his unusual mood, he quickly shifted the conversation to her disagreement with Maggie. When she tried again, he hid his emotions behind the pages of a book. All his actions indicated he hurt something fierce inside and needed someone to confide in. He would have confided in *her* once.

"An evening outdoors does sound lovely," Bianca said. She lifted a delicate hand. "Rookwood, we shall pass on the final course and take our dessert on the veranda."

"As you wish, m'lady." Rookwood nodded to the footmen who immediately disappeared into the butler's pantry.

Lloyd downed the remainder of his wine. "Just as well. I'm off to bed."

Bianca caught his eye as he stood. Even though her voice remained low, Tena caught her question to him. "One o'clock?"

"Not tonight, Mrs. Smith." Then he vacated the room without a backward glance.

With a tiny simper, Bianca leaned towards Tena. "You do know he plans to be with Maggie tonight, don't you? Maybe you should be more like your sister instead of attending parties once again—or should I say *always*—alone."

"I'm tired of your insinuation that I'm unable to capture a man's attention. I was engaged."

"Yes, darling," Bianca crooned, "and now you're not. So, please, Tena, do something to remedy it. We're all getting bored waiting." Her pointed stare swung to her sister. "Edie, I thought a lively game of whist might be in order."

"A perfect match to chocolate soufflé," Edith agreed and the room cleared in a flurry of blonde giggles and Mr. McCoy's hearty guffaws. Tena waited another few minutes, exhaled into the silence, and followed.

The Smiths' grand veranda was directly adjacent to a library whose breadth of knowledge would put Laurence Archer's study bookshelves to shame. She stared in awe of the many volumes, each bound in cloth or exquisite leather, many branded with gold leaf. A rollaway ladder allowed access to the uppermost shelves. She laid a gloved hand on a rung and inhaled deeply. What she wouldn't give for a library like this to lose herself in night after night. What a pity Bianca would never appreciate the luxury.

A breeze tickled her neck when the veranda door opened, bringing fresh April air and the twitter of lively chatter. Edith's giggle cut short as the door closed again.

"I wondered where we lost you to." Tena looked around to meet Mr. Troughton's easy smile. Crossing the room as easily as if he could part oceans, he offered his hand. "Shall we turn about the room, Miss Archer?"

Tena easily returned his smile as she released the ladder to accept his hand. "As you well know, Mr. Troughton, there are only two possible reasons for a lady to take a turn about the room. To speak of others uninhibited or to appear more desirable to the gentlemen watching her. As I have already caught your eye, should I then presume your reason to be the former?"

Mr. Troughton's chin shifted slightly, one brow rising, and Tena considered heading for the veranda without him. It was unusual for her to reference a piece of classic English literature and have her usual literary sparring partner miss the bait. Reuben would never overlook such a blatant reference.

"*Pride and Prejudice?*" she nudged, offering him a second chance. After all, she must continue to remind herself that this man was not like Reuben. In fact, most were not. "It is a statement Mr. Darcy makes as to the rationale for Miss Elizabeth and Miss Bingley's need to walk the room. You have read it, surely?"

Finally, he grinned and said, "Why yes, of course. I was merely caught off guard by the extent of your loveliness. It should be quite clear that I wish to speak uninhibited."

Does he honestly expect me not to recognize such obvious flattery? she thought. Even so, she accepted his arm and allowed him to lead her clockwise around the room.

"It was jolly good luck that Mrs. Smith invited me here tonight, Miss Archer. You are still as breathtaking as I remember from her Christmas party."

Heat rose up Tena's neck and she was grateful for the minimal lamps lit about the room. Most of the light came from the low burning fireplace and moonlight cascading across the floor. "Why, Mr. Troughton, that was well over a year ago."

"I remember every lady I dance with, especially if she is as becoming as you."

She felt her blush deepen despite herself. "Mrs. Smith has a poor tendency to create romantic matches without consent. Although, I do thank you for offering the compliment."

"I hope you can consider accepting more than a compliment from me." His grip on her hand tightened. "It should please me to speak more privately on behalf of what I can offer you, if you will do me the honor of dinner this week."

Tena pulled up short. The veranda doors lay but a stride away. She considered the impoliteness of choosing a game of whist with the Winchester sisters over this man's amorous advances. "Mrs. Smith has deceived you, Mr. Troughton. My stay in England is only temporary. I must return to America in a few days' time."

Only the patio doors separated them from the group eating soufflé and tossing cards at the edge of the veranda. Pale blue moonlight washed over his face and his brazen smile never wavered. "Stealing you may be America's one great folly; however, she does not hold your company tonight." Shifting Tena away from the veranda's potentially prying eyes, he raised her hand to his lips. "May we adjourn somewhere more private?"

The moisture of his kiss cooled upon her fingers, while the rest of her warmed at his touch. He may not be as well-versed in literature as she, but he certainly understood how to craft a story well enough. The words he offered were exquisite, lovely, beautiful ... and potentially a great risk to her heart if found to be false. Yet, she longed for them to be as uncomplicated as they sounded. For tonight, she basked in every syllable.

"Can I be assured your intentions are honorable?"

He drew closer, his already dark eyes lost in the library's shadows. "As honorable as any man. Whether more transpires between us than the shared conversation of two equals, that I leave to your good judgment."

To be a wallflower no more, she thought. To feel cherished and adored after so long trying to not feel. She didn't like the suggestion of an intimate arrangement without commitment or pursue a courtship from opposite shores ... except she could also still remember what a kiss felt like. *Be more like your sister*. Isn't that what Bianca said? As much as Tena wanted the happiness Maggie and Hugo found, she wasn't willing to claim it in the same manner. But one kiss was harmless. Even Charles earned a kiss the night they met. Surely she could give Mr. Troughton that without offering up any more?

"Miss Archer?"

She shook her head, too unnerved to say anything as her heart beat madly. She laid a trembling hand upon his shoulder and her corset pinched when he reciprocated the gesture at her waist. His Adam's apple bobbed a melody of encouragement and that's where her eyes rested.

"Mr. Troughton, you better get your bloomin' hands off my wife, sir, or you won't have any."

The veranda door slammed, the rattle of glass echoing to the ceiling. Reuben closed the twenty-foot gap and eased Tena back against his chest. Fury flared in his features, but his grip on her arm remained gentle. Unlike his other hand trembling violently against her side.

"How long were you listening?" she gasped.

"Longer than would please you."

Mr. Troughton's brow furrowed. "Forgive me, but you're with him? Mrs. Smith never mentioned—"

"She is," Reuben interjected. "Married last month. Mrs. Smith wouldn't let us steal attention from the party." He yanked Tena's hand into the man's face to show their matching rings, the outline of hers visible beneath her glove. When Reuben didn't propose to Hazel after a few months, Tena assumed he would stop wearing it, but he hadn't. "Bands of gold, fool. Take the hint."

"On your right hand, sir?" Mr. Troughton scoffed. "You jest me."

"I'm German. It's the way we do things in *Deutschland*."

"You certainly do not appear German."

"Yes, well, you neither appeared a cad, yet apparently you are one."

The other man folded his arms. "Well, *German*, it may be disturbing to note that your bride has some extraneous desires. It would behoove you to keep her in line."

"Yes, she is most difficult to keep in hand. We'll change that now I think." Reuben nudged Tena towards the door. "Tell Mr. Troughton goodnight, dearest."

"Excuse me, but ... what?" she spluttered as he dragged her from the room with a tight-lipped nod to the group staring from the veranda. Bianca winked knowingly from behind her playing cards.

The instant the door closed, he released her and made for the staircase without so much as a word. She followed, tripping over her glamorous gown on the first step. "Blast this wretched thing!" Bunching the silky material in her hands, she marched after him, her shocked silence now exchanged for irritation. "Reuben Radford!" she hissed. "Stop this instant."

Midway he turned and braced one hand on the banister. He towered over her, bearing down with eyes of steel. *Well, this is discomforting*, she thought and ascended to address him at eye level. "Reuben Radford," she repeated. "Calling me your wife? What in the world has overcome you?"

Reuben exhaled loudly, ran a hand across his slicked back hair, and swore.

"That's all I get?" she said. "Your foul mouth?"

He remained silent, neither his intense gaze nor his body relaxing in any manner. He gripped the banister and stared her down.

"Fine, don't speak to me," Tena spat. "I thought we were friends. Only I suppose not anymore." Gathering her skirts, she huffed up the staircase to the gallery, then immediately turned and stomped back to one step above him.

"No," she said. "I may not be your friend, but you are mine. As a friend, I have a right to know who gave you leave to barge into my affairs as you did?"

Silence reigned. Stone cold silence and eyes just as frozen.

Her chest heaved. "Let me be clear, Reuben. You are *not* my father or my brother. Neither are you my husband; therefore, you do not oversee my decisions. It isn't for you to judge what I do or whom I do it with. If I'm through grieving Charles, that is my choice. If I want to become involved with another man, all you may do is accept it."

Still, he didn't move. The only sound emitting from his mouth was shallow breathing. Finally, he slid his hand from the banister to her shoulder. "Would Charles accept you following a man to his room when you wouldn't even do that with *him*?"

"That's so unfair."

"Is it?"

It was Tena's turn to freeze. She felt tears well and looked to the ceiling lest they fall. She wouldn't cry. Tears meant she was in the wrong, and she wasn't sure that she was. After all, it was only meant to be an innocent kiss. A kiss meant so little, didn't it? Except when Charles kissed her, it hadn't been meaningless. In that moment, she knew someday she wanted more. She had wanted everything. What if a kiss with Matthew Troughton felt like it had with Charles? What if this time she couldn't stop?

Reuben slid his hand down her arm to her fingers, and his eyes finally softened. "This isn't you, Tena. You know it isn't. If you want me to be your friend, then let me. I can't stand by and watch you give away the most precious thing you have."

"You mean like you did with Maggie?"

Reuben frowned. "Now who's being unfair? I loved Maggie. You don't love Mr. Troughton."

"Hazel told me you love *her*. Then you've been with her too?"

Reuben gritted his teeth. "No. I haven't. I decided next time will be with my wife."

"Well, sensational for you. Maggie has been with loads of men, Bianca too, and they enjoy it well enough."

"You want to be cut from the same cloth as your sister? You'll be full of regret."

"I already have regrets." Tena stared down at the hand he held, her glove a secure barrier between their skin. "Until Charles, I always went unnoticed, Reuben. Tonight, someone finally noticed me."

He seemed to struggle with some inward emotion, breathing deeply, his voice strained. "This isn't you," he repeated. "I love you. Please don't be with someone else."

"You *love* me?" With a hiss, she ripped her fingers from his. This wasn't happening. "How can you? You're with Hazel."

"Actually I'm not. We ended things before I left for London."

"You-you-you and Hazel—" Tena stammered.

"Ended things," he repeated. "She thought I didn't love her. She wasn't wrong." He appeared like he wanted to say more, but she kept shaking her head and telling him he was wrong. This couldn't be happening. Hazel loved him. She wouldn't hurt him. You didn't just walk away from someone so perfectly right.

Finally, he pressed a gentle hand to her lips. "Please, Tena. Let's not complicate this. I love you like family. Like Fred or Emil."

"Like you're my brother?" she laughed. She felt both relieved and insulted. "Very well, brother dear, explain how you earned all my father's respect and he left not even a crumb for me."

"Laurence did respect you. Far more than you're respecting yourself right now." He clamped a hand on either of her bare arms, sending goose pimples along her flushed skin. With a tender squeeze, he pressed his forehead against hers and sighed. "With his dying words, your father asked me to watch over you. He trusted me with your welfare, and I'll be hung if I allow you to offer yourself to the first imbecile who sees in you what I've noticed all along."

"Father asked you to watch me?" She pulled back to meet his eyes. "That's what he leaves for me—a nanny? To keep me from swallowing a button and choking to death? Well, in the words of Mr. Washington Irving, 'Ducks and geese are foolish things, and must be looked after, but girls can take care of themselves.'" Reuben was an expert on literary quotations, let him chew on that one for a while. She twisted out of his grip, the flesh where his touch lay now painfully cold.

"No matter what my father may have requested, it does not give you claim over my decisions. And if you noticed something no one else ever did, then you certainly should have spoken up long before now." Her breath caught and she pressed a hand to her throat with a shuddered gasp. "You altered everything by being Abigail's father. If you were really paying attention, you would have noticed *that*."

It had been a guess, a wild suspicion she held since she started adding the pieces of Abigail's birth together, and she immediately knew she hit the mark.

Like a kicked puppy, Reuben stared at her in disbelief, unable to respond to the fact that she knew a truth he never intended her to have. Tena trusted him with her life, while he still didn't trust her with his. The astonishment on his face was like a slap to hers.

"Tena, I'm sorry."

With a turn of her heel, she stumbled up the stairs to her room, unable to speak and unable to escape quickly enough.

THIRTY-SEVEN

REUBEN STARED AT THE WHITE plastered ceiling above his bed and listened to the dresser clock tick. He pictured Tena with Matthew Troughton's hands on her in the library and simultaneously wanted to take a cold bath and light the man's room on fire. It was an extremely confusing emotion.

At least it wasn't Halverson, he thought. Thank God she wasn't as misguided as her sister.

Reuben, on the other hand, was a bloomin' idiot. He should have told Tena that Hazel broke things off before they left for England.

"You're not coming back, are ya?" Hazel had asked while they sat in her parents' kitchen eating apple cream tarts that last Sunday afternoon.

"What do you mean?" he said. "Of course I am."

"But not to me. Why else would you move out so suddenly after Christmas? It was because I told ya I loved you."

Reuben clasped her hands across the little table and traced the distressed lines of her face with his eyes. "No. It was because I couldn't say it back."

He had tried. After Christmas, he tried to make it work with Hazel. He wanted to do as Tena asked when she gave him Charles's ring. Hazel was uncomplicated, and he had hoped he could find it in his heart to deepen his feelings towards her. Then through Abigail he once again came face to face with his poor decisions and life became messy. He had a daughter, and he had no idea how she fit into his life or how he could keep a secret like that from Hazel until the end of time.

Tena figured it out. Of course, she would have. How did he ever think they could hide something so monumental from her when she knew him and Maggie so well? He hadn't really. In more ways than not, it was a relief that she finally knew. He only wished his blind jealousy of Mr. Troughton hadn't been the catalyst by which she discovered it.

He rolled onto his stomach and hugged the pillow into his chin. Tena smiled beneath his closed eyelids, moonlight glinting off her amazing evening gown as she entered Mr. Troughton's room.

Reuben swung out of bed and threw his pillow across the room.

"You need to go back to your life," Charles told him when he was stuck in his dream limbo on the *Höllenfeuer*. After falling into thirty-degree water, Reuben's body lay broken in the ship's hospital and his mind hovered somewhere between life and death. He considered staying peacefully deceased rather than return to a life of turmoil. It was Charles who insisted he leave. "You must go back, because I cannot. I know that is selfish, but I am not sorry for asking it."

Reuben spun Charles's ring over his knuckle and set it on the side table. He reversed the previous image of Tena in his head. This time it was his door she opened.

He wanted to steal the life Charles left behind, the one where Reuben became the husband who smoldered Tena with his stare and any other part of him he chose. She would mother his children, and he never need hide his true identity from them. He would love her, and fifty years from now, he wouldn't regret it, not even once, not even a little bit.

In his dream limbo, Charles had handed Reuben those years, offered them freely, one best mate—one brother—to another. Reuben had three hundred and sixty-five days since to take action and when he finally had the perfect opportunity tonight, he froze.

Why in the name of everything did he say Tena was like a sister when she was the farthest person from?

Because it wasn't Reuben she meant to kiss at the Grand Basin and it wasn't Reuben's ring she still wore. The life he envisioned with her was the one she still wanted with Charles. She could have trusted Charles to not repeatedly withhold the truth from her, especially when Abigail wasn't the only secret Reuben had been keeping.

But what did the rest of it matter now when he had already lost her trust?

"Self-loathing looks quite terrible on you," Mira would say. "Why did you bother saving Tena from the basin if you're going to let her go now?"

"I'm not letting her go."

Reuben would win her back—if not her affection, then at the least her friendship. What they had between them when Charles was alive, they could have again. If she chose Matthew Troughton, he would be as supportive of her decision as she had been when he picked Hazel.

He returned Charles's ring to his right hand. Unrequited love could be stifled. After all, he had already done it once before.

THIRTY-EIGHT

"MISS MARGARET, FINALLY. Where have you been?" Hugo paused in his arrangement of the four poster's top coverlet into a makeshift bed on the floor of their shared suite. He searched her face. "I worried."

Maggie closed the bedroom door behind her. "You shouldn't have. I was only wandering the gardens." *Also, trying not to think and failing.*

"Are you wanting Abigail? I can retrieve her from the nursery." Hugo stretched for his dressing gown.

"That won't be necessary. I nursed her before coming in." She crossed to the window and drew back the curtain. Directly below a motorcar pulled around the circular drive to collect a male and a female passenger, most likely the McCoys, although it was too dark to say for certain. The engine's purr faded as it trailed away, two headlights fading into the darkness until they disappeared. She wrapped her arms around her middle, still sheathed in the glamorous gown, and shivered.

"Something is the matter," said Hugo. Not a question.

"No."

"Something is the matter," he repeated. "Is it that man at dinner? Mr. Halverson?"

"What did he say after I left?" She had been so desperate to escape, she didn't consider what further damage Lloyd could actually cause.

"Beats me. I left the room about a minute after you did and came up here when I couldn't find you anywhere." He paused too long before asking, "Dare I ask, could he be Abigail's father?"

Maggie let the curtain drop back into place. "No," she replied icily. "He couldn't." Hugo's questions invited the potential for conflict, an area he rarely administered to well. Nor would she in the present situation. "It doesn't make a difference who it is."

Stealing a pillow from the bed, Hugo smashed it between his hands, then dropped it onto the coverlet. "Maybe, but I think I should decide that for myself."

Maggie's heart plummeted. It slammed against her feet then leapt back to rattle inside her ribcage. She had spent so long dreading this conversation with Tena and Reuben that she never stopped to consider how to respond when Hugo asked. Maybe a large part of her always assumed he never would. He loved Abigail, so why should it matter where she came from? It was all water under the bridge now, wasn't it?

"Oi." She hated that word. It was awful, like spewing dirt from between her teeth. Except there were no other words to use. Every syllable in the English language failed her. The true father of her child was the same man Hugo worked with at the newspaper, the same man he now traveled with. Reuben slept three rooms away from them, and pacifist or not, coward or not, Maggie didn't want to start an unexpected reaction in Hugo that couldn't be tamped down.

Finally, she managed to squeeze out six syllables. "Don't make me lie to you."

All color drained from his face. "My word, it's—it's—no. It can't be. It's Radford, isn't it?" He didn't bother waiting for her answer. His words tangled, falling over each other in one long stream of consciousness while his fingers never left his hair. They strained against his scalp, tugging upwards then smoothing back in place. Traces of brilliantine forced it out at all angles. "I assumed Reuben was sweet on your sister, but now you tell me he was with *you*? Could that even work? How could that work? I understand Mr. Halverson. I mean, he's a complete nincompoop, so I don't mind hating him, but Reuben? Apple pie, I actually liked him before, and now I can't stop picturing you together. I can only see ... that doesn't matter though.

No, it doesn't. Fish and chips, no wonder he's avoided me since I brought Abbie to the paper. How could I not see it? She looks exactly like him."

Hugo lowered himself onto his makeshift bed, tossed the blanket over his knees, and dropped his face into his palms. "I'm sorry. The wine at dinner must have affected me more than I thought."

"You only had one glass." Maggie turned away from the window and sank onto the dressing table chair, watching the reflection of a young debutante turned elderly matron right before her eyes. She removed Bianca's earrings and necklace then the hairpins and delicate headpiece, piling them all on the table top. Dark curls unfolded down her back. She wanted to slice them all to ribbons.

Pouring water into the wash basin, she scrubbed at her makeup, trying to rid herself of the mask she had been forced into. Glitz and glamour, high society, fancy parties in extravagant gowns. That was what her mother groomed her for, but she didn't recognize herself within it anymore. Now she was a photographer's wife, an unskilled mother with her bare hands in the soil while barges sailed down the Mississippi River behind her and the children ran circles in the garden. Correction, the yard. In America, they called it a yard.

She patted her face dry and lowered her hands to her lap. In the mirror, Hugo remained hunched over on the floor, fingertips pressed to his forehead. She did this to him, she thought miserably. She had done this to them all.

"Forgive me, Hugo."

After another moment, he lifted his face. His troubled eyes met hers in the mirror. "There's something I need to ask you."

Before she could reply, a quick rap interrupted at the door.

"Enter," Maggie called. "And be quick about it."

Rella, Bianca's lady's maid, stepped in with a quick nod. "Shall I assist you for bed, Mrs. Frye?" Her eyes swiveled to Hugo's improvised bed on the floor. Her brow twitched up, but she knew her place not to ask. They certainly wouldn't be the first or even the thirtieth married couple who maintained separate sleeping arrangements.

"No thank you, Rella. I can manage myself tonight. You may

retrieve your lady's gown on the morrow."

"Very good, ma'am." With another quick nod, she backed from the room.

Maggie swiveled to face Hugo, but he had already laid down and arranged the blanket over himself. "What did you need to ask me?"

"It isn't important." He turned onto his side. "Goodnight. I hope your dreams are pleasant for once."

She jumped at the comment, latching onto anything that would keep him talking. Forget her earlier concerns. He had already cracked the door; they may as well kick it wide open. "For once?" she asked. "Do I talk while I sleep?"

"Only sometimes."

"What do I say?" She could only imagine what sort of things she muttered in the night.

Hugo didn't respond. His chest rose and fell far too quickly for normal sleep and his eyelids were clenched together with the strain of the devil. She threw her shoe at his still form where it bounced off his thigh and clattered onto the hardwood. He barely shifted.

"Mr. Frye, are you avoiding another potentially damaging conversation?"

"Yes."

Blast that Rella arriving at the worst possible moment. For a second, Hugo opened up and now he was shying away again. But she had too much she needed to say.

She kicked off her other shoe. "This contract we have ... are you content with the way things are?"

He flipped onto his back and folded his right arm over his eyes. "I'm following the rules and so are you, so sleep in peace."

Maggie swept her hair over her left shoulder as she moved to kneel beside him. "That's the problem. Why am I following the rules? Inviting five men into my bed in less than a year's time and rejecting my parents' every societal fiber is not the definition of devout conformity. I should have broken every word of our agreement by now."

"I beg you don't do this tonight."

"If not tonight, when? You'll ward me off until you die." She hauled his arm back and pinned it to the floor. "I told you a little about my past, but you don't know the whole of it. I betrayed Reuben in the worst way. I broke his heart through a disgusting deal with Lloyd Halverson to find out a few measly pieces of information I didn't even deserve to know. I was the most selfish being alive, everyone else be forgotten."

Hugo lifted himself from the pillow and with a gentle push against her shoulder, scooted out of reach. "Miss Margaret, please don't."

She shook her head. It was important that he know this. "I think it was better to not fully consider the consequences, better to forget how cruel life could be. I knew there would be no coming back from it, but I think I was simply too broken inside to see another way." Her breath hitched and she pressed a hand to her stomach. "Except when I'm with you I don't feel so damaged anymore, and I wish I knew why."

Every one of Hugo's muscles visibly uncoiled as his lips eased gently upward. "You're not damaged, Miss Margaret. Far from it."

There could be no logical reason for the tender smile he afforded her now nor the intimate understanding reflected in his gaze. It made her feel things she didn't want to feel. A hot burn that coursed through her limbs and stabbed her behind the eyes.

"Please don't look at me like that," she whispered.

Hugo scuffed through his goatee. "Would you like to know what you say in your dreams?"

She nodded. Her fingers slid absently over the iridescent blue fabric of her gown. The folds shimmered like ocean waves, like the *Höllenfeuer* and a night she couldn't forget.

"Sometimes you scream," Hugo said quietly. "You ask why he's doing this to you. I never know who he is, but you beg him for all sorts of things. I lay there listening to you sob, and sometimes I'm unable to bear the sound." He shifted closer until their knees sat only an inch apart. His hands rested on his thighs. "So, more often than not, I reach for your hand and sometimes—" He swallowed "—then you dream about me instead."

Maggie's palm rose to her chest, unable to cool the blaze across her cheeks. She couldn't manage to look anywhere except his nail beds, perpetually stained from photography chemicals. She could barely ask the words for fear of the answer. "How do you know?"

Hugo exhaled a long shuddering breath. "Because you love me. Don't you?"

She looked up, startled by the intensity of his tone. "You know that's not a term of our contract, Mr. Frye."

"Can the contract. Answer the question."

"I can't."

Hugo leapt up and dug his handkerchief from the pocket of his trousers. Throwing the pants back over the armchair, he rummaged through her handbag until he found a stick of rouge. He held both out to her. "Write your answer on this. You don't have to say it."

She stared at the items in his hands. She should run. A year ago she would have found Derby—or some other ill-suited man—and allowed him to do all sorts of things to her until the wee hours of the morning. There would be no remorse and no tears to cry over his inevitable rejection. She loathed that part of her, yet even now there was a frightened girl inside that dragged her kicking and screaming towards her former self. Lloyd would open his door if she but knocked. Without commitment and without expectation.

She should run.

Why then did she find herself accepting the handkerchief from Hugo? Why was a word appearing on the fabric made by her hand?

Her heart raced. It skipped. It spun. Could she do this? Say yes to this man? It defied logic. He never said what happened when he went to Utah to look for Emma. What if she gave her heart away and he broke it into a thousand pieces later?

Business partners, nothing more. They agreed on it, made their marriage vows on it, on the mutual understanding that nothing was worse than being too close with another person. But that was before she came to know him like her own skin. Before he laughed beside her every morning and delighted when he returned home in the evening. Before battling the daily chaos. Before her smile matched his.

When had it happened, this longing for her husband? The day Abigail was born? When Molly was sick? The time he chased Henry around the garden as she watched from the window? While he mourned over his divorce papers? What about every night she lay alone in bed, her stomach growing rounder by the day, unable to sleep from the insomnia and kicking in her loins? She had watched him asleep in the trundle bed below her, breath falling through his chest, arms flung above him and mouth open a little as he snored ever so slightly. Perhaps it was then that she first felt it. Or could it even be the day she spied him at the Kischs' with his camera, never uttering too many words and still saying everything? Was it then that she first noticed he loved her?

Of that, she was now certain. He loved her. He may have traveled to Utah for Emma, but it was Maggie he returned to. The way he held her on Christmas Eve breached their contract. How his fingers slid through her hair and traveled her spine—how she didn't push him away—transformed their agreement. She wept, and he never once insisted she remain strong.

He broke the rules by loving her. She broke the rules by wanting him to.

"Maggie."

That was all he said then. One word. One simple word. Her name and nothing else. But how that word swam in her ears. Not Mrs. Frye. Not Miss Margaret. But Maggie. Her given name said in a whisper, in a plea, as tender as a prayer.

"Maggie," he said again. Quickly, quietly, as though speaking the word too loudly might make it break. He sank onto the blanket before her, his hands removing the handkerchief from hers. He balled it into his fist and pressed his fingers to his lips.

"Are you not going to read my answer, Mr. Frye?"

"I don't need to. I know who my wife is."

His lips embraced hers then, and even as they molded around each other like the missing chink in a chain, the entire time he held that handkerchief. He clutched her answer as though dropping it would end the world.

~~~

Eyes closed against the morning and blankets tugged against her chin, Maggie pressed her back into the mattress beneath her and silently recited her daily mantra. *That life was not mine. It was all a dream. When I open my eyes, everything will be upright again.*

She turned her head and slowly opened her eyes, the most tender of smiles easing across her lips. Hugo lay on his side facing her, already awake with a small smile to match her own. "You're still here, Maggie."

"So are you."

This couldn't be real. That she loved someone who also loved her. That she made love to him without conspiracy attached, without ulterior motives drawing her to his bed. The movements had been slow and strange and not as satisfying as she had experienced on other occasions, but it meant so much more. Hugo was her husband. They would have their lives to find perfection. Last night wasn't a symphony, but it had been a song, a beautiful melody composed specifically for them.

As Maggie lay in the same bed as her husband for the first time, she held onto those emerald eyes and leapt arms outstretched into the endless space between them. Space she needed to fill with her stories; words that wouldn't flow quick enough. Tales of the men who once loved her, stories of how she ruined them, ways she sold her own soul in an attempt to save her heart. It was exactly as Reuben predicted when they arrived in New York one year ago.

Someday you'll meet someone who not only makes you face your fears, but helps you embrace them. And him you won't want to deceive.

Even when he had despised her, he still wanted her happiness. What a fool she was to not understand what he offered. How she could throw it back in his face, she would never know. But she had also been a different person then.

Maggie slipped her arms around Hugo and rested a cheek against the wispy hair of his chest. Underneath, his heart beat steadily. She would never have suspected she could find love with a man like him. Or how, upon hearing the unraveling of her life's story, he would merely brush the hair from her eyes and capture her body all over again. That such a man would impossibly be her husband or that she would want him to be.

"I could live like this forever," she breathed. The morning sun glinted off the wedding band he returned to her on Christmas, and she lifted her face to kiss him soundly. "I want to love you forever."

Hugo smiled against her lips. "Good. Because that's how long you've got me for."

THIRTY-NINE

THE SOUTH LONDON BOTANICAL INSTITUTE lay on the lower side of the city, a lone establishment in a broad stretch of open fields. Another day of drab skies and saturated dirt roads melded with Reuben's already discouraged mood and left the two-story brick Victorian even more unimpressive than it already was. He raised the borrowed umbrella as he stepped from the taxi's passenger seat and opened the rear door.

"M'lady?" he said, offering assistance to Tena. Ignoring his outstretched hand, she stepped from the taxi and raised her own black umbrella without meeting his eyes. "You can't possibly stay cross with me forever, Tena."

Due to the previous night's volatile dinner, all four traveling partners had found themselves in complete agreement come morning. They would not return to England a second time. Which meant that this was their only opportunity to decipher Laurence Archer's enigmatic life. If they didn't learn anything in the next few days, they wouldn't learn it, come what may.

Tena shifted her gaze to where Hugo was assisting his wife from the motorcar. "If this is about Abigail, Reuben, you'll need to give me more time."

Didn't he know it. One didn't learn that sort of information and expect glowing acceptance the following morning.

"Only partly. I also wanted to apologize for my outburst over Mr.

318

Troughton. Although I may not agree with your approach, I'm willing to support your decision. If you fancy him, it's surely none of my business."

Her eyes widened slightly. "Truly?"

"I want to fix this rift between us, so I'll do whatever it takes. I broke our friendship when I left last summer, and I don't believe you've ever fully forgiven me for that. But can't you find it in your heart to try?"

She focused on the brick building at the other end of the walk. One front window was aglow; otherwise, the house appeared uninhabited. Hugo shut the auto's opposite rear door and Reuben pressed ahead before they were interrupted. "Please, Tena. Don't make a grown man beg."

At last, she nodded. "I will try." Not the response he was hoping for, but at least it wasn't a flat-out rejection either.

After depositing their umbrellas in a stand near the door, a thin woman showed them through the semi-shadowed entryway of the Botanical Institute into the house's sitting room. Now converted into a miniature lecture theatre, chairs sat in rows with their backs to the windows. Green and white wallpaper hung the length of the room, complimenting the fireplace carvings with its floral pattern.

"I'm afraid Dr. Schweitzer's office is in a bit of disarray for entertaining guests," the woman said with a chuckle. "What business should I convey?"

"Personal matters," Maggie said. She bounced Abigail against her shoulder as she walked the room. The baby had been especially fussy on the ride over and hadn't slept all morning.

The woman frowned. "Nothing serious, I hope?"

"It's a matter of a will," Tena said. "Our father's, Laurence Archer. Were you familiar with him?"

The woman's lips flipped as quickly as they had lowered. "Oh my, yes. We were all quite familiar with Mr. Archer and terribly troubled to hear of his passing. He offered such a generous contribution when we first established in 'ten. Visited twice that year and brought news of his lovely daughters. To meet you both at last. What a joy."

"Of course, a pleasure for us as well. Father was a magnanimous donor," Tena said with an easy smile, but Reuben knew her expressions better than this woman ever would. For every puzzle piece they slid into place, a new hole formed in the picture. How far exactly did the mysteries of Laurence's life extend?

The woman clasped her hands to her chest. "These dear men must be your husbands?"

"Yes," Maggie snapped. Abigail continued to whine against her shoulder. "Please, ma'am, we're on a schedule. Is Dr. Schweitzer available or not?"

She stiffened at Maggie's unladylike tone, which Reuben could only assume did not match Mr. Archer's well-spoken stories. "Of course, ma'am. I'll fetch Dr. Schweitzer now."

"No need, Mrs. Allan. I'm here."

"Very good, sir." With a nod, Mrs. Allan squeezed past him into the hallway.

With brunette hair as peppered as his beard, the man now filling the doorway carried himself as securely as the leather attaché tucked beneath his arm. Fine wrinkles couldn't break the sophistication in his face, nor could narrow spectacles filter his surprise at their appearance. When he next spoke, there was a slight German lilt to some inflections, although faint enough to suggest he had lived abroad a good many years, perhaps even the majority of his life.

His eyes flickered from Maggie to Tena and back again. An inordinate amount of fear registered there. "Why are you here?"

Maggie didn't respond. Her face was ashen. Abigail wailed.

"Did Mr. Weston send you?" Dr. Schweitzer asked. "You tell him that dead men tell no tales and neither will I." He turned for the door.

"Please, sir," Tena spoke up. "We've traveled all the way from America to finalize our father's financial obligations. All we want is to make certain his wealth is in deserving hands. If your research was important to our father, then it's important to us."

His expression softened only slightly. "Your father's vested interest extended to all areas of the Institute, not only mine."

"What of his donations to your work at the Palm House?" Reuben asked.

Dr. Schweitzer's scowl returned with a deadened stare to match.

"As of December, I've concluded my research at the Royal Gardens."

"But why would our father invest in that at all?" Tena asked and quickly amended, "That is not to say that botany isn't important; however, our father never expressed any interest towards it. He preferred to invest time in books rather than the outdoors."

"Your father had his reasons. I can assure you they were sound. Take comfort in knowing that." He tipped his chin. "Now, you must excuse me. I'm afraid I have an appointment at Imperial College I am already tardy to."

"Please, sir, one more minute of your time," Tena chased after him, her voice edging on begging. Abigail's cries had finally died down to a mere whimper, and she shoved Maggie forward as Dr. Schweitzer collected a hat and umbrella from the coat rack. "Maggie," she ventured. "Surely, you have something to include?"

But her sister remained as silent as the secrets in their father's grave. Reuben frowned at her continued silence. Something was amiss.

"He's dead, Dr. Schweitzer," Tena said. "Surely it no longer matters if it's discussed?"

The botanist plunked the hat onto his head and looped the umbrella around his forearm. "Listen, miss, I am truly sorry for your loss. Your father was a man of exceptional character and a fine friend. For my part, he will be greatly missed; however—" When Tena again attempted to argue, Dr. Schweitzer talked over her in that no-nonsense voice. "However," he repeated, "as you yourself have stated, the man called Laurence Archer is deceased, and it no longer matters. Now, good day."

He tipped his hat and turned away. Tena grabbed her umbrella from the stand and followed down the front steps, leaving Reuben rushing to catch up. "No," she cried through the drizzle. "That's not enough. Father hid this from us for our entire lives. Why couldn't he trust us with it? Did he have another family in London? A better daughter? Was he having an affair with *you*?"

Dr. Schweitzer turned so quickly, Tena barely stopped before slamming into him. His eyes flashed, and when he stepped towards her, Reuben positioned himself between them.

"Stand down, doctor."

Dr. Schweitzer ignored him and spoke only to Tena. "First off, *fräulein*, judge not those whom you do not understand. Furthermore, what you should already realize about your father, if you claim to know him as you do, is that he was fully devoted to his family. No woman, man, or possession could ever drive him from you. If you want to know what your father's motives were, only your mother can tell you." His sights shot to Maggie who now stood in the front doorway, staring down at this imposing figure. For a second, his gaze seemed to flicker to something more compassionate, then hardened, so much so that Reuben believed he had only imagined it. The botanist's glare swung back to Tena. "Do not approach me again."

For an instant, they were trapped in Dr. Schweitzer's enormous shadow then he cranked his parked motorcar and spun mud in his retreat.

Tena whirled on her sister. "Explain yourself, Maggie Elaine. After all your grousing with me over uncovering every blasted secret, and then you didn't say a word. Why wouldn't you help me?"

"I hoped it wasn't true," Maggie murmured. She handed Abigail to Hugo and rubbed her eyes as though still uncertain of what she had seen. "I prayed you were right. That the significance would turn out to be nothing."

"Right about what?"

Maggie stared in the direction of Dr. Schweitzer's disappearing motorcar without an ounce of emotion. "That was him, Tena. The man from Shaw's Garden. The man from my dreams."

FORTY

RETURNING TO FONTAINE AFTER over a year away was how Tena imagined it might feel to return home after being away at war. Nothing looked quite the same because she was no longer the same.

This far from London the weather fared more pleasant, and girls in white dresses danced in the sunshine of the town square. Their pigtails swung as they wrapped multicolored ribbons around the ten-foot maypole. It would be but one of many upcoming rehearsals for the town's lavish May Day festival in two weeks time. She missed those days of frivolity, whispering secrets with her friends about who would win the prestigious title of May Queen. Every young girl wished it for themselves, each silently jealous of the one who actually received it.

Except for once. Three years ago, Maggie was chosen for flowers in her hair and it was the only time in Tena's then seventeen years that she felt such admiration for her elder sister. Within the year, Maggie was supposed to bring honor to the Archer name through an esteemed betrothal. Then the spotlight would have shifted and finally, Tena's chance would have come. Their daughters should have danced on May Day together.

How frivolous they were then. As if flowers and ribbons mattered compared to the Pandora's Box they cracked open at the Institute.

Ignorance had been ecstasy. Now Tena was a stranger in her own life story.

An unfamiliar housemaid showed them into the Archers' parlor, now reupholstered in solid shades of tan and crimson instead of the pale florals of her childhood. As expected, Laurence Archer's chosen country landscapes had been exchanged for fresh cream wallpaper and heavy tapestries. She could only cringe at how her mother must have altered the upstairs bedrooms.

Her own eyes ingesting the unfamiliar décor, Maggie eased Abigail to the crook of her arm and claimed the sofa nearest the window. Hugo quickly sat beside her, leaving Tena and Reuben to the settee nearer the fireplace.

"Where is Olivia?" Maggie asked the maid.

The youngest member of staff at twenty-nine, Olivia had been more than a housemaid and later lady's maid. She was a humorous addition to the staff, always smiling, and an overall lovely person—as close to a friend as a servant could expect to rise. After Laurence's death, when staff was significantly reduced, Olivia stepped into forgotten tasks usually meant for footmen and lesser maids.

"Olivia left service," the new maid explained. "My name's Sarah. I started here about six months ago." Still younger than their mother by many years, Sarah seemed a fine enough companion, but simply put, she was no Olivia.

Another unwelcome adjustment.

Beatrix Archer appeared to be the one element that hadn't changed a bit in the past year. When their mother breezed into the parlor a moment later, she still carried her thirty-eight years with the same regal precision and begged the affection of all who might care to gaze upon her. Brunette locks curled delicately against the base of her neck with pearled combs the only hint of silver. Her green tea gown hugged curves like a woman half her age.

"Mr. Radford," she said, her lips flat. "You did not inform me you were coming."

"Why would I need to inform you of anything?" Reuben asked. He leaned into the sofa, crossed one leg over his opposite knee, and crooked his eyebrows high. "You're certainly not *my* mother."

She raised her trim brows to match his. "Yet you appear to have taken quite the interest in my daughters again. If you're searching for my blessing, you've wasted a perfect use of ship's passage."

Reuben frowned. "Let's skip the nonsense, Mrs. Archer. Alois Schweitzer—how do you know him?"

To their mother's credit, she didn't allow an ounce of astonishment to appear on her face. The only indication that she hadn't been expecting this turn of events lay in the slight widening of blue-grey eyes within her otherwise calm expression. She strode to the call rope although, with Sarah having only left the room, summoning her would have been more easily achieved by the use of her vocal cords. Except that was not how things were done here.

Beatrix sat in the armchair directly to the left of Tena and smoothed her delicate skirt over her knees. "Seeing as you have interrupted me at an hour normally calling for High Tea, I cannot have this discussion without refreshments."

"We do not require tea," Maggie said. "We require an explanation."

"You will wait for tea, or you will receive no explanation."

Ten silent minutes later, Sarah entered carrying a tray laden with a steaming teapot and five cups with saucers. Setting the tray on the table, she carefully poured one for each of the sisters and added completely inaccurate amounts of cream and sugar. She turned to Hugo, "How will you take yours, sir?"

"I would prefer coffee," Hugo replied. "Do you have that here?" Maggie gave a quick shake of her head. "Then tea it is." He accepted the cup from Sarah and visibly struggled with the desire to grimace.

After preparing the final cups, with a quick curtsy Sarah removed herself and the tea tray from the room.

"So, Maggie, I see you've gone off and married a Yankee?" Beatrix asked as she reached for her tea. She gingerly tested the temperature and finding it too warm, returned the cup to its saucer.

"Yes," Maggie said. "This is Mr. Hugo Frye and this—" She smoothed a hand across her daughter's dark curls. "—is our daughter, Abigail."

"And you, Tena dear, I suppose you've married *him*, have you?" Beatrix gave a mighty roll of her eyes, and Tena felt her temper flare. Reuben had made a fine life for himself in America. He was far from unworthy.

"No," she said. "No one since Charles."

Beatrix stirred her tea with a sweet saccharine smile. "How terrible it was to hear of young Mr. Kisch's passing. Although, that is the price you pay, dear, for not selecting a worthy partner."

Reuben jerked forwards and only the arm Tena lashed against his chest kept him from launching off the sofa. "I want to be rid of you as soon as I can," he spat. "I've tried again and again to make you see reason, and I'm not wasting anymore time on a venomous shrew." Even through his jacket, Tena felt his heart pulsing, keeping time with the one that thudded in her own chest. What had she honestly expected? A tearful reunion painted with apologies? Not from *her* mother.

She steadied her arm. "Now please tell us how you became familiar with Alois Schweitzer."

Finally, Beatrix deemed her tea worthy to drink. After a long agonizing sip, she said, "How did you even find out about him?"

"That's not important," said Maggie. "We know there's some dreadful secret that everyone's hiding. So enough delay, Mother. Time to tell."

"Very well."

"You won't even deny it?" Tena sputtered. Her arm dropped and she hoped Reuben slapped the smirk straight off her mother's face.

"There's little point now, is there? I promised Laurence I would tell you when you asked. You've asked, and I'm obligated to tell." With another sip of tea, she turned back to Maggie. "As my eldest, you will promise not to use it against me, won't you?"

"Per the day you washed your hands of your motherly duties, you're not exactly in a position to demand such a promise, are you?" Reuben said.

Beatrix smiled around the lip of her cup. "Refuse then. My daughters seem to be securely in your pocket, Mr. Radford, so by all means, convince them to turn their backs. The truth, however, remains with me."

"Believe me, if I held the influence, this would already be resolved." Reuben shoved all ten fingers through his hair and stood up, but instead of throwing a right hook to Beatrix's face, he strode across the room to stare out the window overlooking Union Street.

"Agreed," Tena said.

Maggie nodded. She ran the tip of one finger over the same seam in her dress until Hugo finally cupped her hand inside his.

"I love you," he whispered. He looked up at Beatrix. "They agreed. Now please break the news as gently as you can."

"It all began in the summer of 1892. Alois was a botany student at Kew, fresh off the boat from Hamburg and studying under one of my father's friends, a man by the name of Dr. Raymond. He introduced us one afternoon after a lecture my mother and I attended. The veiled enlightenment of flowers, I believe was the topic. Nonsensical, but how it changed my life all the same.

That entire summer we carried on our affair. At the same time, I allowed myself to be courted by the son of my father's wealthy bank manager. Laurence was endearing with a kind smile. It was obvious from the first that he was absolutely enraptured with me, and I, of course, cherished the idea. We were the highlighted couple of every function, the ones to watch—similar to how Lloyd Halverson became with you, Maggie. Bets were placed on how and when Laurence would ask for my hand. He was a handsome match. Yet, I continued my affair.

One month later, I discovered I was three months heavy with child.

I knew my father would never approve. My mother was from humble means, and my father saved her from the life of mediocrity Alois possessed. Disappointing him would have been the ultimate humiliation. Rather than openly defy them, I ended things even though it broke my heart.

When Laurence proposed, I accepted immediately. He loved me despite what I'd done. More importantly, he had money enough to care for me and my child. I thought perhaps in time, I could learn to love him as I had loved Alois.

Two months after you were born, Maggie, I took you to meet your father, and it was as though no time had passed. Gentle and caring, he brought out a desire in me I never felt before or since. Shortly after, I learned I was carrying again.

Alois didn't seem to mind that I was married. He understood how I only wed Laurence to please my parents. He was delighted to have me any way he could, and I brought you to see him every chance I could. He believed he was getting the very best of me, and being young and foolish, I believed he was giving me the same.

Until the night before we moved from London to Fontaine. Four years after Tena was born, Laurence received an invitation to manage Fontaine's largest bank. London would be too far for me to travel regularly, at least not without drawing suspicion, but I couldn't bear the idea of losing Alois a second time. By then, he had graduated university and was situated quite nicely within the staff at the Royal Botanic Gardens. He could now give me the life I wanted.

It was the Ides of March when I told Laurence; I remember the night so clearly. I handed you both off to the nanny for bed, walked into his study, and slammed my traveling case on his desk. 'Laurence,' I said. 'I'm having an affair and I'm leaving you for him.'

He tugged a ledger out from beneath my case and looked it over. "For Schweitzer," he said calmly. I'll admit I was taken aback that he knew. He never told me how he discovered my lover's identity, but we were never willing to share much with one another. He had his secrets as much as I had mine, and that was the way we were.

I told him, 'Yes, and I'm taking the girls. You cannot stop me.'

'Why would I try?' Laurence set down his ledger and stood to face me. 'Nothing I say would likely affect your decision, Bea. I have some business to attend to tomorrow morning leaving you to pack. I only ask that I spend the evening with my daughters.'

I, of course, had no intention of allowing him to work you girls into a frenzy over leaving without him. He wouldn't return from the bank until nearly six, so the following afternoon, I packed everything as quickly as I could, bundled you girls up, and summoned a taxi straight to Alois's flat as we planned.

Except when I arrived, he had changed his mind. He said he had time to consider and realized what a terrible mistake we both made. He argued that we would ruin my husband's life.

'Laurence cares nothing for me!' I argued. 'He knows I do not love him.'

'But we cannot take his children.' Alois's expression was so stern, I remember that clearly. Never in the many years we were together did he ever seem tall, but on that day, he was a mountain. I sat in his flat while you girls played in the next room, and he glowered down at me. We were through.

'But Maggie is yours!' I cried in one final attempt to sway him. 'Would you deny your own blood?' I think this was perhaps the only time I've wept with such desperation. To look back on it, I acted like a ridiculous child. Nevertheless, by the time Laurence returned home, my face was powdered, and he believed the decision to stay had been wholly mine."

"What about Tena?" Reuben asked when Beatrix finally concluded her story. "Why didn't she matter in your argument?"

Beatrix set her empty teacup in the saucer and daintily poured herself another cup. "For king and country, Mr. Radford, you certainly are thick. Tena belongs to Laurence. I was happy to leave her with him if need be."

Tena felt Reuben's gaze level on her from across the room, but her eyes were moist and her throat sticky with rejection. At one point or another, she had been abandoned by nearly everyone she cared about. At least her father still belonged fully to her. Her heart bled for the woman who was now suddenly her half-sister.

She was grateful when Reuben said the words she wished she could. "If you had a heart, you would have left them both behind."

"As well I should have. Laurence was a doting father, I will grant him that one praise. I never despised him the way I abhorred Alois for abandoning me to a life of—"

"Of what?" Maggie cut in. She slammed her teacup onto the table, and it was a wonder it didn't shatter. "Dr. Schweitzer didn't abandon you to anything! He gave you a wonderful life with Father and with us. I now understand how you developed your German prejudices— although stereotyping an entire nationality due to one man's folly is absurd—but how could you extend that contempt to the rest of us? How could you not tell us?"

"You never asked."

Simple as that.

With a derisive snort, Maggie stood and handed Abigail to Hugo as he rose to meet her. "Thank you for the tea, Mother. We'll take our leave now."

Beatrix stirred her tea as though she had all the time in the world. "A truth like this would have ruined our good name. You would have lived a very different life, Maggie, without privilege and without options. Instead, you received the best of everything. Can you honestly say you did not enjoy it?"

"I had privilege, certainly, but I never had options. That life may have been ample enough for you, but it certainly wasn't for me."

Beatrix smiled. "I am pleased you are not like me. Mr. Frye didn't need to save you like I allowed Laurence to save me. Trust me, Maggie, that's something you would have always resented him for. However ..." Another stir of the spoon. "You could never resent anyone as much as the child who looks exactly like your greatest mistake." Her eyes settled on Abigail, clutched in Hugo's arms. "Thank goodness you will never experience such contempt for *her*."

Such deafening silence was never heard. Maggie rocked back dumbfounded, trying to take it all in and failing. *Say something, Maggie,* Tena thought. *You're made of ash and fire. You can tear people down at the drop of a hat.* This was only one of many days dedicated to protecting Abigail's parentage. If Maggie couldn't defend her to their mother, how could she manage it for a lifetime?

"Get out," Hugo spat, taking them all aback. Disgust dripped from those two words and he appeared to want nothing more than to channel Reuben's inner need for violence.

"This is my house, Mr. Frye."

"Have you taken me for someone who still cares?" Hugo placed a protective hand on Abigail's back. "You won't make accusations about the paternity of my child. I won't stand for it."

"Whoever questioned that, Mr. Frye, except for you this very moment? Who else could even be the father when my daughter hasn't entertained another suitor in over a year? At least none I've been informed of." Her gaze flitted to Reuben for less than a second, barely enough to notice, but Tena knew her sister did. Maggie's expression crumpled in a ball of emotional wreckage.

"You know?" She edged closer to Hugo, and his face burned hot with anger or embarrassment, which Tena couldn't tell.

"Oh, Maggie, I'm your mother, of course I know. Babies always resemble their fathers. It's what saves men from turning out their offspring the day they're born."

Setting down her teacup, Beatrix stood to stare Hugo down from her height several inches above him. "You really are squat, aren't you? Unsurprising my daughter would choose you. Her tastes were never very refined."

Hugo glowered. "I doubt her tastes mattered much once you disowned her."

Beatrix shrugged and held out her hands. "I would enjoy holding little Abbie."

"I'm certain you would."

"She's my granddaughter. She belongs with family."

"Then I sure as a buttered biscuit won't be giving her to *you*." Hugo wrapped both arms around Abigail to hold her into his chest. In her sleep, her tiny fingers grasped the edge of his vest and she released a small hiccup.

"My, my, Mr. Frye, such temper. That was certainly not what I was expecting from Mr. Radford's description of you in his letters." She smiled innocently as both her daughters' lips parted in surprise. "Oh, my, you didn't know? Mr. Radford's written me all year."

Maggie shook her head, edging still closer to her husband. "You're lying. Reuben would never—"

"Oh, no?' Beatrix walked to the sideboard and opened the drawer to remove a thick stack of envelopes tied with pale blue ribbon. "You already stole my most nefarious secret, Maggie. Why would I need to deceive you about a silly thing like fifteen letters?"

Tena leapt from the settee to yank the bundle from Beatrix's fingers. She didn't need any more revelations. Every inch of her was already shaking from shock at learning her father wasn't her father, then relief at learning he still was, and disgust over her mother's persecution towards Charles for sins committed by someone else.

"Mother, have you no shame at all?" she yelled, and Abigail immediately let out a shriek. Tena didn't mind. At least one of them should be allowed to weep openly. "You loved a German man the same as me. You should have understood my wants better than anyone. But if you weren't happy then no one could be. Embittered until the very last. And this?" She waved the letters in her mother's face as she struggled not to break down. Reuben would leap to her rescue, and she couldn't have that. "This is simply more of the same. Well, congratulations on mastering the big reveal."

She turned to Reuben. Her breath rose until she feared she might be overcome. "What was the point, Reuben? You know how we despise her. What exactly did you hope to gain?"

"I only wanted ..." Reuben began. He folded his arms and blew out a breath. "Whatever I wanted isn't about to happen now."

"You really shouldn't be so hard on him," said Beatrix. "The boy had gumption to even bother."

"I believe we're finished here," Hugo said firmly. "Mr. Radford, could you ring for a taxi? I saw a telephone in the hallway. Maggie, follow me." He took Maggie's hand while trying to bounce away Abigail's tears with the other.

They were nearly out the door when their mother rushed after them. She placed a hand on Maggie's shoulder. "You cannot blame me for hiding it. I only did what I believed was best for you."

"No, you only did what was best for you." Surprisingly, Maggie still didn't shrug her off. Her lips formed a sad smile. "But I don't blame you, Mother. It's exactly what I did too."

Still attempting to calm Abigail's whimpers, Maggie and Hugo walked from the room and their mother ascended the main staircase, leaving Tena and Reuben shoulder to shoulder in the doorway.

"Tena—"

"*Don't.*" She held up a hand, effectively silencing him. Then she stalked towards the kitchen, her thoughts on baking pie rather than his betrayal.

FORTY-ONE

LAURENCE ARCHER'S STUDY WAS the absolute last place Maggie wished to be and the only place she longed for as much. He wasn't her father, but on all those lonely nights of her childhood, he had been. Now lost in the room's emptiness, devoid of his belongings and his laughter, she felt unbelievably small. Like a child locked in the cupboard of her nightmares, wondering who would bother to open the door.

Her head reeled. Her mother, a woman who never seemed to care for anyone but herself, actually loved someone once. As a result, half of Maggie's blood belonged to a stranger.

How different life would have been if she had known the truth from the beginning. If Tena had known. If the world had known. Maggie would have been a societal outcast, while Tena became first in line for the parties, the proper suitors, the best of everything. They would never have moved to America, and her baby wouldn't be here. Her beautiful, bright, wonderful Abigail.

Her father's joy ...

Laurence Archer was not her father.

Maggie was the reason Beatrix Archer lost Alois in the end. Why her mother hated Germans. Why her mother hated *her*. What then would become of Abigail with Maggie for a mother?

She met Hugo's eye as he closed the study door, Abigail finally rocked to sleep in his arms. She honestly didn't know what to do, how to act, what she should be allowed to think or feel or say. Without

Laurence Archer as her father, she didn't know who to be.

Stale air coated her throat like chalk dust. She threw open a window, and the fresh breeze ruffled the curtains. The sweet fragrance of peonies brought memories of a floral May Day crown tangled in her hair.

Hugo met her where she stood, so close his forehead pressed against hers while their now sleeping child snuggled between them. No, not their child, she corrected. Hers. Reuben's. But not Hugo's. Never Hugo's.

She turned away, moving to Laurence's desk where her fingers lighted upon the now empty top. He used to keep a lamp against the right edge to disguise the time her seven-year-old self wrote too hard with his fountain pen and carved her name straight into the wood. Maggie traced the lines of each letter with her fingertip. Those marks should have been inscribed onto Alois Schweitzer's desk; his voice should have soothed her to sleep; his hands should have lifted her up for hugs—a father who whispered *"Gute nacht"* rather than "Goodnight."

Whom might she have been with him for a father? Perhaps it didn't matter. Perhaps it would have all turned out the same. Maybe she only set into motion a path that had always been.

Abigail released a contented sigh. Hugo had folded her blanket to barricade her against the sofa back. One tiny fist clasped the cloth, and with a shudder, she drifted back to sleep. She was beyond beautiful.

Void of Abigail, Hugo's hands slid freely to Maggie's waist. He eased her into him, his lips a mirror to her own, meeting like no one's ever had. Not because he carried innate talent or had been schooled on how to place his hands. His lips weren't as supple and pleasing as Derby's and his fingers didn't caress her as Lloyd's had. He couldn't breathe the same poetry Reuben could. Hugo's goatee tickled her chin, rough and scratchy, yet his touch made her feel like they had been that way for years.

"Tell me what you're thinking," he said. She longed to focus anywhere else except those tender emerald eyes, but confound him, he was always in her line of vision.

"Why are you so short?" she demanded.

He frowned. "Heredity. Now tell me what you're actually thinking."

Why couldn't Father tell me the truth in his letter? I never would have married you. I would have given up Abigail before I even saw her. I wouldn't be so infernally weak.

"Heredity."

"Maggie, please don't be like that. No one is here except us, and I love you." He had said those words so many times since last night, and she wondered if he was saying them now to convince her or to convince himself. The ease with which he released them led her to believe he never needed any convincing. Her spirit bled just a little bit more.

Stealing her hand, he laid it palm down on his chest, right against the pounding of the heart she cared so much for. "It's yours and no one else's."

That was when the tears came. Hot and feverish, unable to disappear despite the erratic sweep of her palm. She couldn't even blame pregnancy this time. She could only blame herself.

He held her close, even as her hands moved to push him away. "It doesn't matter," Hugo soothed. "Whatever it is, it doesn't matter."

"It does."

"Only if you let it. Forget what happened this afternoon, Maggie. We have ship vouchers. Let's steam home, and the entire voyage, I'll do nothing but help you forget."

Maggie kept her head lodged against his neck. Salt stung her eyes. He was offering her exactly what she wanted—to sink into a pleasurable oblivion for one glorious week, to pretend like the last three hours made no difference between them. Except they did.

She needed to tell him. She *had* to tell him. Now, before another wave of emotion destroyed her resolve, before her frail heart succumbed to what it wanted. She came here to secure Abigail's future, and that was what she was going to do.

"I can't *steam home* with you," she said. Cold. Unfeeling. Matter of fact. Even she was stunned at how heartless the words sounded and that once upon a time such expression would have been second nature.

"The Atlantic is awfully wide to swim." Hugo elicited a small chuckle with an enthusiasm that didn't even make its way to the end of the breath. "I don't understand," he said slowly even though she knew beyond doubt that he did.

Maggie Archer spoke the next words while inside Maggie Frye buckled beneath them. "I'm leaving you, and I'm giving Abigail away."

Hugo stiffened. "Repeat yourself."

Like a block of stone, Maggie forced the weight of her head from his shoulder. "When I return to the States, I'm taking Abigail to a convent in New York. She'll be safe there. Mrs. Kisch's friend had a cousin who gave her baby to the sisters when she fell on hard times. She wasn't married either."

Hugo stared at her. "But you are married! You're married to me!" His face went ashen, all color draining from his skin. He fisted his hands when they began shaking and lowered himself into Laurence's desk chair. "How could you want to give away our daughter?" he croaked.

"She's not ours or yours. She's mine, and I'm doing what's right."

"For who? You? Not for the rest of us. I promised you—"

"You fulfilled your promise. Abigail was born legitimate. You saved her, but you're still trying to save me, and as my mother said, Archer women never require heroes."

His cheeks flared to the color of his hair. "First of all—you're not an Archer anymore. You're Maggie Frye. You chose to change your name; I never made you. And second—your mother's done this to us, can't you see? She's gotten in your head and swirled it all around like broken eggs. Don't you dare go back there. Back to who you were before you met me." He leapt from the chair and circled his arms around her. His fevered breaths rattled against her ear. "I love you, Maggie."

"Yesterday morning, you didn't even call me Maggie. You hadn't kissed me or—" She flushed, radiating with the thought of his touch roaming every inch of skin with a gentle passion she had never experienced before. "—or anything else," she finished weakly.

"Exactly, Maggie. This morning, you said you loved me, and I can't believe it was the same lie you told all the others." His lips brushed her neck and her hands slid inside his jacket, around his waist, up his back. She found her lips molding to his and couldn't understand how she arrived there.

When he finally eased away, his lips remained inches from hers, but this time didn't press closer. He withdrew his handkerchief from his pocket where her declaration of love was emblazoned in scarlet. "You need me to call you Mrs. Frye again? It's done, Mrs. Frye. You never want me to kiss you or touch you again, then I won't. You want to return to the way we were two days ago? I'll give you anything you ask, except for this."

He moved towards her again, and from some abysmal pit inside her soul, she opened the door that held fast the black ugly pieces of her past. From so deep below, they raised their hands to her. None of them had been erased by one man's tenderness; they had merely been waiting like a volcano on the edge of destruction. Uncontrollable. Regret after regret after regret. Exactly like her parents. Maggie's cruelty wasn't made; it was born. Stained to her forehead like the mark of Cain. Why couldn't Hugo see it?

She yanked the handkerchief from his hand, wadding it back into his jacket pocket. "We can't go back. I can't unlearn what my mother told me. My entire life I was the daughter of Laurence Archer. I was one hundred percent English. I had one whole sister and thought my blue eyes came from my mother. Now I know they're my true father's eyes too, and I'm not any of those other things."

Hugo's hands flew to her face, reining her in with trembling palms. "No, Maggie, no. You're wrong. No ancestry changes who you are or what we are. I have a marriage license to prove it."

"No piece of paper makes a loving marriage, Mr. Frye. I have my parents to prove that. All three of them."

"I disagree."

"Your opinion doesn't matter in this case."

"You can't take Abigail," Hugo stated. "Leave me if you want, but she stays. I'm her father, Emma. How selfish can you be?"

Maggie drew away, his hands falling flat as hers drew tight against her sides. A pain caught in the center of her stomach. "My name isn't

Emma."

"I—what?" Hugo stuttered, then he blinked slowly and folded his arms. "I didn't intend to say that, but I'm not taking it back. Emma would have done the same thing you're doing. I appear to have a partiality towards selfish women."

So, she thought, *he does see what's in me. In the end, no man could possibly overlook it.*

Her entire body ached. If only a chasm would open to swallow her whole. "We have a contract, Mr. Frye, but I can't stay another six years. I thank you for taking me in, and I'll thank you for giving me a quick divorce." She yanked off her wedding ring. "Here. This is yours. Or was it Emma's after all? It was obviously never mine."

Hugo quieted. "It was my mother's."

"Your *mother*? But we weren't even really married. Why would you give me something so valuable?"

He sighed, a deep morose exhale as though he only now realized their arguing went against his usual desire to avoid conflict at all costs. "No one would believe our ruse if you didn't have a ring. I couldn't afford one, and this was all I had. I wrote into the contract that I would get it back so I knew I would."

"But this marriage *was* a ruse. It was a way for us to forget our mistakes, cut our losses. To try to let go. But we haven't, have we? If we keep Abigail, we'll never be free. I'll always be shackled to the memory of where she came from, and you would see me every morning and wish another woman was in my place."

He stood stock still and seemed all of his five-foot-three. He took a step back, curled the ring inside his fist, and sank onto the sofa. "Maybe you're right."

"I am?" Surprise wasn't a strong enough word, nor was it an accurate sentiment for how she felt. She didn't want to be right. Never had she wanted so much to be proven wrong.

Hands clasped upon his knees, Hugo stared into the cold fireplace. "Why did you never ask if I found Emma in Utah?"

"Because I've ruined lives by asking the wrong questions, and I didn't want to ruin ours."

"I wish you would have." His eyes slid closed, his body unnaturally

338

still. For once no fingers in his hair or harried expression on his face. "I found the city, and I found the hotel, all I couldn't find was her. For weeks I searched, asking every soul in town and all the while somehow managing to keep the truth from Henry. There was no Adeline McClay; no one had even heard of her." He opened his fist, flipping the tiny ring against his palm. "Damaris called it 'a dead lead.' A thousand miles for nothing."

With an extra beat of her heart, Maggie claimed the chair across from him, and she could barely say the words. "So, she's still out there?"

"Yes," he murmured. "She's still out there." He stared at the ring, his thumb gently stroking the petite diamond. They could never be a real marriage; that much was now painfully clear. Hugo's desire for the truth was as ravenous as Maggie's once was aboard the *Höllenfeuer*, and just as surely Emma's betrayal would hold him to the flame until it burned him apart.

"We're a perfect match," she told him in jest the day they married. Except they weren't.

He cuffed the ring again and raised his chin to meet her gaze. "Do you know why I married you, Maggie? You were honest. You said you were no good. You warned me from day one. You didn't want me and you didn't think there was any reason I might want you—my sadder but wiser girl. But eventually, I still found myself in love despite never wanting to walk that path again."

He peered up at her, more regret in his eyes than that which Maggie held in her heart. It was the most reckless thing she had ever done, wanting a man whose heart belonged to another as surely as she had always vowed never to belong to anyone. But how she wished that she could have him—him, his family, and Abigail. Abbie was Hugo's little bee, her father's joy, the only thing in this world Maggie might have done right. How she wished she could seal herself off again now like she had so many times before.

"That man thinks the moon and the stars of you," Reuben told her once. Long before Maggie wanted Hugo to want her, long before she even knew herself.

"Even if that were true," she had argued, *"the problem is that the*

moon and the stars are both beautiful, and yet completely unobtainable. What good is loving something if it's impossible to hold onto?"

For Maggie, the stars would never shine so brightly again. But for Hugo, maybe someday they could.

A great tightness ripped at her chest, threatening to heave itself from her lungs in a torrent. She could feel grief pricking behind her lids and with a mighty shove, pushed her anguish aside. "You'll continue to search for Emma, won't you?"

Hugo nodded and the motion held all the angst of carrying a mantle too heavy for his shoulders. His fingers ran along his neck then through his tousled hair. "Only," he said. "I'm afraid that finding her won't matter if I'm still in love with you." He slid the ring into his breast pocket and stood, peering down at her with fresh determination. "But doubt is an old man's game, Maggie. You're young, so don't doubt this decision." He bent low to kiss her cheek. "I'll file the paperwork when I return home, and we'll put the past behind us."

She nodded. "Thank you. I'll come for my things when I return to the States. Please take the children on an outing?" Henry, Molly, Isa— those children so dear to her heart—seeing them again would ruin all resolve.

Hugo paused beside Abigail on his way to the door, watching soft easy breaths rise and fall within her chest. He wouldn't hold her or kiss her goodbye. It wasn't worth the risk of waking her and hearing her cry or worse, seeing her smile.

The door lay half open when Maggie called to him to wait. Hugo abruptly closed it and marched back to kneel before her. Her breath stilled when he gripped her hands in his own, staring up at her with matching saucers of equal parts hope and despair. He shifted until his chest pressed against her knees, holding her hands in her lap as though at a kneeler praying. "Yes?"

She anchored her gaze on their clasped hands, refusing to meet his eyes. "When we met, I meant to ask you my father's infamous question, only I never did. I suppose I didn't expect it mattered so much with you, although I can't exactly say why I thought as such."

She thought of how many times her father asked her which day she would redo. Every time she replied, *"Every day I constantly fail at what you want me to be."* Except that if Alois Schweitzer asked instead, she would wager her life fit quite neatly within his expectations.

"Except now you think it matters?" Shaking his head, Hugo drew all ten fingers through his mess of hair as he stood. "I think you already know the answer." Tipping one finger under her chin, he offered her the same half smile as the day they met. "Take care, Miss Archer."

In four quick paces, he exited the room and with the click of the door, ended their marriage.

With a roll of her shoulders, Maggie wiped both palms across her cheeks and strode to her daughter, clutching Abigail to her with the realization that if Laurence Archer asked her today, her answer would be the same as Hugo's.

This one.

FORTY-TWO

REUBEN COULD STILL FIX THIS. The question was, how?

Taking a notepad from his jacket pocket, he propped a shoulder into the Archers' entry doorframe and flipped through his brief observations since their ship docked three days ago.

"Our readers like international scandal," Smithson said the day before he left for England. "Get me some of that."

Oh, he had scandal. He just couldn't print a word of it.

How had so much happened in so short a time, and how was he—again—powerless to change it? Laurence Archer finally left Reuben with a blessing, and he couldn't even use it. He finally knew how deep his own father's defense of him had gone, and there were no opportunities to express his gratitude for it. He couldn't change Maggie's paternity any more than he could Abigail's. And even after fifteen letters, he still couldn't influence Beatrix towards reconciliation with her daughters.

He realized it was a ridiculous endeavor when he penned the first word from his desk in the newsroom. He sat with only the night sky for company and replayed Tena's gut-punching words, *"Sometimes I wish we'd never met him."* Never before had he felt more responsible for someone's unhappiness or more uncertain how to fix it. So he clung to the only other words he could, the call to action she didn't even know he heard.

"I planned to write Mother hundreds of letters about every way

342

she was wrong. Everything would be different. But in truth, nothing changed. At least nothing except me."

No matter how honorable his intentions in writing Beatrix, he should have known that blasted woman would turn a gesture of goodwill into one of ill merit. Tena had never looked at him in quite that manner before. Although her furious words certainly indicated anger, her demeanor suggested disappointment more than anything else. She believed he let her down—again—when all he wanted was the opposite.

A black taxi slowed to a stop outside the front gate. Reuben recognized the driver, Jeremy Grimes. Now in his early fifties, Mr. Grimes began his taxi service during the carriage heyday then exchanged for a motorcar in 1909. The driver had spread his fair share of rumors in regard to Florence Radford's mental illness, and his sons bullied Mira at every turn.

Returning to the near-anonymity of St. Louis never sounded so good.

The Archers' front door opened, and he fell backwards into Hugo carrying his Brownie and nothing else. Reuben glimpsed an empty hallway as Hugo closed the door behind him. "Where are the girls?" he asked.

"Not coming with me," Hugo said. "Neither are you. I'm collecting my bags from Mrs. Smith and heading home." He nodded to Mr. Grimes who now held the rear door open for Hugo to climb inside. "Rail depot, please, sir." Reuben only managed to hop in the other side before the taxi pulled away from the curb.

"We obviously need to talk," he said.

Hugo faced the opposite window. "I have a train to catch."

"Without your wife or your child?"

Mr. Grimes's chin quirked up as he failed to disguise his eavesdropping. Reuben couldn't care. The man could take news of their endeavors wherever he wished. They wouldn't be around to bother.

Hugo ran his hands over his worn pant legs. "Mr. Radford, you need not worry about your article. You'll get your photographs. You'll keep your employment."

"Seems odd," said Reuben, ignoring his comment. "Usually it's Maggie who does the running away."

"I'm not running. I'm riding to the ticket office and catching a train to London. Then I'm going to collect my luggage and sail very calmly back to St. Louis."

"Without your wife?" Reuben repeated. What in the world happened in Laurence Archer's study? That morning, Mr. Frye still seemed as entranced by Maggie as every other man, and now he was fleeing like a frightened alley cat.

Hugo leaned forward to tap Mr. Grimes's shoulder. "How far to the depot?"

"Quarter mile."

"Delightful. Drop me here, please." Handing the man a coin, Hugo flipped the handle before the motorcar fully stopped. The door swung wide over the walk. "Safe travels, Mr. Radford."

Reuben jumped out to other side, rounding the auto to face Hugo as he closed the door. He waved to the driver. "Mind your own business, Jerry. I know you have plenty of it."

Frowning, Mr. Grimes sped off around the corner.

Hugo crossed the street, leaving Reuben to give chase. His extra inches allowed him to catch up easily. "You're running away from Maggie," Reuben insisted. "Don't argue, because I know the gesture. I've done it myself, and heaven knows how often Maggie did. Yet this time she stayed and you're leaving. What is wrong with you?"

Hugo's pace quickened as the railway station came into view. A black engine stood at the ready beside the platform, passengers scuttling in and out of the adjacent station building.

Reuben grabbed Mr. Frye by the arm, halting him before he ascended the platform. "She loves you, Hugo. She does."

"Why?" Hugo asked. "Why would she care about me at all? Unlike you or Mr. Halverson, I'm not very sophisticated. Look where she came from, why should she have to settle?"

Reuben pinched his nose between his fingers. "Listen, if I had a glove right now, I'd slap you with it. You're supposed to be the smart one here, a decade older than me, so wise up. I'm supposed to be the hothead who acts like a confounded fool when I get angry."

"But I *am* a fool, Mr. Radford. This cloud of doubt hangs over us, and I'm partly responsible. I don't want her to have any misgivings, any more wonderings of what life could have been. She gets a do-over, and she should take it." His expression bled. "Convince her to keep Abigail. She'll listen to you."

"She's giving away Abigail?" Reuben choked. That turn of events he was not expecting. Maggie was so blasted adoring of that little girl; how could she give her up? On the other hand, it afforded him the perfect escape. He wouldn't need to worry about where his daughter fit into his life, or if she even should. Yet, now that he had her, he couldn't fathom life without her somehow in it.

Hugo nodded. "Maggie fears she's too much like her mother. Perhaps there's some truth to that, but you can influence her otherwise. She trusts you. You are Abigail's father, after all."

Shaking his head, Reuben glared at him. "You're an idiot if you think that."

"Don't call me an idiot," Hugo spat with unusual vehemence. His finger crooked between Reuben's eyes. "I may be short in stature, but I'm not simple. You are, however, if you don't believe Abbie is yours. Look with your own eyes, she has the same ones!"

"I know she does, but that doesn't make her my daughter, and you well know it."

"You swine." Hugo shoved Reuben as hard as he could. The gesture barely moved him an inch. "I'm not a violent man, Mr. Radford, but I'm going to wallop you into tomorrow."

Reuben sighed. "No, you're not, because I can bring you to your knees in one and a half moves."

He didn't even see the punch coming. Hugo's fist slammed into Reuben's cheek with enough force to clack his teeth and make his eyes water. Although, he was still far better off than his assailant, who now leaned against the stair rail in pain. Reuben bent to check for broken bones, but Hugo pushed him away. He cradled his hand against his chest and lowered himself onto the steps. People angled past, muttering annoyances at the blocked staircase.

"Come on, Mr. Frye." Reuben pulled Hugo up by the elbow and directed him to a wooden bench on the platform. Reuben rubbed his cheek, only mildly affected even though Hugo had thrown everything he had into that punch. At last the man had found a bit of gumption, although it was puzzling why then he continued to act like a coward.

"Maggie and I won't work," Hugo moaned as he fell onto the seat cradling his wounded fingers. "God knows how I hate it. To lose another wife—plus my child—and it's my own fault? Did you know we literally signed a contract? We wrote down how we would wed for seven years and split everything fairly when the term was over. Business partners, that's what she called us. Not even friends, but partners. Certainly never meant to be more."

"But you love her now."

"Why though? I shouldn't. She's awful. Look at what she did to you. That bout with Mr. Halverson? That's just—that's—well …" He released a breath and winced when he attempted to run damaged fingers through his hair. His hands returned to his lap. "You didn't deserve that," he admitted. "I'm sorry it happened to you, but you must know you weren't the only one she toyed with. She looked in my eyes and told me every horrible thing she did and who she did them to, and do you know what I thought? I thought, stupidly, how can I not love this woman?"

"She looked you in the eye?"

Hugo's eyes were as straight up wild as his hair. "Yes! And I thought, apple pie, she's so honest, she must love me. She wouldn't lie to me like she lied to everyone else, would she? I must be different. Oh yes, I'm different by gum, and it's not an asset."

"Except she looked you in the eye," Reuben insisted. "She never looks anyone in the eye."

"Who cares about that? Isn't it just another trick?" Hugo sighed. "Mr. Radford, I never thought myself incompetent or unworthy until Maggie's actions reminded me how my first wife left me too, without so much as a backwards glance. Emma came from the wealth of Connecticut and stayed for less than she deserved, to remain depressed caring for three children while I traveled the country."

"This isn't the same. Maggie does what Maggie wants. It's different with you."

Hugo stared at his wedding band like it was a foreign object. "It's not. It's only business; isn't that what they say? At least that was the rule we made." Hugo's voice took on a desperate plea. "Please, Mr. Radford, you can offer them so much I never could. If I'm out of the picture, you can sway her to keep Abbie."

With a start, Reuben realized that the man he was speaking to now wasn't so different from the man he once had been. Perhaps everything he went through had led him to this very moment. If he couldn't change time for himself, then maybe he could at least change it for someone else.

"Mr. Frye, sometimes we lie to save ourselves and sometimes to save someone else. But it's both this time. The past can haunt us like nothing else, torture us until we believe the lies it tells. We're not good enough, strong enough, smart enough, deserving enough. So we change. We wall off our hearts from the very people we're trying to save. Then one day we discover that our lies have become the truth, and it's too late to turn back because what we want is gone forever."

The last call sounded, and Hugo stood. Reuben couldn't let it end like this.

"Fear and love are so similar, Mr. Frye. We can do some indescribably regrettable things due to either."

"Sometimes both. Take care of my girls, Reuben." And with those words, so reminiscent of Laurence Archer's, Hugo was gone.

FORTY-THREE

THE SACCHARINE SCENT OF BLUEBERRY wafted over the kitchen as Tena slid the pie plate from the oven into her mittened hands. Laying it to cool, she replaced the mitts on their hook and cast another glance through the open doorway. The hallway still lay deserted. She had demanded that Cook and the two kitchen maids leave while she worked, and they hadn't returned even as the minutes ticked past the usual start to dinner preparations. Maybe they were as afraid of her as they were her mother. More likely Beatrix told them she would dine out and not to associate with the infidel she used to call her daughter.

By her continued absence, Beatrix Archer had made her statement loud and clear—she wouldn't apologize. Repentance expressed openly, even if wholly fabricated, was reserved for those who could still provide something she wanted. Tena was no longer one of her mother's wanted things.

With a roll of her shoulders, she returned to Reuben's letters spread across the preparation table. She unfolded the final correspondence, dated the same night Mr. Goodfellow announced the existence of her father's secret will. The words were poetic, their insistence profound. Reuben was a writer for more reasons than a regular salary.

Mrs. Archer,

Allowing your daughters to sail without their mother's love was your gravest mistake.

There will come a day when you may see that a woman's strength doesn't stem from wealth, privilege, or securing the proper husband, but from the ability to see past the surface as you cannot. Charles enhanced all the beauty Tena has to offer. Her smile, her grace, every step she took with him embodied the same love Laurence had for you. For your daughter, being German was the same as being English. True love is blind to such insignificant difference, and I pray that each of us can hope to one day discover that type of great affection ourselves.

This is the last I will speak of it—seek forgiveness from your daughters. Life is already far too trying to encourage additional isolation.

Sincerest Regards,

Reuben Radford

Fourteen letters preceded that one, full to bursting with more of the same. In between details of Maggie's marriage and Abigail's birth, Reuben told Beatrix in no uncertain terms that she should view her youngest daughter exactly as he always had. To him, Tena was some warrior version of herself who survived shipwrecks, buried fathers and fiancés, and tended to everyone she loved.

Except that wasn't how Tena viewed herself. She did those things because she had to, not because of some extraordinary strength. Most days her heart still felt battered by hurts that healed too slowly and doubted if the wounds would ever fully mend. The last person she saw when she looked in the mirror was a heroine.

And yet, she wished she were. To be a person who settled into the bumps in the road and overlooked the mistakes of the past. Who could forgive her mother without expectation. Someone kind. Someone courageous. Someone Reuben could always admire.

Today was the fifteenth of April, one year since *Titanic*.

Kelsey Gietl

She would admit it now. She had loved him for too long.

When Charles was alive, he liked to often remind her how entranced he was the night they met at the Winchesters' Christmas party. It was the only night he ever witnessed her as a flawless beauty, entirely different than every other day. How truly lucky he was that, even in all her splendor, not a single man in the room noticed but him.

Except Tena never had the heart to tell Charles he *wasn't* the only one. Reuben noticed too. He always noticed her, every day, even when Charles didn't. He became the axis her world spun on, the balm that soothed her soul, the piece of her she couldn't be without. After all the trials they had been through, there wasn't anything she didn't believe they couldn't overcome together. She would cross an ocean for him, and he would turn the tides to keep her safe. The man she loved when she believed love had been all but lost.

He witnessed her ugliest moments and still thought her exquisite.

"I thought I smelled pie."

Reuben strode into the room and braced his hands on the table across from her. He winced as he forced a smile and gingerly rubbed his jaw where a rough red splotch painted the skin.

"What happened to you?" Tena asked, feeling flustered.

Reuben rolled his jaw. "Hugo happened to me."

"Hugo *Frye*? He's too reserved."

"Then I guess a bit of me rubbed off on him." He started opening drawers and closing them as quickly.

"What are you searching for?"

"Peace of mind. Aha!" He pulled a fork from the drawer and made haste to the still steaming pie.

"You'll burn your mouth."

"Since when has that ever stopped me?" He dug into the center, removing a heavy forkful. Steam billowed while blueberry syrup dripped onto the tabletop. Rueben wiped it up with his finger and licked it clean. "Mmm, blueberry." His brow furrowed. "Whose favorite is blueberry?"

"Mine."

The fork paused midway to his mouth. Then he ate the entire

350

amount still steaming and swallowed without a blink. "I suppose there are some things I still don't know about you," he said quietly.

"How could I expect you to know everything?" She reached for his hand, but he shifted away and took another bite of pie instead.

"Hugo's left Maggie."

"Excuse me?" She knew Maggie to be rash, but Hugo? He seemed so genuine in his affection towards her sister.

After another bite, Reuben finally looked at her. "That's why he hit me. When he told me to accept responsibility for Abigail, I refused. I called him an idiot, and he called me a swine. Then he decked me."

"Why would he want you to take Abigail?" Reuben threw her a very pointed look and dug out another heaping bite of blueberry. "Oh, I see. He thinks she and Maggie belong with you." She shook her head. "That's nonsense. Hugo loves them; I'm certain of it."

"He does, and it sounds mental, I know, but only from the outside." Another bite of blueberry and Reuben finally lay his fork down. "I saw myself in him, Tena. I finally understood who I've been for so long. I never realized what it looked like before, living so in fear of losing things. I was so desperate to hold on that I made stupid decisions ... ones that pushed the people I loved even farther away."

"You're being too hard on yourself, Reuben." Tena lay her hand palm down on the table and her fingertips nearly brushed his. It was an invitation, and one she wanted him to take. He meant the world to her and she was ready for him to know.

"Reuben, I—"

Her words were overshadowed when he spoke at the same time. Their fingers remained an inch apart. "Tena, I need to ask your forgiveness."

"You already apologized—"

"No, just listen, please. It's not only for what happened with Mr. Troughton or Abigail or moving out last July. I'm sorry for everything. For what I did with Maggie and not telling you about the letters to your mother. I'm sorry your father gave me the money. I'm sorry I wasn't there when Charles died and I'm sorry I told you Hazel meant more to me than she did. My life has been full to the brim with missed opportunities and words left unspoken. I never wanted you to be one of them, and I fear now that I disappointed you more than anyone. I wonder if that's all I can ever do."

"Oh, Reuben, do you honestly believe yourself so incapable of honor?"

Tena rounded the table to steal the stool beside him. She leaned closer even as he edged away, worry prominent in his narrowed gaze. Her fingers slid over his and held them there. "I read the letters, Reuben. You tried to change my mother's mind for no ulterior reason than my happiness. That is the definition of honor. A man who would do that is someone I could stand beside forever."

"What are you saying?"

Surprisingly, her pulse remained steady beneath the close ribbing of her dress, although each beat flooded her veins with a warmth she hadn't felt for a year. "What I'm saying is, I want the man who noticed me first to be the one who notices me last."

~ ~ ~

Reuben didn't know how it happened. One second he felt lower than the road, and the next Tena's soft lips were on his, her arms around his waist delicately pulling him towards her. He remembered the kiss they shared at the Grand Basin, the one meant for Charles, the one he stole. That moment had been frantic, desperately charged in a way this was anything but.

She was the girl who always stood on the sidelines and always played second fiddle to her sister, but could still light worlds with her stare. Reuben had cowered behind his heart of hearts, fleeing that gaze lest he might learn to love her too.

Yet he always had. Denying it never made it any less true. She was his beacon of hope in the dark stretches of his life. Exactly who he wanted her to be. Not a distraction from Maggie or a replacement for Hazel, and at long last, he could believe he wasn't Charles's replacement either.

All these years they stood mere inches from each other and yet never noticed the wall that separated them. Now that wall had been torn asunder, and they were finally seeing each other for the first time.

He wasn't perfect, neither was she, and it no longer made a difference if they were. The realization made him love her more than he knew was possible.

Tena's eyes shone with her pale fire, exactly as they had in his dream limbo and more stunning than anything he would ever see again. He wanted to capture that gaze in his mind forever and the incredible knowledge that it was directed at *him*. Those eyes made him believe in the impossible more than any book ever could.

Reuben didn't want to settle for mere adequacy anymore. He no longer wanted what made sense.

He simply wanted her.

FORTY-FOUR

MAGGIE WAS HALFWAY TO LONDON before Tena and Reuben even realized she was missing. She left a note with Sarah explaining her whereabouts to them; however, she didn't tell her mother goodbye. There were no appropriate words left to say.

When she disembarked the train, she glimpsed a flash of crimson hair, but when the man turned, his face was unfamiliar. It only affirmed that their decision was the right one. One day Hugo would win Emma back. One day sooner still Maggie's heart would forget she ever cared.

Reuben may have believed that time changed things. Except she simply wasn't one of those things.

After all, how could one stop a flower from seeking the sun? It was simply in its nature.

~~~

The taxi rolled to a stop outside the South London Botanical Institute, a light drizzle falling upon the darkening road. Swaddling Abigail's blanket tighter, Maggie bundled the child against the rain, paid the driver to wait, and stepped onto the muddy street. Ladies hustled from the Institute with black umbrellas held high, fussing about their dress hems being sullied as they were helped into waiting taxis and private motorcars. Maggie edged sideways to allow them passage before ducking inside.

In sharp contrast to the outer weather, the entry hall greeted her with warmth, and bright lamps lit the lecture theatre from which the last of the ladies were exiting. It was set up exactly as it had been that morning—rows of wooden chairs facing a small podium. Only now there was a blackboard containing diagrams of tropical plants being erased by a man with grey-tipped hair and a voice she once believed was only part of her dreams.

In silence, she observed his stance, the firm cut of his chin, and the determined way he held his form. The rag in his hand circled the board, erasing the names of plants even she didn't yet know, and she considered him fifteen years ago removing his connection to her with the same ease.

Edging past those still conversing while they pulled on traveling coats and gloves, she hurried to the end of the hall and stepped through the back door, quickly pulling it closed behind her.

Although relatively small, the glass-enclosed conservatory in which she now stood contained an abundance of plant life. She had noticed the building's extension on their approach that morning and speculated since if it held more than flora and excess humidity. It played like a miniature Palm House with expansive fronds rising against the ceiling and colorful floral flares filling the space between. Although, unlike the Palm House at the Royal Botanic Garden, the compact space brought an intimacy that left Maggie's fingers tingling as she reached out to stroke the edge of a scarlet flower. A year ago, her father stood in this very space, never guessing she would ever do the same.

Shifting Abigail to her shoulder, she descended the few stairs and made her way down the aisle. Brushing away one plant then another, she searched along every wall and while she found a great many flowers that turned her head, none that shared her name. None that matched the surreal Magdalena.

An exterior door led into the outer gardens. She would search there next then the upstairs offices and even the gardening shed if she must.

"I thought I told you not to come here again."

Dr. Schweitzer's narrow voice caught her with one foot out the door. He stood halfway up the aisle, two fronds flanking him on either side. His eyes narrowed. "I told you I have nothing more to say."

Try as she might, Maggie couldn't picture him at home in a garden with dirt trapped in the creases of his slender fingers, coaxing life from nothing. Like Laurence Archer, this man too was one of knowledge, more content to teach the world from behind a podium. *Do as I say not as I do. ... The truth shall set you free, but only when I will it.*

"Perhaps not," she said, stepping back into the conservatory, "but there's more I need to hear." She lifted her chin. She wasn't a child anymore, yet she could remember how he made her cower in her nightmares, the way he owned her there. To a five-year-old, every adult seemed ten feet tall. "You may not wish to speak of it yourself, Dr. Schweitzer; nevertheless, what is still is. My mother told me who you are."

His expression didn't waver. If anything, it drew tighter still. "That is her right. I, however, made a commitment to hold my silence."

"Silence has already been broken. Already I know more than is good for me, more than was ever right." She exhaled a bitter laugh, thinking of the husband she sent away and the daughter she planned to let another mother love. "My life has been irrevocably altered by this truth. There is not a way to return from that."

"I will not betray a promise at the request of a child."

Maggie laid a protective palm upon Abigail's back. "In your eyes, I may forever be a child, but I have a child too. I saw you that day at Shaw's Garden, and I need to know—did you come to America to find me?"

"No." So flat, so completely unemotional. So very like herself, she thought. "It was pure coincidence," he continued. "Henry Shaw based his original designs on the Royal Gardens. It only made sense then that when they planned the addition of a Palm House in St. Louis, I was invited to lend my expertise. Until I saw you that day, I assumed you to still reside in Fontaine." Although his expression hadn't changed, he had the audacity to raise a tender hand to her. "I'm sorry if that disappoints you—"

"It doesn't. You didn't desire to be a father to me then, so why should I expect your affections now?"

He shook his head. "I'm not your father, Maggie. If you're searching for a replacement to the one you lost, you will not find him here. Your father was the man who raised and loved you—"

"Who bribed you to stay away from your own child?"

"Who—who told you that?" He appeared stunned, as stunned as if she slapped him.

Maggie's confidence rose. She had brightened the flashbulb with her accusation and captured the image with his words. Words were all she had left, and Hugo would tell her a photograph was worth one thousand of them. "Laurence manufactured all of this, didn't he? He came to you before my mother could carry out her plan. He offered you money for your research, more than you could ever hope to receive fresh out of university. He promised to contribute as long as you stayed away from us and would withdraw immediately if you ever spoke a word. Fifteen years of extortion; that's the legacy my so-called *father* left for me, isn't it?"

With a great sigh, Dr. Schweitzer's lids lowered and just as slowly raised. There was an awful weight within their depths and an even greater relief of finally setting it at her feet. It must be a terrible burden, Maggie realized, to carry such a secret for so long. How had she ever believed she could?

Abigail's sudden cry pierced the silence, and Maggie felt a surge of milk to her breasts as the infant began to root for her next meal. It had been a blessing, her ability to nurse Abbie without a single complication. So many mothers had a difficult time of it, some never successful, while Maggie, the most undeserving, had been granted a generous supply from the beginning. Her body was equipped with nourishment, while her soul starved from lacking.

She slipped her finger between the child's toothless gums, and after several arguments, Abigail finally accepted the substitute. A sad smile lifted Dr. Schweitzer lips as he watched her slowly suckle, remembering another time and another child. "What do you call her?" he asked.

"Abigail Lorraine."

"She takes after you and you after your mother. As beautiful as I remember." He quieted. "You may believe your father only maintained interest in manipulation or that I exchanged you to further my own personal gain, and that may well hold some truth. But the truth is also that, in the end, Laurence and I made each other better. It was a trying journey to be certain, but rivers of contentment never flow straight."

His fingers moved to cup her chin, and she was staring into her own eyes. More grey than blue today, more dead than alive. "We'll never know if I would have been a suitable father, Maggie. That makes no difference at this point. What we do know is that the day Laurence offered me payment for my silence, I met a man who was willing to sacrifice his soul to keep you with him. I couldn't knowingly ruin a family without bearing that same confidence inside myself."

"It's too late, Doctor. My family is ruined anyway." A sudden surge of panic gripped her middle and a million memories flowed from that contraction. Children's laughter before dawn, tender lips against hers, infinite possibilities not yet believed in. She couldn't believe. Not when she was witnessing firsthand the heartbreak liable to befall her. She was her mother's daughter. She needed to rid herself of Abigail before she led her own child to make the same mistake for a third time.

"Maggie, so often we feel trapped between two terrible choices, but we must hold hope that someday we can find the reason for the decision that didn't make sense. Sometimes the best choice is the one we don't even know why we made."

He motioned for her to follow him inside, leading her upstairs to an office as cluttered as the one in Hugo's studio. She didn't need any additional explanation. Because there they were, exactly as she had seen in her dreams for months. Those violet flowers reached towards the window, their pointed little petals desperate for a touch of light in an otherwise dismal sky. She reached out to touch one, soft and smooth in the middle, slightly rough on the outside. A little bit broken. A little bit beautiful.

A little bit like her.

~ ~ ~

Back in the taxi, Maggie unpinned her hat in order to slide the Magdalena blossom between the combs in her hair. She remembered the torment of being seventeen and having the May crown forced upon her. It was the last thing she wanted then, but how pleased it made her parents and how proud. Would her father honestly be proud of her now?

Although it might have brought temporary relief, she couldn't bring herself to cry anymore. She couldn't even force herself to scream. It couldn't magically return her husband or change her blood to match Laurence Archer's. It certainly wouldn't still the knife that slashed at her heart.

Never had she been more afraid that she had finally received exactly what she deserved.

I don't love myself. That's my own doing, but I don't know if I can shoulder it anymore.

Her actions hadn't saved her from the pain of life; they had only barred her from a life worth living.

Claim your happiness, Laurence wrote. Oh, how she desperately longed to.

She wanted unfailing love like Tena, unabashed passion like Reuben, unwavering devotion like Hugo had for his children. To use her brazen determination to save instead of ruin. To build a home, a family, and a life they would be proud of. Maggie wanted it so much it hurt.

The taxi slowed. "We've arrived, ma'am."

"Come along, Abbie girl. It's time." Looking forward, she lifted her daughter and stepped from the motorcar. One foot in front of the other, one day after the next, one moment at a time until she finally reached the woman she most wanted to be.

FORTY-FIVE

PINCHING THE TONGS AGAINST the corner of the saturated paper, Hugo slid the photograph from the development rinse and hung it on the line strung above his studio workbench. Twelve others preceded it, all moments captured during his time in England.

After his argument with Reuben, Hugo rode the train to London, refusing to allow himself to think about anything. He strode into Bianca Smith's home, collected his belongings, and accepted her offer of a ride to the piers without speaking more than a handful of words. He didn't answer her inquiries about the others' location or when they might return. When she said Maggie deserved someone who could actually hire a servant to carry her trunk, he didn't disagree. When she called him a simpleton, he didn't reply.

He had lost his daughter and his wife; in a mind numb with grief, it was unable to process anything else. He hoped Reuben convinced Maggie to keep Abigail. He prayed she changed her mind.

Upon arriving at the ticket office, Hugo was handed a single berth second class passage in exchange for Mr. Archer's voucher. Not due to sail for two days' time, he stowed his luggage at the nearest inn, grabbed his Brownie, and wandered into the city. It was quite possibly the only chance he would have to visit Europe. Capturing a place so rich in history should have been every photographer's dream.

With eyes closed, he now listened to the city of St. Louis through the studio's open window. Even from behind the confines of heavy

360

darkroom curtains, he made out the clang of a streetcar, a street vendor's shout, and the shuffle of feet on the walk. This was his city, and there was still none better. Why did he ever feel the need to leave it?

It was his worst mistake, telling Maggie he would continue searching for his former wife. Emma's memory wasn't the one who held his attention during the day. She wasn't why Molly cried so often or Henry reverted to being a hellion. Thankfully Isa was too young to understand much, but the others understood all too well. Emma's leaving he couldn't have done anything about, but Maggie he could have.

Even so, he wouldn't convince her to come home; he wouldn't even try. He would give her what she asked for even if it tore him apart.

He wouldn't leave home again. It wasn't more of the world he wanted, it was less of it. Despite what he said, he wouldn't hunt for Emma anymore. Instead of paying an investigator, he would hire a suitable nanny and remain right where he belonged. He would be a father to his children in all the ways his own father hadn't been for Damaris. Between portraits in the studio and sales to the *Mid-Mississippi*, they could make ends meet. If Emma wanted to rejoin their family, he would allow her to do so, but he wouldn't continually seek her out in vain.

"If you think that is what's best," Damaris said when he broke the news after dinner last night. There was fire in her eyes; however, to Hugo's relief, her tone remained steady. He had expected more of an upheaval.

"I do. Too much bad happens when we leave St. Louis. Emma disappeared, Molly got sick, then Maggie. We should take it as a sign that we're meant to stay right here." He squeezed his fingers around his thighs to stifle another bout of emotion.

The first night back from England and also the first spent in his own bed since the wedding, he wept himself senseless surrounded by all the photographs he took when Maggie wasn't watching. The second night he shoved them into the bottom drawer of the desk in his studio. He hadn't opened it or cried since.

"If you think that is what's best," Damaris repeated. She stretched her hands towards him upon the tabletop. "You're my brother. You know I would do anything to keep us together."

Hugo's hands slid to hers with a smile. "I thank heaven that you've always been here."

Dredging the final photograph from the solution, he clipped it on the line beside the others. He would deliver them to the *Mid-Mississippi* first thing in the morning before Reuben arrived. Hugo rubbed his knuckles. They still twinged from his uncharacteristic bout of aggression, but not nearly as deep as the ache in his heart.

Bells tinkled at the downstairs parlor door. Hanging his apron up, he pulled on his jacket and smoothed his hair back. His four-fifteen sitting had arrived right on time.

"Mr. Carson, I presume?" Hugo asked as he entered the parlor. A young couple stood near Damaris's vacant desk admiring a framed California mountain range.

The man turned with a broad smile. "Right you are." He shook Hugo's hand then drew the attention of the slender woman beside him. "My future bride, Miss McClay."

Hugo nearly choked as he accepted her hand. *McClay*? What could the odds be that she bore the same name as his former wife's alias? *Calm down, Hugo*, he scolded. McClay was a fairly common name; it was a complete coincidence. With her dark brown hair, this woman obviously wasn't Emma, yet something about her was startlingly familiar.

"Have I photographed you before, Miss McClay?" Hugo asked as he released her hand. "It feels as though we've met."

She gave a slim smile. "I'm afraid not, Mr. Frye. Although perhaps I have served you before. I'm a waitress at the Nightingale only a few blocks over."

A waitress? Hugo spun on his heel, throwing open the door to the rear office. He ran to the desk and shoved a crate onto the floor to shuffle through stacked papers. Invoices, session requests, more blasted bills. Where were they?

He yanked open the bottom desk drawer, strewing broken

photography accessories across the floor as he tossed them out. Not there either. He pulled at his hair as he racked his brain for where he left those photographs.

"Excuse me, Mr. Frye?" Hugo's clients stood in the office doorway with alarmed expressions. "Are you quite all right?"

Grabbing his satchel from the chair, he upended the bag onto the desktop. Stacks of paper shifted and sheets cascaded to the floor. There on top of the pile was the envelope from the investigator and Adeline McClay's photographs stored within. Sliding them free, his eyes shifted between the woman in the photograph and one watching him. The angle of the frame left plenty of room for doubt before, but not when he had the subject. The Miss McClay in his studio and the one in the photograph were indeed the same woman.

No wonder there was no information when they went to Utah. No wonder everyone in the city looked at him like he was insane. He had visited every café, every boarding house, every last hotel. He wasted precious time chasing an illusion when he could have been at home not destroying any chance at happiness with Maggie.

He slapped the photos face down on the desk and pulled his handkerchief from his pocket. Smeared like a blood stain was Maggie's, "Yes." *Lord in heaven,* he thought. *She loved me once if only for a minute, and I threw it all away for a dead lead.*

A *dead* lead, he thought. Those had been Damaris's words, not his.

Terror could have stopped his heart. *Oh, my Emma, you never wanted to leave me, did you?*

Hugo snatched his billfold and house key from the mess and pushed past his bewildered clients. "I'm sorry," he said without glancing back. "We must reschedule. I have an emergency."

"At a discount!" called Mr. Carson as the studio door closed. Hugo raced for the streetcar, jumping for the back rail and barely able to pull himself onto the landing as it rounded the corner. He flipped a coin into the bin and prayed there would be no delays.

The magnitude of his ignorance seemed so terribly obvious now.

Emma hadn't left him. She was dead.

FORTY-SIX

TRAFFIC WAS AN ABSOLUTE NIGHTMARE.

"Come on, come on," Hugo muttered. Ever since automobiles had gained popularity, adding their numbers to the already congested streets only made travel times worse. He had expected some delay, but the streetcar was currently at a complete standstill and had been for a good ten minutes.

He shuffled his way to the front of the car, attempting to see what the hold up was.

"Delivery wagon flipped onto the tracks," the conductor told him. The man settled back in his seat and folded his arms. "'Fraid we'll need to get comfortable, 'cause we ain't going anywhere soon."

"Bread and butter, I don't have time for this."

Leaping from the streetcar, he ran two blocks to the next junction and stepped onto the National Railway line as the streetcar started up. He dropped a coin into the till and himself onto the nearest seat, his knee bouncing in agitation.

It felt like the streetcar stopped at every intersection, for every passing wagon ... the conductor even waved a friendly "hello" to a passerby on the walk. Hugo combed his hair back, raking his knuckles across his scalp nearly to the point of pain. He couldn't believe what a colossal idiot he had been. Damaris had the know-how to frame her story; even on her worst days, she could capture a photograph every inch as good as his. It would be easy enough to cover up a murder by

364

appealing to her brother's ignorance and affections. But why? His own sister ... why had she done it?

His children were at home with an aunt they could no longer trust. *Dear Lord*, he prayed, *keep them safe.*

Rather than switch lines again at the final junction, he raced the remaining mile on foot, his chest heaving when he sped onto the front walk and a stitch pulsing in his side. Sweat pasted his shirt against his back and his neck stung where the starched collar had rubbed it raw.

That was when he saw the smoke.

A grey fog billowed from the kitchen windows on the backside of the house. Although the flames appeared to be contained to the northern wall, it was only a matter of time before they engulfed the kitchen and worked their way into the master bedroom directly above it. Why hadn't any of the neighbors rang for help? he wondered. Perhaps they had. It took the fire department longer to respond this far out. Then again, maybe no one even noticed. The acrid smell could be assumed as someone burning the wrong sort of wood, and the house wasn't fully visible from the road.

Halfway up the walk sat a lone traveling case, and standing calmly to the side, Damaris watched the results of her handy work.

The sound of his home crackling fell hollow as he stumbled forward. "Damaris, what have you done?" he gasped.

She jerked, unable to conceal her surprise at his appearance. "You're supposed to be at the studio."

"Why? So you can burn my house down?"

"Our parents' house," she corrected then grinned as though she expected commendation for destroying the house their father built. Thinking on it, she probably did.

More important matters first.

"Where are my children?" he shouted. When she didn't respond, an unfamiliar curse left his mouth, this time unmasked by any culinary reference.

"Daddy?"

Hugo blinked at Isa's innocent voice. Her frightened eyes peered out from behind Damaris, tiny fingers clutching fabric while her father burned hotter than the fire. She had never seen him this way before. He didn't even know he was capable of it.

Then again two weeks ago he hadn't deemed himself capable of smarting off to his mother-in-law or walloping Reuben either. He always taught his children to turn the other cheek.

"Isa ..." He started towards her, but Damaris shifted the child farther behind her and raised a hand to halt his pace.

This was his most loved sister. She helped their mother raise him while their father was away. She traveled the country with him, laughed with him at their sisters' weddings, and mourned with him when their parents passed ... first one then the other. He was her Hugh, and she was his Mare. There wasn't anything they wouldn't do for one another.

Until she murdered his wife and set fire to his home.

"Let her go." He grabbed Isa's arm, but Damaris held on tighter. He should have given it more thought when she insisted on always being the one to haul the studio's delivery crates in from the alley. But why would he ever think she had a reason to keep herself in fighting shape? Damaris was only a fighter when it came to him, and even then, she always relented eventually.

Until today.

"Your house is burning," she sneered.

"I can see that. Can you tell me why?"

Damaris tightened her grip until Isa whimpered. "You're wasting precious time with questions, Hugh. Who knows how many minutes remain before the flames break into the upper bedrooms?" Gently she smoothed her free hand across Isa's crimson curls with a thin smile. "Seems you have a decision to make. Which child do you love the most?"

All the rage drained from Hugo like the Mississippi River water far below. He looked up at the second story windows. She couldn't have trapped Henry and Molly in there, he thought. She wouldn't be that truly twisted.

"You could call my bluff," Damaris said as though she heard his thoughts. She lifted the traveling case. "You could decide to not believe that I locked your precious angels inside. Or that I emptied our account of all the company's assets and am now leaving you destitute. You could deny my candor as dishonesty, yet you would be unwise to do so." She jerked Isa's arm and Hugo lost his grip. In shock, he watched her back his youngest daughter towards the road.

"You can keep the money, Mare, but why do you need her?"

"I know you, Hugh. You won't let anyone harm me as long as I have her."

"Daddy?" Isa asked timidly. "Why fire?"

Damaris eased the girl against her side, her words switching to syrup. "Your daddy has behaved very badly, Isa dear. Unfortunately, bad people need to be punished."

"What about murderers?" Hugo asked. "Should they be punished?"

His sister simply smiled.

He swiveled between the house and his youngest daughter. The children weren't in there. Damaris took them to her apartment or hid them in the carriage house. This was all a trick to get him killed. She would ditch Isa somewhere along the way and leave all three children without any parents.

He needed Maggie. He needed her wits and her steam engine ferocity.

"Why did you kill her? When?" He knew it was stupid to waste time with questions. Every second another flame climbed the wall. With each pop of ashen wood, they came one inch closer to the children he prayed were somewhere else. He crushed his fingers through his hair.

Damaris took another step down the walk, and without deciding to, Hugo followed her. God help him, if this was his final moment to learn the truth, then he needed to learn it. It was exactly the choice Maggie would have made. Truth over decision without facts.

"When?" he repeated.

"The night before we left for Seattle. When you went to sleep at the hotel, I returned to the house."

"How did it happen?" Hugo held up a hand before Damaris could speak. "No details. Isa can't know."

Damaris's eyes flicked towards the river, and Hugo didn't need her to say more. He doubled over and with his hands on his knees, struggled to restrain his horror. Emma hadn't been able to swim, but even if she had, the Mississippi rarely spared its victims. She would have drowned quickly.

Someone he loved didn't deserve that end. No one did. Not even a murderer.

His voice emerged as a man who lost years in a single moment—all his possible futures stolen because of a relation he trusted all his life. "What happened to you, Damaris? You were the tame sister, not some suffering lunatic."

Damaris slid back another pace, her expression nostalgic. "You always underestimated me, Hugh, just like Papa. I wasn't like our sisters, not pretty or personable and could certainly never fetch a man with twelve thousand a year. I was plain ordinary Damaris. Good enough to be your assistant and follow on your travels, but when it came down to hard facts, there was always someone better. Emma. Maggie. The children."

She offered him a simple smile, full of nothing but the sweet sister she was all those years growing up together. "To me," she said, "we were Tom and Huck. Frank and Jesse James. All I wanted was us and the world. If something stood in our way, I eliminated it." She looked to the house. "It's a shame, Hugh, the way this needs to end. You were always so nice to me. Although that was your downfall. You were always too kind to everyone."

Tentatively, she set the traveling case on the ground and extended a shaking hand. Her lips curved into a warm smile. "You can still come with me, Hugo. There's so much world left to see."

He stared at her hand, at the glow on her face, and the warmth in her voice and had no idea who he was seeing. The sister he knew was lost.

I thought Emma's betrayal was the worst pain I could ever feel, he thought, *but I was wrong. This is a thousand times worse.*

Hugo tilted his chin to meet his daughter's frightened stare. Tears stained her cheeks. There was only one logical choice.

"I'll come for you, Isa," he whispered.

Barreling into the house, he launched himself towards the stairs, the scent of charred wood now mingling with that of fabric and furniture. Smoke eased from under the kitchen door like fog on the river, rising to wrap the upper level in a thin haze. It tingled his nostrils as he reached for the hook at the top of the stairs, already knowing the little metal key would be missing. Damaris's intention was to destroy his life for attempting to ground her in St. Louis. The surest way to succeed in that was to harm his children.

Panic threatening, he reached for the knob to Henry's bedroom, mentally preparing to break down the door and instead stumbled when it swung inward unlocked.

"Move outside!" he yelled.

Molly and Henry looked up from where they sat cross-legged upon the bed, Henry's toy cars lined up between them.

"She's gone then?" Henry asked. He glowered at the miniature Model T in his hand.

Molly sniffed, her eyes red. "Aunt Damaris wouldn't even let us say goodbye." Her nose wrinkled at the smoke. "Smells bad. Did you burn dinner again?"

"We need to go. Now." Yanking them both up, Hugo pulled them out of the room and down the stairs faster than Molly's feet could carry her. She tripped on the last step, and he hefted her into his arms as she began to cry. For some unexplainable reason, the kitchen wall remained intact, sealing the flames from the hallway.

"Come on, we need to phone for help."

That was when he heard screaming directly above him. His eyes rose with the sound of an awful banging that, thanks to Henry's tantrums, he instantly recognized as fists against a bedroom door.

It was then that Hugo finally heard his children's earlier words. "Who else is here?"

Molly's tears fell harder, and Henry glared at his father. "Miss Margaret, of course. Aunt Damaris sent us to my room right before they started fighting."

FORTY-SEVEN

MAGGIE COULDN'T BELIEVE SHE allowed her emotions to run away with her. More so, she couldn't understand how she allowed Damaris the upper hand so easily.

She had planned everything out to retrieve her belongings without encountering any of them. Damaris answered when she rang on the telephone that morning. "Of course, I'll take the children out. I certainly don't want to see you."

But when Maggie knocked on the door that afternoon, Molly answered. Her wide eyes turned up in excitement, and it took all Maggie had to push the child off. "I'm sorry, Molly. I can't stay."

Damaris appeared from the living room. "Figures. My brother has a knack for losing wives."

"You told me they wouldn't be here." Not waiting for a reply, Maggie hustled up the stairs only to encounter Henry on the landing.

He didn't say a word. The metal toy car he held folded into his fist.

Blinking away hot tears, Maggie stepped around him and made for the master bedroom. It was exactly as she remembered, and she tried not to focus anywhere except the fruit crates piled with her belongings. What she hadn't taken to England only filled two of them. Hugo even packed the tea tin he bought her for their wedding night.

They never had a real wedding night.

Maggie stumbled against the bedpost as someone shoved her through the doorway. Spinning, she saw Damaris pull the door shut and heard a key turn in the lock. She jiggled the handle to no avail. "Damaris!" she screamed. "Let me out!"

The elder woman laughed. "You think you're getting out of this? Not this time, darlin'."

With another scream and a slap to the door, Maggie sat on the bed she never once shared with her husband and ran her hands over the quilt seams. Hugo would be home eventually. He would unlock the door, and she could go home.

Home ... where was that? Did she even have one anymore?

Yes, she amended, of course she did—with Tena and Abigail. Keeping her daughter was hopefully one good decision in the midst of too many bad choices. She had to believe Dr. Schweitzer was right, and someday she would understand why she did it.

It wasn't until smoke started to seep through the floorboards that she realized Damaris's intentions were far darker than instigating a row between her brother and his former wife. The grey wisps filtered up near the wall behind the writing desk, twisting past the windows towards the ceiling. A putrid odor followed shortly after—the scent of life about to burn down around her.

Spinning, she pounded on the bedroom door, yanked at the handle, kicked at the grimed and worn hinges until her toes went numb. "Damaris! You can't leave me in here! Damaris!" No response and the spare key was stored in Hugo's study. She would never get out this way.

Dashing to the window, she unhooked the latch and shoved. It only raised its usual five inches, not nearly enough for her to squeeze through if she dared. She was still two floors up and liable to break both her legs if she were to jump. Were the children still in the house? She couldn't climb back up the stairs or run for help on broken legs.

Yanking open the dresser drawers, she rummaged through each one. If she couldn't find another key, there might be something able to jimmy the lock. But her search quickly came up fruitless.

"Beans and Bacon!" shouted a voice from the hallway.

"Hugo! Thank goodness." Running back to the door, she yanked on the handle in vain. "It was Damaris. She locked me in here."

"I know. She also murdered Emma."

"Emma? But—are you certain?" After so many weeks of unbelievable events, this one shouldn't have surprised her. Damaris told her once that life was like a game at the fair. From that first round of thievery at Charles's funeral, the witch had shown every card in her hand. Why did no one bother to look?

"We can discuss it later," he said gently. "Now, I need you to move as far from the door as you can."

"Tell me how to take the hinge pins out of the door."

"They're too old and they're not coming out. Now back away."

"Do you have the key?"

"No, but I have a means to open the door."

"Where are the children?"

"Safe. Now please, Maggie, just do as I ask."

A breeze whipped up outside, thankfully drawing the smoke through the window, but also apparently drawing the fire. She pressed herself into the far corner and the wall shook when something slammed against it.

"Hugo?" she cried. "Are you hurt?"

"I'm fine," he grunted. "I have an ax." Another slam against the wood, another groan. The wall trembled with the impact, although the door appeared intact.

To her right, the curtains caught flame. "Hugo, hurry!" She promised Tena she would never leave her again. She needed to keep that promise.

The next strike resulted in a crack to the wood, but not enough to push it open. He struck again. "When I find Damaris, I'll slap her senseless. I was so angry I actually used language in front of Isa." His next swing fell short, and the ax dropped to the floor with a metallic clunk. Between the smoke and the strain, his breathing had become labored.

Another hit of metal against wood, not nearly as strong as the one that preceded it.

He would never crack through that door in time. If Reuben were here, perhaps, but Hugo simply wasn't built for it.

The room's heat intensified as the fire finished with the curtains and clawed at the window frame. She imagined the garden below with its little shoots pushing through the soil. Come June there would be a multitude of blooms from bulbs chosen especially by Molly. She wondered if her stepdaughters would forget the classifications she taught them. She wondered if they would forget *her*.

Abigail was only four months old; she wouldn't remember she ever had a mother.

Maggie pressed both hands to her mouth to stifle a sob and the effort momentarily blackened her vision. She couldn't use more air; her head was already fuzzy with the fumes filling the room. But what good would conservation of air do now?

She pressed her cheek to the wallpaper. Across the room, the flames finally caught the ceiling and started to spread.

"Remember the day we married?" Hugo asked. Maggie nodded; it was all she could manage. He would finally leave when he realized it was all he could do. She slid to the floor, her eyelids heavy. Her head hurt and someone's breathing sounded too ragged. The thrum of ax swings beat in time to the blood pulsing in her ears.

Hugo continued speaking. She wanted to commend him for such clarity in his voice. If she were out there trying to save him instead, she doubted she could remain so calm. "Even in black," he said, "you were beautiful. Given the chance, I would marry you all over again."

Given the chance? They were out of chances. Her fingers landed on the scuffed toe of Hugo's boots and she smiled. Everything about him had always been a little tattered. Wherever she was headed, she hoped she remembered him.

"Maggie?" Hugo's tone was suddenly intense. "Maggie, keep talking so I know you're still with me."

What was he on about? Words only landed them in unfortunate situations. Talking wasn't so important. Sleep was important. Her attention drifted. What was that orange glow? Why was the room so warm? St. Louis certainly was a distressingly hot city. Too much brick, not enough trees.

The banging stopped. "Maggie?"

She meant to answer with something important, maybe that she loved him or maybe that she had been wrong to leave, but darkness tugged her onward, and she no longer felt the need. She had found a quite comfortable place curled up on the floor.

Her eyes slid closed.

She would tell him in the morning.

~ ~ ~

Hugo lowered the ax and drew short shallow breaths. The wood around the door had splintered, the knob bent at an odd angle, and he feared he had done more damage than good. "Maggie?" he called again.

No answer.

"Maggie?"

Still nothing. Even the soiled shirt tied over his mouth and nose could no longer keep out the smoke rising in the stairwell and creeping under the bedroom door. How much worse it must be inside.

Drawing on every ounce of strength, he managed to drive his compact frame with enough force to split the door's mutilated wood. With a final kick, it finally swung inward, and his arms raised against the oncoming wave of heat. Tiny scraps of seared wallpaper and curtain danced by in the breeze from the window. That air might have been the only saving grace from the thick smoke filling the room.

Beside the wardrobe, Maggie lay silent.

He fell to his knees and pressed a hand to her lips, thankful to feel strong, although too rapid, breathing.

"Maggie, wake up." He jerked her shoulder. No response and he didn't have time for a second attempt. With a groan, he hooked his arms under hers and dragged her towards the door only to waste seconds when her boot hooked the frame. Pushing it aside, he pulled her into the hallway and ran straight into his son.

"Mother of omelets, Henry, I told you to stay outside!"

"No!" Two hazel eyes glared at his father from over the shirt collar held up against his face. "You need me."

"Leave, Henry! I won't have you dead too." Coughing, Hugo pushed his son towards the stairs and in the process dropped his wife. Sweat dribbled into already watering eyes as he rushed forward and slammed closed what was left of the bedroom door. That would hold the fire for a minute longer, maybe two, but not enough. He reached again for Maggie's arms.

"You need me," Henry repeated. "If you die because you're stupid, then I'll hate you forever."

His only son blocked the stairwell. Hugo would either need to let him help or push him down it.

"Take her legs."

Half carrying, half dragging Maggie's body, they managed down the stairs and across the yard, finally collapsing onto the grass. Hugo tugged the shirt from his face while Molly danced beside them, great tears cascading down her cheeks.

Something shattered in the blaze, the sound splitting through the air and drawing the children's attention. Hugo focused only on Maggie as he pressed a palm to either side of her face to force her chin up and mouth open. Her breath shuddered as though it were being drawn through the rock of a riverbed. She needed clean air; she needed to open her eyes. *He* needed her with him.

"Henry, take your sister and run to the Kincades'. Tell them to phone for help."

"What if they're not there?"

"Then keep moving until you find someone." He met his son's determined gaze. "I love you, Henry."

"I love you too, Dad." Taking Molly's hand, he led her away still crying.

Flames and smoke billowed ash into the air. Their house would be little more than memories by the time the fire had its way. Everything they owned would be destroyed. "We'll sort it out together," he imagined Maggie would say. She would have the answer. She *was* the answer.

His forehead pressed into hers, her face gently cradled between his fingers. "I know I can do this without you," he shouted over the din. "I can, but I don't want to. I never wanted to. Please don't make me."

Hugo didn't doubt he could face tomorrow, then the next day, and each one after that on his own. That had been the plan two weeks ago when he walked out the Archers' front door. He had married a resilient woman who in turn taught him how to finally be resilient. He just didn't want that to be her final gift to him.

"Hugo."

He felt the word more than he heard it. Maggie's lips moved against his chin and to him, her rasp was the sound of angels singing. When he raised his face, her irises reflected the bright blue sky above. Gasping, she folded handfuls of his undershirt between her fingers and wrenched him to her. They lay on the grass side by side ... holding on, never letting go.

"Your photographs ..." Maggie breathed. "Can we save them?"

Hugo could only stare at the life in her eyes and the breath on her lips, and marvel at how during such a time, she could think only of him. How much this woman had changed ... and changed him. He was the most fortunate man alive.

"Leave them. We have each other. We've already saved everything we need."

FORTY-EIGHT

THE POLICE CAUGHT UP TO DAMARIS at Union Station. She waited on the railway platform with a one-way ticket to Chicago, carrying only a camera and a single worn traveling case. $187 lined her pockets—the exact amount now missing from her and Hugo's shared account.

They located Isa in a corner of the central terminal, unharmed although babbling uncomprehendingly through her tears.

Tena too wept when Hugo rang from the hospital. While the doctors couldn't determine if there would be any long-lasting health effects from the ordeal, thankfully Maggie would live. Reuben could only watch Abigail asleep in Elsa's arms and think how close she came to losing her mother.

In the weeks that followed, Hugo refused to even set foot near the courthouse prior to the trial. His only words to his sister came in a note sent to the jailor: "You were supposed to be on my side." All she returned were, "And you were supposed to be on mine."

Reuben attended the trial. He listened to Damaris explain how Emma's death was necessary for the sake of her brother's overall well-being—as though heaving someone from a cliff in the dark of night was the same as extracting an infected tooth. When he read back over his notes in an attempt to make sense of them, he simply couldn't. What malice needed to be in a person to commit such crimes against their own blood?

The proceedings became front page news. His words were read in households around the city, and sales of the *Mid-Mississippi* were the highest since his piece on *Titanic* one year ago. Eric Smithson at long last offered his lowly obituaries writer a place in the front section, right below the fold.

"'Bout time you climbed out of the muck," Stanley teased when Reuben told him about the promotion. He clapped a hand to his friend's shoulder. "You'll get used to writing grizzly details. Eventually the sight of blood won't make you vomit."

"I turned him down," Reuben replied.

"What? After all the grousing you did about wanting your own beat?"

Reuben chuckled at the shock on Lee's face. He knew his response didn't make sense after receiving exactly what he wanted. Even Smithson had turned a darker shade of red than he usually wore when Reuben rejected his offer.

"And exactly why not, Radford?" Smithson shouted. "You got another paper schmoozing for you? Is it the *Post-Dispatch*?" He reached for the telephone. "I'll give them a piece of my mind. They've stolen too many of my best reporters already."

"Put the receiver down, Mr. Smithson. It's not the *Post-Dispatch*."

The chief editor returned the mouthpiece to its cradle. "Then who is it? I'm doing you a favor here. I won't do it again."

Reuben pressed a finger to the open ledger on Smithson's desk. "If you want to do me a favor, you can hire Hugo Frye as our official staff photographer. No more one-off work. Pay him a decent wage. Children should be proud of their father and a father should be able to provide."

"Frye's never complained. You're out of your tree if you think I'm upping his rate."

"He'll go elsewhere. The *Post-Dispatch*, perhaps, or the *Globe*. I'll see to it."

"It sticks me to admit that Frye's work influences our numbers. But I'm not running a charity case here. I know what the *Post-Dispatch* pays their designated staff photographers. The *Mid-Mississippi* can't compete."

"You can if you take me off the payroll."

Facing Stanley from across the desk, Reuben packed the personal contents of his desk drawers into his satchel. "Priorities change, Lee. I'll have my beat, but today someone else needed the money more." He slung the bag across his chest and held out a hand. "Enjoy the violence beat, Lee. Take no offense, but I hope I never see you in my line of work."

Stanley gripped Reuben's hand and his lips folded into their usual good-natured grin. "Just so long as I see you sometime."

"Blimey, Lee, that goes without saying."

~ ~ ~

The following Sunday, Reuben walked the two miles from the boarding house to the Kischs', surprised he hadn't yet encountered remorse at his hasty decision to quit his job before securing another. It had been the opposite of wise—outrageously foolish in fact—yet it hadn't brought him the worry he imagined it should. Probably because Tena kissed him the previous night when he told her his reasons, and even after six months together, he still couldn't get enough of her. Charles had given him a gift and he would try to never take it for granted.

"You did this for Abigail, didn't you?" Tena said when Reuben told her.

"Some for Abigail, some for me. Mostly because it was simply the right thing to do."

Isa attacked him as he walked through the front door, her little arms stringing around his knees. "Uncle Reuben, play with me?" Since the fire, the Frye clan had boarded with their neighbors, the Kincades, but attended every Sunday night dinner with the Kischs. Within a few weeks, they settled in as an extension of the family. With the strange web already between him and Hugo, Reuben found their quickly-formed amity an incredible relief.

He ruffled Isa's hair and pried her arms away. "After dinner, Isa. I can't play on an empty stomach."

"Okay!" She raced off to join her brother and sister on the living room floor. Henry bounced a small ball and scooped up an entire handful of jacks, while Karl and Hugo sat on the sofa watching the excitement. Through the window at the end of the hall, Reuben observed a heated game of improvised cricket between Emil and Friedrich, the former of whom was obviously cheating the latter. From the smells wafting out of the kitchen, the women had not allowed Maggie to assist with dinner. Even with Hugo's—and later Elsa's—help, her skills had only marginally improved.

"Would you care to hold her? She's crawling her way into everything."

Before he could respond, Tena slipped Abigail into Reuben's arms and pressed a kiss to his lips. She smiled. "Thank you, love." Then she was off down the hall and back into the throes of dinner preparation.

It wasn't the first time Reuben held his daughter. He fought through the inevitable many months ago. Unfortunately, familiarity still couldn't lessen the emotion he experienced every time he encountered his own flesh and blood.

For a man who always wanted children, he never fully comprehended how much he would care about the one he never planned on. This little child, now ten months old, with her dark hair and even darker eyes had stolen inside parts of him he wasn't even aware existed. He may have lost Mira all those years ago, yet here she was returned to him in the face of this precious child. Abigail laid her cheek against his chest and when she nuzzled closer, he knew that someday his own children would bring him completely to his knees.

He prayed he could be a father his own would admire. Harris Radford hadn't expressed enough of his hidden faith in his son. Reuben would make certain that his children always knew.

Abigail wriggled her little hand out from under her, those wondering eyes bending upward to find him as she toyed with his jacket buttons. Her incomprehensible babbling sent his heart fluttering. It wouldn't be long before those sounds took meaning and she, like the other Frye children, would call him Uncle.

Could he truly allow another man to father his child? he had asked himself a thousand times.

Surprisingly, it was always Laurence Archer's voice to reply. *"You will, Reuben. You already have. What is done is done."*

"I wish you could meet your grandfather," Reuben whispered to Abigail. "He would have done anything for his girls." With a tender kiss to her brow, he entered the living room to set the child on her father's lap. Grinning, Hugo bounced her on his knee to the child's delighted giggles.

And I will do anything for mine, Reuben thought. *Even if it means giving you up.*

Maggie always told him everyone deserved a good story for their lives. Thanks to her, he now had a beautiful one.

~ ~ ~

From the dining room doorway, Maggie observed the Kischs' living room in silence. Her life was one she stumbled into, and she wouldn't forget how she ultimately found her happiness—through the sad chocolate eyes of a boy in a cemetery who loved her when she was less than lovable. She owed Reuben a debt she could never repay.

Entering from the front hall, he handed Abigail off to Hugo as though it was the most natural thing in the world, although she knew better. It still crushed him every time, but he did it because he had to.

"This is how it was always meant to be," Reuben told Maggie only a few weeks after the fire. "I'm satisfied being the doting uncle, and you need to allow yourself to be at peace with that. I'll never come back and ask for more; I'll never tell anyone the truth unless you want me to. You don't owe me anything, and I want nothing from you. Letting Abigail go only hurts because I know it's right."

"Still ..." she said, "There may come a day when Abbie needs to know. What do we tell her?"

"The truth—how much she's loved. Blood doesn't make a family, Maggie. Love does."

Creating a child did not make you a parent any more than your parents' mistakes didn't destine you to do the same. A person was more than a sum of their parts. She understood that now.

Maggie's father was the man who raised her when she wasn't even his. He was the man who taught her to walk, who read her *Journey to the Center of the Earth*, and embraced her at the railway station for what would be the final time. He looked like Tena, but always understood Maggie best. That man was her father.

She had a choice, as her mother did before her, of how to raise Abigail, and she could have done it alone. Instead, she gave her a father who loved his daughter in the same way Laurence Archer loved her. Every day she would tell Abigail the truth—that Reuben Radford was her uncle, sometimes people make all the worst mistakes on the path to happiness, and above all else, a home was only as happy as the love that filled it.

Hugo Frye was Abigail's father. Laurence Archer was hers. And no amount of blood would ever change that.

Maggie caught Hugo's gaze as he approached. He ran a hand through his crimson hair with a shy smile, those locks not unlike the man whose true fire lay inside. With her own eyes, she counted the specks in those emerald irises, one for every piece of her happiness her husband claimed. Then she traced the thin hazel line that rimmed their worn edges and marveled at what a wonder they always were.

Hooking a hand around her waist, he drew her close, and when he kissed her, his lips lingered a moment even in the crowded room. "I could live like this forever, you know."

"Good." With a slow smile, she lifted Abigail from his opposite hip. "Because that's how long you've got us for."

Nothing was ever impossible, she thought. *There were merely possibilities we hadn't yet believed in.*

~~~

The story continues in
Hope or High Water Book Three: Broken Lines

HISTORICAL NOTES

I HOPE YOU ENJOYED taking some new twists and turns with Maggie, Reuben, and the rest. They sent me on a wild ride, forcing sharp turns from my original outline. For instance, Hugo was supposed to be wealthy, Stanley's character barged his way in when I wasn't looking, and there were no plans to send anyone back to England. In the end though, I'm glad I listened to my characters' demands.

While *Across* Oceans will always hold a special place in my heart as my first novel, *Twisted River* was even more of a joy to write. It was wonderful to visit so many locations within my hometown, learn new facts about them, and then introduce them to you, the reader. St. Louis is a city of fantastic history, amazing people, and hidden gems, and well worth the visit. I have always loved living here, and writing this novel gave me so many more reasons to stay.

A few interesting facts about the locations in *Twisted River*:

Shaw's Botanical Garden, now known as the Missouri Botanical Gardens, was built by Henry Shaw. He did, in fact, consult with the Royal Botanic Gardens at Kew, as well as many German botanists both in St. Louis and abroad. The Palm House at Kew and the South London Botanical Institute still remain to this day; however, St. Louis's Palm House was replaced by the Climatron in 1959. Alois Schweitzer's character and the Magdalena flower are completely from my imagination.

Cave Hall was one of the premier dance halls of the time and for many decades after, under the name Castle Ballroom. Built in 1908 by Cornelius Ahern and Herman Albers, the hall was completely non-alcoholic, allowing it to thrive even throughout Prohibition.

According to records, the infamous Morality Squad only visited one night in December 1911, hoping to enforce laws against inappropriate dancing. Supposedly forgetting that the hall was closed on Monday, they simply left. Otherwise, they may have witnessed the dances performed by Reuben, Tena, and their friends: the Grizzly Bear, Turkey Trot, and Lame Duck, amongst others. After many years in disrepair, Castle Ballroom was demolished in 2012.

All the World's Fairs Hugo attended were actual events, including the 1904 fair in St. Louis. The Flight Cage (within the St. Louis Zoo), Palace of Art (now the St. Louis Art Museum), *Apotheosis of St. Louis*, and Grand Basin are still visited year-round. In 1912, the Basin sat around ten to fourteen feet deep, making it a legitimate hazard for those sledding on Art Hill. After updates in 2003, its depth was raised to around four feet and the hill is considered the most popular sledding spot in the city.

The *Mid-Mississippi Daily* is not a real newspaper but was based on many newspapers of the time. The *St. Louis Post-Dispatch*, which Reuben mentions always gets the best stories, was founded in 1878 and is still in circulation to this day.

In addition, some of my early readers asked me about how slowly the Fryes' house seemed to burn. How did they have time for those lengthy conversations and still make it to safety? According to my research, it would have been far more possible in 1912 than if a similar fire occurred today. One hundred years ago, a home's framework and furniture were constructed of more natural materials instead of the synthetics we tend to use now. Therefore, without the use of a stimulant, an older home could take thirty minutes for one room to completely burn into the next. If the fire began shortly before Hugo arrived, he would have had just enough time for a little chit-chat and still be able to save his wife. Although it did cross my mind to have Maggie perish, I love happy endings, and it only seemed right for she and Hugo to *finally* claim their own.

Finally, I love connecting with my readers! To send me a line, or for updates on future projects, visit: kelseygietl.com

ABOUT THE AUTHOR

Photo by Valerie Boaz

BORN AND RAISED IN ST. LOUIS, Missouri, Kelsey Gietl grew up with a love of books and excessive use of her library card. She earned a Bachelor of Fine Arts in Theatre Design and Graphic Design from Stephens College in Columbia, Missouri, and has made a career in fields from event planning and proposal writing to product management and communications.

In her free time—when she's not writing, reading, or researching—she enjoys yoga, musical theatre, beach vacations, and gallivanting around St. Louis with her amazing husband and two beautiful children.

You can connect with her online at:
kelseygietl.com